Looks that Deceive

A Novel

Braxton DeGarmo

Christen Haus Publishing

Copyright

Cover design by Rocking Book Covers

For more information, go to
www.braxtondegarmo.com

DEDICATION

This book is for all of the EMTs, paramedics, nurses and pilots who are involved in pre-hospital care, both flight and ground crews. You *do* make a difference.

Two

Amy Gibbs sat at the antique, round maple table in her breakfast nook and sipped her Slim·Fast breakfast. The kitchen was spotless, for a change—a sign of her not cooking in over three weeks, not of a penchant for housekeeping. Unlike the kitchen, the rest of her modest three-bedroom ranch home, purchased three years earlier in the community of Saint Peters, reflected her "penchant" for housekeeping. Friends teased about her "early landfill" style of décor.

Despite their opinions, her home was her dearest symbol of freedom and independence. She had been in college while her father completed his last tour of military duty overseas, but she lived with him for a long, quarrelsome year when he retired to the city and she started her nursing career. She wanted to spread her wings of adult autonomy, yet he clung tight. A widower and single parent for over a decade, he had displayed enough empty-nest angst for several sets of parents, and retirement had added to his anxiety. So, to help him "move on" and to regain her sanity, she moved out to share a home with two friends for two years before striking out to buy her own place. This was it, her castle.

She stared at the paperbound Pre-Hospital Trauma Life Support, or PHTSL, manual opened across the tabletop, reviewing yet again the sections on field immobilization and intubation of head trauma patients. Her brain couldn't absorb anymore. Normally, she didn't

7

doubt her medical abilities, but . . . She flipped another page and arose to pace the floor, mentally reciting the steps involved in rapid sequence intubation.

The phone rang. She didn't need any interruptions, so she glanced at her Caller ID before picking up. *The trauma center?*

"Hey, girlfriend. You ready?"

"Hi, Macy." Macy Johnson was one of her closest friends, having worked together for over a year in the E.D., the Emergency Department, of Mercy Medical Center, a regional trauma center.

Amy, still walking a tight circuit between the table and farthest counter, mulled over Macy's question before answering. Despite five years of experience as an Emergency Department and Critical Care nurse, the concept of pre-hospital care was a new dimension in her healthcare universe. She had always appreciated the paramedics, bringing patients into the E.D. immobilized and splinted, airways secured, blood samples drawn, and intravenous access established—most of the time. But she had never fully recognized their working conditions. For her, the lighting was nearly always ideal, the supplies readily on hand, the conditions clean and dry. Now, reflecting upon her work over the last two months, she had a newfound respect for the people who worked in all weather conditions, across all forms of terrain and water to deliver the ill and injured to the hospital.

"I don't know. I guess I'm as ready as I'll ever be." *I'd better be*, she thought.

Eager to start her new job, she'd been flying the

Three

❧ ♦ ❧

Amy's heart pounded as she reviewed the test and her answers. More than half of the attendees had already left for lunch. Her own gut grumbled. Should she go through it one more time? No. She gathered her things and arose, walked to the front of the classroom and handed in her answer sheet, managing a feeble smile at the test's supervisor. He gazed up from the test he was grading and smiled back.

As if reading her mind, he said, "I'm sure you did fine."

"Thanks." Amy exited the room and liberated a long sigh of relief. At least that was over. She wondered if the E.D. had any open shifts the following week. She doubted she'd be flying.

Outside, she saw Brad with a platoon of paramedics, some of whom she knew, arranged on and around a few cement benches adjacent to the building. The gorgeous, late August day, with a combination of azure skies, warm sun, and brightly planted gardens surrounding the benches, beckoned her to join the group. From her vantage point through the glass double doors, the conversation looked animated. They all seemed to join into the discussion, which appeared to center on the newspaper passing from man to man.

"Hey, Amy. Please join us. Have a seat." He pointed to the place he had just vacated, right in the middle of the throng. "We were just talking about the article I showed you this morning, and about lawyers in general."

"Yeah. Sure won't miss that face on early morning TV," another medic offered.

A number of others made comments, typically in the same vein. One man, however, stuck out of the group by his silence. Amy focused on him as the others bantered back and forth. He remained remarkable by his stillness in the animated group. He also looked familiar, but she couldn't place where she'd met him.

A tall, redheaded man said, "Looks like someone took the bumper sticker seriously. You know the one. Help keep America great: kill a lawyer!"

The others laughed, prompting the silent one to speak up. "You guys are sick."

"Oh, c'mon, Reilly. You gonna stick up for these personal injury bozos who sue at the scent of money?"

"No. The guy might really be obnoxious on TV, and he might make a ton of money off the unfortunate, but that's not reason to celebrate his death."

"Give us a break, Reilly," another man stated. "We all know you're in cahoots with these lawyers."

The group went quiet, all eyes on the paramedic as if he were a spy in their midst. Amy had run into a few scouts at the hospital and had mixed feelings about these people who received finder's fees from lawyers for passing on the names of potential cases. Yet, such a person had succeeded in ridding the medical community of one grossly negligent physician by collecting a series of names of people injured by the drug-impaired surgeon, a man with powerful political connections. That one

14

To Lynch, death might have been the favorable alternative.

He couldn't image the horror these victims' families now endured, to see their loved one "living" like that, maintained by feeding tubes, managed by catheters and adult diapers, and repositioned on a regular basis to avoid bedsores. Lynch wanted to get this guy so badly it had affected *all* of his relationships. He hadn't dated since leaving Amy. He had no desire to do so. Just like he'd lost his desire for beer with his buddies, or a Sunday Rams' game, or a relaxing jaunt into the countryside with his camera. He hadn't even seen his own parents in over a month.

Lynch scanned each photo to get an overall image of that portion of the scene. Then he homed in on specific facets of each photo, looking for details, which he listed and categorized in a meticulous relational database he had developed on his laptop computer. He had the critical data on all of the crimes he had ever investigated. Obvious evidence went into one of several categories such as blood, DNA, prints, or weapon. He categorized a perp's methods by means of access to the scene, types of injuries or item stolen, cause and manner of death, and other factors that might be useful in defining a *modus operandi*. Items that seemed out of place were listed one way, while normal household items were listed another. Some were cross-referenced more than one way. He then had a series of search algorithms that could pick up items common across all selected crime scenes. With each new case, he added more information to the database and refined his own methods for analyzing that data.

For the "LA Rapist," a clear M.O. had emerged, and his latest suspected case, plus the lawyer killed in the blast of the previous night, were outliers. Lynch wondered whether or not they even belonged with the earlier, serial cases. Yet, he couldn't simply dismiss that possibility. Serial assault could graduate to murder. The latest female victim, Patricia Shriver, was not a legal assistant but a lawyer, and she had been found dead at her home, not in the expected vegetative state. She was also in her early forties, but physically she fit the profile of the other assault victims. Edward Payne clearly did not match that profile, but he did share two common traits with the female attorney. Both were big in medical malpractice torts, on the side of the plaintiffs, not the doctors. And both now rested under the brown side of the grass.

At ten 'til one, Lynch pulled into the back parking lot of the Richmond Heights police department where the Major Case Squad maintained its temporary op center for the Shriver case. He skirted past a handful of remote transmission television vans in front of the station and hoped he had passed by unrecognized. The political pressure bearing down on the MCS would jump logarithmically with this violent death of a second prominent attorney.

At this early stage, Lynch could see no commonality between the two victims or the mode of death except their area of legal specialty, and he had no desire to stand in front of the media and stonewall them. He disliked standing before the media. He liked being a sergeant, sticking the PR work to the lieutenants and higher ups. Unfortunately, his rank hadn't helped him avoid that task. Compared to *his* lieutenant, Lynch was eloquent and photogenic, movie-star material.

Inside the building, he plopped his gear down onto a ten-foot-long, folding leg table where he could spread out as needed. He loosened his tie, opened his collar, and prepared to work.

"Cully! Fix the tie. You're heading out front with me," said Colonel Albert Dandridge, the chief of the Webster Groves police and current commander of the MCS. Dandridge, known simply as the "Chief" by most who had ever served with him, was nearing retirement. He no longer stood quite as erect as in his "glory days" as a military intelligence officer who found his way into civilian police work and had distinguished himself as the lead detective on a number of very high-profile cases of national interest 20 years earlier. His white hair made him look older than his stated years, and the paunch across his middle told of the many years since he had seen active fieldwork. Still, he hid the years well, his always-crisp, starched uniform and well-trimmed mustache providing a distinguished image that matched the man's famed intellect. He was a man whom Lynch fully respected and admired. Dandridge sat on the squad's board of directors and had personally taken command of the investigation into the serial assaults because of its high media profile.

"And I hope you have your quota of B.S. stored up for these media yahoos."

Lynch rebuttoned the shirt and tightened his tie, and then looked for a mirror, window, or anything offering enough of a reflection to check his appearance.

"It's straight enough. Let's go!" Dandridge waved him on while holding open the door.

The two men strode toward the waiting media.

"Talked with Janick this morning. Your colonel has formally asked for our help in this Payne case. Janick doesn't think the case has anything to do with our ongoing investigation, and he asked that I release you back to help him. So, what's your thinking on it?"

Lynch pulled up short in the hallway and stopped. He rubbed the left side of his jaw as he thought. "It's only been eighteen hours, and we don't even have a definitive cause for the explosion yet. You want an educated response or my gut?"

The Chief smiled. "Lynch, we've worked together on what, nine major cases since I took over this squad? Do you think I want an educated guess when we have no facts yet? I keep asking for your services because I respect that gut of yours." He smacked Lynch in the abdomen with the back of his hand. "Not Janick's, or Powell's in Chesterfield, or any number of guys who'd likely make up the Who's Who of local detectives. You can give these media folks your best educated gobblygook; tell me what you really think."

Lynch not only admired the man, he liked Dandridge

others in the house. And Matthew? *No, not Matthew!* If Matthew caught him there, what would happen? He rushed back to the bed and crawled beneath its covers.

Seven

❧ ✦ ✦ ❧

Amy woke early, unable to sleep, her confidence renewed. Today was the day she had been waiting for— her first shift, solo, as the team's flight nurse. She had packed and repacked her duffel the night before, making sure she had two extra flight suits and a change of clothes, toiletries, reading material, and her portable brain, the small reference notebook she had used to make notes, copy algorithms, and list memory aids. Under the stress of an emergent situation, she didn't always like to rely on memory alone and batteries in a PDA could fail at the worst possible time.

She scurried about her small home, watering plants, tidying up, and double-checking window locks. She would be gone for 36 hours, thanks to a midday meeting in the city following her shift, and wanted no surprises or untended chores when she got home.

She walked to the spare bedroom she had turned into an office and turned on the TV, switching to the Weather Channel to catch the day's forecast. Despite the cooler than usual weather over the past week, August's weather had been typical so far, with temperatures nearing 100 degrees Fahrenheit and intermittent runs of thunderstorms. Following a night of storms, Amy didn't want weather to ground her on her first day. The forecast came on within a minute, and finished two minutes later. She still had 20 minutes before she'd have to leave, and her attempts to fill that void weren't succeeding. She flipped through the local channels and was about to turn off the set when the newscaster mentioned the recent death of Edward Payne. She focused her attention on the television as it showed a replay of the previous day's broadcast from the Ladue police station.

"We're here at the Ladue police headquarters where an announcement is about to be made about the death of Edward Payne, a prominent local attorney. We understand that the detectives here have been under significant pressure to solve this case, but they have not revealed the nature of the announcement. It's been 72 hours since the attorney, whose ads were prominent on late night television, was the victim of an explosion that destroyed his and his partners' legal offices.

"Although not confirmed by authorities, it has been postulated that this is a case of arson and homicide . . ."

Amy tuned out the reporter for a moment, thinking back two days to Reilly's comment about the man having kids and a wife. Her heart reached out to the family whose grief she understood so well. The recent death of her brother, Chad, in Afghanistan had been hard on her family. Where her mother's death to cancer, when Amy was thirteen, was expected and had brought her family closer together, the unexpected death of a sibling had been particularly rough, to the point where she required a month's leave of absence from work. It was during that month that her world crumbled. From a sniper's bullet fired from a mosque on the outskirts of Kandahar to the emotional missile to her own heart when Lynch Cully just stopped calling. No phone call to say it's over, no cowardly email or "Dear Jane" letter. He simply stopped calling and hadn't returned her calls.

She stared at the TV until it faded into a blur as she recalled the day she first saw Lynch Cully. She was on duty at the E.D. when this haggard-looking detective arrived to take the statement of a shooting victim. The officer had been up for 48 hours straight, and the circles under his eyes and the uneven rubble of a half-hearted shave with an electric razor proved it. She had noted right away that his height and age were "a match" to her list of desirous traits. Despite her mental recognition that it was nothing more than cultural inbreeding that said the man should be taller than his mate, she still wanted someone upon whose shoulder she could lay her head, and men shorter than her had never moved past the role of "friend" in her life. And at five-foot eleven, she had many male friends.

Plus, she always searched a man's eyes when the slightest flicker of attraction arose within her, and this detective had caused just such a reaction. Surrounded by a face full of fatigue, his distinctive chalcedonic eyes exuded a confidence and fire for life. It was his eyes, not his stature, which intrigued her.

And on their second chance encounter, also in the E.D., that brilliance hadn't left his eyes, although the fatigue was gone, and she then saw a whole new set of features that appealed to her. That was soon followed by an admiration for his intelligence, by an appreciation of his zest for adventure, by approval of his subtle sense of humor, and finally by an affirmative answer to his first request for dinner together. That first date led to a year and a half of "firsts" for Amy, culminating in the ultimate "first." Lynch Cully became the first man she believed she could spend a lifetime with, only to have him disappear from her life.

The newscast disrupted her thoughts of Lynch. She recognized Bob Janick, the lead detective Lynch Cully worked with, but no Lynch Cully in the background.

". . . here today to confirm that the explosion that leveled the law offices of Brumly, Grimshaw, and Payne was indeed intentionally set and was responsible for the death of senior partner, Edward Payne. The case has been officially labeled a homicide and arson."

"In addition, we have a strong lead in the case and expect to make an arrest within the next 48 hours. . ."

Amy tuned out the newscast and picked up the remote control to turn off the TV. So much for the ulcer she half-heartedly wished upon the errant detective from her past.

The first five minutes of Amy's 24-hour shift had produced an adrenaline surge unlike anything she'd experienced, thanks to being punked by Lyle, their pilot, and Reid, her paramedic. They had, however, calmed her first-day jitters and given her something to ponder during the next eight hours on the ground, first due to dense fog and then to too low a cloud ceiling. Payback would be sweet.

As the day eased toward dusk the skies brightened,

and Amy's mood lightened to match. Although the place was comfortably furnished, she had had enough of reading and television. She was halfway through her book, which, since she first started reading it that morning, she considered a cheerless footnote to her first day. The sky was clear for flying, and she was eager to lift off.

Fifteen minutes later, her day changed with their initial request for service.

The dispatch radio tones designating an EMS call were distinct from those used for police or fire, and she heard them first. She hustled into the "office" where they maintained their logs, monitored the weather, and kept their collection of local and regional maps, as well as supplies.

"Lyle," she called out to the pilot. "There's a MVA with injuries on McIntosh Hill Road, just east of Little Sandy Lane. Family van rolled over, one ejected. Let's get ready for a call."

Dispatch came back on the air, upgrading the EMS call to a 'Charlie' response with the addition of a second EMS unit and the EMS supervisor.

"Crash scene's gonna get crowded real quick," Reid said. "I'll grab our flight bags and go tell Lyle." He didn't give her time to protest, but jumped up from his chair, grabbed their two duffels and stormed out the door.

Amy tried to calculate the response times of the ground EMS units. Even with dry roads, the curves and hills remained a challenge for the top-heavy, box-like ambulances. After a glance at her watch, she figured it would be another two, maybe three, minutes before the first unit would arrive. With luck, that day's paramedic supervisor might have already been on the road and able to reach the accident ahead of the ambulances. The lead medic's SUV could navigate the rural two-lane road much faster than the fully equipped, advanced life support rigs.

She hated the wait, but her real frustration was born of her desire to get into the air, to do the job she'd spent the past two months preparing for, and to eliminate her first solo flight jitters. She had an in-bred need to prove herself, a trait she only now began to recognize and understand. Being the only girl in the family hadn't meant special treatment or Daddy's favor. Competing with four brothers for her father's attention hadn't been easy, and she'd not had a mother to turn to after her mom's cancer had advanced and incapacitated her.

She watched Lyle and Reid prepare the aircraft, and waited. A moment after the business phone rang, Amy was out the door and running to the helipad. Lyle saw her coming and gave her a thumbs up through the window, while Reid climbed into the back. The blades beat the air, ready for take-off, as Amy jumped into the back with her paramedic partner, buckled in, and donned her headphones.

"County sheriff's on scene and has secured the LZ for us."

Four minutes later, Lyle circled the crash scene and scouted the field where he was expected to land. He noted no wires or other obstacles. Landing was a "go."

An in-flight report told them that a family of five was

involved, and a teenage daughter had been ejected from the van, suffering an apparently significant head injury. After landing, Amy catapulted from the Bell Ranger's side bay door, and turned back to the helicopter to grab her flight bag. Slinging it over her shoulder, she moved away from the whirling blades and set off at a jog toward the lead paramedic's Yukon. The collective smells of jet exhaust, spilled gasoline, and wet clay combined with the deep breathing of her exertion to create a dizzying effect in her, causing her almost to stumble. Regaining her balance, she continued on. They still had a quarter-mile ride to the crash scene.

In the dimming light of dusk, the scene was one of semi-bedlam. While two county sheriff's cars cordoned off the road, two ambulances and the lead paramedic's Yukon were parked close by, the flashing lights of all five emergency vehicles stabbing the growing dark like dueling light sabers.

"What've we got?" Amy asked, as she knelt next to the victim. The paramedic briefed her on the known injuries and treatments applied so far. Obvious scalp wound on left side. Upper extremity deformity on left as well. Unconscious since their arrival. Amy pulled a penlight from her shirtsleeve pocket and scanned the teen's pupils. Ipsilateral pupillary dilation.

"How long has the pupil on the injured side been dilated?" She again scanned the eyes with her light to show the ground medic. There was a distinct asymmetry to the pupils. *This girl's going down the tubes,* she thought.

"They were equal right before we started this new line."

Reid joined her with a stretcher and their monitors.

"Let's get her tubed." Amy unzipped her bag and retrieved her intubation set. With the paramedic's help, they prepared their equipment and had portable suction and oxygen ready for use. From another pocket, she removed her rapid sequence intubation, or RSI, drug kit and quickly administered Lidocaine, vecuronium, and Versed to the teen prior to paralyzing her with succinylcholine. These pretreatment drugs would help prevent heart arrhythmias and sedate her in preparation for total paralysis, a terrifying event for someone conscious enough to recognize they were unable to breathe on their own. Her hands trembled as she placed the laryngoscope into the young girl's mouth and slid it down to search for her vocal cords. As the paramedic applied some gentle downward pressure on the teen's larynx the cords popped into view, but Amy lost sight of them as she slid the endotracheal tube toward her trachea. She pulled back the tube.

"Shoot! Lost them. Ventilate her before I try again."

After several administered breaths, she again slid the laryngoscope back through the girl's pharynx, but stomach contents came bubbling up from the esophagus and blocked her view. And again, she retreated.

"Suction!"

Reid quickly slid the suction tube into the girl's mouth and removed what he could. He whispered, "Want me to try?"

Amy was exasperated, feeling the pressure of time. A patient, paralyzed for rapid sequence intubation, had only minutes to get intubated before gag reflexes and other natural responses kicked back in to make the process more difficult. And being paralyzed, the patient could not breathe unassisted. This girl's life was quite literally in Amy's hands.

"One more try." She repeated the process, doggedly moving the scope into position. Ignoring a new influx of stomach fluids, she went ahead, intuitively knowing where the cords should be. "A little pressure on the larynx, please." That did it. The vocal cords appeared, and Amy deftly slid the lubricated plastic tube down between them into the teen's trachea. A quick listen to her chest and belly confirmed adequate placement of the tube, and she inflated the tube's balloon to hold it in place and block the airway from aspirating any gastric fluids. She released a mental sigh of relief. Her first emergency intubation, but not without a hitch.

"Let's secure the tube. Reid, start hyperventilating her. Guys . . ." She looked at the ground EMS crew. ". . . help get her onto the stretcher, and let's get her loaded up. I need to get the equipment ready on the aircraft."

Amy took another look at the girl's pupils and was relieved to see there'd been no progression, but now time was critical. With the lead paramedic, she raced back to the helicopter and prepared their ventilation equipment, getting the in-line carbon dioxide monitor ready. Once airborne, she would contact the regional trauma center and ask for further instructions, but for now, hyperventilating the teen was their best option for a possible brain herniation in progress.

Five minutes later, MedAir-12 lifted straight up in a max power lift-off and headed southeast toward the medical center. As she called for medical control, a familiar voice replaced the nurse on the radio.

Oh great, Amy thought, *just what I need. God's gift to women is on-duty.*

Eight

"MedAir-12 to Mercy."

There was no immediate response.

"MedAir-12 to Mercy. Three minutes out and inbound directly from the accident scene."

"Go ahead, MedAir-12."

"We're on final approach. Please turn on your pad lights and have security standing by," Lyle requested.

"Security's on the pad."

A moment later, with the day's light failing, the helipad's landing lights flared on. After landing, Reid beat Amy out of the aircraft and opened the patient bay doors. Amy and Reid transferred their stretcher to the top of the E.D. gurney and allowed the hospital team to take over. Amy's "first" patient was officially in their hands now, and she experienced an emotional catharsis. The girl had survived and, in fact, seemed to have stabilized. For that, Amy was happy.

Amy glanced about her old stomping grounds as they entered through the ambulance bay doors. The department was in its usual state of chaos. Amy saw the young girl surrounded by staff as they emerged from the department's CT scanner room and headed back to the trauma room. She watched from the doorway as one nurse shaved the girl's head, and a doctor prepared for the procedure of drilling a burr hole into her skull. That would release some of the pressure on the brain while providing a portal for placing an intracranial pressure monitor. That they were performing this in the E.D., and not the O.R., was not a good sign.

An arm around her shoulder suddenly disturbed her observations.

"Hey beautiful, I get off in an hour. Up for dinner?"

She'd been so absorbed in the neurosurgical procedure, she'd forgotten about the voice on the radio, the E.D.'s well-known Lothario.

"Doctor Royce." She picked up his hand with her index finger and thumb, and removed it from her shoulder, as if picking off some contaminated biohazard that had fallen on her. She turned to face him. "I don't care when you get off. The answer forever remains no."

"But, Angel Eyes—"

She held up her hand as a command for him to stop, shook her head "no," and walked away. As she neared the doorway of the small workroom set up for paramedics and flight personnel, she saw Reid laughing quietly, along with a petite black nurse with hair plaited into cornrows.

"But, Angel Eyes," the nurse whispered as Amy walked past her into the room.

"Cut it, Macy. And you, Reid, keep it up, and I'll talk Lyle into making you walk home." The paramedic stopped chuckling but continued to smile.

"Whew, girl, you told me living with four brothers equipped you for handling almost any man. I just loved the look on Romeo's face when you—"

"Macy, pulleease."

"He'll be talking about you for the next week, and by the following week, he'll have us believing you were holding his hand."

"Macy!" Amy picked up a large paperclip from the worktable and threw it at her old friend. Macy had been with her the first time they worked with Doctor Royce, and the inside jokes at his expense were numerous. She was tired of doctors hitting on her—interns, residents, attendings, unmarried, married but available, divorced, and even one female internist. Macy knew Amy had sworn off dating doctors ever since a minor skirmish with an ardent resident while she was a nursing student. Yet, even without that oath of abstinence, she had way too much class for that philandering doctor. One other nurse had tried charging him with sexual harassment, unsuccessfully. There was so much off-color banter within the hospital environment that she could never prove the "harassment" aspect of her charge. Most of the nurses, while irritated by him, saw him as harmless.

"Excuse me," a vibrant male voice said from behind Macy. Reid, after turning to see who was speaking, stepped aside in deference to allow the man inside. "Are you the flight crew that brought the young girl in?"

Reid nodded hesitantly, while Amy scrutinized the man attired in scrubs and a surgical head cover. He appeared to be mid-to-late thirties, lean and athletic with a squared-off jaw and pro-athlete's five o'clock shadow. Amy's gaze zeroed onto his eyes, rich chestnut pupils flecked with green and exuding sincerity and confidence. She was shaken by the reaction they ignited within her.

"Yes, I'm Amy Gibbs and this is Reid McCormick, our paramedic."

"Just wanted to say good job. I think she's going to do well and—"

Amy interrupted. "But you just did a burr hole on her in the E.D."

He smiled, which Amy found equally distracting as his eyes. "True, but she's doing well, and I'll go out on a limb early and predict a full recovery." His eyes held an obvious sparkle. "By the way, Ms. Gibbs, your reputation precedes you. Nice meeting you."

"And you are—"

The doctor didn't wait for introductions, but backed away from the door, turned with a loose military precision and walked toward the Radiology Department.

Amy smirked and said, "Nice meeting you, too. Whoever you are."

Macy raised her hands to shoulder level, palms forward. "You don't want to know."

"And just what did he mean by my reputation?" Amy furrowed her eyebrows and cocked her head, waiting for the rest.

Her friend continued, "Seriously, you don't." After 30 seconds of silence and Amy's withering glare, she went on, "Okay. Okay. That was Doctor David Koettering, the neurosurgical attending. He came to us from Harvard . . ." The name pronounced without any R's. ". . . and a long line of big money New England blue bloods. Rumrunners during the Prohibition. He's been in town for a couple of years, but joined the medical staff here about three months ago."

The memory of Doctor Koettering's eyes absorbed

Amy. If the eyes were truly windows to the soul, she wondered what his eyes could reveal. She had sensed seriousness and self-assurance. What else was the man made of?

started to say something, but remembered he was only auditing this meeting, not kibitzing, and stopped. Colonel Halbert apparently noticed his reaction and studied Lynch as Janick continued.

"Phosphine, a highly toxic gas that would have poisoned Payne if it hadn't exploded. The killer figured he'd get his target one way or the other."

Colonel Halbert raised his hand to signal Janick to stop and looked at Lynch. "Lynch, you have something to add? What can you tell us about phosphine?"

Lynch felt unsettled. He hadn't intended to steal Janick's thunder. It would only add to the tension between them. But, then, the big boss asked him a direct question.

"Phosphine is the phosphorus analog to ammonia. Where ammonia is three hydrogen atoms attached to a nitrogen atom, phosphine is three hydrogen atoms and a phosphorus atom. That makes it extremely explosive. It can even ignite just by contacting the oxygen in air. In an office setting, it'd be unlikely there was any attempt to just poison the victim, though. With all the electrical equipment, it was sure to explode." Lynch turned toward their arson investigator. "Roscoe, what'd you find? Phosphorus pentoxide? Maybe some orthophosphate after all the water from the hoses?"

Roscoe nodded. Janick scowled.

Lynch ignored the look from his team leader and moved on with a question. "Bob, anything on the medical report about orthophosphoric acid in Payne's airways? That's what you'd find if he breathed the stuff in before he died."

Janick answered, "Don't have the final medical report yet. Anyway, this stuff is used in the semiconductor industry, which put us right back onto someone with a computer connection. We started askin' folks in the law firm about people who might have held a grudge and who were computer types, and right away three people remember this guy. Payne represented the family in a wrongful death lawsuit against some doctor and lost. I guess in their Arab culture, they figure he'd dishonored them or something, and the deceased's brother threatens Payne in front of several witnesses at the firm. They also recalled he was involved in computers and had worked for Intel when he first came to the States from Saudi Arabia."

Lynch knew what was coming next and rolled his eyes. "*Bingo, two and . . .*

"So, bingo, two and two makes four, and we got a prime suspect." Janick puffed out his chest and smiled.

The agent from the Justice Department asked, "So, why did you consult our database?"

Janick continued to smile. "Well, I learned that phosphine is on the FBI's list of most likely chemical agents to be used in a terrorist attack, and since the guy's Arab I figured it was worth checking into."

"Profiling?" the agent asked, egging Janick on.

"Hardly. We didn't single him out just 'cause he's a certain race or ethnic background. We already had motive and a history of verbal threats, so we was trying to learn more about him. Cover the bases." Janick paused, but no one else spoke. "And we was right, weren't we? You guys have him on your watch list 'cause he has known ties to an Islamic group that's known as a front for raising money for terrorist activities. You even gave us surveillance footage of him at a meeting with some religious leader that you later detained and arrested. Seems our boy had some training and isn't above killing someone."

SAC Culbertson confirmed the information Janick had just given with a nod of the head. "It's true he has connections, but we haven't confirmed that he's had training or that he has the character to even carry out such activities. He might just be sympathetic to the cause and donating money, bad enough as that is. We'd been hoping that through our surveillance, he might lead us to something, someone, bigger. Now you've screwed that up." The other agent leaned toward the SAC and whispered. "Excuse us a moment." The two men left the room.

Colonel Halbert spoke, "Good job, Bob. Anything else you didn't tell them?"

Janick turned toward the police chief. "Nothing of substance. We're still trying to find the phosphine source and a way of tying him to it. But we have enough to hold him."

The Colonel nodded. "Okay." He turned toward Lynch. "See any other loose ends?"

Lynch had been quiet. This wasn't his show, and he didn't want to seem critical of his team leader in front of everyone else. Nor did he want to embarrass him, but he saw several holes in the case besides the lack of a phosphine source. Janick had once again jumped ahead of the facts in the case.

"Well, sir, maybe I missed this part, but what about opportunity? How did he get the phosphine tanks into the building, and how did he set them to release the gas at a specific day and time?"

Janick jumped in. "There was some repair work being done on the air conditioning system. The building's maintenance guy just figured the tanks was part of that work."

"So, your suspect, the one everyone remembered as a threat, simply rolled those tanks into the building and hid them with the other equipment? And he was there long enough to rig some kind of timer-activated valve, but no one saw or recognized him? You're going to need concrete evidence he was there and had the opportunity. Or you're going to have to consider he had an accomplice."

Lynch sat through the remainder of the meeting, saying no more, but suffering through the glares from Janick. Good thing he was still assigned to the Major Case Squad. Even working the streets with a patrol unit might be preferable to working with Janick again. Then Lynch recalled some of his days on patrol and thought otherwise. Still, Janick would make life miserable until he finally saw that Lynch was right. That sometimes took a few hours, sometimes days.

SAC Culbertson ended the meeting, saying. "Okay, we have no specific charges to hold this man, so we'll back off and let you work it. But if you find anything that would interest us, I expect to be notified ASAP."

The Colonel nodded as Culbertson and the other agent stood to leave. Janick smiled. No, to Lynch he looked smug as he gathered his papers and left the room with the Colonel and other detectives. Lynch was about to leave when Culbertson called him aside. He had worked with Culbertson on another case and found the man to be fair, even though his superiors often asked him to play the "Fed card" to trump whatever the local law enforcement folks had. Lynch's first impression of the other man was less favorable.

"Lynch, this is Aaron Masterson, Justice Department."

Justice Department. Lynch had been right. And if Justice was interested in this case, there was more to this Arab suspect than met the eye. Had Janick stepped on some big toes? Masterson extended his hand. "Aaron, this is the guy I told you we needed to talk to, but he's not working the case. Yet." Culbertson smiled. "Look, Lynch, I know you're up to your eyeballs on this serial assault case, but I've asked your boss to bring you in on this one. Besides totally screwing our surveillance, Janick doesn't have what it takes to bring it to court. For one, we don't see motive or real opportunity here."

Masterson cut in. "I don't know what you know about Islamic or Arab culture, but Janick's statement about the man holding a grudge isn't very likely. Based on cultural mores, they'd hold the doctor responsible, but not the lawyer. If 'an eye for an eye' and 'a hand for a hand' are in this man's belief system, death is beyond any justice the lawyer might be deemed to deserve."

Lynch nodded in agreement, but thought, *Jihad approves the killing of infidels for any reason or no reason.* Still, they were right. Motive and the apparent lack of opportunity were not clearly established. Nothing more had been said about opportunity, or phosphine sources, or any other potential gaps in the evidence, all of which could culminate in the release of their suspect. Janick still had time to fill in those breaches if his case held together. But there was also time to watch those breaches erode into chasms that could swallow Janick whole if it didn't. A not entirely unpleasant thought.

"I have a question for you," Culbertson continued. "How hard would it be to rig a phosphine explosion like this one? We're looking at national security implications if this thing's a no-brainer."

Lynch pondered the means by which the killer might have activated the gas cylinders. "Well, it would be relatively easy to configure a valve system using an embedded computer chip that held a specific date and time for opening the valves. Contact with oxygen would trigger the rest. But to hit a specific target, the killer would have to know for sure the person was in the building. That would require a much more elegant solution."

"How much more elegant?"

"One way would be to have a network link capable

of recognizing that the primary target's computer was in use or an infrared sensor showing a warm body in the target's office at a certain time. If he wanted to avoid injuring anyone else, he'd have to know that everyone else was gone. If we're dealing with a computer expert, none of this would be difficult, but it would require some level of inside knowledge of the computer network or building security system. Or both. I don't see our suspect having access to either one."

"Or just basic surveillance. Payne was always last to leave the office," Culbertson noted.

Lynch couldn't disagree. "True. A simple timer, set for a likely time when he would be alone in the building. Maybe it's that simple. For that matter, the guy could have been watching. He could have triggered with a cell phone, but I didn't see anything in the report where anything close to cell phone components had been found at the scene." Lynch paused as Culbertson shook his head to confirm the negative. "But it's not that simple. The firm's entire data system was destroyed. This guy had to have access to the company network, along with certain security codes. This guy required inside information, and since all of the law firm's employees have been cleared, it seems this guy had access to their computer network."

Culbertson and Masterson looked at each other as if communicating telepathically.

"I have a question," Masterson said. "Why phosphine?"

"Yeah, that concerns us," Culbertson added. "A couple of bricks of C4 could have taken out the building and would have been a lot easier to place in the building. We'd like your thoughts on that."

"My first thought is availability. It's hard to get C4 or Semtex in this country. Access to these has been really clamped down since 9-11. Bringing it into the country is almost equally difficult. Phosphine? Any number of common industries use it. Janick's reference to the semi-conductor industry doesn't hold water. We don't have any nearby chip manufacturers. But other common uses include pest control, particularly bulk grain fumigation. We have dozens of grain silos in the area. With the right credentials, you can almost walk into any gas supplier and buy it. So why not? Isn't that one of the reasons you have it listed as one of the top ten chemical agents of concern?"

"Our thinking exactly. Thanks."

The men shook hands and parted. Lynch felt a sense of relief that he didn't have to deal with issues of national security on a daily basis. Managing local crime seemed difficult enough. Lynch walked directly toward the detective bureau and caught up with Janick outside the bureau offices.

"Hey Bob, had a couple more questions."

Janick stopped in the doorway to his office and turned to face Lynch. He didn't look happy. "You trying to ruin our case, or what? We've got this guy dead to rights."

"Hey, I'm not the enemy. You got holes in a case, they need filling before you go to the DA. And it's meetings like this one where we discuss the potential problems. I was asked a pointblank question, and I answered it."

Janick didn't appear placated. From experience, Lynch knew it might take a while before Janick saw things reasonably, if he could get past what he saw as personal jabs at his integrity.

"So what's your question?" Janick's voice held a subtle growl.

"Payne's hard drive. Any chance I could check it over?"

"It's at the county's computer forensics lab. I'm sure your buddies there won't have a problem with your taking a look at it." With that, he turned back into his office and left Lynch standing in the outer office. Lynch sighed. Why was working with the man always so difficult? During confrontations like this one, he always felt like a bear trying to tiptoe on eggshells in a glass factory.

Lynch discussed Janick's case, as well as the Fed's interest in it, with the Chief. He hoped his frustration with Janick hadn't been too obvious. Yet, the Chief knew the man and his foibles and suggested that Lynch simply let things slide. Janick was a big boy. He'd get over it.

After clearing it with the Chief, Lynch drove to the county's computer labs and headed to the supervisor's office. Lynch was well known to everyone at the lab and, as a member of the regional computer forensics group, had been called upon for help on numerous occasions. The facility, identified by a block-lettered sign similar to those of all county offices, was housed in a nondescript red brick building only a block away from the county's other forensics labs. Inside, the lab appeared indistinguishable from any electronics tech support facility with metal shelves stacked errantly with miscellaneous hardware, computers in various stages of assembly and disassembly strewn across a half dozen work benches, and a myriad of instruments, monitors, and cables scattered everywhere. At first look, the curious bystander might wonder how they could keep track of specific cases amidst the apparent chaos. Yet, when it came to specific hardware related to a particular case, the storage location, condition, tests performed and test results of each piece were meticulously noted and filed. A documented chain-of-custody roster secured each item like any other evidence or medical data.

Mike Jurgesmeyer, the supervisor, had his back to Lynch as the detective approached his office door.

"Hi, Lynch. Been expecting you."

"How'd you . . ."

"We ID'd you by the time you entered the front door. New face recognition software we're playing with." Jurgesmeyer swiveled about in his chair and faced his friend. "Everyone with any contact to this place is in the database, and the software now limits access to the facility. Has a few bugs, but once we iron those out, you'll be recognized and the door unlocked for you automatically, 24/7. And it'll log you in and out."

The technician appeared as anything but the stereotypic engineering nerd with a bad haircut, pocked face from a bad case of teen acne, and T-shirt and jeans.

Mike's skin held a flawless, almost feminine complexion and his sandy hair, pony-tailed to the middle of his back, had the luster of a shampoo spokeswoman. Yet, there'd be no mistaking him as female from behind. In contrast, he was broad shouldered and well muscled, and held numerous body building titles. He was the type few bouncers would tangle with, had he a propensity for bar hopping, which he didn't even though he was highly extroverted and a social gadfly. Lynch had often wondered what led this man into the introverted world of computer technology and forensics.

"But, that's not what I meant," Mike continued. "I knew once you got wind of the computer aspects of the Payne case that you'd come calling. I've got Payne's hard drive ready to inspect in one of the locked investigation rooms, along with the company's network and backup servers. I've seen some screwed up hardware in my days, but this one has stumped us. Follow me."

Jurgesmeyer stood up and led Lynch across the main work bay to a short hallway leading to half a dozen locked rooms used for special forensics cases.

"Smile at the camera." He pointed to a camera at the end of the hallway. A light panel at the side of one door turned from red to green, while the others remained unchanged. "The system IDs both of us, checks the permissions file, and opens any doors that we both have access to. You've got permission to enter this room so, voila, it unlocks. Of course, every once in a while I still get called to override a lock because the system failed to unlock a door, but it's getting better."

The two men entered the small room containing a single six-foot-long, grounded work bench along one wall, a couple of metal stools, and all of the testing equipment a technician might use. Mike started a video camcorder set up to document all tests so that the video footage would be available to develop video presentations that might be used in court. Mike sat down on a stool positioned off to the side, leaving the front and center one for Lynch.

"Boot up disk's already in the external drive. Go ahead and power up."

Lynch double-checked the box's cable connections and then hit the power switch. A couple of minutes later, after booting from a portable CD drive, the monitor displayed the cursor prompts of a variation of MS-DOS, which was all they would need to analyze the hard drive at this time. Lynch rummaged through the directory on his thumb drive and selected a diagnostic utility.

Mike reached over and handed him a different flash drive. "Here, try the second program on this one instead. See if you find what I found."

The analysis began, and the display revealed line after line of ones and zeroes, the kind of binary gibberish Lynch expected when files are erased and then overwritten to make sure they can't be retrieved. Lynch sat there, chin in hand, watching the useless code run across the screen. Fifteen minutes later as the utility program neared the end of the 40-gigabyte hard drive, a series of random appearing digits appeared. Lynch hit the 'Pause" button to stop the code mid-screen for review. Uninterrupted, he sat there a full two minutes scrutinizing the display.

Mike reached over and hit a key to resume the analysis. "There's just a little bit more, and then it goes back to garbage." A moment later, he hit the key to pause the program again. "There. That's all of it. And I have some hard copies of it, somewhere . . ." He pushed aside some papers and cables. "Here."

Lynch couldn't see anything useful in the data he saw on the screen. Parts of it looked familiar, but it had been a long time since he'd done any work in straight binary code. Who needed to? There were a dozen excellent, high-end program generators on the market to do the grunt work of creating the code.

"Looks like straight binary code to me," Lynch said after taking a copy and scanning it again.

"Me, too. But I couldn't make heads or tails of it. I mean, who programs in plain binary anymore? Javascript or VB script I might expect, but not binary. Anyway, tried to decode it and came up with nothing."

"Do you have—"

Mike pulled an ancient-looking textbook from under the clutter. Lynch recognized the nearly 30-year-old book as one of the old standby texts on binary programming from the early days of MS-DOS. This text had been old already when he took his first programming classes, but he'd gotten to know it when he started studying computer forensics. It was like using a dictionary to create a story. Today, like Mike had stated, most viruses were written in some script language. To program in pure binary these days took time or a Mensa level intellect.

He flipped through a few pages and reviewed some of the basic commands, then returned his attention to the paper copy of the code. Jurgesmeyer was right. The binary code seemed to make no sense. Lynch concentrated on the code, and then he saw it. The code was simply offset by one digit. Several minutes later, aided by the textbook, Lynch completed a written translation of the binary code into standard machine code instructions. And after a couple more minutes, he had copied the machine code program onto a clean flash drive. He didn't want to risk compromising his secure thumb drive.

"Wish you'd stopped by sooner. You could have saved me a whole day." Mike grinned. "What now?"

"Got an old hard drive that you can afford to erase?"

"Be right back."

Five minutes later Mike returned to the room with another computer case. Together they set up the box and booted up the drive's copy of Windows, followed by an older copy of a word processor.

"Okay, shall we see what this does?" Lynch placed the flash drive into a USB port and, from the command prompt, initiated the program. Nothing. The system froze. He rebooted the computer, loaded in a debugging program and restarted the machine code program. Several lines of code were executed, and the program, and system, froze again. Lynch tried again, this time using the debugger to bypass the first lines of code and get around the line where it had stopped before. The program tapped into the system's BIOS and a moment later, a digital clock appeared with the current time.

"Well, that's exciting." Mike grunted in frustration. "All this to find a digital clock in binary code? Whoopee."

"Let me try something else," Lynch replied.

As he rebooted again, Lynch accessed the BIOS and reset the clock to read 6:58 p.m. This time as the program ran, something was different. The program unsuccessfully attempted to access another program, but continued, and then at 6:59:45 a message appeared, "Goodbye Edward." Ten seconds later, the clock reappeared.

Eleven

Currently camped outside the city, his plush 40-foot Fleetwood motor home—its windows lightly mirrored and exterior stylistically painted to rival the road home of any rock band—provided him all of the comforts and conveniences of a traditional home. Yet, his dwelling bore little resemblance to those of retirees who flooded the highways each summer with their motor coaches, travel trailers, and campers. A contemporary, Scandinavian style with lots of sleek curves and soft, molded leather splendidly furnished the interior. A variety of trim in mahogany, teak, and walnut lent rich wood tones throughout and made it easy to suspend the belief that one was standing inside a motor home. Inside, its appearance was that of a highly paid CEO's office suite, which in a way, it was. After selling his shares of the dot.com business he helped found, he had established a number of smaller enterprises. These he controlled from right there, wherever "there" was at the time. Although he had spent more time in this region since starting his latest endeavor in the city, he had moved a number of times, both to avoid detection and because he soon bored of playing the same role, keeping the same identity, for too long.

A 42-inch plasma screen hung from one wall, connected to a state-of-the-art multi-media system that included his computer network, Internet telephony with full visual capabilities, satellite television and high speed

Internet access, and an array of video and DVD equipment, both recording and playback. It was similar to the many systems one of his companies had installed in numerous law firms, medical clinics, and businesses across the country, although on a much smaller and significantly more individual scale. The system used server software that he had personally modified and improved. Little did the clients know that he had a well hidden back door embedded within that operating system, a point of access that had enabled him, and him alone, to glean insider information, personal data, and trade secrets from the dozens of installations under his umbrella. It was information he used to further his net worth. Only recently had his back door become a trapdoor for an ex-client.

As the markets closed on the East Coast, he monitored his portfolio and smiled in approval. Despite the ups and downs of the Dow and NASDAQ, his personal profits were ever escalating. Unlike so many others whose incomes had suffered the losses of threatened deflation and a major stock market retreat, neither the extreme recession of 2009 nor the anything-but-laissez-faire economy of the following years had fazed his income. He continued to live without financial worry as he traveled in his Class-A coach.

He prepared a quick meal of pasta and vegetables, and dined comfortably, alone, as the local news continued its early evening broadcast. Then, with a glass of wine in hand, he retired to his bedroom, where he exercised a sordidly different type of business. Lady Law.

Legal Eagle. Queen of Torts. Hot Suit. Ribald Rainmaker. The banal chat room handles had shifted more times than he had changed locations.

Even the briefest glance around the bedroom, an inner sanctum that few ever saw and even fewer would leave capable of talking about, showed that he was a man familiar with role-playing. Images of S & M, bondage, and erotic esoterica, some of it so bizarre as to defy the average person's imagination, were prominently on display. Tonight he would again be Lady Law, an established author of textbooks for legal assistants, fighting for the expansion of the role of the assistant in the legal process, and particularly the role of female assistants under the control of male dominated firms. It was a soapbox he had found especially useful with the Internet law forum he was accessing at that very moment.

Twelve

Amy found herself back in Mercy's E.D. an hour before her shift was to end. An early morning accident involved a young mother of three, who while driving unrestrained along a gravel road had rounded a curve and confronted a garbage truck lumbering toward her in the middle of the road. It won. Who was right and who was wrong had played no role, and life had not been fair that morning. Speed had played no role either, but seatbelts, or the lack thereof, had.

By some fluke of luck, Amy's first weekend off was to be an extended weekend, and it promised to be fair and mild, ideal flying weather for her and her father to spend a day in the air. He had promised a trip to Flying Jake's Steaks, a small restaurant right off the runway of a small community airport just over two hours flight time away. Jake had been a military test pilot whose eyes had deteriorated and washed him out of everything but flying small, fixed-wing aircraft and grilling the best ribeyes, fillets, and T-bones Amy had ever tasted. This was her dad's treat for attaining full flight status.

As she turned to leave the E.D., Dr. Royce blocked her way, hands up in front of his shoulders.

"Truce?" He made no move to stop her as she dodged past him and headed for the door. "Please?"

Amy stopped out of politeness, unsure why he deserved any, and turned to face him. He had a look of contrition she'd never encountered before, at least with him. He approached her to within a few feet but came no closer. That suited her just fine.

"Hey, I mean it. A truce. No more 'angel eyes' or pick-up lines from me. In return, no more personal digs or badmouthing me from you. Okay?"

Amy considered his request, doubting he could live up to his end of the deal.

"Prove it with your actions, and I'll consider it."

"Fair enough. I'm a changed man, you'll see. Thanks."

With that, he simply turned away and returned to his workstation. That move alone surprised Amy. *Once a womanizer always a womanizer*, she thought as she continued out of the E.D. into the ambulance bay.

Two hours later, Amy waved at her father from a distance as she parked nearby at the small municipal airport where he father maintained their Cessna 172 Skyhawk. In a unique way—maybe God's way of easing the pain of losing her brother and Lynch—her father had emerged as a "new" man in her life. Not in a chronological sense, but new as in different, changed. He had taken Chad's death more emotionally than she thought possible of him, and his unusual behavior since had become a concern among her siblings. Yet, she had found the change remarkable. Where he had been aloof and quiet as she grew up, awkward and apprehensive in raising a teenage daughter without the benefit of a wife, now he was much warmer and compassionate, even more talkative. Yes, she had decided she liked the change, despite her brothers' disquiet, and in its way, the new warmth of their relationship had eased her heartache.

She grabbed her day bag and purse and jogged to the grassy plain where the smaller private planes were tied down. She stopped short after getting a full frontal shot of her father. Something was wrong. As a military aviator, he had always been trim and toned, and he had carried his physical exercise habits into retirement, but he looked ill, his face gaunt and his weight noticeably down from her previous visit. And in need of a haircut. Still, she saw no hesitation in his movements, no sign of weakness. He possessed the same vigor and assurance in his actions. She watched him untie the plane, waiting for a twin engine Beechcraft to pass along the taxiway between them.

"Hi, sweetheart. What took you so long? The sky's awaitin'." He smiled broadly, his eyes bright and alert.

"Hi, Daddy." She gave him a quick hug, but long enough to feel a difference in his size. *He's probably lost 20 pounds*, she thought. She pushed him back to arms' length, her hands remaining on his upper arms. "You look, uh, different."

"Yeah, probably the weight loss. Figured if you could afford to lose some, so could I. It was on purpose. So don't worry, nothing's wrong."

He broke free from her grip and turned to the plane.

"You sure?"

"I'm sure. Besides, had to make room for Jake's Steaks. I called ahead and talked with him. He's saving the best for us, so get your stuff on board. Already filed the flight plan, pre-flight's done, and we're ready to roll. You want left seat on the first leg? Thought we'd stop by the Bircher's farm, too. Land on their grass strip and walk down to the lake."

He started to turn, but Amy put her hand on his and stopped him.

"Dad, are you sure you're okay? I'm getting a little worried about you."

Her dad glanced at his watch. "We'd better take off, if we want to eat."

"Dad?"

"Sweetheart, I'm okay. It's just really hit me that life's so short. Sometimes there are things you hide, or hide from, all your life. Some things you always say you'd like to do but never do. Some things you want to be but never are. I guess I'm trying to decide which of those things I want to be or do before it's too late. I'll be fine. Don't worry about me."

And that comment alone worried Amy.

Thirteen

The law forum had accepted 'Lady Law,' the "author," without doubting "her" identity. In fact, many of the women expressed their eager anticipation of Lady Law's visits to the forum. They lauded "her" contributions and noted that "she" had been such a great inspiration to them. Matthew played on the fact that they thought Lady Law was the online handle of a well-known lawyer and author, one that Matthew knew was traveling and not easily reached.

He typed, "My research is going well, but I need more participants. Please encourage any legal assistants you know to go to my website and complete my survey."

He watched as a dozen replies streamed into the chat room. As far as the forum members knew, "she" had another book in the works detailing the working conditions of legal assistants, both male and female, with a greater focus on the plight of the female assistant who tried to juggle work, home, and parenting responsibilities within the time demands of the profession. The previous evening, almost a dozen new surveys had been completed. Perhaps more would arrive tonight.

With Markie asleep, he poured another glass of wine, took a sip, and navigated into one more unsuspecting woman's computer. He found the usual garbage in her temporary Internet cache, the results of surfing the Net. Healthy recipes she'd never make. Exercises she'd never do. Clothing she'd never buy because of her sedentary lifestyle and high-fat diet.

He had no real interest in the survey's results. He was more engrossed in the things his survey software provided as a side course. He denigrated most virus authors as rank amateurs. His "virus" was undetectable because he wasn't trying to prove anything to anyone else. While these childish hackers loved to see how far their viruses and worms could travel and how many systems they could "infect," he sought only information. And since there was no widespread distribution of his code, he remained under the radar of the government and anti-viral software consortiums. The new age hackers depended upon the higher-level code scripts to effect their goals. His code was pure binary and guaranteed to remain undetected by all but the very brightest. Unless you knew what to look for, and where to look, you'd never find it. And even then, you'd be unable to figure out what it did, open a back door into the system that no firewall or anti-viral software would discover or block.

His surfing came to an abrupt halt. Someone was at the computer and keying in text to a letter. It was some banal letter to a distant relative who remained computer-phobic and in the dark ages of snail mail. He watched for a few minutes, hoping she would finish quickly and move to the Internet. Or leave the computer altogether, so he could navigate into her digital photo files without any risk of detection. The risk was slim to start, but he took no chances.

Yes, his software was unique. By the time a survey

was completed, the opening had been secured, and another program launched itself through the door into a system eager to reveal its secrets. He had little use for personal financial information. Credit card data and the like, if he were to use it, would draw attention to him like flies to an outhouse. He sought more intimate personal data: age, height, weight, address, phone number, professional titles, usernames, passwords, and most of all, digital images. Most of this he found on the hard drive, while some data waited for discovery online. His spider software could utilize the usernames and passwords he retrieved to access those sites and search for the additional information. Or, he could sit and watch the hapless dupe as she surfed the Net, just as if he was watching over her shoulder. His latest version even detected the presence of a webcam and allowed remote access to it. His vicarious voyeurism had revealed delicious secrets, but he resisted the temptation for blackmail. That would surely alert them to the fact that someone monitored their computers. No, all he sought was information, and from that data, he culled out the select few who met the strict criteria for inclusion in his research group.

The previous night had been successful in more than the number of surveys completed. One in particular had already caught his attention as a potential member of the club. As he sipped his wine, her computer virtually lay before him, displayed in 32-bit color. She reminded him of his mother, slim with silken, long dark hair. A photo of her and her paramedic brother first earned his attention.

Her affiliation with a recently deceased lawyer made him hesitant.

Lynch sat at his own desk, twiddling and twirling a pencil in his fingers as he mentally reviewed the events of the previous few days. He jotted several notes on the sheet of paper on his desk, and tried to organize his findings in a way someone with less computer knowledge would comprehend.

At one time, Lynch had had trouble dealing with his peers. It wasn't that he had some sort of superiority complex, and he'd never been smug with them. He just couldn't understand why they could not see what to him was so obvious. But Amy—again, Amy drifted into his mind—had made him see that all people had different gifts. "We are all uniquely gifted by God," she would tell him when he got frustrated with someone. Could he hit a fastball? Could he play the violin? Could he run down a criminal as fast as some of his fellow officers? Heck, he couldn't run as fast as she could. He had learned to see each of his peers for his or her talents, and he had become a better police officer, thanks to her.

He shook his head to clear her from his mind, picked up the phone, and hit his speed dial number for the computer lab, followed by the four-digit number for Mike Jurgesmeyer's office.

"Jurgesmeyer."

"Hey, Mike. I need your advice."

"Where are you?"

"Huh?"

"My caller ID didn't pick up the number, and I want to figure out why."

"I'm at the squad's Ops Center, and the numbers are temporary."

"Oh. Okay, shoot. What can I help with?"

"Look, I need a way to tell some of my less computer literate partners about the importance of what we've found so far. Suggestions?"

"Hmmm." Mike paused. "It's kinda like presenting this information to a jury. Keep the words simple, but present it in as straightforward fashion as you can."

"Like, we found some software code on the law firm's network server that was similar to what we found on Payne's hard drive, and it linked the computer's BIOS to a rarely used port to open a back door—"

"Whoa. Way too much computer lingo. Server, BIOS, port, back door. No jury would ever understand that. Keep it simple or explain as you go. More like, we discovered some programming that would stay hidden from off-the-shelf, retail software that detects holes in your computer's security. It was on Payne's hard drive as well as the law firm's main computer. This programming opened what we call a back door, a way of accessing someone's computer without detection. We think this program also erased all of the data on the hard drives and then triggered some kind of wireless device that opened the valve on the phosphine tanks and caused the explosion. The forensics experts have found wireless components in the building debris that would fit that explanation."

"Seems a little wordy."

"Sure. But then, every job has its own lingo to use as verbal shorthand. You have to bypass that to explain things to the layman."

"Never thought of it quite like that," said Lynch.

"Think about testifying in court. You simplify your information all the time, and what you don't make easier to understand, the lawyer makes you repeat in basic terms."

"That's for sure."

"So what'd you find?"

Lynch was still thinking about explaining their discoveries to the detectives and, ultimately, a grand jury.

"What?"

"At the lady lawyer's office. Did our little search program work?"

He and Mike had concocted a search program that looked for binary code from the two discovered fragments, as well as several logical subunits of the code. They reasoned that the killer, like any programmer, would reuse code for certain functions in every program he wrote. As Lynch left the law offices the day before, his assumptions were no longer theories.

"Like a charm. I found identical code strands that appear to tie the two cases together. It's as good as a programmer's fingerprints, like finding DNA, although its use in court is questionable."

"Yeah, been there," replied Mike.

As a result, the Major Case Squad had taken the task

of assisting in the Payne murder investigation, a fact that had Janick stewing. And Lynch smiling. Janick couldn't bear the thought that his boss, Colonel Halbert, had called in the MCS when Janick was convinced he had nailed the case, and his suspect would be looking at life in prison.

"Hey, thanks for the feedback."

"Anytime, Lynch. We're here to serve."

Lynch could see Jurgesmeyer's wry smile as he said those words, and returned to the task before him. He took a moment to sketch out a diagram of how their software parsed the binary code on a target computer, looking for a specific pattern of bytes. He would need such a diagram later in court, to show the jury how they found the suspect code. He would also need to prove that the code was somehow unique, that it couldn't possibly have been left over from some popular business software or game. He put his pencil down and launched the search software from a separate flash drive. While the program churned, looking for a binary match, he returned to his ruminations and notes.

He frowned at the thought that his lucky streak had stopped. He stood up and stretched, working out the kinks in his back and the tension in his shoulders. He'd forgotten to ask Mike about the computers used by previous "LA Rapist" victims. They had never been given more than a cursory inspection. He reached for the phone to redial his friend, but it rang before he could lift the receiver.

"Sergeant Cully."

"Hey, forgot to tell you about the other computers.

We batted zero. Zilch. Two of the computers were donated to charity or sold to anonymous buyers in yard sales. The others are still in possession by family members, but they've all been reformatted and updated with new software. Sorry."

How did he do that? That had not been the first time Jurgesmeyer had read his mind remotely. Maybe together, instead of facial recognition, they could come up with thought recognition software, and both retire. He chuckled at the thought.

"Thanks for checking, Mike."

Lynch hung up the phone, upset at the reversal of his fortunes. Had only one, just one of those women's computers been found to contain the suspect code, he would have been able to tie all of the cases to one suspect and to lay a variety of traps designed to snare him.

Lynch plopped back into the chair at his desk. Although still assigned to the Major Case Squad, with the addition of the Payne homicide he could resume working from his own office, and he needed to get there. He took his notes and reworked them into a final version on a fresh sheet of paper. In 30 minutes, he was to meet with Janick and the other detectives working the Payne case. He would lay out all of the computer and other technology findings and blow Janick's allegations against Ahmed bin Abdul Aziz bin Saleh al-Harasis into the landfill with the rest of 1535 Ladue Road. The man remained in jail, with charges pending, and bail set understandably high for someone accused of the crimes he was suspected of having committed. With the new evidence, they would now have to prove the man's involvement in two murders—two motives, two opportunities, two entirely different methods, on two people with very little in common. The county prosecutor's office would have al-Harasis home for dinner. And Janick would likely want Lynch's head on the platter.

Fifty-five minutes later, Lynch prepared to emerge from the meeting with new respect for Janick's incompetence and narrow field of vision—and pure luck.

"In summary," Janick droned, "the FBI's raid on the mosque of the imam videoed with al-Harasis, the one with fund-raising ties to the terrorist organization Ansar al-Islam, found a small tank of phosphine what had allegedly been used as a rodenticide and left behind by an exterminating company. So we have our link between al-Harasis and his source for the phosphine."

Lynch would never understand how Janick convinced the FBI to pull the raid. They had pulled in the imam and two others affiliated with him and held them all on federal charges related to homeland security, a fact that bolstered Janick's case. The help was circumstantial, but it improved Janick's ability to sell the prosecutor on detaining the man and calling for a grand jury.

Lynch could see the media spin already and determined to stay out of the limelight at all costs. This was Janick's case, and Janick alone would hang out to dry when it fell through. Lynch wanted as far from that as possible. He had nothing personal against the man, he simply didn't care for his arrogance and saw him as a politician first, policeman second. Unlike Mike Jurgesmeyer, Bob Janick wasn't there to serve; he expected others to serve him. Lynch shook his head. Maybe he was being a little too judgmental.

As Janick finished, he gave Lynch a self-righteous look and on his way out of the room said, "Like I always say, Cully, one and one make two. It's all comin' together."

No, he wasn't being too judgmental at all. Janick's case was going to fall apart, and he wouldn't even see it coming. Yet, he wouldn't hesitate to blame others for their shortsightedness.

Lynch followed the others out of the conference room, but after seeing Janick leave the building, he returned there. On a large, wall-mounted dry marker board, the case against al-Harasis was laid out in diagrams, photos, and notes scrawled in the handwriting styles of several different people. Lynch drew a line vertically down one end of the board and in large block letters wrote "Cons" at the top of his column. He then added his own notes, and hoped a certain supervisor wouldn't erase them before the next morning.

At the other end of the room was a detailed map of Ladue, and adjacent to that, a similar-sized map of the metropolitan area, both secured to a corkboard. Lynch noted the local map had seen better days, its paper well perforated by pin sticks and beginning to fray at the heart of the community's business district from all of the tiny holes. The metro map was new and untouched. *But not for long*, he thought.

He searched the conference room for a box of colored plastic pushpins, but finding none, rushed to his desk and retrieved a box buried at the back of one of his drawers. He remembered that some time back, one of the other Major Case Squad detectives had used area maps to see if the "LA Rapist" had any pattern. The maps were so detailed they'd been split into three sections for hanging on the wall, but no pattern had been detected. They had entered the address data into a software program designed to predict such patterns. It, too, had failed to assist their hunt. But that was three or four cases earlier, so Lynch decided to do the same thing on the smaller map in front of him. It was a lark, something to kill time before going home to an empty house, but it was the kind of simple, single media display that often got overlooked in the current age of multimedia computers.

Lynch pulled a small spiral notebook from his back pocket. He noted the spiral wire had been slightly flattened, but with a little effort he flipped several pages over to find what he wanted, the list of victims' addresses. Slowly, he placed a pushpin in the general area of each victim's home or apartment, as close as he could get to the address on a map scaled to show major roads only. Once done, he pulled a chair from the conference table and placed it about six feet away from the map. Then he simply sat and stared.

No good, he thought. *Can't see the pins well enough. Not enough color contrast.*

He returned to the front office looking for their secretary, but as it was five-fifteen, everyone had left for the holiday weekend. Not finding what he wanted there, he moved to the supply closet, but found nothing helpful there either. The desk sergeant and dispatchers wouldn't know where to look. Maybe someone on the City Hall side of the building remained to help. As he headed toward the connecting hallway, a familiar voice stopped him.

"Lost, Sergeant Cully?"

He laughed. Of all the people in the building, he had run into the one he was sure could help. She had worked in City Hall before taking the job as Police Analyst, and he had the highest respect for her. Her work ethic matched his, although she seemed able to put family and others at a higher priority than her work. How did she manage that?

"Look who's still here."

"Yeah, little overworked me. You guys are asking for the moon on this Payne case. I'm still trying to get the stats they need for Tuesday. Almost finished now."

"Say, Paula, do you know where I can find some plastic film to overlay on a map and write on?"

"Sure. Not in the supply room though. Planning and Zoning or Engineering are most likely to have it. Follow me."

Lynch followed the svelte sixty-something lady with short salt-and-pepper hair past a dozen cubicles in City Hall and into an area marked "Engineering." Sure enough, next to a large slotted case filled with maps, she pulled out a roll of plastic film.

"How much?"

Lynch replied, "About three feet should do it. Thanks." With plastic in hand, he escorted her back to the Colonel's suite and thanked her again. He then turned and rushed back to the conference room. He placed the plastic over the map and used the pushpins, each in its right location, to secure it. Then with a red marker, he extended a half-inch circle around each pin. He sat down and scrutinized the map again.

"Still not enough," he said aloud to the empty room.

Returning to the wall, he enlarged each circle to double the original size. He sat down and bounced back up, realizing he had failed to add Patricia Shriver's home to the map. He added the pin, drew its surrounding ring, and sat back down. He thumbed through his notebook, cursing the bent wire when it caught his attention for a different reason. His eye bounced back and forth between the binder and the map. Ten seconds later...

"Well, I'll be!" he muttered. "Is that real?" He walked over to the board and used his finger to trace what he thought he saw. Could this guy really be that smart, or was his over-worked mind seeing things? He took the marker and followed the route he had traced with his finger. Yes, it *was* really there. He grabbed the phone in the corner of the room and dialed the Chief's cell phone. The man actually answered this time. "Chief? Lynch. Our guy has a pattern. I think we can find him."

Fourteen
❧ ✦ ✦ ☙

Lynch led detective Paul Flannigan into the conference room where he and another squad member, Jim Boyerton, had been working earlier. Flannigan was in his mid forties, divorced, short and round, with a flattop buzz for hair. The man was willing and able to spend long hours to get the job done and preferred pounding the streets for an answer over shuffling papers. Boyerton, on the other hand, was younger, slim and blond, and one of the "new breed" of police armed with a criminology degree and a love for new tech toys. Like Lynch, he saw the crime lab as a second home, although he favored technology that advanced older, tried-and-true forensics methods such as fingerprint detection and matching, and materials analysis. In similar dark clothes, the duo looked like Arnold Schwarzenegger and Danny De Vito in the 1988 movie, *Twins*. But, in fact, they perfectly complemented each other.

Lynch had personally asked the Chief to call in these two men. He'd worked with them before and knew their strengths and weaknesses, and how they related to each other. More importantly, he understood how they could relate to him, to *his* strengths and weaknesses. Plus, it didn't hurt that they got along well on a personal level.

They had committed themselves to spending a good part of their holiday weekend working toward the goal of catching this unsub—unknown subject. Lynch was committed because he thought they would succeed.

Flannigan, because he had eagerly volunteered after Lynch called. Boyerton's girlfriend had to work, so he had no plans and happily agreed when he got tapped for the task. On a personal level, all three saw the task as a way to avoid many hours alone over the holiday. More importantly, their professionalism called, and they saw a chance to bring this guy to justice, finally.

As they regrouped in the MCS op center, Lynch knew he needed his partners to believe in what they were doing if he was to get the men's all-out effort necessary to make it happen. Telling them over the phone what he had found and what he had planned had gained a certain level of dedication. He needed them to see it as he had, to get their true commitment. And he needed that loyalty now, not down the road. The "LA Rapist's" timetable had been a rough one, a female victim about every seven to ten weeks. With the Shriver case now over a month old, they didn't have much time.

Lynch sat for a moment, thinking. How could he make this simple, or, at least, simpler? He hoped the visual aids would be enough because he hadn't a clue as to how to make others see what he saw without them.

"Paul, Jim, here's the map I set up yesterday. Look closely, the victims' locations fall into a spiral pattern. Here. Here." He took a pointer and moved from point to point.

"Sorry, Lynch. I don't see it. The first victim wasn't where you started, and the order of the victims falls all over the place on that map. One here, the next one across town, the next one north of the city. I don't see a spiral forming."

"Don't take them in order, just look at the pattern."

Paul shook his head again, but Lynch was prepared. Although the Chief had seen it as soon as Lynch pointed it out, Lynch had anticipated others on the squad failing to do so without help. He walked over to the table and picked up two sheets of plastic. He removed the sheet that was currently overlaying the map, the one that had originally enabled him to discover the pattern, and placed a second one over the map. It was almost identical to the first overlay except that it had numbers next to each colored circle representing the chronological order of the victims. Then he took a marker and slowly connected the dots, starting with the case at the far bottom of the map.

"I don't believe it. A spiral."

Lynch smiled. "Like I said, the cases fall into a spiral. They don't move along it case by case, but they all fall somewhere along the curve. It looks like the chronology is scattered, and I thought it was, too—at first. Look at this." He then placed the second piece of plastic sheeting over the map, on top of the current sheet.

The other detective shook his head. "What're you doing being a bum detective? How'd you see this?"

Lynch shrugged his shoulders. "Don't know. Just saw it and then remembered some of my analytical geometry from college. It's an equiangular spiral, first discovered by Descartes in 1638, and involves Fibonacci numbers to . . ." The look on Flannigan's face stopped his geometry lesson. "Well, anyway, see how the cases map out chronologically? Cases one through four map out along this set of secants moving toward the inside of the spiral . . ." He pointed to the progression. ". . . and then case five starts back out on the wide part of the curve and the next three cases follow that set of lines toward the center. He's done that three times and now he's into his fourth set."

Flannigan kept shaking his head, rubbing the back of his neck at the same time. "Man, I see why the Chief calls you a genius."

Lynch frowned, but his voice belied a level of admiration for their assailant.

"No, what's scary is that *this* guy is a genius. I mean, what normal serial rapist or killer could find victims of like size, age, and color, the same profession, and then plot their assaults in a complex way like this? One big question, how does he find the vic within a certain area so that his geometry works?"

Indeed, the man they were hunting was Mensa material, despite his affiliation with the dark side. Lynch saw him as a mental equal, maybe even superior, and a true challenge. The latter aspect had already been borne out by their failure to find him so far. Yet, Lynch hoped the man—and he was now totally convinced they were dealing with a male—saw himself as superior. That meant they could use his ego to trip him up.

Jim shrugged his shoulders, and Lynch nodded. He had no answer either. "Want to see something else interesting? Take a look at the center of the spiral."

Flannigan and Boyerton leaned forward to look more closely at the map.

"Look at that. It's centered right in Ladue."

Lynch felt relief that his visual aids had worked. He still had no idea how to show his colleagues how the pattern worked otherwise.

"You got it. And what can that mean? Does the man live here? Profile would fit—intelligent, well educated, likely very successful in what he does, and probably financially secure, maybe even quite wealthy. A man who knows he's smart and is eager and able to take control. That fits a lot of the homeowners in Ladue. Possibly a scientific leaning. Could mean something else, too, if you add the Payne murder to the list. Payne's at the center of the target, so to speak. Purely coincidence? Could Payne have been a target all along? If so, this guy's been planning it for a long time. What if it's both? Payne lived and worked here. His killer might have known him from the country club for all we know."

"You still think these cases are related, don't you? You know the Feds are backing Janick's case now."

"I know. I'll go on the record saying they're wrong."

Lynch knew in his gut that al-Harasis wasn't the killer. But so far, the circumstantial evidence continued to mount against the man, and Janick was pulling no punches in going after that evidence. Even the Chief agreed with Lynch's assessment, but politics had stayed his formal involvement and muffled his comments to anyone but a select few internal police officials. Lynch's efforts were to remain focused on the serial rapes and Shriver murder, while splitting out a small part of his time to assist Janick. Janick needed more time than that, but Lynch wouldn't offer it freely. He would get nothing but headaches from Janick. Why be a masochist?

"Okay, so do we start looking for our guy there? That could raise some hackles."

Flannigan was right there. To begin an investigation and to make allegations that their killer was a resident of the city's most economically and politically powerful neighborhood would create a firestorm throughout the metropolitan area. No, Lynch agreed with the need to keep a low profile, something best accomplished by focusing on the serial assaults and catching the man at his own game.

"Nope. Take another look at the spiral. If the guy's pattern holds, his next victim will come from here." Lynch pointed to an area on the map. There was a mix of middle and upper middle class communities in the vicinity he pointed to, as well as one or two large, nicely appointed apartment complexes. It was an area where a large number of young professionals resided.

Lynch then walked over to the table and picked up a stack of computer printouts about a half-inch thick. It was paper-shuffling time. He divided it roughly in thirds and tossed a section in front of each man. "It's a listing compiled from the Bar Association and county court system of all legal assistants and secretaries in the metro area. Now, we just need to find the ones that live in this area, and from that subgroup, find the ladies that fit our man's personal tastes."

Boyerton groaned.

* * *

Amy rode along as Macy drove down the tree-lined lane leading up to the old estate's home, a hundred-year-old colonial of white brick and large four-over-one windows. Mature oaks framed the front portico's two-story-tall columns and driving toward the house invited images of visiting the home during an earlier period, an era of horse and carriage, long skirts and bonnets, and chipping blocks of ice for the festivity's hand-cranked ice cream.

Cars lined both sides of the drive as they crawled along looking for a parking spot.

"Thanks for asking me to come," said Amy.

"Wouldn't be the annual Labor Day picnic without you," replied Macy. "And your mom's four-cheese potato casserole."

Amy chuckled. "So that's the only reason you asked me to come, huh?" She pointed to an opening ahead and to the right. "There's a spot."

The saliva-stimulating aroma of barbeque and charcoal smoke invaded her car through the open window along with faint strains of country music. The musical genre would shift around over the course of the afternoon, providing something for every tuneful taste. Amy waved to two other nurses emerging from a car ahead to their left.

"Hi, Krista, Tammie. How are you guys?"

"Hi, Amy."

"We're great. Hey, meet you out back. Got lots to tell you." Krista held up her left hand and wiggled her fingers to show the diamond on her ring finger.

With a four-year history of memorable Labor Day picnics with friends and co-workers from the hospital, Jeannie Harbinger's gala was not one to miss. Despite her earlier misgivings, Amy now looked forward to seeing old friends and catching up on their lives and families.

Amidst a steady flow of familiar faces and friendly greetings, Amy found her way to the kitchen and from there to the back patio where the food was on display until the barbeque was done and everyone lined up to eat. Beyond the patio, covering the backyard, an area that looked small compared to the expanse of grass and trees that comprised the front two-thirds of the property, were three tents with tables and chairs. The center tent had a small stage for live music after the meal was served. Until then, recorded music usually took center stage. At the moment, however, a familiar face had usurped the country music and commandeered the stage, and microphone.

"Yessiree, ya gotta love it. Where I hail from, ya ain't one of the boys lessin' you a great fisherman . . ."

Amy tried to tune out Brad and search for others she hadn't seen in a while. But she smiled at his recent good fortune, having been picked up by a local comedy club for a standup routine based on his imitations.

Well, he is improving, she thought as she meandered into an adjacent tent and caught up with Macy, Krista, and Tammie and a half dozen other nurses she had worked with in the past. For the next hour, they enjoyed updating each other on their social and family lives, while others came and went, joining the group for a few minutes and leaving again. Freshly restocked with the details of her old friends' fortunes and misfortunes, as well as enough new gossip to fill a master's thesis, she grabbed Macy and directed her back to the patio where a line was forming in front of the food tables.

"Hey, thanks for inviting me. I'm having fun, and what a rock on Krista's hand."

"Me, too. I work there and, yet, I haven't seen some of those people since the last party. I—" Amy grabbed Macy by the elbow and spun them around. "Hey, I thought we were going to eat."

"Yeah, and I thought you said he was working."

"Wha—"

"Royce. He's waiting by the food table and just waved at us. You said he'd be working."

"That's what the schedule said, but . . ." She broke free of her friend's grasp and looked her straight in the eye. "Look. You've brushed him off enough times to make that Guinness book. What's one more time? And besides, I thought you wanted to see if he's gonna stick to his deal. How you gonna know if you keep avoiding him?"

Amy sighed and dropped her arms to her side. Macy was right. How would she know? And why had she developed such an aversion to the man? She'd confronted a lot worse, a few of them being a lot more physical than Royce's occasional arm around her shoulder and verbal banter that remained one notch below qualifying as harassment or inappropriate advances.

"You're right. You're right. He's a changed man, right? Okay. So, let's eat."

They turned back toward the patio to find a line twice as long and Royce nowhere in sight. Macy glared at Amy and shook her head. The line inched forward, and the two women chatted with various people who passed by. Yet, while some people came and went directly to one spot or another at the table, getting seconds on specific items, no one came to the line behind them.

Seems we're last in line, Amy thought, wondering if her delay would cost them their meal. The table's selections were looking sparse. Macy must have read her mind.

"Don't worry. I know there's plenty of barbeque. I just hope you didn't have your heart set on trying any specific dish though, because from the looks of it, there's no guarantee it'll still be there."

Amy thought about her recently ended diet and realized she needed to be careful not to rebound from it. "That's okay. Moderation, remember? I'm into sensible portions—"

"Nurse Gibbs. Nurse Johnson. Nice to see you both again."

The resonant male voice from behind seemed familiar to Amy, but she couldn't place it. At least it wasn't Royce. And again, she wondered why she let him bother her so much.

Amy turned to find the new neurosurgeon from the night of her "first" air-evac patient. She couldn't say they'd met because he hadn't introduced himself to her, nor had anyone else for that matter. For some reason, Macy had felt it important to learn everything about the man and call Amy with the scoop. One grandfather had been into electronics and computers, back when they were built with tubes and filled entire rooms. The other had been a U.S. Senator from Massachusetts. His father had helped found Boston's version of Silicon Valley, while his mother played the socialite and philanthropist. As for the good doctor himself, he had a rebellious streak, attending Stanford University, followed by Duke's School of Medicine, instead of Harvard all the way, as was expected of him. But he had returned to Harvard for his post-graduate medical training, and was nationally known as a highly talented surgeon and researcher with ongoing work in both traumatic and anoxic brain injuries. Amy had been impressed, but she wasn't about to let him know that.

Standing before her, without the loose scrubs and surgical hood, he appeared to be about six foot two with a more muscular, athletic body than she had first noted. His wavy, brown coal-colored hair was long by most conservative medical standards, parted right of center, and combed rakishly back. He was well tanned and smartly dressed in olive green dress slacks with a nicely contrasting silk knit short-sleeved shirt. Amy remembered being impressed with his eyes, but today they lacked the fire of their first meeting.

"I'm sorry. Have we met? I—" Amy asked, before Macy's elbow in her back interrupted.

"Sorry. Maybe you don't remember. I'm David Koettering, a neurosurgeon at the medical center. I picked up the Whiteside case you flew into us a week or so ago."

"Okay, sure. You popped into the workroom and complimented our care, but you never introduced yourself."

Macy and Amy moved to one side of the serving table and moved along filling their plates. Doctor Koettering worked his way down the other side, but was unable to keep up with them due to the slower moving line. As they sat down, Macy gave Amy a quizzical look. Amy thought she was looking at her plate and realized that her goal of reasonable portions didn't quite work out as planned. Her sensible servings, of ten or twelve different dishes along with the barbeque, had resulted in a culinary mountain on her plate.

"Girl, what's with this 'have we met' stuff? You know who he is." A small grin eased across her face. "Do I sense a flicker of interest? Is the cardinal rule against dating doctors about to be broken?"

Amy frowned. "I doubt it. And technically, we haven't been introduced. Right?" Her friend was smiling and shaking her head in disbelief. "Well, right?"

"Whatever you say. But be careful, 'cause he's coming this way with his food."

A moment later, he was standing across from them. "May I join you both?"

Amy looked up. "Umm, I'm not sure." She looked at Macy and asked, "What was it we heard about him? A reputation for what?"

Macy's eyes widened enough to be perceptible, as if not believing Amy had just said what she'd said. Amy didn't care. In her opinion, he'd been rude that first encounter, and she wasn't going to be at a disadvantage again, whether or not the medical staff Grand Pooh-Bahs were grooming him to become director of neurosurg when old 'what's-his-name' retired next year.

Doctor Koettering stood there silently for a moment, unmoving, until a sign of recognition became evident on his face. "Oh. Please, my apologies. You're right, I failed to identify or introduce myself last week. As for the comment about your reputation, it was purely professional. I'd asked about the flight crew bringing that girl to us and was told you were one of the best, that the medical center had lost a great asset when you left. I can see now how that comment, from a complete stranger, could have been taken. If I seemed rude, I apologize. I was preoccupied."

Macy kicked Amy under the table.

Amy looked up again at the man standing across the table from them. "Apology accepted. Have a seat."

Doctor Koettering placed his food on the table and sat down. "Did you hear we sent the Whiteside girl home yesterday? She did really well, and—"

Amy held up one hand. "Doctor, if you want to sit with us, we have one rule at these parties—no shop talk." She waited a moment to see what effect her comment had, which was none. "But I'm glad to hear she went home."

"Okay, but I have a rule, too. Outside the hospital, it's first names. Okay? I'm David."

Amy felt awkward. From the beginning of nursing

school, their instructors drilled into the students that doctors were to be given the respect due their standing, and that, as professionals, nurses were to address always them as doctor. And after that fracas with an overtly passionate and testosterone-charged resident when she was doing her nursing school clinicals, she had found that using the professional title up front helped her keep them at arm's length.

She hesitated, but finally said, "Okay." She took another bite of food, but he kept looking at her, eyebrows raised and hand gesturing toward her, palm up as if to say, 'and...' "Oh, I'm Amy."

"And I'm Macy," her friend added.

"Amy and I went to nursing school together and then started here at the medical center. So, that makes it about ten years now. We also worked together in the ICU and E.D. for the last three years before she left."

"And why did you leave? Was there a problem at the hospital?"

Amy was on the spot now. She finished chewing. "Not at all. It was a way to combine two things I love, critical care medicine and flying." She took another bite, hoping to delay any further questions. She had another reason for leaving, but avoiding contact with an old flame was not an excuse she was about to share with a stranger.

"Do you fly? I mean, like, do you have a pilot's license?"

Amy nodded. She knew what the next most likely question would be, so she added. "My dad was an Army aviator. I've been flying since I was old enough to look over the console and have had my license since I was old enough to get one. Now I'm instrument rated as well."

Macy interjected, "She co-owns a Cessna with her dad."

Amy nudged her friend. He didn't need to know that.

"Really? What kind?"

"A 172 Skyhawk."

David smiled. "That's a great plane. Reliable and stable. I remember the first one I ever saw, original white paint with green trim."

Amy eyed him closely. Did they have flying as a common interest?

"Do you fly, too?"

"Well, yes and no. I don't have a license. Never had the time and even now I wouldn't be able to keep current. Had a FAA friend tell me once that the highest casualty rate in flying involved doctors. They have the money, but not the time to get the hours they need to keep up the skill. Decided I wouldn't be one of those statistics." He took a sip of his soda. "But my family has a couple of planes, so if I ever have to go anywhere I just make a call home and set it up."

Amy couldn't resist asking, "What kind of planes?"

"Oh, a Beech King Air 350 for shorter trips and a Lear 45 for anything else. When I was a kid, our pilots would show us around the airport and I learned about all kinds of planes."

"Wow, nothing like going first class. Must be nice." Amy tried to look uninterested, but she'd fantasized many times about flying a Lear. Even the King Air would be a major step up from her humble Cessna.

Amy took a bite and gazed at the man sitting across from her. She was amazed that in so little time, he had gotten so much out of her, and that she had given the information so freely. That's when she sensed it, like a form of internal radar picking up a familiar blip on its scope. She'd managed to avoid Royce, but now, someone else, a man she'd just met, was about to hit on her.

He stared at her for a moment, then said, "You have the most amazing eyes."

As night closed in on the motor coach, 'Lady Law' paced the floor between the living area and bedroom, impatient, frustrated, and atypically anxious. Matthew's half-finished glass of Merlot had not calmed him and, in fact, tasted bitter. Every sense seemed finely attuned to his surroundings. He could feel the coach vibrate in unison with the rush of the evening breeze through the canopy of trees that enveloped his abode and hid it from detection above. The electronics filling his "control center" hummed with their cooling fans and rarified the air with electrically generated ozone that irritated his nose. The sound of an approaching car on the nearby road made him turn nervously and face that direction, even though he knew he was invisible to them, hidden by a hundred yards of densely wooded hillside. As the car continued past the turn-off to the gravel road where he was parked, he returned to his computer monitor and scrolled through the list of user names currently signed into the legal forum's chat room. *She's still not there!*

He'd been watching for her for almost a week, but she'd not signed on. She had taken the survey several weeks earlier, and over time, his spyware had gleaned the information he sought and brought her to his attention. He focused on her now, eager to grant her admission to the club, to ease her through the initiation rite. But she hadn't come back, and to contact her by any other means would raise suspicion. She'd made no mention of illness or of a vacation break. What if she had left the firm for another position? He disliked the notion of having to make the effort to find a replacement. Perhaps they were having network problems at work, or her boss had cracked down on using the office computers for personal reasons, even those creatively related to work. Surely, she had a system at home she could use; yet, maybe she had reasons for not accessing the forum from home. He had noted a trend where more of his contacts were limiting their links with the forum through work computers. Why that was, was open only to speculation.

He felt a compulsion to act, and his disquiet stemmed from that need, as well as from the fact that for the first time in his life, his sense of superiority as a programmer and technician had been challenged. Following the demise of that Payne-in-the-ass lawyer, and realizing that a kernel of code would remain on an otherwise blank hard drive, code that might provide a signature to someone astute enough to find it, he prepared a sentinel program and launched it into the systems he continued to monitor. He had been confident it would remain silent, never to be triggered by anyone searching for his code. But he had been wrong, and almost too late. Within two days of preparing the sentry, it had already signaled a warning. Someone had searched for his code on the Shriver computer, someone smart enough to suspect a link between the two deaths, even though to him one was personal and the other a favor to someone close.

It disturbed him to think that someone else was possibly as clever as he was in technical terms. And this disturbance translated into his pacing, an act of repetition that was out of character, reflecting an unfamiliar agitation. Even more upsetting was the thought of becoming the hunted, when he was accustomed to being the hunter.

In quiet rage, he again searched the user names in the chat room and again failed to find her name. But that would change. She would be back. It was time for the hunter to remain calm, steady, and perseverant. It was also time to tie up some loose ends, and for the hunter to backtrack and set a snare for whoever was stalking him.

Fifteen

❧ ✦ ✦ ❧

Two nights later, Lady Law was glowing.

"Thank you so much..."

"You're oh so sweet to say that..."

He typed feverishly to keep up with the compliments. "Her" online charm and saber-sharp wit had the women of the law forum, who delighted in seeing the preliminary results of the survey, which had become the basis for the "new book's" introduction and first chapter, tapping "her" praises onto their keyboards. Both were now available online for the forum community to read and critique, and the early comments revealed little but admiration for "her" efforts. None of the forum members had reason to suspect that this was all they would ever see of the "new book."

Tonight's praise heightened his awareness that he needed an out, a legitimate exit strategy that would prevent suspicions from developing when no book evolved. Of course, the publishing industry was such a fickle one. In a few months Lady Law would announce the book's completion, follow that with a few months of spurious lamentations about rejection after rejection, and soon after disappear from the forum altogether. No one would be the wiser.

The chat room's current discussion, however, turned somber as one of the round-table directors turned the "conversation" into a memorial for one of their own, Patricia Shriver. Lady Law moved to sidelines to observe as tributes to the deceased lawyer emerged from an angst-ridden group that had only recently learned the details of the death and saw it as a homophobic attempt to silence a leader in their lesbian push toward "equal" rights. Descriptions of her death as the victim of a "hate crime," while being the most succinct and frequently used epitaph, were blasé compared to the more descriptive, and sometimes pornographic, phrases used by the hard-core activists in the group.

Lady Law diverted the video output to his large plasma screen, sat back, and delighted in watching the community bond disintegrate before his eyes. As the activists crawled from the woodwork, the straight faction within the forum expressed dismay and offense at the language being used.

"Hey, we don't need language like that here," wrote one.

"Yeah? What we really don't need is a bunch of lesbophobic straights on this forum spewing more hate speech," answered an activist.

"Wait a minute," wrote someone else. "What is the real purpose of this forum?"

"Have I been duped into supporting a group that uses my membership to promote a questionably moral political agenda?"

The verbal barrage exploded between the two groups, and it was nearly impossible to read and keep up with the exchange. It was such fun to monitor, he now wished he had started the whole thing.

And then nothing. The chat screen blanked out.

"STOP!" wrote the forum director who had initiated the discussion as a tribute to Ms. Shriver. "I'm using my SysOp privileges to put an end to this. All messages are coming through me, and I will only allow the civil ones through. No, this forum isn't for promoting a single political cause, but we have a diverse group and there are several subgroups here that use the private chat rooms to discuss their specific issues. We MUST respect everyone here . . ."

She continued to admonish those members who had remained online, a significantly smaller number than just fifteen minutes earlier, about the goals and purposes of the forum.

"This forum has a lot to offer our profession. Lady Law's book research is a shining example of what this community can contribute to the law profession as a whole. We should embrace all who chose it as a career, whatever their social, political or moral beliefs."

A few statements of contrition were displayed, tightly controlled by the system operator and allowed to pass through in order to moderate the tone of the night.

"Party-pooper!" Lady Law stated to empty air. He was about to sign off as well when a statement came through from a user he'd not "talked" with before.

"Ladies, I wish to alert you to a danger that faces not just the women we know in the legal profession. Pat was my boss and a close friend whom I miss terribly. But another personal injury lawyer, a man, was also recently killed, apparently for revenge. Some in our local police believe the killer is the same person who killed Pat. It is unlikely to be a hate crime if the killer has crossed gender lines with no regard for sexual orientation. This individual . . ." The SysOp allowed her to continue.

Lady Law perked up. He watched as the community absorbed her comments, and the chat room discussion regained the sensibility and civility it typically displayed. Ruffled fur seemed smoothed and the whitewater calmed as the discussion took on a new tone, a tone that now gave his skin tingly gooseflesh. Mere suspicions or not, more was known about his activities than he had ever anticipated might come to light. And should these suspicions ever become buttressed by fact, he would face a new threat of exposure. He read the completed message and waited for more. He had quickly deduced who this person was. He could even picture her in his mind. The big question was, just what did this person know?

He monitored the room briefly and noted that she had returned to the shadows. Her contribution had ended, but she had not signed off. Yet, what she stated exposed that she knew more about her boss' death than she openly revealed. He stood and began pacing, a trait that was becoming uncomfortably common. Again, for a moment, he wondered what she might know and then decided it didn't really matter. She simply became another loose end to deal with, and for that, he had an idea. He took the opportunity and signaled her to request a conversation on a private channel. A moment later, they were sequestered in their own confidential chat room.

Assertively he keyed in his first comments and hit 'Return.' "Legal Grief, I wish to express my sincerest condolences to you and those at your firm. I also knew Pat Shriver professionally."

"Thank you, Lady Law. I've followed your work online for the past week. I look forward to your book." There was a pause in the typing, but Lady Law resisted interrupting. "How did you know Pat?"

In response, he debated how heavy to lay it on and decided to go for broke, risking the chance she might call his bluff. "I met her two years ago at a conference. Her death is such a horrible waste." He left it vague and open-ended on purpose, a tact that rewarded him with validation.

"Was it the conference in New Orleans? I missed that one."

"Yes, New Orleans. It was a wonderful conference. Sorry I didn't get to meet you as well." He loved it when they filled in the blanks and added veracity to his claims without being aware of doing so.

"Me, too." Her reply came quickly. She was hooked.

"Say, my husband and I are traveling in our motor home and could swing through your city in two days. Could we treat you to dinner?"

After some hesitation, Patricia Shriver's legal assistant agreed to dinner, and arrangements were made for meeting. Legal Grief, already known to Lady Law by her real name, Elsa Dunleavy, suggested a location where they could park their motor coach for the evening. She would meet them there at seven.

* * *

124

Lynch, Flannigan, and Boyerton had waded through the computer printout culling the names and addresses of legal assistants and secretaries whose listed birth dates fell within their designated range. This was the typical, tedious scut work of a policeman's duties that television shows never portrayed. Still, that was the easy part, and it had taken the better part of their available time over the holiday weekend. Now, as the shortened workweek ensued, Lynch looked back and realized he had missed yet another holiday. He was mentally exhausted and feeling like a social misfit. His mother had called daily over the three-day weekend, and he'd failed to call back.

In the past, missing a holiday weekend's festivities never bothered him. With the increased police workload over an extended weekend, it had always seemed easier to just go with the flow and be part of the weekend duty roster than to arrive back at work and face a new mountain of paperwork and new crime reports he would have to absorb secondhand. Why did missing this particular holiday seem to bother him? It was just Labor Day. Not even an important family holiday.

He'd been invited to two Labor Day gatherings and turned down both, one being an annual picnic held by a nurse at the trauma center. He'd been afraid you-know-who would be there and, well, he had work to do. But, maybe *she* was the reason he felt so downcast. Thoughts of Amy had been gaining control of his consciousness for the past week or two. Or, so it seemed. And they'd had such a good time together at the previous picnic that the holiday seemed to trigger more memories of their time together. He needed to focus, solve this case, and then deal with his emotions. First things first.

As the trio of detectives resumed their effort, the next step was to cross-match those names with addresses falling within a three-mile radius of the suspected target area. None of the three men was from that part of town and the going was slow, as they had tried to correlate street names to a detailed city map. The Chief came to their rescue by requesting the assistance of the field operations sergeant from Sunset Hills, the larger of the communities located within their target zone. By the end of the afternoon, they had assembled a roll call of names and developed a list of questions.

But for Lynch the real work was just beginning. Expecting it would be easier to find the women at home in the evening, he was at his temporary desk in the Case Squad's op center shortly after his evening meal. The first three numbers he dialed reached answering machines where he recorded a brief message and requested a call back. A deep, but distinctly feminine, voice answered his fourth call.

"Ms. Atheridge?"

"Yes," came a hesitant reply.

"My name is Lynch Cully, and I'm a detective with the Major Case Squad. As you probably know, we're working on the series of assaults involving women in the legal profession. Would you be willing to answer a few questions?"

There was a pause, followed by an even more

tentative reply, "Maybe. H-how'd you get my name?"

"Through the Bar Association and county courts."

"Okay. I guess."

"Thank you. Now, all we have is your name and birth date, but this assailant follows a certain profile. Could you please describe yourself?"

"What do you mean?"

"Well, um, describe yourself physically. Height, weight, hair color."

"Yeah, right, pervert. You think I'm going to fall for that. What's next, heavy breathing? Beat it."

Click!

He chuckled. "Well, that didn't go well," he said to no one in particular. He scanned their list of questions and considered a revised approach. Then he arose from his desk and crossed the room, tapping on the shoulders of detectives Boyerton and Flannigan. As each man completed the call he was conducting, he stopped and swiveled his chair toward Lynch, who was partly leaning, partly sitting on his desk. Having their attention, he described his most recent call.

"Yeah, Cully, we always wondered what you did for fun!" joked Flannigan.

Boyerton cut in. "So far, all I've done is create a small panic. Two of the women on my list got frantic, thinking we were calling because we thought they were next on the victim list. I'm pretty sure every legal assistant they know has been called and alerted by now." He shook his head.

"Paul?"

"All I've gotten so far is answering machines."

Lynch smiled. "That might be the best approach yet. At least, when they call back they can be assured we're the police and not some prankster or pervert." He paused. "It might be best if we leave the questions about personal appearance 'til last, and even then we might want to list the physical attributes we're looking for and then ask if they fit that description."

"Might work better. We might also want to let them know right up front that if they have any concern that we're who we say we are, they can call back at the number here. Front desk might not like us, but it should reassure the women."

Lynch liked Boyerton's suggestion and nodded. "Good idea, Jim. We can refine this process as we go."

All three men returned to the phones and continued until the late evening news. Lynch succeeded in remaining focused until his fifth call. The voice on the other end sounded so much like Amy, he had to repeat himself. His pace on all of the calls after that one showed he had lost his concentration. Only the lateness of the hour saved him from embarrassment.

The following morning Lynch met with the Chief to discuss the previous night's results. Lynch paced the room while the older man reviewed the collection of names and Lynch's quick handwritten tally of their efforts so far. In the adjacent room, Flannigan was back on the phone, but Boyerton had been tasked with other duties. The Chief sat drumming his fingers on the desk, his lips pressed sternly together.

"Not much to go with, Lynch."

Lynch had already come to that same conclusion. He also worried about the negative responses they'd received. It wouldn't take too many complaints before some judge might call to clamp down on their inquiries.

Yet, despite the poor outcome so far, he marveled at the suspected proficiency of their unsub. Did he go through this same process to find his victims? If so, how did he get the names? Did he have access to bar association records? What ruse did he use to learn more about each woman? Or had he figured out some other way? Social media, perhaps.

"I know, sir. Out of just over two hundred names, we found about 30 in our target area and made actual contact with roughly half of them. Not one of them matched the physical attributes we're looking for. We left messages for the rest, minus a couple of disconnected numbers. Flannigan is handling those callbacks."

The Chief nodded. He rummaged through his 'In' box and pulled out some papers. "Here's what we have on nitrogen sources. I don't see anything unusual, but glance over it and see if anything jumps out at you, okay?"

Lynch took the papers and thumbed quickly through it. He wondered how much nitrogen would be required to precipitate the brain injuries they had seen in the victims. For once, he felt stumped. The delivery system would dictate the amount of gas needed, and they had no clue as to how the gas was administered. If, indeed, that was the cause of these injuries.

"Any additional thoughts on what we're going to do after we find our potential victims?" asked the Chief.

Lynch hoped the field of candidates would quickly shrink to one or two, but with a lot more female legal assistants living in the target area than he'd first estimated, this hope was a dim one. He'd been considering several options, of which the simplest was his first choice.

"Well, assuming we find someone who fits our profile, I'd like to use her as bait . . ." The Chief's eyes widened. "Sorry, not her actually. Her identity. If this guy's been using the women's law forum to scavenge victims, then he's obviously role-playing. So, let's do the same by borrowing the woman's identity to set the trap."

The Chief sat there, elbows on the desk, palms together, tapping his fingers, a habit Lynch recognized as one of contemplation while the man formed his next question. Lynch smiled. The game was about to begin.

"Okay. So, what if . . ." the Chief began.

The banter was brisk for the next fifteen minutes, and Lynch was surprised to realize that he, like Janick, had narrowed his field of vision and had failed to look outside the blinders. He had criticized Janick for the speck in his eye without removing the log from his own, an attitude he determined to change. That revelation came when the Chief had asked one simple question: "What if he knows you're coming?" Lynch hadn't considered that turn of events. A man intelligent enough to use his victims' computers to his advantage must certainly have an ace to pull from his sleeve.

Amy tried to catnap in the back seat of the helicopter as they returned from yet another call, the sixth since noon. With the chattering and rumbling vibration of the aircraft, the best she could accomplish was to close her eyes and practice deep breathing exercises for whatever relaxation she might achieve. She knew that the aircrew was not alone in its growing fatigue. The ground crews, too, had been busy all day.

They were returning to base to allow the pilots to change shifts. Although the nurse and paramedic typically worked 24-hour shifts, the pilots worked twelve. And after a day of non-stop flying, she knew that Glen, the third pilot on their roster, needed the rest. They had the toughest job on the air-evac crew.

Five minutes out, a radio request for the nearest helicopter to the Creve Coeur Lake County Park came across her headset. Without missing a beat, Glen answered that they were over the park and available. Amy smiled. She loved flying with a crew that shared her desire to serve and willingness to ignore the clock if they were needed. She glanced out the window and saw the rotating beacons of the on-scene EMS and police. Long shadows stretched across the lake and adjacent picnic area like death's pall reaching out for whoever lay below requiring medical air transport.

As they descended into the flare-lit landing zone, she could see a compact car parked at the far end of the picnic area's parking lot, with emergency personnel huddled around it. Staccato bursts of light illuminated the car and its occupant as someone took photographs of the scene, an action usually reserved for the dead, not someone in critical medical condition and requiring air evacuation.

Upon landing, Amy opened the door, jumped from the aircraft, and then turned to get her bag before jogging toward the scene. The bag felt twice as heavy as normal, and her pace was noticeably slower. Yet, she persisted, pushing her endurance, knowing someone needed her assistance. As she approached the car, one of the ground paramedics restrained her.

"Let me warn you. It's not pretty, but we've checked her vital signs and they're stable. she's breathing on her own. We should be able to move in and get her as soon as the crime lab guys give us their okay."

"Uh, I don't get it. If she's that stable, why do you need us?"

The paramedic gazed toward the ground. "You'll see. The Major Case Squad is all ready for this one in isolation at the medical center. They don't want to risk any problems during ground transport."

Amy felt a twinge of expectant revulsion at the comment. She looked toward the car just as the crime lab technician waved them in, and the paramedic walked slowly to the car with Amy following.

"We'll need to take care extricating her, but we can handle that," he added.

When Amy reached the car, the sight confronting her

left her aghast. Sitting in the middle of the back seat was a young woman, maybe mid-thirties, with short copper hair, disheveled and showing multiple three to four centimeter areas where hair had been pulled from the scalp. That hair lay on the seat and floor around her. She was clothed only in her underwear, and that was disheveled. A blindfold covered her eyes. But the most agonizing aspect of the scene was the woman's left hand, raised to the ceiling of the car, holding a set of brass scales. Amy looked closer and cringed as she saw how both were held to the ceiling. The scale was off-kilter with screws weighing down one pan of the small balance.

The image was a mythological one, of the Greek goddess Themis, known more commonly in modern times as the model for "Lady Justice," blindfolded and holding her scales, meting out justice without favor. The symbolism was clear: justice had been screwed.

The woman was carefully freed of her bond and lifted to a stretcher. Amy sadly attended to her, first checking her vital signs and then covering her with a blanket. There was no sign of pain. Her breathing remained even. Amy reached up and stroked her cheek, feeling lost, unable to care for this poor woman in any way that could restore her. She reached up to remove the blindfold and check her pupils. The paramedic stayed her hand and looked at her questioningly. Amy again moved her hand to the strip of cloth and thought she saw a tear run from under it. She slowly slid the cloth up and gasped when she saw the woman's eyes.

Sixteen

❧❧✦✦❧❧

Lady Law puttered home, inconspicuously riding a small, light blue Vespa ET2 along the two-lane road through a subdivision in the Maryland Heights community. Who would think twice about someone riding along at 25 miles per hour on the popular motorbike with a bag of groceries strapped to the back rack? It was surely not the 'getaway' vehicle expected of a serial 'rapist.' On the contrary, it was a common site throughout the summer, and even now, the week after Labor Day, the warm weather brought out the cyclists and scooter enthusiasts. He had driven his latest test subject to the park in her car, retrieved his Vespa from the backseat prior to posing her there, and was now using the scooter for a casual ride home.

As he rode, Matthew smiled and whistled, nothing recognizable, just a tune that came to his mind. He hadn't felt so calm, so at peace, in the months since he'd arrived in town. There was a singular pleasure, almost giddiness, in the symbolism he'd left behind. Once again, justice had been screwed by law. Blinded and screwed. Of course, no one would understand it. No one knew him as Lady Law. They would be scratching their heads over this one, wondering whether or not it was a copycat, questioning the message he'd sent. Surely, they would see the message. He'd stated it clearly enough so that even the dumbest cop could get it. But without the other side to the equation, they'd never understand it. The lawyers would, if they had that critical half of the formula. After all, weren't they taught that the law superseded justice? Hadn't western civilization, a collective assembly of nations no longer legislated by a diverse cross-section of society but by lawyers and special interests, taken the concept of the 'rule of law' to an extreme, pushing justice and common sense aside?

The law had failed his mother—and then she failed their family. She had petitioned, argued, and pleaded for the courts to see life as she saw it. Yet, in the eyes of the law, her husband had done no proven wrong, even though he abused them behind closed doors, physical torment bordering on real torture. Things he had seen, learned, and experienced in Vietnam. Things that should have stayed in Southeast Asia had come to haunt their home and destroy the innocence of their childhood. Over time he won control of her mind, a control so total that she joined him, became an abuser, and finally a killer. Yet, she also knew overwhelming despair, loathing her actions, and allowing regret and remorse to consume her until he handed her the loaded gun, and she took her own life. Suicide—the ultimate act of abandonment. Even as an adult he had trouble comprehending, although he had learned his father's techniques very well.

In time, he recognized that justice now urged him to amend that wrong. And yet, it was the law once again that had purged his juvenile record and freed him to satisfy some newly discovered appetites and his strong entrepreneurial spirit. He had been smart enough to avoid any further entanglements with the police, using stolen identities in each new community he 'worked' in.

He was also smart enough to realize it was time to move on. He had been right about this assistant. She knew more than she'd let on. That meant Patricia Shriver had told her of her suspicions. Had his spyware not alerted him to the fact that the lady lawyer was investigating the real identity of Lady Law, he would never have learned how close he came to being unmasked. But there was still a page missing from the brief. Had the assistant told anyone else?

Lynch had received a call from the detective on the scene of an apparent assault in one of the county's northwestern parks. The description of the victim and how she was found had affronted every sense of morality and decency he possessed. He thought he had seen the worst the human race could dish out on each other, but this mockery of justice jumped right into his top ten list, near the top. If this was the same perp, he no longer had a shred of respect for the man's intellect. He felt nothing but revulsion at what had been done to this young woman, an act that strengthened his resolve to find this guy.

At first, he had seen no connection to this case and the "LA Rapist" series, and had wondered why he had been called. The woman was in the appropriate age range, but she was redheaded and overweight. Not even close to the typical victim profile. Add the symbolic posing and an unexpected location to the picture and there was nothing that would suggest this to be the work of their unsub. He had been thinking 'copycat' until he heard the main reason he'd been called. The car was registered to none other than Patricia Shriver. Lynch didn't need n-dimensional calculus to do this math. Although there had been no ID at the scene, his eyes were the only tool he'd need to confirm the woman's identity in the E.D. And if her medical status matched their profile, she would be added to the MCS's caseload, but as an outlier like Edward Payne.

With the helicopter still in the air, he raced to beat its arrival at the medical center. Moving through heavier than usual evening traffic, he pushed toward the Emergency Department, running through signals and intersections with full lights and siren. As he drove, he realized it had been months since his last visit to the E.D. There had been a time he had eagerly rushed to the E.D. for purely personal reasons. He had used any excuse he could to stop by. Now he avoided the place, and the emotional distress it produced, even though he'd heard through the grapevine that she no longer worked there. He often wondered if part of her reason for leaving lay in the fact that they had met in the E.D.

He slowed to enter the parking lot and pulled into a slot reserved for police vehicles. As he climbed out of his car, he could hear the crescendo 'whomp-whomp' of descending helicopter blades. As he watched the bird land and its door open, he saw a helmeted female figure in a standard flight suit jump down to the blacktop. Even from a distance, he knew it was her. He'd arrived just in time, to confront his emotions.

As the aircraft approached the hospital's helipad, Amy's energy levels dropped along with their altitude. Adrenaline had supported her from the moment of the call until now, as her role in the care of this unfortunate woman was about to end. She noted a catharsis after delivering every critical patient. This time her sense of letdown was more acute than usual. Was it the unusual nature of the victim's plight? Maybe low blood sugar. She hadn't eaten since breakfast. Whatever the cause, she felt vulnerable.

With less than her usual zeal, she slid out of the helicopter and assisted the E.D. crew in loading their Jane Doe onto the gurney and running her into the department. Lightheaded for a moment, she steadied herself at the door to the patient bay. The emotional toll of the past two weeks had begun to tear at her somatically.

"Hey look, we can deal with the hand injury, but we're not taking primary responsibility on this one. This is a case for Trauma or maybe Neurosurg."

Amy walked into the E.D. as three residents were quarrelling.

"Yeah, neurosurgery should take it. Call Miller," the Trauma Service resident argued. "Only trauma is the hand and eyes and there's nothing surgical we can do for the eyes other than wound care. With the apparent brain injury, this should go to Neurosurg."

"I'll ask, but if they pass on it, it's going to fall on your turf, Nichols, and you know it." The E.D. resident turned from his colleagues and entered the trauma room.

Amy shook her head. The entire exchange was based on Amy's advance report. Not one of them had seen the patient yet. It remained the role of the resident or Emergency Department attending to do the initial workup and command the coin toss. Whoever said patient care was simple and free of politics?

"Hi, Amy."

"Hey, Rebecca. You got here quickly."

Rebecca Wilson was an E.D. nurse who had joined the Sexual Assault Response Team, SART, as a Sexual Assault Nurse Examiner. She would have first crack at the patient once she was deemed stable. In addition to examining the patient, the SANE would collect the specimens needed to confirm a sexual assault and to perform the forensics to be done on both hands prior to any corrective surgery.

"Yeah, lucky me. I was in the building following up on a case from yesterday. Is this what I think it is?"

Amy nodded. "Most likely." Amy had been working full-time in the E.D. when the first victims of the "LA Rapist" came in, and she had personally cared for one of those unfortunate women. She recognized a characteristic facial shroud of an anoxic brain injury in her current patient.

"Guess we can chalk this one to practice 'cause I doubt I'll find anything."

While little had been made public, the E.D. staff all

knew that those victims' SART evaluations had been clean. The only facet of rape that clung to these cases was the media's hyped-up name for the assailant.

"Any idea on a name, yet?"

Amy shook her head and replied, "No idea. There was no ID at the scene."

"Name's Elsa Dunleavy. Birth date, November 23rd, 1975. And I suggest you page Doctor Koettering on this one. Not his resident, him."

Amy's heart regained all the weight she'd struggled to lose over the past month and plummeted to her gut. It was a voice she both longed to hear and hated to hear at the same time. Her mind whirled in uncertainty at the maelstrom of emotions unleashed by this unexpected meeting. Yet, she was certain of one thing. The E.D., in front of friends and co-workers, was not the place to confront Lynch or lay bare her feelings. She turned and brushed past Lynch in a beeline to the refuge of the women's locker room, but escaped only ten feet before she heard him again.

"Amy? Please, don't—"

In agony, Lynch watched her walk away. It had taken only one more look into those crystalline cobalt eyes, eyes so deep he could fall into them, eyes that could make him dizzy with desire, to realize that he could ignore her no longer. He had been running scared, afraid to admit his feelings for her, afraid to make a commitment to someone, when his commitment to something else, his job, might very well shortchange her. He had seen his mother fend for herself as a 'widow' to his father's medical practice and his sister abandoned by a husband whose business travels led more to philandering than business. He'd sworn he would never do that to someone he loved, and yet that's exactly what he had done.

Amy continued without looking back and reached the inner room of the locker area before breaking down. For two months she had fantasized about what she would say when and if she ever ran into one Lynch Cully again. And the words weren't going to be kind. But now that it had happened, the words were gone, replaced by a longing for what they once had together. It wasn't just Lynch. Her unease over the hapless woman she'd just delivered to the hospital and vague worries about her father also burdened her. Perhaps had she been prepared to see Lynch, had she seen him across the E.D. before actually facing him, then she might have found better control of her emotions. But instead of preparation, there was surprise.

After several minutes, she composed herself and emerged from the locker room, relieved to see he wasn't waiting outside the door. She walked to the workroom, hoping to finish her paperwork quickly. They'd already worked past one change of shift. It was selfish of her to delay the pilot any longer because her emotions were playing an internal tug-of-war. She hunkered down in the back corner of the room, the furthest point from the door and continued the field report she had started en route. In a few fortunately uninterrupted minutes, she completed her task and began to gather her things.

"Hi, Amy."

She hadn't finished them quickly enough. She looked up to find Lynch at the door, her only way out of the room. She had an urge to get up and barge past him, ignoring him, but knew that the unsaid things would haunt her longer than anything he might say to her, or she to him. For so long, she'd wanted to know why—why did he stop calling, why had he ignored her, why did he not have the courtesy to return her calls—and the air needed clearing. Now and not later.

"That's it? We date for over a year and you just up and vanish from the face of the earth. No calls, no letters, nothing. And now it's 'Hi Amy'?"

Amy stared at him, noticing his look of fatigue and lines around the eyes where there had been none before. And she noted an air of contrition about him. Or was she just projecting that upon him? Did she want to forgive him, or not? Did she want to risk more heartbreak?

"How about . . . I'm a coward . . . full of feces . . . I'm really, truly sorry . . . and I've regretted it every day." He offered her a wan smile, before visibly taking a deep breath as if waiting for the storm to follow.

But there was no storm to conjure. Not even the slightest breeze remained to stiffen her sail.

"Yes, you have been . . . you sure are . . . and I'm not sure I believe you." She paused to see his reaction. His smile faded, and there was a slight nod to his head. "Why should I believe you?"

"I . . ." He paused and inhaled deeply before continuing. "Look, I won't give you any excuses because I have none. A reason maybe, but no excuses. All I can say is that there hasn't been a day this past couple of months that I haven't thought about you. I think—"

"Amy, there you are!" Reid entered the room, squeezing between Lynch and the doorframe. "Glen's waiting to take off. We need to get going."

"Um, okay. Be right there." Reid took off for the helipad, as Amy arose and picked up her report and gear. She looked at Lynch. "I have to go." She moved to walk past him, and he stepped aside, but didn't let her walk by.

He grabbed her elbow long enough to say one last thing. "Amy, I mean it. If you'd like to talk, I'm ready. But I'll leave it up to you. You call me, and I won't ignore you. I'll do whatever I have to do. Honest."

She gazed into his eyes and saw sincerity. "Okay. I don't know when that will be, but I'll call. One chance. That's it."

Seventeen

❧✦✦❦

Markie found himself wandering along the gravel road again. As his rock-throwing aim improved, the boredom increased. He found a partially rotted log along the berm, and flipped it over. Centipedes, ants, roaches, two crickets, and dozens of roly-polies ran for cover to escape exposure in the light. Markie, on the other hand, hoped for exposure and longed for the light. Matthew would return soon, and Markie would again be forced into that motor coach. Matthew acknowledged Markie, and cared for his needs, but it seemed he wanted nothing to do with him. There was no relationship, as if something physically prevented them from sharing the same room together.

Markie was only nine, but he was no dummy. He knew about the things Matthew did. He had learned about Matthew's surfing habits, the ones Matthew never allowed him to watch. And he knew about some of the women, although not what they did with Matthew in the coach bedroom. It had something to do with David's work. Matthew didn't know that Markie knew about David, but he knew enough to know that David was a doctor, someone who helped people. And that Matthew was somehow trying to help David with something David was trying to understand better. If David had been there, he might have saved his sister. If only Markie could make David aware of him. David would help.

*　*　*

Amy stayed quiet throughout the flight back to base, and the 20-minute flight took on intercontinental proportions. Her thoughts wandered along a circular path that reflected on the past twelve hours. Flight-by-flight, case-by-case, she relived her day, always ending with Elsa Dunleavy and weighed down with Lynch Cully. And her ever-present worries about her dad seasoned these contemplations.

As they retired to their quarters, she ignored the call for pizza and walked straight to her call room. She closed the door and lowered herself to her bed, sitting knees drawn up to her chest. She was beyond sobbing, but the tears escaped somehow.

"Darn you, Lynch Cully," she muttered. Why had he come back into her life? And at that, she realized that maybe he was back because deep inside she'd wanted it to be so. The outward animosity was a natural means of coping. It released pent-up emotions that her friends expected. It put the onus of guilt on the other party. But it truly did little to ease the insecurities, to assuage the inner guilt that maybe, just maybe, she had driven him away. Nor did it mend the heartbreak.

At the time, she had questioned God. Why? What was he trying to teach her? She had considered themselves equally yoked. Maybe they weren't. Was it patience she had to learn?

She had told Lynch she'd give him one more chance. Had that been the right thing to do? One thing for sure was that she wasn't about to cave in and call him at the first opportunity. She'd waited for him to call for months.

Now it was his turn, and a week or two wait was the minimum.

She wavered. Again.

Maybe she should go ahead and call, to see if he really meant what he'd said. She'd accept no excuse. He could take a bullet for the President. Terrorists could threaten the city. A madman could be shooting innocent strangers in random strikes along Market Street. If he didn't show, he would be out of the picture for good. Maybe. Again, her resolve dissolved.

She tossed and turned on the bed, unable to find a restful position, and mulled over calling her dad, hoping he had some guidance or insights that could help. In the past, she would never have considered confiding her affairs of the heart with him. What could he know? He was a guy—and her father. But he knew and liked Lynch, and with this newly displayed level of sensitivity, maybe it was time for his fatherly advice. She pulled her cell phone from her bag, powered it on, and entered her pass-code to log onto the system. Then, using her speed dial, she rang her father.

On the second ring, a feminine voice answered the phone. Amy looked at her phone. The number was correct. Had there been a misconnection by the system? Why was a woman answering her father's phone? *Surely, he would have told me if he was seeing someone. Wouldn't he?* It had to be a wrong number.

"Uh, is Andrew Gibbs there?" she asked.

"Umm, uh . . . yeah. Just a minute, please."

Eighteen
❧ ✦ ✦ ❧

Lynch looked through the crime scene photos and the technician's initial report before proceeding one more time to the preliminary statement by the SANE at the E.D. He had to make sure there were no discrepancies, and no source of contamination of the scene. He had asked for DNA samples from all of the police and EMS personnel who had been on the scene, but those findings would not be available for two weeks at the very earliest.

Once again, he found it difficult to concentrate. Thinking of the SANE exam brought him back to the E.D., and that turned his thoughts to Amy. She had looked wonderful. Slimmer than he recalled. Her hair shorter, but he liked the look. And her eyes. He had fallen into those deep blue wells before. They trapped him again. How could any man not be mesmerized by her eyes?

Lynch clenched his fists and took a deep breath. He had to refocus. They had a major case to solve and distraction was not an option. He sighed. As if he had any control over it.

Returning the reports and photos, Lynch prayed the Dunleavy assault might be the break they needed and called on the lab for a favor. Prematurely and unnecessarily, it turned out. Because of its macabre nature, the story had leaked out to the press, and theories ran rampant as to whether this was the work of the "LA Rapist" or some potentially worse offender. As a result, every police chief and politician who had the authority to make such a decision gave this crime the highest priority. Even the Governor had made a point of requesting the immediate processing of all specimens they had sent to the state lab.

"It's late. You still here?" Boyerton walked into the room, grinning and waving a thin sheaf of papers in the air. "Hot off the press," he stated. "Looks like we might have some DNA from the victim."

If the "LA Rapist" had perpetrated this assault, such evidence would be a first.

"What's that?" Lynch asked, hopeful.

"The hairs found with Dunleavy's pubic combing are head hair, and at least three had intact follicles for DNA testing. Results aren't official, but so far there's no match to anyone at the scene."

Lynch was incredulous. How? What kind of pressure had been applied, and where, to get DNA results so quickly? They must have sent them to the CSI lab on television, the only place in the world with same-day DNA testing. He chuckled inwardly at that thought. Maybe they could solve the case in the next hour, too.

Like with the previous victims, they discovered no semen, but if this hair came from the head of her assailant, it was just as critical. Had he gotten sloppy? Unlike the other victims who had been found at home, Elsa Dunleavy had been posed in a public place. Had he been interrupted? If so, was there someone out there who might have seen him?

"They're sure? I mean, her extrication was a problem

148

with cramped quarters and her body exposed. If that hair matches anyone who leaned over her during her recovery from the vehicle, we again have a victim with no usable DNA evidence."

"Like I said, nothing official yet, but c'mon, Lynch, it has to be our guy. Same M.O. The woman's left with a fried brain and a needle-stick wound in the crook of her left elbow."

Doctor Koettering had informed him that her PET scan and MRI angiogram were similar to those of the other victims he had studied. She appeared to have suffered an anoxic brain injury. The significance of the needle mark was questionable. They had found no drugs in her urine or serum, or in that of her predecessors. Maybe the needle mark was just this guy's signature, like placing a playing card on the body, or taking a finger as a souvenir.

"Not necessarily," Lynch answered because at the same time, she fell squarely outside the M.O. of their man. "She was plump and redheaded. She didn't live anywhere along the spiral, and she had a distinct relationship with another victim."

"Don't tell me you're changing your mind on this one. I thought you said you didn't think it could be a copycat."

There were those on the Major Case Squad who leaned toward that theory, that someone was using the victim's relationship to Patricia Shriver as a smokescreen, a means of misdirecting their inspection toward the chain of assaults and not to this single attack.

The Chief argued strongly for this possibility, and while Lynch could see their side of the debate, the anoxic brain injury was simply too specific. Lynch couldn't believe there might be two attackers with the medical knowledge to pull off such a feat. Still, she was redheaded, overweight, and posed in a public place, factors that placed her well outside the M.O. of their unsub. Lynch had no choice but to wonder just how difficult it would be to replicate the anoxic brain injury. Information on anything and everything was available on the Internet. Even though they had no clue as to how the unsub had inflicted this injury in these cases, there were alternative methods, just as he had discussed with the medical examiner.

Lynch shrugged his shoulders.

"Okay, whatever," Boyerton responded. "Tell you what, if the night shift stays slow I'll hop over to the lab and see if they have anything more. Okay? Want me to call if anything shows up?"

"Nope. Unless it tells us the guy's real identity, it can wait 'til morning."

Boyerton tossed the papers onto the desk in front of Lynch and turned to leave the room. Lynch picked them up and read them through once, drumming his fingers on his desk, but stopping after becoming aware that he was unconsciously imitating the Chief's nervous habit. *Phew! He's rubbing off on me a bit too much.* He stood up from his chair and stretched, twisting his shoulders from left to right and back again to work a kink out of his lower back. He glanced at his watch to discover it was approaching midnight. *Best be heading home.*

He gathered the materials from his desk and organized the stack prior to jamming them into his briefcase. To one side of the desk lay the last two days' front-page sections from the local paper. The Dunleavy attack had been front-page material on both days and had provided various groups the fodder to attack verbally the many police departments involved in the string of attacks by the "LA Rapist," as well as the Major Case Squad, for their failure to find the culprit and string him up from the nearest tall oak. That, in turn, had spurred a furious response from the anti-death penalty crowd.

As Lynch picked up the top paper, he didn't bother with the print. He focused on the photo above the fold on the front page. Someone had captured a photo of Amy and her crew unloading a patient from the helicopter onto a waiting gurney at the Medical Center's helipad. Whether the patient was Elsa Dunleavy or not could not be seen in the photo, and the picture could have been an old stock photo, but it gave the appearance that the newspaper had been right on top of the emerging story.

And it put Amy right back at the top of Lynch's thoughts. Not that he needed much of a nudge. He hadn't really stopped thinking of her since running into her at the trauma center. If he'd found it hard to subjugate those thoughts and focus on the case earlier that night, seeing her picture only added to his problem. If he were to dream that night, she'd be at the center of them.

It had been three days. No call. But then, he deserved

it. It had been roughly three months since he'd stopped calling, two months since he'd ignored her last call. What would he have said? That he needed time alone to find himself? In reflection, he wasn't sure he liked what he'd found. Could he tell her the truth? That he'd fallen head-over-heels in love with her and it scared him beyond anything he'd ever experienced before. Scared that she'd reject him. Scared that he'd be unable to hold up his end of a committed relationship. Scared that he would fail her somehow and drive her away. Scared that one day he might not make it home and would leave her a widow. And after witnessing her grief from the loss of her brother, afraid she'd not be able to live with losing her spouse in the line of duty.

It was one game of "what if" he didn't like playing. It was easier to run away, bury himself with work, and never have to confront it.

He laid the paper back on the desk and closed the top of his briefcase. As he picked it up, his cell phone began to vibrate. He put the case back down to unclip his phone and with a quick look saw that it was Janick.

"Cully," he answered.

"Yeah, hey, we got a problem. Where are you right now?"

"Bob, it's . . ." Lynch started to protest, but knew it would make no difference. "At the MCS ops."

"Yeah, figured you might be when you didn't answer at home. We got a problem."

Lynch wanted to make some sarcastic reply, but was tired enough that nothing came to mind. "You said that once."

"You know we was waiting on the guy who did the air conditioning job at Payne's law office to come back from vacation." Lynch knew Janick had been champing at the bit to interview the man, suspecting he had been al-Harasis' accomplice. "Well, we got word he was flying back from Vegas this evening. Traced his accounts there and he lost a wad of money."

"So, that's good for your case, right? He spent the payoff money. So?" Lynch figured maybe he could humor Janick and push him to get to the point quicker.

"Yeah, yeah, right. And—"

"And the problem is you've lost him. Should I act surprised? Bob, why are you calling me with this at midnight? Pick him up in the morning."

"Crap, Cully. We were at the airport to pick him up. Ralph saw him get off the plane, and the guy up and vanishes. Luggage unclaimed. Car still in the lot. Gone."

Lynch was tired and irritated. "Okay, I see your problem. What's that got to do with my case?"

"We searched his car and found red hair and some women's slacks in the trunk, and a map with that spiral stuff you been talking about drawn on it. But it shows a victim in the South City area, not Sunset Hills. As I hear it, you're setting your trap in the wrong spot."

Nineteen

Lynch arrived at the Major Case Squad Ops Center to find a euphoric, almost jubilant atmosphere. Even the Chief was smiling. What had he missed? Had they found the alleged accomplice?

"Lynch, did you hear the news?" he asked as soon as he saw the young detective.

Lynch shook his head.

"Good news. Got word from Janick that the hair and slacks found in his suspect's car belonged to Elsa Dunleavy. This is our first really big break."

Lynch couldn't disagree. Well, not totally. Evidence in the trunk of a car, particularly a car that had been parked in the airport's long-term parking lot, could quickly be argued to be circumstantial. It would be a big break if they found the guy, or if they found a DNA match. In a case that had spawned more political and media heat than any in recent history, such evidence could be case breaking.

"But, what about the map? Janick said we're setting up our trap in the wrong spot."

The Chief waved his hand dismissively.

"We've got an all-points bulletin out for an Art Barklage. The B&G Heating and Cooling offices and his home are being searched as we speak, and we're setting up 24/7 surveillance for both places." The Chief turned and retreated to his office.

Lynch couldn't ignore the map. Something didn't fit.

Neither Dunleavy's home nor office fell along the spiral, so why would the map be there? In fact, if this guy was as smart as Lynch suspected, why would he leave such a map behind? It had to be a plant. But that added a new dimension that startled Lynch when it came to mind. How did the perp know they had worked out his spiral plan? Did they have a leak in the squad?

At this point, the drill was typical. Detectives would interview Barklage's family, workers, and neighbors. They'd scrutinize his spending habits and charge card receipts. One or two detectives would get the tough task of going to Las Vegas to reconstruct his activities there and inspect casino security video that might have caught him off and on throughout his stay in "Sin City." To cover this expansion in their investigation, Lynch soon learned that the Chief had recruited eight more detectives, all of whom were eager to help.

But to Lynch they were again on a first-class snipe hunt. Barklage failed to meet the assailant's profile in numerous ways. He was a high school graduate who learned the HVAC trade through an apprenticeship and was fortunate enough to marry the boss' daughter and become a partner in the business. He had no military or other experience to account for the expertise in explosives required to take out Payne's law offices. He had some computer proficiency, but not at the advanced level Lynch expected. He had no medical knowledge and probably couldn't even spell 'anoxic' by Lynch's best estimate. And there was the simple fact that he was in Las Vegas when Elsa Dunleavy was assaulted. True, he might have set up some alternate means of travel to return home for the sole purpose of adding Ms. Dunleavy to the garden patch and then return to Vegas to cement his alibi, but Barklage's reputation at work as a "simple good ol' boy" made that quite unlikely.

Lynch was also concerned that the Chief had taken this line of reasoning. It was out of character for the man, a man who had excelled as a detective because he considered all possibilities.

Lynch knocked on the doorway. "Chief?"

The older man swiveled around in his chair to face Lynch. He was on the phone, but motioned to Lynch to take a seat. A minute later, he hung up and turned fully toward the younger detective. His smile disappeared as he cocked his head and took in Lynch's body language, which by any interpretation screamed, "I don't believe this!"

"Ahh, you must think I've caved to the pressure, huh?"

Lynch shifted uncomfortably in his chair and tried to relax his body position.

"Lynch, I know what this looks like. And I know how you think, so I'd have to be pretty dense to believe you could agree that this man is our perp. For the record, I doubt he is either."

Lynch started to say something, but sensed that the Chief was not finished.

"I realize the evidence from his car is at best circumstantial, but this is the first break we've had in months. Even if this guy isn't the real thing, he's the single best lead we've had thrown our way since this series of assaults started. And that's got everyone motivated, whether they believe him guilty or not."

Lynch eased his body's position in his chair. He was relieved to hear the Chief say that and to know that the political pressure hadn't pushed the Squad ahead of the evidence.

"Look, I don't want you getting wrapped up in this hunt for Barklage. The others are likely to ask for your help there, but I want you to stay focused on what you're doing now. We need to get this guy, and sooner, not later. From what we've seen, assuming he really is behind these latest cases, his rampage is escalating, and he's likely to strike again real soon."

"Yes, sir, I'd agree. But even without these three recent cases, his pattern says he's due for another strike any time now anyway. What do you make of the map from Barklage's car?"

The Chief rummaged through a stack of papers on his desk and pulled out a photograph of that map. "I've looked at this several times. Probably a plant, to point to Barklage and to throw us off. That means three things."

"Sir?" Lynch had surmised that the map was a red herring. What else did the Chief see?

"First, he thinks we're dumb enough to fall for the planted evidence and go after Barklage as the 'LA Rapist.'"

Lynch nodded. That would fit the profile of someone so intelligent he saw himself elevated in station and beyond the law, as someone unstoppable. It was also the unsub's best-case scenario, to throw the blame elsewhere with just enough evidence to make that case plausible. Then, as the hunt progressed, he could unveil more evidence to the police to make it believable.

"Second, he's probably orchestrated Barklage's disappearance and will strike again while the man is missing. That assures Barklage won't have an alibi when we're finally allowed to catch him."

That fell in line with what Lynch was thinking. Plus, the phrase 'finally allowed' didn't escape Lynch. The Chief was on target, as usual.

"And third, he knows we're getting closer. Thus, the attempted decoy, and he's likely to know when we're coming for him. That makes him especially dangerous."

Lynch tensed a bit in his chair. This was the second time the Chief had commented on that possibility, and it unsettled Lynch. The Chief wasn't just telling him to be careful and to avoid getting complacent. He was telling Lynch not to fall into the same trap as the assailant, not to get so cocky about his intellect and skill that he became overconfident about getting his man. Yet, Lynch saw something else in the man's statement, something he would have to contemplate. How would the man know they were coming? Intuition? A tap into the police computers? Or more disturbing, was he one of their own?

After leaving the Chief's office, Lynch drove toward the Central West End neighborhood, a chic community within the city limits known for its art galleries, antique shops, sidewalk eateries that formed a bright tapestry of umbrellas and awnings, and trendy boutiques that catered to young professionals and nearby university students. Tall, stately oaks and elms that were lively with color and the early shedding of leaves, lined the streets, a rambling mix of cobblestone and asphalt. The area had undergone a renaissance in recent years with restored and updated older homes making it one of the more fashionable areas to live within the city. That also made it one of the more expensive areas to live, and Lynch was unsure how Elsa Dunleavy had afforded a small home there.

The community was a liberal one, even by modern standards, and popular in the gay and lesbian community because of its "enlightened tolerance." Many, if not a majority, of the restaurant workers and clothing store staffs were part of that sub-culture. He had not confirmed that Elsa was of that persuasion, but the buzz coming from more than one source said that she was. Perhaps Patricia Shriver, with whom rumor held that Elsa had a more-than-working relationship, had financed her home, totally or partially. Perhaps she'd inherited it. That wasn't unheard of. Under the current circumstances, however, how she obtained the property was irrelevant. Its only importance to Elsa now was that its sale would help provide her the cash needed for a lifetime of full-time nursing attention in one of the better long-term care centers.

Lynch drove down the business district's main thoroughfare, his wheels chattering over the restored cobblestone lanes. The beautiful early September weather typically brought the sidewalk cafes to life, their outside tables crowded with lunchtime patrons, and the delicious aromas of grilled meats and hearty spices could catch your attention blocks away. As he drove, he thought about how much, right now, he'd love to be rid of this case, to be able to enjoy lunch with Amy at one of these eateries. Then maybe they'd walk to Left Bank Books and lurk among the shelves to find the right book to take on a weekend get-away.

Yet, today, being midweek and with classes in session, the streets were nearly devoid of university students, and the sidewalks and shops were noticeably less crowded. Lynch turned down a side street in time to see two tall women emerge from a clothing store, fashionably dressed, well made up, and carrying shopping bags.

The taller of the two turned toward Lynch as he passed them and seemed suddenly surprised. Lynch, too, was unexpectedly taken aback. He stomped on his brakes to avoid rear-ending the car in front of him and once stopped, turned to look again, but the duo had hurried into another store. She looked remarkably like an older version of Amy. Should they stand next to each other, they might appear as sisters. Lynch waited, hoping to catch another glimpse, but the car behind him honked, and he moved on.

Man, I think I've really lost it this time, he thought. Amy had reclaimed his thoughts. He saw her in unrelated people on the street. He debated not waiting for her to call and calling her that night, but he knew he couldn't force himself back into her life. She needed to make the decision about granting him one more chance. He could only pray for her forgiveness. After another fitful night's sleep, he had finally admitted to himself that he was head-over-heels in love with Amy. He would do whatever it took to regain her trust.

Lynch turned left down the next street and pulled up in front of the home of Elsa Dunleavy. The home was a typical row house from the turn of the last century, two and a half stories with two dormers built into the roof line, matched by two four-over-one windows on the second floor. A covered stoop announced the front door on the left side of the first floor, while the right side held another window matching those above. A short concrete walkway led from the front sidewalk to the front door. Yellow police tape blocked the front door, but someone had recently cut the grass, as evidenced by still-green clippings on the sidewalk. He retrieved his two flash drives from the seat beside him and headed for a side door, for which he had the key. Immediately inside, he signed a register on a clipboard, indicating his time in and, as he left, his time out.

He had not been to her house before this, so he took several minutes to walk through and peruse the place. Despite the home's rather traditional outside appearance, inside it was succinctly more modern with furnishings of Scandinavian flavor, hardware of brushed chrome, and light woods for moldings, baseboards, and the like. Area rugs over light oak floors were abstract and colorful. Lynch took time to scrutinize the framed photos on the bookshelves and mantels, as well as those running up the wall along the main stairs. From the pictures, it appeared conclusive that Elsa and Patricia had been more than assistant and boss. But those images were of a younger Elsa, with a different hair color, dark brown, and a much slimmer figure. From those pictures, she would have fit the "LA Rapist's" preferred victim list. *Which is her natural color*? he wondered. He made a mental note to ask the lab about whether her hair was colored or not.

More current photos, those showing her as Lynch knew her, revealed a different person of prominence in her life. He also made a note to try to discover who that was. Perhaps she knew something of Elsa's fateful night. Perhaps one of the other detectives on her case had already interviewed the young woman. He picked up a photo that seemed current and placed it on a table near the side door so he wouldn't forget to check on it.

On the second floor, he discovered the room that was her home office and found a reasonably up-to-date desktop system with thin-screen LCD monitor on a sleekly styled but cluttered workstation. He checked the cables and turned it on. According to the crime lab report, they had inspected her system and combed her hard drives for information the day after discovering her at the park. Supposedly, no one else had used the machine, yet a quick inspection of the system logs revealed that someone had turned on the machine the day after the crime technicians and had accessed her MS Outlook program. Lynch's first thought was of someone removing their contact information, but that made little sense unless that person was unaware that the crime lab had already gathered such information from the hard drive so that the detectives could use it to find friends and relatives. It also was unlikely that the person using the computer was their man. He would have erased everything.

That was a mystery that would remain unsolved for now. Lynch's main purpose for being there was to scan the drive for their culprit's signature code. He pushed a thumb drive into the USB port and started the utility program designed to find the code. About halfway through his scan, the screen blanked and a message appeared, "Not this time." The keyboard and mouse failed to work, but the hard drive LED showed it was fast at work. Faster than Lynch.

"No! No! Not now!" said Lynch, frantic as he tried the power button to turn off the machine. Nothing. The button did nothing. He scrambled to move the computer and find its power cord. He pulled it from the socket and the machine died.

Twenty

❧ ♦ ♦ ❧

Lynch had a bounce in his step as he rushed from the university's Parking Lot G toward the academic quadrangle holding the Psychology Department, a collection of century-old buildings with which he was all too familiar. He had loved attending school here and walking among the buildings brought back some great memories. Yet, he resisted any thoughts of what it would have been like to attend college knowing what he now knew. His parents had used that clichéd statement way too many times when he attended there.

His own academic mentor, although semi-retired now, still had an office on the second floor of the building to Lynch's immediate left. He wondered if the elder statesman of abnormal psych still held court on the benches outside the quad. He laughed at the sudden memories of some of the impromptu "psych experiments" he and his friends had performed over the lunch hour right there along the main walkway toward the central cafeteria, stunts more reminiscent of *Candid Camera* than serious, controlled tests, all under the watchful eye of their own Allen Funt. Herr Doktor-professor Hessling, as he jokingly called himself with a perfect but cartoonish German accent, had earned his PhD in Austria, but Freud and Jung could never have made the study of abnormal psych so much fun.

He smiled at the security camera as he neared the door, wondering when face recognition software would become de rigueur for campus security forces. As he reached for the door, his cell phone rang, and he stopped, retreated several yards away from the building, and answered it.

"Hey, it's Mike."

Earlier that day, he wanted to kiss Mike Jurgesmeyer's feet, but was afraid to comment from the fear that Mike might actually remove his shoes. At Lynch's suggestion, the computer techs had checked the drive for usable files, had lucked upon finding the Outlook.pst file intact, and were able to compare it to the same file, as it had existed a few days earlier. Lynch's guess had been on target. Someone didn't want police associating her, or him, with Elsa, and, in fact, a single name and address had been erased from her 'Contacts' list. Lindsey Parrish. After a few calls to local detectives in the Central West End precinct, Lynch learned that the young woman had avoided making it onto their list of contacts in the case. He had volunteered to remedy that omission.

"Just wanted you to know we finished comparing the hard drive image we took from the Dunleavy computer on our first inspection with what was left after you pulled the plug. Looks like the overwriting pattern is the same as the one used to wipe Payne's computer."

Lynch clenched his fist with a subtle jerk down. *Yes*, he thought. "Sounds like another puzzle piece pointing to our guy."

"Yeah. Besides the altered Outlook file, we also found a handful of jpeg files that had been deleted from her photo directory. They all had the same girl in them. Mid-twenties, short blond hair, prominent freckles. Might be the one who tampered with the computer."

"Well, I'll find out shortly. I was just going in to meet with her. I'll let you know."

After a few more pleasantries, Jurgesmeyer hung up, and Lynch headed for the door. Lindsey Parrish was a university graduate student, working on her own PhD in Psychology. Lynch found her in the department, presiding over a developmental psych class as a teaching assistant, a freckled, blond assistant in her mid twenties. She expected his visit, although she seemed most unhappy that she'd been discovered. Lynch politely waited outside the classroom for the few minutes until the session ended, and then introduced himself after the last of the students emerged from the room. She led him to a cramped office on the upper floor of the old building. He guessed the floor had little, if any, air conditioning in the summer, making it undesirable by the tenured staff. And being the upper floor, it was probably equally as hot in the winter with the old steam radiator system evident in the building as they walked the floors and stairs. As he entered the office, three separate fans in the room confirmed his guess.

"Ms. Parrish, thanks for meeting with me. I guess this has been awfully hard for you."

She closed the door and opened a window for ventilation instead. "It's a nightmare. I mean, I still can't believe Elsa was . . ." She broke down and Lynch grabbed a box of tissues from his side of the desk and offered it to her. "Thanks." She struggled to regain control. "Elsa was a really good friend. I . . ." She paused. "I'm sorry."

Lynch was unsettled as to how to start, so he thought it best to begin with something a bit trivial.

"I had a chance to see Elsa's home and the pictures she had displayed. Saw you in a few of them."

"Yeah, she loved photography. I don't think she went anywhere without her digital camera."

Lynch paused for a moment to think through the evidence list. He did not recall the recovery of a camera from her car, and he hadn't seen one in her home. If, indeed, she did not go anywhere without it, had she taken it with her to her ill-fated meeting? The task of finding that camera found itself etched into the "higher priority" category of his to-do list.

"I don't think we found a camera. Do you know what kind she owned?"

"A little point and shoot. A Nikon, I think. She always had it with her, even though her phone took pictures, too."

Lynch made another mental note. They hadn't found a phone either.

"I also noticed two Elsas, one dark haired and one redheaded."

The young woman smiled. "Amazing difference, huh? She was a natural redhead. She had colored it at the request of someone else."

That cleared up one question in Lynch's notebook. But it raised another. Did the assailant know she was a natural redhead, or had he only noticed her as a brunette? If it was the former, then her relationship to Patricia Shriver alone was the motive for her attack. With the latter, her assault could have been because she fit the attacker's preference profile. Lynch considered that for a moment and leaned toward the first case. The message sent by her "Lady Justice" posing took this case out of the realm of the "LA Rapist's" standard M.O., if they could believe he still held to a pattern. Recent cases certainly showed a man capable of breaking the mold.

"I understand. Look, um, I don't know how to ask this other than straight up. We know that Elsa was involved in at least one lesbian relationship. Were you two—?"

Lindsey sat up straight in her chair. "Were we involved? Not as you might think. Patricia asked her to color her hair. She didn't fancy Elsa's red hair. She was pretty controlling in other ways as well." The woman paused. "I was also involved in a lesbian relationship at one time. I loved it and hated it at the same time. I mean, my partner was kind and caring. She had the qualities I wanted from a lover and figured I'd never find in a man. But I hated the secrecy from my family and the isolation from friends who disappeared after they found out. One day, one of those friends approached me, and we talked of heavenly things, eternity, and I gave my life to God. I've been out of the lifestyle for two years now and am happier than ever. And I have a boyfriend who has proven to me that the qualities I sought really don't have any gender barriers." She paused and gazed out the window.

"And Elsa?" Lynch prompted.

"Last year I joined a group called Exodus International. Are you familiar with it?"

Lynch shook his head.

"We work with those seeking to leave the gay and lesbian culture. It's not easy. There's a lot of handholding, in a, well, you know what I mean. I was working with Elsa."

Lynch had to admire the woman's stand. She was one of a few in a profession that endorsed the homosexual lifestyle and that condemned anyone who suggested that someone could leave the culture and change their sexual orientation.

"Did you access her computer and erase your name from her address book?"

The woman nodded. "Pretty stupid of me, I guess. I know I shouldn't have crossed the police tape, but I just didn't want to get dragged into any investigation. And I didn't want any of her old friends somehow learning that I was helping her to leave the lifestyle. It's hard enough without facing their threats and taunts."

Lynch debated whether or not to bring up the fact that she could be charged with trespassing, or worse, tampering with evidence. He reasoned that a good lawyer could argue that since she had accessed Dunleavy's computer *after* the crime techs had collected their data, she hadn't really tampered with any evidence. No, she was cooperating. He would let this infraction slide.

"Did you notice anything strange while you were using it?"

"Um, I'm not sure. I only signed on for maybe five minutes. She's connected to a DSL line, and I noticed that the computer was exchanging data through that network connection even though I wasn't doing anything online. You know, those little computer monitor symbols in the bottom right of the screen that show you have a network connection? They were on almost the whole time I was there, even when I turned off her Outlook program. Now that I think about it, I couldn't turn off the computer until those icons showed the Internet activity had stopped. Is that normal?"

Lynch couldn't be sure. Every system had its peculiarities, but he suspected that her use of the computer had given their man time to download his hard drive demolition software. He would be smart enough to know that they would search her computer the day after her assault and had been confident enough to expect someone else might turn it on for him after the initial investigation. Yet, Lynch realized that he, too, might have triggered the event. He had been checking out her computer for more than fifteen minutes before he started his scan for the binary code. He had focused on his inspection and had paid no attention to any Internet activity while he was there.

"Tell me, did you talk to Elsa anytime that day, the day of her assault?"

The woman looked teary and nodded. "I did. She called in the middle of the afternoon, all excited. She was going to be joining a very prestigious lawyer and her husband for dinner. The woman has written several of the textbooks used by legal assistants and had known Patricia. She and her husband were traveling, by a large motor coach, I think she said, and had offered to swing into town to talk with Elsa and help her deal with Patricia's death. I don't recall if she said anything about where they were going or how late they'd be out. Sorry."

"Do you recall this woman's name? Or how Elsa met her?"

"Hmm, she did mention the name, but I'll have to think about that a little, try to remember it. I do know they connected through the Internet."

Lynch felt a surge of excitement. Did she just help confirm his theory about the legal forum being used by the unsub to find targets? And a motor coach? This was a new piece to play with, like finding all of the edges in a jigsaw puzzle at once.

Lady Law took advantage of the excellent weather and jogged to his destination, hoping the exercise would clear his head. He was unaccustomed to failure of any kind, and it unsettled him that he had failed to monitor Elsa's computer usage patterns, and in so doing, had failed to anticipate one tiny, tiny detail—that she'd turn off her computer after their last chat and not use it again prior to their meeting. The result of which was that he'd not had an opportunity to send her system a simple command, the one that erased all possible traces of their online conversations, as well as his spyware.

He attempted to correct that error at the first

available opportunity, only to have someone astute enough to pull the plug on Elsa's computer before his program had completed its task. It was one thing for the police to have a full, hard disk image with trillions of bytes to parse and analyze. That could take weeks. Having a partially erased drive to compare to a fully restored drive now made their job a lot easier. This was a failure he could only hope to minimize by careful planning of his next steps.

His breathing became labored as he climbed a long hill. The incline was gradual, but enough to tax him. Yet, he smiled at the thought of taunting the police. He loved the message he sent to Elsa's computer. "Not this time." Not at anytime was more like it, but the message should have been enough to mock whoever was looking for him. And the evidence he planted in the trunk of that fool air conditioning man's car surely had them working overtime. Not that he expected them to suspect the man of being their 'LA Rapist.' No, they likely had a profile that such a simpleton could never fulfill. Still, he enjoyed the thought of leading them on a merry goose chase.

His jog eased to a walk as he entered a gravel lane that penetrated the far south end of Creve Coeur County Park. The overgrown service road, rarely used, led to a small supply cabin, no longer used. There was graffiti on the walls and lovers' initials carved into the rustic, heavy wooden door. The area's use as a teen lovers' rendezvous stopped when a rumor started that two teens had disappeared from there, a rumor that started about the same time as the first assault by the "LA Rapist."

He fished some keys from the pocket of his jogging shorts and unlocked the new padlock on the recently installed heavy-gauge metal accordion gate designed to keep vandals from breaking in the old wooden door. He quietly slid the gate back and unlocked the wooden door. Muffled grunts greeted his entry into the dimly lit cabin.

"Ahh, you're awake." The reply to his words was a frantic shaking of the rusty metal cot in one corner of the room. "Whoa—careful. You might hurt yourself. You really don't want to break open those stitches. The scarring would be awful, not to mention the risk of infection in an environment like this. Here, let's take a look."

As Lady Law held a small battery-powered lantern over the man's body, the look of terror in the fully restrained Art Barklage's eyes brought pleasure to his tormentor.

"Good. The sutures are intact and clean. Hold still while I disinfect them again." A muffled groan of pain emerged as the drips of now-banned Mercurochrome touched the incisions and initiated a stinging pain much more intense than alcohol on an open wound. Lady Law dabbed the substance around each one and taped clean four-by-four gauze over each. "There, that should hold until my next visit." The muffled sound of swearing followed. "That's enough! You should be pleased with the enhancements I've given you. Would you like a more permanent alteration?" Barklage's eyes widened in horror as he shook his head violently. "I didn't think so. Well, time to sleep. Goodnight."

Lady Law picked up a vial of sedative, drew up a precise amount, and slowly pushed it into a port on one of the man's intravenous lines. He then added three new bags of fluids and examined the man's urinary output through the Foley catheter taped to his leg and draping over the edge of the bed. It was sufficient. Each plastic bag of normal saline dripped slowly enough to last until the next visit, yet combined, provided adequate fluids to prevent dehydration. Barklage had no need for glucose, or amino acids, or fatty acids, or vitamins, or anything else expected for complete parenteral feeding. No more loose ends. The man would only live long enough to hear Lady Law boast of his next initiate, the next addition to his collection.

The information from Lindsey had been of great value. Elsa might have had dinner with such a couple, and met her fate after that engagement. Or the dinner date might have been more role-playing by their assailant and a lure to snatch the unsuspecting woman. The value in her information lay in three facts: that Elsa had a camera and cell phone that had not been located, that she met with someone who owned a motor home, and that she had connected to this person through the Internet. Regarding the latter, Lynch knew just where to look and who to contact. As he sat at his desk, the interoffice memos piling higher each week as he focused on his main case, he fingered through his case file and found the list of women lawyers who co-directed the Internet forum with Patricia Shriver. His first contact attempt found the lawyer in court, but his second was successful.

"Ms. Straus, my name is Sergeant Lynch Cully, and I'm investigating Patricia Shriver's murder. Do you have a moment for just a few questions?"

"Certainly, Sergeant Cully. I was told to expect a call, but I honestly thought I would hear from someone earlier than this."

"I'm sorry. We had no need to bother you or anyone else involved with your law forum until now. It seems the case has taken some new and tragic turns." Lynch proceeded to inform the woman of Elsa Dunleavy's assault, without going into detail. He also told of their suspicions that the assailant, Patricia Shriver's murderer, had been using the law forum to meet and connect with the women he subsequently attacked.

"This, this is horrible. I can talk to my colleagues and shut down the forum if we must. We can't let this go on."

"Actually, Ms. Straus, we need you to leave it in place. We'd like to discreetly bait the individual and draw him out if we can. We have a plan, but first, do you know of any participants who have authored one or more major textbooks for legal assistants?"

There was a long pause at the other end. "I-I'm sorry. Your question floors me. But to answer it, yes. Alice Wespike is a distinguished member of our group. She's authored the major text used by almost every program in this country. Certainly, you don't . . . I-I just can't believe this. I've known her for years. She and her husband are wonderful people."

175

"Do she and her husband travel frequently, in a motor home?" Lynch heard a sigh of relief through the earpiece.

"Thank God. For a moment I thought you suspected . . . you don't, do you?" There was another pause. "Howard travels some, but by plane mostly. Alice has been wheelchair bound for almost three years thanks to a drunk driver."

"Does she participate in your forum?" Lynch was beginning to see the truth.

"Well, I didn't think she liked computers, even though she's been forced to adapt and use one for her books. But for the past year, someone using the handle Lady Law has been promoting a new book for legal assistants. I simply assumed it was Alice, but I never confirmed it directly with her. Omigod, are you implying what I think you are? Some kind of identity theft?"

Lady Law? he thought. His gut assured him they had found their man, but it added some new twists to their profile. The symbolism of Lady Law versus Lady Justice was confirmation of that. That the law had "screwed" justice revealed someone whom justice had failed, maybe thanks to some legal technicality. How, when, and where were simply targets for speculation, but the 'who' wasn't. Lynch snorted a half laugh to himself. *It's always the mother, isn't it,* he could hear Doctor Hessling saying. The profile of his victims implied a direct relationship with the man's mother. A strange noise from the other end, followed by quiet sobs, drew him back to the current conversation. "Ms. Straus?"

"Poor Patricia. If only we'd listened."

"What's that?"

"On the forum we've never required any kind of formal registration or proof of identity because we figured it was such a specialized group, and we wanted to encourage candor in the discussions. Not to mention that as lawyers and legal assistants, we felt a need to protect our right to privacy. For the past six or eight months, Patricia argued that we needed to have some sort of registration; some means of doing identity checks on anyone whose behavior seemed out of place. I led the move to protect our privacy rights, and we never changed our policy. Oh dear God, if only I hadn't been so insistent, so smug about our rights, Patricia and her assistant might still be alive."

The anguish in the woman's voice was palpable. Lynch could feel her pain six hundred miles away, and although he didn't like the idea of playing on her emotions, he had to. "Ms. Straus, I'm sorry. I mentioned we had a plan. Briefly, we want to set up one or more decoys using your forum. Bait, you might say. Can we enlist your cooperation?"

The woman's voice steadied as she replied, "Most certainly." It possessed an edge of courtroom steel as she said, "Let's nail this S-O-B."

Twenty-one

As was typical of the area, the weather in September shifted from summer's relentless heat to a pattern of moving fronts. Beautiful blue skies and temperatures in the upper seventies dominated the five consecutive days of the workweek. And as usual, she worked three of those five days and slept away the better part of the other two.

Amy finished her shift and drove home as the early morning light yielded to a fast-moving frontal system and the increasingly ominous clouds that led its charge. She carried her bag into her bedroom and unpacked prior to taking a leisurely hot shower. She debated plugging the tub and letting it fill with water so she could lie back and relax in its womblike warmth, perhaps accompanied by a packet of soothing, floral bath salts.

But she didn't have time. Some mysteries needed solving sooner rather than later. After the woman who answered gave her father the phone, he'd said simply that she was an old friend seeking to sell her vintage sports car and wanting his advice on pricing it. Okay, plausible enough. But, why had Amy never met this old friend? And if he was inspecting a used car, why was she there at ten o'clock at night, after dark? Maybe he was evaluating *her* chassis. Maybe her imagination wasn't as fatigued as the rest of her. She tried to clear that last thought from her mind. It didn't bother Amy that her father might be seeing someone. Her mother had been dead for fifteen years, and her father needed someone in his life. But, why hide it? She didn't want to think her father was hiding something, someone, from them, but the thought kept asserting itself, battling her thoughts about Lynch for pre-eminence.

I don't need this right now. She seemed to be jogging on a wheel even a hamster would avoid. As her relationship with Lynch dissolved, her once distant father filled the gap. Now, as her father seemed to distance himself once again, Lynch was trying to re-enter her life. At the moment, convent life struck her as the best way off the treadmill. But she was unaware of any Southern Baptist convents.

One issue at a time. She intended to pay her father a surprise visit, and she would most likely find him at home before noon as opposed to after.

What if, what if, what if. The phrase replayed itself in her mind, and she recalled Lynch's passion for the "what if?" game when on a case. He was another "mystery" to be solved. She remained unsure as to what had actually happened in their brief encounter in the E.D. Was he just trying to cover his tracks, to improve what others might think of him after dumping her? He had never really been one to worry about what others thought of him. So, why would he start now? Perhaps he felt bad for how he had broken off their relationship and now wanted to apologize, but nothing more. But, what if he truly was remorseful and wanting to reconcile? What would she do then? Delays on her part wouldn't deliver the answers she needed.

Her father's home was less than an hour away, and

she drove as quickly as she dared considering the weather had materialized into a gauntlet of constant drizzle interspersed with heavy torrents of rain. The clock ticked past eleven, and she began to worry that he might not be home, but, upon arriving, she gratefully saw his car parked on the drive in front of the garage. *Funny, he always parks in the garage*, she thought.

She dashed through the rain to the front door and, protected by the portico of the stoop, she checked her hair in the reflection from the windows at the side of the doorway, put on her best 'surprise' face, and rang the bell. Normally, when he knew she was coming, she would ring the bell and let herself in with her own key. Under the circumstances, she thought that might not be her best move. She wanted to gently surprise him, not induce a heart attack.

The door opened.

"Amy! What a pleasant surprise!"

The look on his face belied the words. In fact, the look of his face was noticeably different. Her brother, Grant, had left a message saying Dad looked awful. His face was gaunt and drawn, yet . . . Amy couldn't pin it down. He didn't look ill. Certainly, he appeared thinner than at their last encounter, and his face showed the weight loss.

"Surprise! I thought I'd come over and treat you to lunch. The rain makes it a perfect day for a luncheon. You can't do yard work. We can't go flying. And it's cleared my allergies so I feel hungry for the first time in over a week. How about it? Maybe 'The Flying Goat'?" Neither of them knew the origins of the name, but both loved the eclectic atmosphere and excellent food there.

Her father appeared uncertain for a moment and glanced to the back of the house. Amy followed his gaze and looked past him. Was someone else there? She hoped so.

"Umm, I'm, uh, not interrupting something, am I? Do you have company?"

"Oh no, not at all. I was just planning on a bit of work in the garage, but I can start that later." He stepped back and motioned her to enter. "Let me go change. And I did hear you right, you're treating?"

Amy nodded.

"In that case, how can I say no? This is a first. The First National Bank of Dad gets a deposit instead of another withdrawal." He smiled, his composure back to normal. "Be right back."

While her dad changed clothes, Amy nosed around. Nothing seemed out of place. Nothing she could see indicated someone else living there, or even frequently visiting. From the kitchen, she opened the door to the garage and discovered an old sports car. Actually, "exquisitely restored" described the bright red MG better than "old," right down to the chrome luggage rack on the back. She stood in the doorway admiring the lines of the car when she felt a tap on her shoulder.

"Beautiful, eh? It's a '64 MG-B. Sat in a garage for the last ten years. Engine needs some work, but I should have her ready for the road by the end of the month. That's what I was going to start this afternoon."

The reason for her dad's car being parked in the drive was answered. And his mention of a vintage sports car had proved honest, although the tag, "old sports car," was somewhat misleading. She turned to say something to him and did a double take. His hair had been roughly pulled back when she arrived. Now, as it hung freely, it was almost as long as hers and the gray had been colored out while retaining his natural blond color. Sure, they were family, but his resemblance to her was eerie.

He handed her his brush and a rubber band. "Could you give me a hand? I still don't quite have the hang of pulling it back smoothly." Amy stepped behind him and brushed his hair into a low-riding ponytail appropriate for a man.

She handed him the brush and stood facing him, arms crossed in front of her.

"Okay, Dad. What's going on?"

She grabbed his hand and led him to the kitchen table, the scene of many, many family and individual parent-child discussions. She sat down, and he hesitantly followed, taking a deep sigh as he did.

"I guess you're curious about the hair." He gave her a wan smile.

As she faced him, she noted the redness on his face also appeared to involve his upper chest, at least the part she could see through the V-neck of his Polo shirt. "And the sunburn?" she added. "And the old friend whom I've never met?"

"Boy, you don't want much, do you?" His smile was a bit brighter. "Okay. But over lunch. You're not getting away without treating." He stood and moved to leave the room. "Let me get the rest of my things and I'll meet you at the front door." He left the room, and left Amy to all sorts of wild thoughts. The "what ifs" procreated within her mind.

Ten minutes later, they pulled into the parking lot of the old firehouse-turned-restaurant, parked and dashed between raindrops to the entrance and lobby. A hostess seated them right away and, being familiar with the menu, they ordered when their waiter brought them water and fresh, homemade, honey-wheat bread. Amy ordered a glass of Merlot, while her dad ordered his favorite Dewar's on the rocks. After the barman delivered their drinks, both took a sip and settled in for lunch.

"So, what first?" her dad asked.

Amy took a longer sip and then said, "You. The hair and the sunburn, rash or whatever that is." She waved her finger at his chest.

"Okay." He paused a moment as if collecting his thoughts. "Call it my mid-life crisis, if you want to, complete with a red sports car, which is now mine, by the way." He smiled, but quickly turned serious when Amy didn't respond in kind. "Remember our talk by the plane?"

Amy nodded. "I believe the take home message was something like life's too short."

"That's right. When I was growing up, your grandfather was a strict taskmaster and Calvinist, whose hand didn't spare the child if we didn't conform to his way of doing things. I entered high school with a buzz cut when all of my friends were sporting Beatle cuts. As soon as I graduated, I joined the military and remained unfashionable throughout the end of the Vietnam War and subsequent global engagements. But that was okay. The military fit me, and I served it well, I think." He paused for a sip of scotch. "Even though I retired from active duty several years ago, I kept a reserve commission, and, well, last year I finally retired from that commission and left that life behind for good. In simple terms, I guess I'm doing something I've wanted to do since I was sixteen. I've never grown my hair long and decided to give it a try. And I like it, although it made the gray more noticeable, so I decided to color it as well. Does that bother you?"

Amy scrutinized her father with his hair pulled back, and she had to admit the look suited him well and gave him a cosmopolitan flair that fit the international life he—they—once lived. She had met all types of men over her life, from athletes to geeks in high school and college; to hoo-rah marines, hot shot pilots, CIA "spies," consular attachés, defense industry sales reps, and, of course, doctors of every size, shape, and dexterity. She inspected her father once again, the clothes he had chosen, the shape of his face, and the changes in hairstyle. Yes, this style fit her father.

"No, not at all. In fact, I kinda like it, too. But it's driving the boys a bit crazy."

Her dad chuckled. "Yeah, Grant was stumbling all over his words when he stopped by with the kids the other day."

would pick up the call. The latter proved to be true.

"Lynch, it's me. Sorry I've missed you, but here's your last chance. I work on Tuesday and Friday this coming week, so we should be able to get together, if that's what you want. Give me a call when you can."

There, short and sweet. The ball's in his court. Of course, the proverbial ball had been in his proverbial court for three months, so she resigned to his not calling back.

She picked up the phone again and dialed Macy, hopeful that her friend was home to share the good news about her father.

"Hey, girlfriend, whatcha know?" Macy answered before Amy could utter a greeting. Caller ID.

"Just got back from taking my dad to lunch."

"And..."

"Well, some of the mysteries are solved. Don't know that my brothers are going to like it, but . . ." Amy proceeded to tell her friend about the conversation with her father, but instead of a supportive reply, Macy let out a low whistle. It was a signal Amy knew all too well, a sign that Macy was about to launch into another story involving her widespread family. Macy's living family included great-grandmothers, great-aunts and two great-uncles, parents and stepparents, twelve siblings, some 30-odd aunts and uncles, and over 100 first cousins, not to mention nephews and nieces. If you needed a service or some kind of merchandise, one of Macy's relatives could provide it. And books could be written on the hijinks, misdeeds, and philanthropy of her family members, living and dead. After years of friendship, Amy thought she'd heard all of Macy's stories and wondered which one was about to be repeated, not that Macy would let you stop her from telling it again.

"Girl, reminds me of my Uncle Maurice. He came to our annual family reunion one year sportin' long hair and a new slim figure. Told everybody about gettin' in shape and findin' himself and stuff. The next year he shows up as a she, going by the name Diamond, with a surgically sponsored chest rivaling my mama's and legs every woman in the family envied. It took six months before anyone in the family would talk to her. Some still won't. Now though, I gotta admit she's a much better aunt than he ever was an uncle. Even my mama says she's easier to buy Christmas presents for."

Amy was wrong. She'd never heard this story and didn't know whether to scream or reach through the phone to strangle Macy. The violent winds of Hurricane Macy had just assaulted the emotional safe harbor where she had anchored her worries about her father.

Twenty-two

❦✦✦❦

"The jerk's playing us big time, Lynch," Flannigan stated, his face reddened and left fist clenched.

Lynch couldn't agree more. Yet, he hoped Flannigan calmed down before elevating his blood pressure up to stroke levels. They sat in the Ops Center double-checking the list of women who matched their working profile of potential victims from both the Sunset Hills and south city areas. Despite his convictions, Lynch floundered on this one. He knew the old saw about the word "assume" making an 'ass' out of 'u' and 'me.' Still, he was 98% sure.

"Yeah. I'm sure this map pointing to south city is bogus, but—"

"No kidding. If this guy's so smart, does he really think he's going to throw us off that easily?" Flannigan shook his head, more in irritation than disgust. "Doubling our work load is all he's doing."

"Maybe that's all he wants to do," Lynch said, nodding as he scanned another sheet of names and addresses. Both men knew that, in good conscience, they couldn't ignore the map. Were they to write it off as the red herring they believed it to be and the next attack occur in south city, the entire Major Case Squad would be back to walking a beat—if they were lucky. At the moment, however, both men might have found that option favorable. Despite the Chief's attempts to protect them, the political "pressure" flowing downhill had reached their level and threatened to make both men

189

scapegoat stew.

For Lynch, this was becoming a personal game now. A game where 'cat and mouse,' 'the tiger or the lady,' and 'hide'n seek' were all rolled into one. Fortunately, in his hunt for the rat, he didn't have to choose one door; he could cover both choices while trying to flush the rodent from his hiding place.

Lynch set the last page on his stack and looked at Flannigan.

"Find anyone else?"

Flannigan shrugged his shoulders and shook his head. "Naw. We still got five women in Sunset Hills and nearby communities, and three women in the south city area."

Lynch had considered asking all eight women to come to a meeting that evening so they could discuss the potential danger and solicit their assistance, but instead they had warned all of the women by telephone because, in the final analysis, they needed only one woman as their virtual bait, and one woman in particular stood out from the rest. And she had a personal interest in the case.

Meghan Reilly not only fit the physical profile, she had been the legal assistant to Edward Payne and had left work just minutes before the building exploded. Lynch saw that as an advantage. He reasoned that their unsub had gone after Patricia Shriver's assistant, Elsa Dunleavy, so maybe Payne's assistant would also hold a special attraction. They deduced that Dunleavy had become a target because she knew something dangerous to the assailant. Did Ms. Reilly also hold that knowledge, even if consciously unaware of it? Would he see her as a threat? He also considered other factors. She no longer worked for the law firm, and the news accounts of the explosion had not mentioned her. If the attacker was unaware of her name and past employer, would she hold the same appeal? Of course, the downside was that he had discovered that Elsa Dunleavy was no real threat and would assume the same of Meghan Reilly, and avoid her like feral cats running from a pack of liberated dogs. That was a gamble Lynch and the Chief were willing to take because she held one other distinct advantage over the others. She was a member of the Internet law forum and had a better-than-good chance of having been "spotted" by Lady Law already.

"So, you getting anything from this Internet law forum?" Flannigan asked.

Lynch stared at the distant wall. "Not much, so far." We think this guy is using the handle 'Lady Law,' and even though he signs on often, he's not there long enough to trace. Our one attempt led to a dead-end."

Lynch was frustrated. At first, the forum offered no way of seeing who was signed in without doing so oneself. After seeing the sporadic pattern of access, Lynch had arranged with the moderator and SysOp to log all entries by Lady Law and to page Lynch's computer whenever 'she' was there. A pattern of use had evolved from this monitoring, and Lynch hoped to use it in preparing his trap.

* * *

At two p.m., Lynch and Flannigan returned from a late lunch to meet with Meghan Reilly. Lynch felt as if he had chowed down on butterflies. He had never asked a civilian to help in such as way as to put her potentially in harm's way and hoped he'd never have to again. How would she receive their request?

Ms. Reilly awaited them in the front lobby of the police station with a man attired in the uniform of a local paramedic unit. The detectives approached the couple.

"Meghan Reilly?" Lynch asked. The young woman nodded. "I'm Sergeant Lynch Cully and this is Sergeant Paul Flannigan. Thanks for coming."

The woman extended her hand in greeting. "Nice to meet you. This is my brother, Sean Reilly. He's a paramedic for Patterson Fire District." The men also shook hands in greeting.

"Why don't you both follow us? Chief Dandridge wants to join us so we'll use the conference room," Flannigan said.

The detectives led the way, and after seating their guests at the large table, Flannigan left to get the Chief. After introductions to the older officer, everyone took a seat around the table. The younger detectives deferred to their commander to open the discussion.

"Ms. Reilly, please accept our condolences regarding the death of Mr. Payne and our thanks for assisting us."

Sean Reilly broke in. "She hasn't decided to help yet. I insisted we hear you out first, before she makes any decisions."

"And I appreciate my brother's concerns," she

stated.

Lynch turned his attention to the Chief and watched as the older man stared at the two siblings, his face inscrutable as he measured his next words. Lynch, too, appreciated the brother's concern. He liked that the man watched over her, as a father, husband or brother should. Did Col. Gibbs or Amy's brothers watch over her as protectively? How would they react to his desire to renew their relationship? He fought to refocus his attention on the Reilly siblings.

"Well placed concerns, I'm sure," the Chief replied. "I can assure you, we have no intention of putting you in any danger. Has Sergeant Cully explained his plan?" The Reilly siblings shook their heads. "Then, it's his turn to do so." The Chief turned to Lynch and yielded the floor to him.

"As the Chief said, our intent is not to put you in harm's way, simply to borrow your identity to flush this guy out. We have a pretty good idea of how he lures his victims into his snare. What we don't know is where or how he actually accomplishes the assault." Lynch proceeded to give the Reillys a synopsis of the victims' fates and their suspicions about the use of the law forum. "Tell me, Ms. Reilly, do you frequent the forum?"

"I used to, before the explosion. Not so much anymore."

"And have you ever been approached by an individual regarding your opinions on your profession? Perhaps regarding a new book?"

"Why, yes. A lawyer with the handle Lady Law has

been researching a new book. But we all know her, at least by name. Most of us used her texts in college."

Lynch nodded. "We don't think it's really her. We think someone, most likely male, has usurped her identity for his gains. Has he contacted you directly?"

Meghan looked shocked, but thought for a moment before responding. "No, not that I can recall. But there was a website for the research, and I filled out a survey. Did—" She stopped abruptly, looked at her brother and back to Lynch. "Is that how he's checked us out?"

Lynch appreciated her insight. He, too, saw the link. Download a survey, and you've downloaded a cookie that opens the computer to reveal whatever information the programmer is looking for. Spyware was the common term. The program could also search out holes in any firewall software in use and follow the computer user's surfing across the Web. Any and all information about the user—digital images, financial data, passwords, and more—could ultimately be sent to the programmer, Lady Law in this case.

Lynch nodded and explained his theory. "Could we examine your computer?"

Meghan shook her head. "It's gone. Destroyed in the explosion and fire. I've been to the forum once or twice from my home computer, but I've never visited that website from home. But if you want to examine that computer, sure. Anything, if it helps."

Lynch mentally debated the possibilities. It was unlikely her home system would help, unless . . .

"Did you ever chat with Lady Law, in a private chat

194

room? Particularly from home."

Meghan again shook her head. "No. I'm sorry. Not much help is it?"

Lynch leaned back in his chair. Anything they found on her computer would be just one more piece of the puzzle. But the puzzle could miss a number of pieces and still reveal its picture. Or in this case, the trap could still be set.

Lynch pondered another idea. Could they set up a computer for her use at home and install it with its own set of traps? Traps that could help them locate the guy. Would that even be possible? Would it be possible within a reasonable amount of time? He would have to approach Mike Jurgesmeyer about that idea.

"That's okay. Look, this is what we want to do. Hear me out, and then you can decide if you want to participate. You don't have to give us an immediate answer, but the sooner the better."

Lynch spelled out his plan. The Reillys promised to give an answer the next day.

Lynch caught the Chief at his office door, preparing to leave for the day.

"Sir, got a minute?"

"Sure, Lynch. What's on your mind?"

"Did you get any impression about Meghan Reilly? Do you think she'll help us?"

The Chief laid his briefcase back on his desk, sat on its corner, and nodded. "Yes, I think she will. But I doubt her brother will leave her side during all of this. Can't say as I blame him."

Lynch shifted his stance. "I agree. But let's say she doesn't. What if we can't set the trap I've proposed? And what if the bait isn't taken?"

"And what if he smells the trap and finds a way to end run us? Are we really doing what we have to do to protect this girl?" The Chief paused, but Lynch had no reply. "What if the brother does stick to her side, and that scares off our offender? What if this guy takes them both out? Lynch, the 'what if' game is a great exercise, but at some point you just have to let loose and act, and let things fall where they may. I think we're at that point. We also have some other leads, like the motor coach angle and Dunleavy's missing digital camera. Have we accounted for that yet?"

Lynch had forgotten about the absentee camera. "Uh, no sir. I'll work on that first thing tomorrow. Speaking of the motor coach, I've been thinking about where could you park a bus like that and go unnoticed for months. Probably not on public property. Maybe a campground or RV center. Any thoughts? You still have yours, don't you?"

Lady Law hadn't remained free by taking chances. There was a new law forum attendee who appeared to be online all the time, and that was atypical of the members of that group. It didn't take a neurosurgeon to deduce that Patricia Shriver's role as a moderator on the forum might lead police to monitor it. It also didn't hurt to have inside information. As a result, he took no risks and stopped by sporadically and only briefly, looking for one specific member of the group, someone who seemingly had vanished from the forum. Tonight he would go online once again, and if she was there it was fate informing him that she was the one, the next initiate into his club. If not, he would extend his invitation to an alternate.

Lynch arrived home after a late evening meal to find the message he'd been anxious to receive. ". . . Give me a call when you can," ended the message, and this time Lynch had no reluctance, no desire to procrastinate in returning the call. He picked up the portable phone in his kitchen and walked into his home office to deposit his briefcase. He had no need to look up her number. Even after a three-month hiatus, he knew it by heart. He felt as though he would never forget that number. He punched in the first three digits and paused. His computer was being paged.

He put the phone down and turned on the dormant monitor. On the task bar, a link to the law forum gave him access with a single click of the mouse. "Lady Law" was there, not actively engaged in the public chat, but apparently sitting on the sidelines. He signaled his presence to the sysop, and a reply message informed him that Lady Law was currently in a private chat room with a member by the username of Research Roxy. A brief moment later, both names disappeared from the roster of those signed onto the forum. *What the. . .?* He instant messaged the sysop once again, only to learn that she had been unable to monitor the private conversation, but would try to find out who Research Roxy was.

Lynch was already familiar with the name. It had been one of their interview questions, and one of the women they had talked with had mentioned the name as her online handle, one she used for several chat rooms she visited. But which woman? Lynch tried mentally to recall each woman he'd personally talked to. They had warned them all to avoid just such an encounter, so why had she ignored their warning? Maybe she had been on Flannigan's list.

Lynch felt torn. He needed to call Amy, to set that ball in motion. Yet now, another life could be at stake. He grabbed his phone and cleared the previously started number before entering Flannigan's cell phone number.

"Flannigan."

"Paul, it's Lynch. Quick. Do you recall any of the women on the list with the username Research Roxy? I think our guy is making a move."

"Yeah. Yeah, I do. But I can't recall who. She's not on the final list, but I can't remember why we disqualified her." There was a pause. "Oh, c'mon brain. Lynch, I can't remember. My list is at the Ops Center. Yours?"

Lynch was already rummaging through his briefcase. Photos. Medical reports. Nitrogen suppliers. Lunch receipts he needed to file. No list.

"Also at the office. I'm on my way."

Lynch felt a sense of urgency bordering on panic.

This was the closest they'd ever come to being proactive, to stopping the man, and the delay of driving to Richmond Heights, even with lights and sirens, and finding a name on a list of dozens of women, could make all the difference in another woman's life.

Lynch could almost hear the same turmoil running through Flannigan's mind. The rustle of a coat, the opening and closing of doors, the start of a car engine from Flannigan's side of the connection told Lynch his partner was already on the move.

"Meet you there." Click.

Lady Law had taken the motor coach from its secluded site north of the city to a RV campground southwest of the city. It was there he was to meet Research Roxy, a.k.a. Esther Jacobs. The young woman was ecstatic to meet Lady Law in person and eagerly accepted the dinner invitation for that same night. He pulled the coach into its designated overnight mooring and hooked up to the nearby utilities. He then rolled down an awning at the side of the coach and set up two camp chairs and a small table. The site looked as though he'd lived there for the past week.

Shortly before her scheduled arrival at seven-thirty, he placed a chilled bottle of wine in a cooler and positioned it beside the table. He had filled his own glass, however, from the bottle in the refrigerator inside the motor home. His guest was prompt, slowly driving past the coach on her first look and backing up to park adjacent to the home. He stood to greet her.

"Esther?" She smiled. "Hi, I'm Howard Wespike. Welcome to our home away from home." She approached cautiously, looking around and up to the coach's windows. "Please have a seat." He motioned to the chairs by the table. "I'm afraid Alice was detained briefly. She was talking to some folks at the law school, and when she tried to leave, her wheelchair lift in the minivan malfunctioned. I just got a call from her, and she expects to be here in about fifteen minutes."

The young woman relaxed. "Thank you. It's just, well, I was expecting her to be here."

"I understand. Believe me, I'm harmless, but we can stay out here in the open until she arrives if that makes you feel safer. Can't be too sure these days. Lots of crazies doing weird things." He laughed and nonchalantly pointed to the chairs. "I'm not being the best host, am I? Would you like something to drink? I'm having a glass of chardonnay. Care for some? Or something else perhaps?"

He already knew from her computer profile that chardonnay was her favorite, down to the detail of which brand.

"I'd love a glass of wine. Thank you." She sat down on the opposite side of the table, seemingly more relaxed. She accepted the glass and took a sip. "Umm, that's good wine. Thanks." She took a second sip. "So she, um, I mean Alice, still drives? Someone told me about her accident. Sorry."

"Please. Don't show her any concern; she gets mad. Alice may not play tennis anymore, although she tried it in the wheelchair, but the accident hasn't dulled her intellect or determination. We have a specially equipped minivan that she handles well. I operate this monster . . ." He pointed to the motor home. ". . . but she drives for just about everything else when we travel."

The young woman was obviously more comfortable. He had designed the conversation, the non-threatening outdoor encounter, and the wine to put her at ease. She took a longer draught of wine as the conversation focused on her and her work. Within five minutes, she had drained the glass.

"Wow, I'd better be careful. I'm thirstier than I thought."

He smiled as he refilled the glass. The wine held nothing noxious; nothing that would show up on a toxicology screen, just a short lived but potent diuretic. She would begin to feel its effects quickly enough.

The conversation moved to Alice's new book, and Howard did his husbandly best to discuss it. "I'm sorry. She tells me over and over about what she's writing. I've even read the first couple of chapters. But I'm not in the legal profession in any way, shape, or form so a lot of it's Greek to me. Maybe I should leave your questions to her. I know she has a bunch for you." He took a small sip of his wine and noticed she was squirming a bit in her seat.

"Um, I, could I use your bathroom? This wine has worked overtime on my kidneys."

"Why sure. Ever been in a motor home before?" She nodded. "Well, they're all pretty much alike. Take a left toward the back of the bus, and it's on the right."

She excused herself and climbed the makeshift ramp to the coach's door. As soon as she had entered the home, he pulled out what appeared to be a small portable television, complete with the Casio trademark. But its screen revealed no broadcast signal, just a closed circuit image from the small bath of the coach. He had no voyeuristic intent, just a need to confirm her presence in the confined space. As she adjusted her clothing and sat on the toilet, he flipped a switch on the console and the door double-locked and sealed itself silently. Then, in an equally stealthy mode, pure nitrogen replaced the air inside the chamber. He watched as she stood from the toilet, clumsily pulled her panties and hosiery into place and, lowered her skirt. As with all the others, her breathing became labored and she teetered a bit. Then frantic, she tried to open the door. Two minutes into her initiation, she no longer had the strength to scratch or claw at the doorway. Seconds later, with the little remaining control she had, she tumbled to the floor. He flipped another switch, and the monitor showed her heart and respiratory rates, as detected by sensors in the wall of the chamber. Four and a half minutes after the release of the nitrogen, her vital signs began a precipitous fall, and he sent another signal to the chamber, one that quickly flushed the nitrogen from the space and unlocked the door.

He rose, drained the wine from his glass, and took his "toy" with him into the coach. After securing it with his other electronics, he donned a surgical hood and gloves, moved to the bathroom, and picked Esther from the floor. He took her into the bedroom and lovingly placed her on the bed. He stroked her short blond hair and smoothed it into place on her head. It wasn't anything like his dark-haired mother's wavy locks, but after taking redheaded Elsa Dunleavy, he recognized the need for a change. He would no longer consider hair color in finding new initiates.

A quick neurological assessment revealed a satisfactory level of anoxic damage, and he administered oxygen to safeguard the heart and other organs. Then he collected a rainbow of blood specimen tubes—red, blue, green, and purple-topped tubes along with a few special ones. A courier, who was well paid not to ask questions, would pick these up at a designated site and deliver them to the lab at the medical center, where they would be anonymously mixed in with other samples. He would later tap into the medical center's network to find the results of the tests on these specimens, as well as the results of other diagnostics he was sure would be performed after she was discovered at home.

And that was his final task, getting Esther Jacobs, his newest initiate, back home. He loaded her into her car and put his Vespa in the back. There would be no assault, no rape, although he had certainly assaulted her in a legal sense. And unlike his sister, who had lived in a vegetative state under the poorly financed custodial care of the State until she died shortly after his 25th birthday, Esther would have the best of care and the benefit of new investigational drugs.

Twenty-three

Doctor David Koettering walked slowly out of the room of his newest patient, Esther Jacobs, dismayed at the prospect of dealing with yet another victim of this serial assailant and possible killer. He had a special interest in hypoxic-anoxic brain injuries,. and his research in that arena focused not just on surgical techniques that might improve cerebral function in such patients, but also in the basic science and medical aspects of these injuries. The development of near infrared spectroscopic monitoring for adults, the use of hyperbaric oxygen therapy, medications such as magnesium sulfate, vitamins and diet, high-dose antioxidants, and more were all being investigated for their potential in helping those who had suffered such damage, whether from shock, near-drowning, asphyxiation, cardiopulmonary arrest, poisoning or any other means of depriving the brain of oxygen. He aimed his research at these forms of acquired brain injury and did not touch on injuries such as penetrating or closed head trauma. At their large tertiary care center, he had enough accidental cases to study that he didn't need the 'assistance' of some deranged whacko in finding new patients.

David sat down in the dictation carrel at the nursing station and picked up the phone. His secretary picked up on the first ring.

"Carol, would you track down Dan and have him

meet me here, on the ward? Thanks."

His research team's neuropsychologist, Dan Diehl, Ph.D., would be next to examine her, to provide a detailed assessment of cognitive and functional impairment. There would also be a CT scan, which would function primarily as a baseline for comparison with later scans. The CT might show some small "watershed" or pseudo-laminar infarcts at the confluence between the anterior, middle and posterior cerebral arteries, but David expected nothing more. The protocol also included both functional MRI and SPECT scans, which hopefully would provide some indication about the levels of function of various parts of the brain.

David proceeded in writing his initial progress note and stopped to ponder one finding from his follow-up exam. In the E.D., her pupils had been active, though sluggish, and she had retained her oculovestibular reflexes and basic cranial nerve function, so evidence of brain stem damage was minimal. But now she had exhibited an unusual eye twitch, something not seen in any of the previous victims of the "LA Rapist." He tried to recall the twitch because at one point it impressed him as not being sporadic or random. She was unable to follow him around the room with her eyes, and when he watched from the side, the eye spasm seemed diminished or absent. Like the others in a vegetative state, she failed to respond to verbal or tactile stimuli, or to pain. But when he was in front of her, with direct eye contact, the blink almost seemed purposeful. He flipped to the doctor's orders page and added a request for an electroencephalogram. Perhaps it was seizure activity.

"Hey."

David looked up from his contemplations to find Dan Diehl standing on the opposite side of the counter. Just then, Dan's pager went off. He looked at the text message and laughed.

"Guess you're looking for me. That was Carol."

"Good morning. I think." He noticed the notebook in Dan's hand. "Have you had a chance to review Esther Jacobs' chart?"

"Only briefly. I pulled up the E.D. record on the computer, as well as some test reports. Glasgow Coma Scale was a six out of fifteen. Not good. Glasgow Outcome Scale is consistent with a vegetative state, and the Rancho Level of Cognitive Functioning Scale confirmed the severity of her condition. Her reaction to external stimuli was limited, nonspecific, and non-purposeful. Not looking good for her prognosis."

David nodded. The patient's family had agreed to enroll her in his study group. So, after completing a battery of tests under the protocol, she had gone straight from the E.D. to the hyperbaric oxygen chamber. David's early morning assessment of these factors had shown no change from that in the E.D., but . . . He thought about the unusual eye twitch.

It was early in the treatment course and hope . . . well, hope was something he left to the family. He was caring for eight of the ten living victims of this monster who remained loose to assault other women. One of the ten had already died. The families of two other victims were anguishing over the ethical dilemma of discontinuing care and feeding. He could give them no objective findings that their loved ones would someday 'wake up.' No, hope was something he couldn't afford to indulge in lest he risk total emotional burnout.

Dan shook his head. "I hope they catch the S-O-B soon. Poor lady. Anything different with her this morning?"

David paused for a moment before responding. "I . . . well, I'm not sure. I've ordered an EEG to check out something. It's just a twitch, in her right eye mainly. Might be seizure activity, but it was weird, almost a pattern to it."

"Okay. I'll keep my eyes open for it." He extended his hand toward David and flexed his fingers a couple of times. David smiled, closed the chart, and handed it to him. "Thanks. Are you going to be around?"

"I should be. I don't have any surgery scheduled for today, and I have three more patients to see up here. So, I should be on the floor for at least half an hour, 45 minutes."

"Good. Why don't you check back with me before you leave the unit? I might be done by then. If not, I'll be in Jacobs' room."

David nodded and picked up the next patient's chart. He watched as Dan walked down the hall to examine Esther Jacobs. Dan's contributions to the team had been immeasurable. Having joined them just fifteen months earlier, Dan showed an extraordinary interest in their patients. He had suggested never-before-attempted

207

therapies that were well rooted in the basic medical science of brain injury. And David knew they shared a personal interest in the subject, an interest born of afflicted family members. Yet, rumors floated among the other research team members that Dan was bored, eager to move on. David hoped he would settle in. He would be hard to replace.

Thirty-five minutes later, while David completed the exam of his last patient, Dan found him and knocked on the doorpost to the room.

"David, I need to see you. Like, ASAP." The urgency in Dan's voice was clear.

"One minute. Be right out." David finished his exam and replaced the dressing over the man's right parietal scalp incision. He made a couple of quick notations on the chart and walked out to the hall. Dan was leaning against the wall just outside the door, but quickly stood upright as David emerged. He grabbed David by the elbow and started leading him toward Esther Jacobs' room.

"That twitch is more than a spasm of the eyelids. Were you ever a Boy Scout?"

David shook his head. "Ever learn Morse code, for any reason?" Again, David shook his head. "Well, you'd better learn 'cause that's what I think it is. I don't think she's in a vegetative state after all, and that, I'm afraid, is also my biggest fear." They stopped outside the room. "Look, I saw in the chart that this lady was found very shortly after the assault, or at least that's what was postulated by the police based upon the last time she was seen at work, the time of a credit card charge for gas, and the time she was found at home. They found all the others maybe a day, or more, later. I think our early intervention with the hyperbaric oxygen may have made a difference. I just pray we haven't moved her from being in a vegetative state into having locked-in syndrome, 'cause in my opinion, it would be a whole lot worse to have awareness of what's going on and no way to do anything, than to just be oblivious to everything."

The thought caused David to shudder involuntarily. He had to agree with his neuropsychologist.

"Okay. And the Morse code?"

"Well, when I placed my face squarely in front of hers, the twitch noticeably changed. It was a bit inconsistent at first, but then it clearly became an S-O-S, three dots, three dashes, and three more dots. As I kept watching, the pattern changed. I've got her nurse looking up Morse code on the Internet so we can get a printout to refresh my memory, but she might have been saying 'help.' " Dan took a step into the doorway. "C'mon, let's check again."

Together they approached the young woman's bed. Dan moved to her first, and as he moved into her field of view, the eyelid spasm took on intentional action. Three short blinks, followed by three longer ones, and again by three short. David stood there, shocked. Had their actions to help her only worsened the situation? In brightly colored scrubs, a nurse walked into the room and handed Dan a two-page printout. He looked at David.

"Here. You face her, and I'll decipher."

David moved into her field of vision, and the blinking stopped for a moment. Then, more slowly and deliberately, the blinks changed. Dan watched from the side, scribbling on the paper. After several minutes, he pulled David away from the bedside.

"Whoa, man. Did you do something to hurt her? 'Cause I don't think she likes you."

"What?" The statement took David aback. He'd done nothing out of the ordinary or unprofessional in dealing with her. "I don't follow you."

Dan held the paper up to him. Underneath a series of dashes and dots, in rough block letters, were the words, "You bastard."

Twenty-four

Lynch slinked into the Ops Center, self-conscious and dejected. He and Flannigan had failed, and he cringed at the thought that Ester Jacobs' condition could actually be worse than that of the others. They had found her name and contact info. They had called and talked with her, to learn she was heading out to meet someone for a drink. She wouldn't divulge who, and they tried talking her out of it. They even rushed to her home, to talk to her face-to-face, but no one was there, and her car was gone. They waited a while to see if she returned home, but after an hour realized the futility of that. They had no way of knowing if she'd actually accepted an invitation to join the spider in his lair or not, much less where she might be. Maybe she truly was meeting a friend or friends for drinks. Yet, two hours after they left, a concerned neighbor called police, who found Ms. Jacobs just like all the others. Almost.

He knocked on the Chief's door after being "ordered" to report the latest on Ms. Jacobs. The Chief had never been so short or treated him so curtly. There was talk the Chief would pull the plug on their plan, but he had yet to say anything to Lynch about it. The Chief was on the phone and motioned Lynch into the room and to have a seat while he listened. Even from a distance, Lynch could hear the anger and volume of whoever was on the other end. He quickly realized that the heat he was receiving from the Chief was only a small fraction of what the Chief faced daily.

Without emotion, the Chief hung up his receiver and faced Lynch.

"So, what do we have?" he asked.

"Well, it looks like Ester Jacobs might not be in a vegetative state after all." Lynch shuddered to think of the alternative, to be conscious of what's happening around you and be unable to interact. Such a life would be a garish nightmare. "I've gotten word that she seems to be able to communicate in Morse code. Seems her dad is an avid ham radio operator, and Esther learned the code almost as soon as her alphabet."

"Well, that's certainly hopeful. Maybe she can identify her assailant." The Chief looked less defeated with that statement.

Lynch also related how they had discovered her ability to communicate, and what it had yielded earlier that morning. Doctor Koettering's team and others "in the know" were debating her slur of the doctor. Had she been recalling her attacker, unaware of her present surroundings? Was she cursing the doctor for saving her and allowing her to live in such a condition? Had the blinking been misinterpreted all along? Dr. Diehl had admitted to having trouble deciphering the 'code.' What if the EEG revealed seizure activity? Could this be the cause, with the 'code' just being the projected wishes of a zealous healthcare provider?

"Maybe, but at the moment she's lapsed back into a semi-conscious state and is no longer communicating. She's scheduled for another hyperbaric oxygen session this afternoon, and Doctor Koettering hopes it might reawaken the nascent signs of improvement."

But did he hope to duplicate that morning's event? That episode had to have been unsettling for the doctor.

His report completed, Lynch returned to his workplace. As he reviewed the initial forensics report from the scene, he realized he had been in the process of calling Amy when he had been interrupted. He muttered something unintelligible as he recalled that she had said in her message that she would be working that day. He picked up the phone and dialed anyway, realizing he would be better off leaving a message than letting her call slide away once again.

She answered the phone on the third ring. "Hello."

"Uh, Amy? It's Lynch. I thought you were working today."

"Oh. We had a last minute schedule change. I, uh . . ."

Lynch could hear her shuffling around in a chair, its distinct squeak revealing the exact chair in her home. She was in the spare bedroom that she used as an office and reading room. In his mind, he could see her sitting in it, her legs coiled up beneath her. She always curled up in the same way when she talked to someone while sitting in that chair.

"Look, I, um, I couldn't get back with you last night because we got busy and—"

"I know. I read about it in the paper this morning. I'm sorry."

Lynch envisioned her playing with her hair as she talked. That was another habit of hers that he found endearing.

"You have no reason to be sorry. I'm the one who needs to apologize, for everything."

"No, I mean about the attack, that this guy is still on the loose. I know how this must be eating at you."

She was right about that. And he was surprised she understood him so well. He didn't consider himself easy to get to know. "You don't know the half of it." They had been so close, knowing the neighborhood where he was likely to strike, even talking with the victim beforehand. They hadn't anticipated the change in M.O.—his attacking a blonde. That added a completely new twist to the case. Lynch recalled Flannigan's earlier words, "The jerk's playing us big time."

"So, what's next?" Amy asked.

"Well, we have some leads we're working on—"

"No, Cully, what's next with us? You have your second chance. There won't be another."

Lynch knew that to be true.

"What about dinner? Tonight. Pick you up about six."

"Okay. I'm free, but I need to be home by nine since I work tomorrow. Ten at the latest."

"Fair enough," he replied. "Wear something dressy. I'm sparing no expense to make amends."

By mid afternoon, the hunt for Art Barklage had intensified. The DNA results from the stray hairs found on Elsa Dunleavy's body during her SANE workup had come up as a perfect match to hair taken from Barklage's hairbrush at home. Barklage didn't fit their profile, but Lynch couldn't argue with the Chief's decision to intensify the search for the man by formally involving the Major Case Squad in his disappearance. Their guess was that he was some sort of accomplice or thug to do the heavy lifting. If that was true, he was the best lead they had in locating the real killer. And if it wasn't, they needed to clear him from their suspects list.

"Lynch."

The detective turned in his seat to face the Chief standing in the doorway behind him. "Yes, sir."

"Where's Boyerton? I need to talk with him."

"He's out for a little while, helping to coordinate the search for the motor home."

Based on the information Lynch had obtained about Elsa Dunleavy's evening dinner date, word had gone out to every law enforcement agency in four adjacent counties to stop all motor homes in search of Barklage. From trucks towing campers to full-sized Class-A coaches, they were to be stopped and the owner identified. They hadn't the manpower to search all of these vehicles, but hoped that they might get a break, find Barklage, and flush out the real culprit. They were closing in and Lynch sensed that he would soon meet the man he'd been hunting, close enough to see the whites of his eyes.

"Good. Look, if you see him before I do, tell him to stop by my office. I should be in all day." The older officer turned to leave, but stopped and faced Lynch again. "Anything on Dunleavy's camera?"

"Nothing new. It wasn't mentioned on the evidence list from her car. The lab has returned most of her personal belongings to her family, but the car's still impounded. Thought I'd check out her home again and then the car."

"Don't let me stop you," the Chief replied before turning and leaving the room.

Lynch was about to reply, but the Chief was already gone. Something seemed off with the Chief. He couldn't put his finger on it, but the man seemed tense and was more curt than usual with his subordinates, even with Lynch. Maybe the political pressure from this case had found a chink in the man's crisply starched armor. Shaking off a nagging feeling about Chief Dandridge, he filed the papers he'd been reviewing, picked up his keys and gear, and headed for his car.

Twenty minutes later, he worked his way through late afternoon traffic within the Central West End neighborhood. The street in front of her home had already filled with local residents, so he worked his way around to the alley behind the house and parked in her home's parking area. As arranged, someone from the family was there to let him in, since the police had released the house to the family. Lynch climbed out of his car and approached the vehicle next to his where a young woman sat in the driver's seat. Her red hair and facial features bore a strong family resemblance, and she was close in age to Elsa, so he guessed her to be Elsa's sister. He flashed his credentials through the window and heard the door unlock. As she opened the door, he introduced himself.

"Hi, I'm Sergeant Cully. Thanks for letting me in. I won't be long."

The woman didn't bother to introduce herself. She looked tired and scared. She nodded her head and slowly walked to the side door of the house where she unlocked the door and stepped aside.

"Umm, I-I can't go in there right now." Tears formed at the corners of her eyes. "Do I need to?"

Lynch nodded in understanding and smiled weakly, unsure how to reassure the young woman. "No, you don't need to. I shouldn't need anything else. I just want to look around for her digital camera. Do you know what kind she had?"

The woman swallowed hard. "Yeah, it was a Nikon Coolpix. A 5700, I think. Silver. About this big." She held up her index fingers and thumbs to approximate the size.

"Someone told us she always carried it with her. Is that true?"

The sister nodded. "Yes. She always had it in her purse. She took pictures of anything and everything."

"Thanks." He started into the door and then paused. "I can lock up if you like. You don't have to stick around for me."

She looked up to him and smiled wanly. "Okay. You don't need a key to lock it; just flip this . . ." She flipped a small latch on the inside of the deadbolt. ". . . and pull it shut. The lock in the door handle is already locked. Thanks." She quickly turned and walked to her car.

Lynch saw her wipe her face with the sleeve of her

sweater and realized how hard it must have been for her to come to the home of her sister, a place where she no doubt remembered all the good times they'd had there. And now it was a place where she'd no longer hear her sister's laugh or share a meal together. It was not the first time he had seen the emotions of family members whose lives had been disrupted by the wake of the "LA Rapist."

Lynch entered the small home, remembering the one other time he'd been there. Little had changed. Paperwork on the dining table remained there, now accompanied by a box of items returned by the police lab. The dishes in the sink and drying rack had not magically moved to the cabinets. It looked as if no one had been there since he had left, other than to drop the box on the dining table. Quietly and efficiently, he moved from room to room, looking for a camera. Even though he expected it to be obvious, in a place where she could quickly grab it for a spontaneous photo, he made a point of looking everywhere—behind pillows on the couch, inside cabinets, within drawers, under the beds. His search was thorough, but tidy. He was not ransacking the place, just trying to find a camera. In one closet, he thought he'd succeeded in his quest, but the camera was an older 35mm SLR, not digital.

After searching each room and the small utilitarian basement, he had come up empty handed. He moved back through each room and surveyed each closely, looking for any place he might have missed the first time. A few spots he inspected again. Yet, once again, he came up empty—only the 35mm SLR and it was void of film.

Yet, this finding encouraged him. She *must* have taken it with her. And that led to two potential conclusions. On the negative side, she had it, and the perp now possessed it. On the positive side, though, the perp didn't have it, and since the techs hadn't found it in her car, there was a good chance she hid it somewhere in the car. The techs would not have known to look for a hidden camera. And there was only one reason for her to hide it. She'd taken pictures that she didn't want the assailant to find.

He also found it curious that despite Elsa's predilection for state-of-the-art electronics he found no PDA, cell phone, or digital recorder, all items he would commonly expect of someone active in her profession and comfortable with modern electronic gadgets. He climbed the stairs and reentered the woman's office. Although the computer remained in police custody, he rummaged through the various cables scattered across the desk. He found two USB cables compatible for use with a PDA and digital camera. He was now on the hunt for more than just a camera and a cell phone.

Oh no, he thought, as he glanced at his watch and realized what time it was.

Twenty-five

❧✦✦☙

The shortening days of early autumn forced Lady Law to start his evening jogs in the park a few minutes earlier every day. He hoped to remain inconspicuous, using the cover of fading light to dim anyone's chance of getting a good look at him. Yet, he couldn't wait too late and risk a Ranger stopping him after the park's close at dusk. This evening he ran hard, pushing himself beyond that comfortable pace where he might still converse in sentences if he'd had a running partner, to a level where even single words would be difficult to gasp. He concentrated on his breathing, forcing the accumulating lactic acid from his muscles as his body struggled to convert the acid to carbon dioxide to exhale. He wanted to feel the coming cramps in his legs, the stitch in his side where each breath stabbed at his chest. He wanted anything that might distract his mind from dwelling on the potential danger he faced.

Never before had revelation been so close. Esther Jacobs was down but not out. He laughed when he first learned of her insult to her doctor, but then the realization that she might regain enough communication to identify him settled in. She had become another loose end, or perhaps a split end that simply needed snipping away, although that task was much more difficult now. He would have to give serious thought as to how to remove her, and soon.

He felt the first twinge of a cramp in his left leg and

pushed through it, taking longer strides to stretch the muscle. Yet, that distraction lasted only seconds. His mind remained focused on the reams of data he'd recently acquired about the Major Case Squad. He had run a check on this detective, Lynch Cully, and saw that for the first time, he faced a formidable hunter. But he wasn't interested in games. No mouse to Cully's cat. No dodging a dozen balls while encircled by police. He could no longer be the chameleon that simply blended in. No, the prey that typically lived to run again was that which went to ground. He needed to do that, to get away.

He had also learned that they were searching for Elsa's electronic toys. Her cell phone and PDA were safely in his possession, removed from her purse shortly after her trip to the toilet. He had taken care to remove the battery from her cell phone and thus eliminate any ability to track the device. Her PDA was antiquated by his terms, and he had easily erased its contents and reprogrammed it, even to the point of altering its embedded serial number so no one could trace it to Elsa. He hoped the police enjoyed their hunt.

As he ran toward the old park supply cabin, he realized he needed to clear up the loose end at the hut as soon as possible. Maintenance activity in the county park was increasing in preparation for winter, and with the cooler days, the odds of someone trying to enter the old place increased, whether it was a park employee baffled by new and unexplained locks, teens seeking seclusion from parents while enjoying sexual or pharmaceutical experimentation, or some drifter looking for shelter from a sudden autumn storm. By the time he reached the cabin, he had decided that good ol' boy Art's hours were numbered.

Twenty-six

Amy glanced at the reproduction 'Regulator' clock on the wall above the front hall table. She didn't know whether to scream or cry. She spent the better part of the day letting anxiety run amok. Why had she agreed to a dinner date for that same night? It was a complete and inexcusable lapse of judgment. It had taken her an hour to realize she had nothing to wear, and another half hour to grasp that she had no time to shop and would have to come up with something from her existing wardrobe. After finally deciding on a hunter green strapless silk dress she could live with, she spent yet another hour trying to decide what to do with her hair. It had been easy to change looks with long hair, but since cutting it for the new job, she had had no reason to dress up, much less play with elegant hairstyles. It was then that she recognized she was so concerned about how she would look because she really wanted to turn Lynch's head, to convince him that he'd made the biggest mistake of his life in almost passing her by.

But now, at six-thirty, with Lynch a half hour late, she wanted to give his head a few extra twists.

She took one last glance out the front window and sighed. Pacing the floor consumed another ten minutes and that was all she needed. She started toward her bedroom to undress and resign herself to jeans and a quart of Häagen-Dazs for the evening. As she slipped off her heels, the phone next to the bed rang. She debated

223

answering it, but finally yielded to its plaintiff sound.

"Amy, please, please forgive me. I'm two streets away and will be there in a minute."

Amy took a deep breath before answering. "Okay, Lynch. Needless to say, I'm ready to go." Her voice was flat and tired. Again, she wondered why she had agreed to this date.

Two minutes later, she heard a car screech into her driveway and looked toward the front window to discover red lights dancing across her curtains. A moment later, they disappeared. It struck her oddly, but in a pleasant sense. The Lynch she knew was a real stickler for some things, the proper use of official equipment being one of them. If he had caught a junior officer using his lights to run traffic for personal reasons, the reprimands would have known few bounds. Yet, he had just broken that rule for her, and she wasn't sure quite how to take it. Had he unknowingly flattered her, or not?

Seconds later, there was a knock on the door, and Amy opened the door to a red-faced Lynch Cully sporting a suit on a hanger over his shoulder. He rushed past her into the small foyer.

"Sorry. Can I change someplace? We can still make it to the restaurant and get you back here on time."

She stood there, hands on her hips, staring at him in disbelief. He had talked of sparing no expense, yet stood there in the rumpled slacks and hound's-tooth check sports coat he had been wearing all day, maybe even slept in it from the looks of it. He sported a five-o'clock shadow that could sand wood, and the shoes he wore would compliment the suit over his shoulder like a bed of sauerkraut under an expensive fillet of fresh, wild game salmon. If expense wasn't an issue, poor taste could become one. More importantly, though, as it was nearing seven o'clock, it was improbable they could drive to any of the area's higher caliber restaurants, get seated, eat, and return to her house before ten. Did she want to chance a late night before a 24-hour shift?

Lynch let out a heavy breath and suddenly focused on Amy, his gaze scanning her from head to toe.

"Wow! You . . . you look gorgeous." He pulled the suit from his shoulder and held it out in front of him, scrutinizing it. He frowned. "Sorry. Guess I won't be much of a . . ." He shook his head. "Seems all I can do for you today is apologize."

Amy noted the look of defeat that crossed his face, a look that aggravated the lines of fatigue. And it tugged at her heart. Yet, she couldn't give in to her desire to embrace him, to reassure him.

"Lynch, be realistic here. We don't have time now to go to whatever restaurant you had planned. Why don't you put your stuff back in the car and go pick up some Chinese or something? We can eat here. Then we need to talk."

He hesitated, looking more dejected than before. "Are you sure?"

"Yes, I'm sure. Do you remember what I like?" She paused, but his response was not immediate. "Well, never mind. Whatever you get will be fine. I'll change into

225

something more suitable while you're gone." She stepped aside, leaving a clear path to the front door.

"Okay. I'll be right back. Promise." He started through the door, then stopped and turned toward her. "And I do remember." He smiled.

Amy watched from the doorway as he backed out onto the street. Was she crazy? Probably, but she would not let the temptation of his being there lure her into anything prematurely. There was too much that needed explaining, too much to talk through.

Lynch alternated his gaze between Amy and the road as he backed out of the drive. Yet, he almost backed over her mailbox as he watched her standing in the doorway. She looked beautiful. And the fact that she had gone to such lengths after the way he'd treated her spoke volumes.

He berated himself over losing track of the time, scolded himself for using his police vehicle in an inappropriate manner, and wanted to kick his own butt for having put himself in this position in the first place. Why had he been late? Was he subconsciously trying to avoid her again? He couldn't begin self-analysis at that point. He wouldn't dare. It would be much too incriminating and depressing. Yet, to continue in the same vein risked losing her altogether and without her, his sanity.

The nearest Chinese restaurant was only one to two minutes away, but he recalled something she loved even more than Chinese food. Greek. The nearest place with carryout was another ten minutes away. At the first stop sign, he popped out his cell phone, connected to the Internet, and retrieved the eatery's phone number. He then called ahead and placed his order for grilled lamb, a Greek salad, pastitsio, moussaka, shrimp tourkolimano, spinach pie, and baklava. She would have a Greek smorgasbord. With a little luck, they would have the order ready within minutes of his arrival, but first he needed to stop at the nearest supermarket for a bottle of chilled white wine and fresh-cut flowers, if they still had any from that day. If all went as he envisioned, he would be back at Amy's before 30 minutes lapsed.

Amy retired to her bedroom, slipped off her dress, released her lower body from the vise grip of her pantyhose, and pulled on her favorite jeans, soft and comfortable from frequent wear and washings. After donning an equally comfy fleece top, she went to the bathroom, unclipped her hair and let gravity take control, with some help from her brush. She removed her makeup, but replaced it with a light coating of mascara and a lighter shade of lipstick. It was as if she had removed a mask and revealed her true face. If only her life could be remade so easily.

She anticipated Lynch being gone for at least half an hour. It took that long for her to place and retrieve an order from the local Chinese place, so she couldn't see him being able to move any faster, even with lights and sirens. The hiatus gave her time to reflect. She had written Lynch Cully out of her life, only to have him return. What did this mean? Was it a sign from heaven or the Devil wreaking havoc upon her life? With her Baptist upbringing, she chose to believe the former, yet feared the latter. So, if that were true, what came next? She trusted God to lead her. His Word said her footsteps were ordered by Him. Which stepping-stone should she take? The obvious one, or one requiring a small jump to reach? She knew what she personally desired, and having Lynch close at hand, in the comfort of her home, made that a tempting possibility. If only he hadn't messed up their relationship so royally.

Lynch stood in front of the register at the Greek carryout area, tapping the toe of one shoe randomly on the floor. Nothing was going as hoped for, and he feared Amy would once again believe he had stood her up. He had picked the shortest line at the supermarket, only to have the woman preceding him place several unmarked packages on the conveyor, each requiring a price check by a different department. Two items rang up with prices differing from the weekly sales flyer, and to top it off, her check needed approval by the acting manager. Then he arrived at the Greek restaurant to discover his order would require at least ten additional minutes. All he wanted was something, anything, to take to Amy's house, now, not later. He didn't want to apologize for being late yet again.

Ten minutes later, the hostess announced his order as ready and acted as if she had done him a personal favor to speed things along. He paid the tab and ran out the door, but he resisted the temptation to flip on his lights to race to Amy's home this time.

Amy glanced at her watch and wondered what was taking so long. It was midweek, and the carryout line couldn't be that long. She was about to move to the kitchen and retrieve some plates and utensils when she saw his car turn the corner. She steeled herself not to open the door prematurely, as if she'd been waiting there for his return. Instead, she walked to the kitchen, pulled out two plates and glasses, chopsticks, forks, and spoons, in case he had purchased soup as well. She was grabbing a few paper napkins when the doorbell rang. She paused, and when it rang again only fifteen seconds later, she walked to the front door and opened it.

"Surprise!"

Lynch held a bouquet of fresh-cut flowers toward her. Inwardly she sighed. At least he was making an effort. She took the flowers and stepped aside to allow him in. That's when she noticed the large brown paper grocery sack in place of the Chinese restaurant's custom bags. Evidently, the flowers weren't the only surprise.

"Sooo, no Chinese?" she asked.

"I told you I remembered what you liked. And Zorba's was more than willing to provide." He juggled the paper sack in his arm and nodded toward his elbow.

"Could you grab the wine as well? Thanks."

Amy complied, smiling. He was working his D minus for effort toward a strong B. "I have plates ready in the kitchen, but I guess I can put the chopsticks away." She was feeling a bit more relaxed. It was beginning to feel like old times, the good times, yet she couldn't afford to let their relationship simply renew itself as if nothing had ever happened.

Lynch watched Amy closely as he followed her to the kitchen. Her walk, the way she tossed her head as she turned, the distinct allure of her perfume all aroused in him a desire for her that was stronger than he could ever remember. A good detective required sharp observational skills, and he had the talent for divining the smallest of vibes. His angst eased at seeing a genuine smile cross her lips, and he discerned the release of tension in her shoulders. Maybe this evening would turn out even better than the posh bistro he had originally planned. It would certainly be easier to talk in privacy here than in a public space. And talk was all he had in mind. He knew her too well to presume anything about their relationship, or even that their relationship might resume. He had already decided that his best tactic for breaking down any barriers between them would be a frontal assault of total honesty and openness. But, like all battle plans, deciding on the plan and acting on it were two different efforts, and the latter one was the hardest of all for him.

* * *

Amy opened the paper bag Lynch had set on the counter, and a Mediterranean perfume of spices engulfed her. She closed her eyes and inhaled deeply. The pungent aromas of cinnamon, cloves, garlic, and other spices abundant in their food brought back memories of her one brief visit to Athens and a small island whose name she couldn't pronounce back then and couldn't remember now.

"This smells sooo good," she said.

She arranged the containers across the counter and moved the bag out of their way. She noticed that Lynch went directly to the correct drawer and retrieved her corkscrew to open the wine bottle. She wondered if, after the gap in their relationship, she could do the same in his kitchen. She pushed a plate in his direction and laid serving utensils before each Styrofoam box.

"After you," he said, stepping back from the counter. "Where do you want to eat?"

She nodded toward the small maple table at the other end of the kitchen. "Right here."

He picked up the wine and two glasses and moved them to the table while she served herself. As she sat down, he returned to the food and dished out smaller servings of a few of the items. She laughed inside, thinking he probably wished he had picked up a steak as well. He walked to the table and sat in the chair to her right, which she found curious. In the past, whenever they ate together they'd always sat facing each other. It

231

was easier to talk that way. And she quickly decided it needed to be that way again that night. She stood up, moved to the chair across from him, and pulled her plate and silverware in front of her. She nodded her head for a short silent grace and then tucked into her salad.

"Ummm, tastes good. I'm glad you remembered." She smiled.

He stared at her, not touching his food. "You've changed," he finally said, furrowing his brows just so slightly.

"What?"

"Something's changed about you. Oh, not just your hair. I really like it shorter by the way." He continued to scrutinize her, lifted his nose a bit, sniffed, and then smiled. "Your perfume, it's different."

She sat back, cocking her head a little to the left, amazed he had noticed. "Yeah, I switched about a month ago." She wasn't sure she really liked the new scent as much, but was too frugal not to use it up.

"Used to be Marc Jacobs. What is it now?"

"Burberry Body." She took a bite of the lamb and savored the flavor.

"Doesn't suit you as well."

She looked at him with curiosity, but said nothing. They both ate in silence for a while, with Amy enjoying every bite while Lynch seemed to pick at his food. It seemed he wanted to say something, as he stopped chewing and looked as if he was about to speak, only to take another bite and chew slowly.

"There's some leftover lasagna in the fridge if you'd

rather—"

"Thanks, but this is fine. I . . ."

The silence resumed, and now even Amy found her appetite waning. She wanted *him* to break the ice, to explain himself, to sell her on why he should get another chance. Yet, sitting there, eating together, was like old times, except for the awkward silence. And except for the fact that he had avoided her for months. She restrained her desire to act as if nothing had happened. Yet, the confrontation ahead might not be pleasant, and to act that way would certainly be the easier route.

She looked up and saw Lynch smiling wanly at her.

"This lamb is pretty good . . ."

She couldn't take it any further. If she left it up to him, she'd be left waiting yet one more time that night. She put her fork down, pushed back from the table, placed her hands in her lap, and asked, "Cut to the chase. Why, Lynch?"

"Huh?"

She saw him squirm in his seat and knew that he was perfectly aware what it was she was asking. She inhaled sharply and sighed, shaking her head a little.

"I think you know what I'm asking. Why? Why did you stop calling? Why did you avoid me? Why didn't you answer my calls?" Small tears formed in the corners of her eyes. "Why did you give up our relationship, just when it was going so well?" She grabbed her napkin and dabbed her eyes.

Lynch leaned back into the chair, pushing his legs out in front, and rubbed his forehead with his palms before dragging them down across his eyes and cheeks. He let out a deep breath.

"I was scared," he replied timidly.

"What? I didn't hear you."

"I was scared," he stated and then paused. "Do you remember what I once told you about my mom? And my sister? Both married men who put their careers first. My dad is married to his practice. My sister's husband was so dedicated to the job he got tired of hearing her complain about the hours and left her. In different ways, both had to fend for themselves, to raise families alone. I was scared one way or the other I'd do the same thing to you."

Amy took that in and mulled it about. "Soooo, you just abandoned me *before* the wedding, is that it?" She saw her words wound him, and the thought crossed her mind that she was not telling him something he didn't already know. She turned away, wondering which would be worse, to lose him now or to invest her love and life in him only to have it ripped away at some time in the future. It was clear which of the two options he thought to be the worse. And that angered her, that he wouldn't give *her* the choice, that he'd made such a decision for her.

Her mind rushed and tumbled through a myriad of emotions and questions. It was clear that he loved his job, but did he love it more than her? If so, why was he back? Why had he asked for a second chance? Did she love him so much that she'd accept second fiddle to his job?

The realization that maybe she didn't, and wouldn't, hit her hard. Since his return to her life, she had grown to accept that she loved him. A renewal of their relationship and a hope for going back to the way it had been had become her daily fantasy and nightly dream. Instead, maybe it was a delusion born of loneliness after he left.

Or maybe it was God's way of saying, "Put Me first."

She hadn't heard Lynch leave his seat, but sensed his presence beside her. She turned to find him kneeling next to her chair. As she turned back to him, he grabbed her hand and placed it between his.

"Amy, I was also scared of making a commitment, of loving you so fully, and of fearing I'd hurt you somehow, and scared you might ultimately reject me. Not at first. I wasn't blind to how well things were going between us. I was scared that after you saw how much I loved my job, you'd wonder what my priorities would be and decide you didn't want to risk taking second place, and that you'd leave *me*." He paused and with one hand, took her free hand and joined it with her other, so he was now holding both. "When I saw you again in the E.D., I realized I was living a lie. I thought that if I could just avoid you, my feelings would eventually diminish. They didn't. All it took was seeing you again to make me see how much I still love you." He looked directly into her eyes. "Oh man, how your eyes still captivate me. I feel like I could fall into the well of your soul through them, and I'd never want out. I love you, Amy."

Amy's tears flowed freely, and she liberated one hand in order to wipe her cheeks with her napkin. Then, freeing her other hand, she leaned forward and wrapped them under his arms and around to his back, laying her forehead on his shoulder. His hands instinctively moved to hold her, and she welcomed his awkward embrace. A moment later, she straightened up a bit and gazed at his face.

"I love you, too, Lynch. But . . ."

She saw a look of concern wrench control of his face. There was always a 'but.'

"But you're right. I won't take backstage. If I'm not first in your life, just like if you weren't first in my life, it would eat at and poison our relationship over the years. Maybe not to a breaking point, but certainly to a point of creating doubts, maybe make us ask ourselves what we were thinking when we were young and foolish in love." She pulled her arms from behind him and sat upright in her chair. "I know who would be first in my heart. Do you?"

He started to say something, but she stopped him by placing her fingertips over his mouth. "I don't want an answer right now. I think you need to search yourself for the answer, to know for sure it's an answer you can live with for a long time, until death do us part, if that's where we end up."

She slid her chair away from him, just far enough to be able to stand. But instead of standing up, she reached for her wine glass and took a sip. Her mouth felt dry despite the cool nutty liquid. With another drink, she emptied her glass and then stood, Lynch following her lead. He took both of her hands again.

"Okay. I think I know my—"

"No, Lynch," she interrupted. "That's part of the

problem, you *think* you know. Give me an answer when you *know* you know."

She leaned forward, kissed him softly on the cheek, and pulled away. Lynch sort of shuffled his feet and looked both ways around the room, as if unsure where to go from there. She glanced at the clock and noticed he had caught her doing so.

"It's getting late. I, uh . . . Maybe I better get going. Um, when can I see you again?"

She studied him for a moment, unsuccessfully trying to catch his thoughts by osmosis.

"The rest of the week is pretty tight. I work tomorrow, then off a day and work again the next. If the weather holds, I plan to go flying the day after that. Want to come?"

Lynch looked at the backs of both hands and then at his fingertips. He grimaced.

"Not going to be another white knuckle flight is it? I think my fingertips have healed from the last time."

She laughed and gave him her best pout.

"Maybe, but the finger holes are still in the sides of the passenger seat where you latched on. Dad refuses to fix 'em."

"Look, I know you're a good pilot. Just promise me, no acrobatics on this flight, and I'll join you. You don't have to show off for me."

"Fair enough. I'll let you know what time."

Lynch started toward the door, and Amy followed. She appreciated his joking about her flying because it removed the earlier tension. She preferred they part on friendly terms. No, she *preferred* they not part at all, but . . . There was that troublesome conjunction again.

At the door, she allowed him a kiss, hoping it would help persuade his decision, while dreading it would cloud his thoughts. She yearned to be chosen, to know she would always win out over his job. Yet her requirement was only that he put her first because that's what he truly wanted, not because of a hormonal response. In high school and college basketball, she had been a forward, always on the receiving end of the pass. This time, despite the open shot given her, she had passed the ball across the lane to Lynch. Only time would reveal if they were playing in the same game.

Lynch sat in his car, his hands trembling, and watched as the lights in Amy's front room went out. He wasn't trembling at the thought of flying with her again.

He had accomplished what he wanted to do, being totally open and honest about his feelings for her. He took hope in the fact that he hadn't scared her away. In that sense, the evening had gone better than he'd realistically expected. But what next?

A thought hit him. Maybe he could have the best of the two worlds he sought. Maybe teaching—criminology, criminal psych, and computer forensics—and consulting could keep his interest as much as active police work, yet allow him the life he wanted with Amy. Yes. Maybe this was his answer.

He had never thought about *teaching* criminology.

Could that really be a workable solution to his dilemma? Could he find the same level of professional fulfillment in teaching as he did in active police work? He decided he would start looking into that option ASAP. He took a deep breath and started the car.

He made choices all the time. Sometimes he had to make a command decision with minimal data on the spur of the moment, based on his instincts. He couldn't afford to make a gut decision this time. This time, he had the most important decision in his life to make.

Twenty-seven
❧ ✦ ✦ ❧

Lynch, Flannigan, and the Chief sat in the older man's office debating their next course of action. The meeting had already passed the 30-minute mark, not that Lynch had noticed. Earlier that day, he had made his first move and inquired about positions at the University of Missouri–St. Louis, the only full-fledged criminology program in the area. He had Masters Degrees in Sociology, as well as Forensic Science, but he had not pursued a Ph.D., which he would need to become a professor. He mulled over what that would require.

"Earth to Lynch. Where are you today? You need to focus here."

The Chief sat, staring at him. He was right. His thoughts were elsewhere, and they needed to be concentrating on the problem at hand. He nodded.

"Are sure you want to go ahead with this? I don't want this lady put in jeopardy," the Chief argued. His previous comments made it clear. The Chief's primary concern focused on Meghan Reilly.

Lynch contemplated his next statement before speaking.

"Sir, this guy is starting to run scared. His pattern is wavering, and his timetable has accelerated. "He—"

The Chief interrupted. "He outsmarted us on this last one. I don't want her used in any intentional trap."

"But, sir, she fits his profile to a tee. She's in danger one way or another, and we're in a better position to

240

protect her if we have a plan than if we leave her to fend for herself."

Flannigan looked like he was at a tennis match as his eyes oscillated between the two men volleying back and forth. Lynch saw him fidget when the Chief finally turned toward him.

"Flannigan, what do you think?" the older man asked.

He shook his head. "Sir, I sure won't be discussing the next mystery novel I read with either of you. You two throw more red herrings and stir up more muddy water than any bestselling author."

The Chief huffed. "I didn't ask if you could read. What do you think?"

"Chief, I see both sides, but I tend to agree with Lynch. The Reilly girl will be better protected with us than if we just let her go on her own. She's pretty headstrong. Who can say she might not try to bait this guy with the help of her brother if we don't work with her. It's like she feels she owes something to Payne's family to find this guy."

Lynch nodded. Despite their discussion, Flannigan had come up with an angle neither Lynch nor the Chief had mentioned.

The Chief paused a moment and finally nodded. "Good point. Okay, keep it going, and let me know what you finally come up with. You don't have my final blessing yet." He paused, and then looked Lynch squarely in the eyes. "Nothing better happen to the girl, or her brother." His tone was clear.

Lynch realized he had been premature in sending out feelers about teaching. He had to concentrate on the case, and on protecting a young woman who had volunteered to help. The plan was his. He was responsible—for the plan and for her safety. Yet, he had initiated something that could evolve into a major distraction. Amy had already become a major distraction—in a good way. He didn't need another one. She understood the need to rid their city of this "LA Rapist" and Lynch's key role in the case. She would understand any additional delays on his part. Yet, he owed her more. He wanted more.

With the Chief's decision made, the two younger detectives stood to leave.

"Lynch." The Chief stopped him before he stepped through the door. "Anything on Elsa Dunaway's camera or cell phone?"

"No, sir. We tried a trace on her number, but none of the local towers are picking up its signal. Knowing this guy's proficiency with electronics, he probably disabled it. Her PDA's likely wiped as well, which doesn't look good for finding her camera."

"House? Car?"

"I rechecked the house. Nothing there. The car's still in the county impound lot, but the report says they did a complete exam of it, fingerprints, tests for body fluids, pulled the seats and lining of the trunk. Vacuumed everything. Everything I'd do. No camera or gadgets."

"Did you examine it yourself?" The Chief's tone was explicit.

* * *

Amy's day had started much too early. She'd had a hard time falling asleep, tossing and turning, her mind racing from one thing to another, mostly about Lynch. The second act of grace was that the policeman who flagged her down for speeding knew her, discerned from her flight suit that she was headed to work, and let her go without even a warning. She arrived at base only one minute late.

As she reached to open the front door of the doublewide, it burst open before her and both Lyle and Reid emerged through the doorway, stopping abruptly to avoid running her down.

"Whoa! Watch out!" Lyle yelled.

"Me?" Amy responded. "You're the ones who can see out the door. I can't see in. What's up?"

"Stash your stuff and let's go. Got a call for Creve Coeur County Park. Another weird one," Reid said. "I got your flight bag."

Susan, the nurse she was relieving, stood behind the two men. "Glad you're here. Thought I was headed for some overtime."

She backed away and cleared the path for Amy to enter the prefab home, where without further conversation she threw her bag onto a chair. She unzipped it and grabbed her stethoscope and "pocket brain." She turned and flew out the door, breaking into a full run to the helicopter. The sudden surge of adrenaline eradicated whatever fatigue she'd had earlier. As the

243

blades increased their revolutions, she climbed into her seat, buckled in, and donned her helmet. She moved the microphone boom around toward her mouth and pressed the talk switch on her cord.

"What've we got?" she asked.

"Another assault. Another weird one. Worse than that lady in the car you went out on." Reid proceeded to fill her in on the details as they had them so far. "Paramedics on the scene thought it was a DOA, but one of them detected a weak pulse and an occasional weak gasp for air. At that point, someone discovered a possible bomb, so they had to clear the building. I just hope we don't have more than one victim when we land."

Six minutes later, they circled the landing zone once and descended rapidly before Lyle made another of his celebrated barely-discernible touchdowns. As they jumped from the helicopter, a park ranger waved them on.

"This way. I'll drive," he screamed over the noise of the aircraft. "It's a quarter mile down this gravel road. Ambulance is already there."

Amy and Reid dumped their bags into the back seat, and Reid sat down next to them while motioning Amy to the front passenger's seat. Moments later, they pulled up next to the ambulance, its crew pacing nearby. Amy climbed out of the squad car and rushed to the paramedics.

"What's up?"

"Police got a call this morning. Jogger said he saw some vandalism at this old service building. A Ranger drove up to check it out and found the door open and our victim inside. He thought he might pass out from the sight, but managed to run back to his car and radio for us. It's not—"

At that moment, a bomb squad officer yelled from the small, nearby service building. "No bomb. You're clear."

Amy and the medic ran toward the building and rushed through the door. Amy stopped dead in her tracks upon entering the small building.

The coppery smell of blood permeated the structure, and as her eyes adjusted to the dim light, her first thought was that they had another victim of the monster roaming their city. The victim profile fit, as she saw a long, dark-haired figure bound to an old rustic wooden chair, head drooped forward, arms dangling to her sides, with wrists cut and blood slowly dripping into two small pools that had coalesced beneath the chair. A bloodstained lace bra that appeared much too small stretched tightly around an unusually flat chest. A tattered skirt, also blood soaked, strained at the waist and across the thighs. At first, it appeared as if someone had carved random slashes into her skin. But as Amy moved closer, the wounds showed a pattern of systematic torture.

Amy took command of the wave of nausea that hit her and forced it aside. Donning her gloves, she moved to the woman's side and started to search for some sign of life.

"Here," Reid said as he tossed her the necessary

personal protection gear: face shield and paper gown. "Too much blood. Cover up."

She put on the face shield, ignoring the gown that would take too long to pull on, and used her stethoscope to listen for heart sounds. They were faint, and the pulse thready, but at least her heart was still ticking.

"First line in," yelled the paramedic who had entered the building just ahead of her. He grabbed the liter bag of lactated Ringer's solution and squeezed, forcing the precious fluid down the tube and into the waiting vein. His partner had already started searching for a site for a second large-bore line.

"Reid!" she stated. "Go for a third line, wherever you can put it!"

Amy gazed past the swollen, brutalized face and felt for a carotid pulse, and that's when she noted the rough, almost straw-like texture of the woman's hair. She looked closely, but had to use her penlight for a better visual. *This isn't real hair*, she thought, puzzled. She moved her fingers along the scalp and felt the rough cap of a wig. She tried to remove it gently, but dry, clotted blood glued the wig to the scalp. Using a bit of saline to soak the cap, she managed to pull the wig free. Blood began to ooze from freshly re-opened scalp wounds.

She gently supported the person's neck while tipping the head upright and felt the prominent Adam's apple.

"Oh God," she moaned. "Folks, our 'lady' here is male."

One male paramedic groaned.

The female paramedic announced the second line was running, and another bag of Ringer's soon poured into a different vein. She then took her bandage scissors from their small pocket on the thigh of her pants and snipped both bra straps and then the main band across the back. Evidence of more torture. She shifted forward to remove the skirt.

Reid grimaced. "I don't want to know . . ."

She cut down the front and the fabric fell beside the victim's legs. She saw no genitalia.

"I think I'm going to be sick," grunted Reid.

But as the medic examined the perineum, the male genitals appeared. They had been tucked backward, but not altered. Amy saw the color return to Reid's face.

"Third line in," he yelled.

A park ranger appeared at the door with the backboard from the helicopter and the gurney from the ambulance. Together all four EMS members gently lifted the mutilated man onto the board and then onto the gurney. The first bag of lactated Ringer's was empty, and the male paramedic pulled a new bag from his box. Onboard the ambulance, while the ground crew retrieved and secured their gear, Amy used their portable Doppler to check again for a blood pressure. The fluids appeared to be working. She found a systolic pressure of roughly 60 millimeters of mercury.

"Let's start dopamine," she yelled over the noise of the engine as they started down to the service road toward the waiting helicopter.

While Reid pulled a pre-filled plastic bag of the

blood-pressure-raising drug from his duffel, she double-checked the dosing in her notebook, guessing at the man's weight. By the time the drug was running, they were out of the ambulance and moving to the aircraft. Two minutes later, Lyle performed a max-power lift-off and cleared the tree line in seconds.

Amy radioed in her first report, one received with disbelief and shock by the staff at the ED. They reassured her that the trauma team would be standing by and informed them the Major Case Squad would be waiting as well. As she tended him, she considered the explicit medical procedures someone had perpetrated on this man, their John Doe. Whoever did this had more medical knowledge and skill than made known to the public. And that bothered her. What more might he be capable of?

She leaned forward in her seat to check the blood pressure and saw a flicker of eye movement on the man's face. His pressure was up to 90 systolic. That would suffice until they arrived at the medical center. Again, she looked at the poor man's face, beaten, bruised, and swollen. What had he done to deserve this? She wondered how much he had suffered. Had he been awake when the incisions were made, when the cuts were slit into his skin? Was he even aware of what had been done to him? She doubted she would ever see anything more unjust and inhumane done to another person.

As she stared at her patient, his eyes opened, and his

mouth moved. He whispered something she couldn't hear over the engine. She knelt over him and faced him directly, placing her index finger over her mouth, encouraging him to remain still and quiet. But he persisted. She leaned closer and put her ear next to his mouth.

"No . . . time," he gasped.

She moved to the side of his head and talked into his ear. "Save your strength. Quiet. We're heading to the medical center."

Slowly he shook his head, and his mouth again moved. She strained to hear him over the whine of the turbine.

"I'm . . . dead. One way . . . or other. He won't . . . let . . . me . . . live."

She switched positions again. "Who? Who won't let you live?" she asked.

"I . . . need . . . confess . . ." He paused and closed his eyes. ". . . my sin." His heartbeat seemed erratic on the monitor. He continued. "Edward Payne . . . took easy money . . . 10 K . . . to leave . . . some tanks . . . Didn't . . . know . . . what . . ."

His breathing became more labored. Amy quickly checked the fluids. *Two liters in.* She listened to his lungs. They sounded wet and diminished. Had they given him too much too fast? *Not possible,* she thought. *He was in shock.* They couldn't have overloaded him with just two liters. Something else was going on. She double-checked his chest, removing the light dressings to scrutinize the visible wounds. That's when she saw the deeper wound.

It appeared to be a narrow stab wound in the left fifth intercostal space, right above the heart. By increasing his blood pressure, she guessed they had succeeded in reopening a wound in his heart that would pump what little blood and fluids that remained right into his chest cavity and lungs.

He tried to speak again.

"Lord . . . forgive . . . me."

She again spoke into his ear. "Who? Who did this?"

"Never . . . told . . ." Again he paused for breath. "Saw . . . picture . . . in paper . . . Name is—"

His eyes rolled back, and one long sigh escaped his lips.

"V-fib!" Reid yelled. "Charging!"

Twenty-eight

❦✦✦❧

Lynch, intent on personally examining Elsa Dunleavy's car, had just pulled into the county's impound lot when the call came. Dispatch, seeking to keep this new case off the police scanners, had tracked him through his cell phone and alerted him to the latest assault at Creve Coeur Lake. Sergeant Flannigan was in route to the park and had asked the dispatcher to have Lynch call him. He parked in the nearest slot and fumbled with the small phone to find Flannigan's number and dial it.

"It's Lynch. What's up?"

"Another assault. Heavyset woman. Long dark brown hair. She was found bound to a chair in a remote service building, blood everywhere. Paramedics are there, and police are clearing the scene, but no details yet."

Lynch's first reaction was to question the call.

"Paul, our guy doesn't use the same place twice. I don't—"

"Hey, getting another call. Let me get it."

Lynch sat in his car, debating whether to get out and go find the Dunleavy car as planned or to flip on his lights and speed out to the park. Their perp had been breaking out of his pattern lately. Maybe this was another attempt to throw them off his trail.

"I'm back. You aren't going to believe this one."

Flannigan proceeded to give Lynch the latest details.

251

They were sparse, but bizarre. Bizarre enough for a copycat crime. There was no similarity between this hideous mutilation and the others. Bizarre enough to make Lynch question whose handiwork this was. Yet weird enough, hateful enough, and medically sophisticated enough almost to guarantee it was their guy. And if it was him, Lynch had a strong gut feeling about the victim's identity.

Amy's crew had been involved, and he suspected she would have more to tell him than what might be stated in a written report. Plus, he was concerned about her. He did not want to see her further caught up in this case. She had already been involved with the Dunleavy case.

"I'm heading to the medical center, Paul. Keep me in the loop."

The county government complex was not far from the medical center so he saw no need to push through traffic, which was light enough after the morning's rush hour. He expected Amy to be there. They had requested she and the paramedic provide formal statements, just like the three ground medics would be providing statements to Flannigan. But, request or not, Lynch knew she'd stay and knew she'd tell him more than she'd tell someone else on the squad.

Minutes later, Lynch pulled into the medical center E.D. parking lot to find it packed solid. He recognized Janick's car filling one of the slots reserved for law enforcement. Squad cars from several jurisdictions occupied other spaces, but it was the network affiliate television stations whose vans, most of them double-parked, and remote broadcast equipment crammed the blacktop and lent a circus atmosphere to the area immediately outside the E.D. Hospital security, with the aid of several uniformed officers, kept the news crews at bay and maintained an open lane for ambulance traffic to move in and out of an inner lot. They had not been as successful in securing the helipad, but Lynch noted two guards running to the pad to intervene and remove the interlopers, while a member of the crew, whom Lynch presumed to be the pilot, watched over his aircraft.

He pulled up to a series of plastic barriers where a security officer was checking identification and turning unauthorized cars away. Lynch flashed his badge, but it was unnecessary. The guard, a veteran of fifteen years at the center with regular duty in the E.D., recognized him and waved him through. Lynch stopped to say "hi."

"Hey Dell, you invite your family over again?"

The guard laughed. "Yeah, well, they make as much mess as my kids do anyway. Good to see you, detective. Ain't been inside, but I hear it's a doozie."

"Looks like you're not the only one to hear about it."

Dell shrugged his shoulders and nodded.

"You need a place to talk with these folks?" He waved toward the growing crowd of news people.

"Not me. Not my show today, unless you know something I don't." Lynch smiled and held up his hand to give a terse wave.

The guard nodded and walked back toward the curb where he had a stool.

Lynch hadn't made it ten feet inside the department

when he heard an all-too-familiar greeting.

"Hey, Cully. Over here."

Lynch turned to find Janick and their boss, Colonel Halbert, huddled together with the director of hospital security. As he approached the trio, he was surprised to see the Chief walk around the corner from an intersecting hallway and join them.

"Doctor's still trying to bring him back. Haven't been able to positively ID him yet, but—"

"Yeah, it's probably him," Lynch agreed as he scanned back and forth across the open space of the E.D. "Flight crew around here somewhere?"

Janick grinned mischievously. "Lookin' up an old girlfriend, huh? She's in the room helping with the code. Anything happen to me, I'd sure like to wake up and see her pumpin' on my chest."

Lynch let the comment slide. It wasn't worth a retort. He looked over at the Chief.

"Surprised to see you here, Chief."

"This was one victim I figured I'd better get a firsthand look at. Press is going to be all over us, and I don't want to be in the dark about what really happened here." He paused, gave his head a little nod, and smiled. "Besides, I'm no stranger to emergency medicine. Did I ever tell you I grew up wanting to be a doctor? I was a medic in Nam. Saw more than I ever want to remember there. Trauma, field surgeries, stuff these new doctors will never see. Hopefully. Anyway, Nam cured me of wanting to be a doctor. But I still have the hands for it." He held out his hands to show them rock steady, not a quiver.

Lynch smiled. "You continue to surprise me, sir." He turned toward his boss, Colonel Halbert. "You here for the same reason, sir?"

The man nodded. "Sure. Thought I'd better see this through myself as well."

Lynch had no problem with the brass being there. Both men trusted him well enough to let him work without interference. Plus, they'd be there to handle the press and let him slide past that chore.

At that moment, there was a commotion on the opposite side of the E.D. where Lynch knew the trauma rooms to be located. The glass doors and curtain to Trauma A opened, and a dejected Doctor Royce and two technicians emerged. The doctor looked over to the waiting policemen and shook his head, frowning. Royce walked to a point about halfway between them and stopped to address the men from there.

Lynch knew that look. He'd seen it too many times in the E.D., and from Amy's past accounts, he knew that no one there liked losing. Calling the code on a kid was the worst, but conceding to death for anyone before their time put a damper on all of the staff for the rest of their shift. Yet, as Amy had also pointed out, all men and women have their appointed time to meet their Maker, and who were we to say when that was.

"Give the nurses a few minutes to clean up and you can go in."

He then turned and walked to the doctor's dictation desk, picking up the chart for the patient in Trauma A on the way.

Amy and a young man in a flight suit were next to leave the room. Both looked over at the police, and the young man walked directly to the group, while Amy lingered near the room. Lynch heard him introduce himself, Reid something-or-other, the flight paramedic, but his attention focused on Amy. He heard Janick ask the paramedic to stick around for a statement as he left his fellow officers and approached Amy. Another nurse came out of the room behind Amy, caught sight of Lynch, frowned, and put her hand on Amy's arm while whispering something to her. Lynch remembered Macy for her saucy spirit and as one of Amy's closest friends. Her reaction to him was not unexpected. He half expected her to walk up and kick him in the shins or punch him in the nose, while exclaiming she was doing what Amy was too polite to do. That would be Macy. Amy nodded to her friend and walked toward Lynch as Macy retreated to the nurse's station.

Lynch took her hand and placed it between both of his.

"You okay?" he asked.

She nodded. "Lynch, whoever did this is a monster." Tears welled up in her eyes. "Nobody, absolutely nobody, could do anything to deserve what happened to this man. Do you know who he is?"

Lynch released her hand and gave her a quick hug, which she accepted without hesitation. As he glanced over her shoulder, he noted Doctor Royce watching his actions. He knew of the man's reputation among the female nursing staff and found the look on his face curious, quiet and reserved, yet covertly jealous. A sense of possession ran through him. *She's mine, man. You steer clear*, he thought.

Amy backed away and motioned for Lynch to follow her into the room. He fully understood her comment when he saw the bloody, disfigured torso and heard about how it had mocked womanhood. A bloody wig sat on a nearby stand. Amy explained what she had encountered upon entering the service cabin, gave a detailed presentation of what they did for the victim, and how he had arrested in flight. She made it clear that they had been fighting against all hope to save the man. He had simply lost too much blood and had too many serious wounds to survive. Lynch took a good look at the swollen, purplish face. There was little doubt that it was Art Barklage.

A voice spoke from behind them.

"Ms. Gibbs, good to see you again." Janick and the two senior officers had entered the trauma bay. "We'd like to get a complete statement from you before you leave. I'll—"

Lynch interrupted. "I'm taking care of it, Bob."

As Lynch ushered Amy from the room, he heard the men gasp.

"My God," said the Chief.

Janick responded, "Yeah, it's him."

Amy grabbed Lynch's arm and led him to the workroom where Reid was already busy completing their transfer forms. She shut the door and looked at Reid.

"Reid, nothing I say leaves this room. Got it?"

The paramedic nodded and continued to write.

"Lynch, we revived him long enough to get a few things." She proceeded to tell Lynch word-for-word what the man had said. "The folks here know we revived him briefly, but I've told no one about his deathbed confession. Right now, we're the only three who know about it because I wanted you to decide whether it's information that should be released."

The paramedic had stopped writing and looked flushed.

"Umm, Amy?" Amy and Lynch looked at him. "I screwed up, I think." He looked chagrined. "You didn't say anything about keeping it secret, so I mentioned it to Royce and the nurses in the room at the time. I didn't tell them *what* he'd said, just that he'd awakened enough to mumble some things."

Twenty-nine

Amy watched Lynch leave the room to confer with his colleagues. Lynch had agreed that it was best to hold the information about the man's deathbed confession in confidence. For one thing, the information was too vague. If asked, they were to say it was all gibberish.

Amy walked out to the main work area and watched the comings and goings as the staff moved on to other patients. There were still times she missed the hustle of the E.D., but this wasn't one of them. Losing a patient was never a positive experience. Seeing someone suffer never produced warm, fuzzy feelings. And knowing some monster capable of torturing and carving up people remained on the loose was not the stuff of heaven-sent dreams.

Doctor Royce arose from his desk, grabbed a new chart, and headed toward Amy. There was none of his usual cockiness showing. In fact, he brushed by her with only so much as a grunt. Macy stood to the side and smiled.

"What's with him?" Amy asked.

"He saw you hugging your old beau. I think he's been hoping for a chance for a date ever since you and Lynch broke up."

"I wasn't hugging Lynch. He hugged me."

"Girl, I saw it all. You were definitely hugging back. Looks to me like the old flame has been relit."

Amy felt her cheeks flush. "Well, maybe. We've come

to an understanding. Now all he has to do is make some hard decisions."

"Oh? Like, you've already made your hard decisions?"

Amy shrugged.

"Girl, you're hopeless. I hope he knows what a gem he's getting."

"Like I said, he's got some decisions to make first."

Doctor Royce emerged from the exam room and approached the two women. He seemed in a better mood.

"So, Amy, what'd that guy say when he came to in the chopper?"

"What?"

"Reid told us he revived briefly in flight and was talking. What'd he say?"

Amy rocked a bit on her feet. She was unaccustomed to lying.

"Gibberish mostly. Couldn't hear much over the engine."

"That's it? Gibberish?" Royce seemed skeptical.

"Uh, yeah. That's it." She squirmed a bit more and hoped she was convincing enough to avoid further questioning.

"Hmmm," he replied, nodding his head as he returned to the doctor's work zone.

Macy looked at her. "Girl, I seen that look in you before. Might have convinced Royce, but I know better." Macy leaned forward to search Amy's eyes. "Police said not to say anything, right?"

Amy nodded just slightly.

"Okay. No more 20 questions. Gotta get back to work."

"See ya," Amy said, as her friend moved toward the clean utility room.

Amy noticed that the police presence had evaporated, including Lynch. Reid was waving at her from the ambulance entrance. Time to go. She started across the main floor when Doctor Koettering appeared and marched right up to Royce. Amy couldn't hear the first words spoken; she was too far away. But the tone was assuredly unfriendly. She knew it wrong to eavesdrop, but her pace slowed as she neared the doctor's work area. She heard something that sounded derogatory come from Koettering about E.R. physicians.

"I may work down here for the extra cash, but I'm still the senior fellow on the hyperbaric medicine service," stated Royce. "If you're going to keep her in a barbiturate coma, she's not coming into my chamber. Take it up with Doctor Cassidy."

"I'll do just that. In the meantime, I want Esther Jacobs to get her HBO session today, as scheduled." Koettering sounded as arrogant as he was persistent.

"Only if my boss overrules me. And if he does, I'll remove myself from the case. I won't be a party to injuring that poor lady any further."

David sat in the doctor's dictation booth on the neuro floor, door closed, rubbing his temples and forehead with his fingertips. There was a knock at the

261

door.

"David? You in there?"

It was Dan Diehl. David wanted to ignore him, let him think the booth was empty so he would move on. He didn't feel like facing his associate with his head pulsating.

The door cracked open wide enough for Dan to see him.

"Another headache?"

David nodded.

"So, I take it the meeting with Doctor Cassidy went nowhere."

David nodded again. "No arguing, but he supported Royce. No hyperbaric treatments for Ester Jacobs as long as she's in an induced barbiturate coma."

Cassidy had backed Royce 110%. Their concern centered on the potential for additional brain injury by subjecting the patient to the increased pressures of the chamber while such high levels of medication remained in her system. Cassidy had pointed out in clear terms that the use of barbiturate coma as a means of protecting the brain was under scrutiny and numerous studies now claimed it was dangerous. This wasn't news to David. His was one of the approved on-going studies where one arm of the study was designed to look at that very question. Until Esther Jacobs, however, they had never exercised the use of both therapeutic modalities in a single patient.

"But our protocol allows it, and we were approved by a dozen committees to include that arm in our study." The neuropsychologist looked angry.

"Not so loud, please." David pleaded with his eyes for the vocal volume to go down. "Look, I told you when she arrived here that we'd get resistance."

"I know. I pushed you into it, but her SPECT scan showed extensive injury, and I didn't believe either barbiturates or HBO alone would affect her prognosis positively. She's the first one suitable for both and with that Morse code episode, I figured we needed to go for broke."

David understood. The man's arguments had been sound enough to convince him to order both therapies knowing there would be opposition.

"That blinking code may have been a fluke. We never saw it again, even before starting the barbs."

David had ordered the drugs, knowing that with the sedative on board she would no longer be able to blink in code. Since then, he struggled with the thought that maybe he had agreed because subconsciously he didn't want her to communicate. It had unsettled him that she'd called him a "bastard." Was he simply soothing his own ego? He didn't want to believe he was capable of something so selfish.

"I'm going to go check on her. Want to join me?" David asked.

"I think I'll head back to my office. Maybe I can find some other argument, some other approach to convince Cassidy."

David nodded, but he knew Cassidy and Royce would stand firm in their conviction. He walked out to the nursing station, retrieved Esther's chart from the rack, and eased his way down the hall to her room. Once inside the room he sat on the edge of her bed, looking at the serene face before him. There was something special about her. He felt she held the key to new treatment guidelines, but he was at a loss without the total cooperation of the other physicians providing her care. Methodically, he again assessed her neurological status, checking her eyes, testing for reflexes and an induced pain response. He listened to her chest and abdomen. The exam revealed only what he would expect from someone so deeply sedated.

It was at that point he made a decision. Her earlier improvement had been the result of hyperbaric oxygen, not barbiturate coma. And if they were prevented from being aggressive, from providing both forms of treatment, then HBO would be the better alternative. He flipped open the chart to the physician's order section and scribbled in his distinct but not always legible script, "D/C pentobarbital—Reschedule HBO."

Lady Law awoke with a start, not recalling how he arrived at his motor coach. Yet, he found himself prostrate across the bed, his temples throbbing, and his mouth parchment dry. He arose and staggered from the bedroom to the kitchen. He glanced forward toward the living area. Markie had left his usual mess at the video game console, but he would leave it to Markie to clean it up. After rummaging through the cabinets, he found the ibuprofen samples he wanted and quickly downed six hundred milligrams with a full glass of water. After refilling his glass with ice and water, he moved to his media center and sat down, eyes closed, willing the medication to work more quickly than his experience told him it would. He sipped on the water to ease the desiccation in his mouth, although it did little to remove the gummy aftertaste reminiscent of a morning following a night of too much wine.

The ebullient mood of earlier in the day had evaporated like alcohol on a warm surface. He was irritable, frustrated, and anxious, and had no outlet for his emotions. He detested the moodiness that had overcome him in recent days. Part of the problem was David. Why couldn't he see the benefits of and graciously accept the test subjects he was being given? He was such a wimp, unwilling to move boldly in his research. While history had been unkind to the Mengeles and Raschers of Nazi Germany, their contributions to the understanding of the human body had been great.

Another distinct problem was his dislike of being the hunted instead of the nameless hunter, and the manhunt had come dangerously close to home. He picked up a remote control and flipped on the television, followed by the digital recorder that monitored his "home" while he was away in the city during the day. Re-indexing the replay to nine a.m. that day, he again watched what his outside camera had caught, a police officer nosing around, knocking on the door and trying to peek into the windows. He fast-forwarded the replay to four p.m. and observed the same man returning for a visit. There was little doubt that he or one of his compatriots would return again, and again, until they found someone home. He smiled for the first time that day as he thought about an appropriate present to leave for them to discover.

If he'd had any previous reservations about moving, they were gone. It was time to move. But where? There were few places where he could park his rig, maintain a required level of anonymity, and still have easy access to his current work in the city. He would have to move farther out and simply accept the longer commute time until his task was completed, and he could leave the area.

And his task would never finish until he dealt with the procreating loose ends. Barklage was supposed to be dead by the time the rangers and EMS arrived at the cabin, but Lady Law had learned that he had survived into his flight to the medical center. There was even talk that he'd revived briefly in the helicopter and had talked some gibberish. Lady Law would need to confirm that, and if it turned out that the man had said more than nonsense, then one loose end had divided itself into two, in the guise of a paramedic and a nurse. The image of an amoeba splitting in two filled his mind, and just like that dysenteric microbe, these two would need curing.

Thirty

୨๑✦✦๑୧

Lights flashing, Lynch raced north through the congested early morning traffic toward the police station in Maryland Heights, Missouri, the suburb where the Creve Coeur Park was located. The phone call hadn't awakened him. Sleep had evaded him for most of the night as thoughts of Art Barklage and images of his mutilation usurped counting sheep. Amy had been right; no one deserved that.

But, what had been the man's actual role concerning the gas tanks he'd left at the law firm? Perhaps his wife knew more than she'd let on. Amy had agreed that neither of them would tell anyone about the man's last words in the hope that damage control would be unnecessary. Besides, the information was the kind the police liked to hold back so that the killer remained unaware just how much they knew.

By four in the morning, he had given up on bed and retreated to the recliner in his home office. By five, he had started scanning the previous Sunday's paper.

When the phone rang, Lynch glanced at the clock. Five-thirty. *Oh well*, he thought, *another day begins*. But he was ready to start, ready to do anything that would get his mind off the previous day.

"Sergeant Cully?" It was an unfamiliar voice.

"Yes." He yawned unexpectedly.

"Sorry to bother you so early. This is Sergeant Wilson with the Maryland Heights Police. I was told to

267

call you directly and to keep this off any police radio."

That perked up Lynch's attention and erased the sleep from his brain.

"What can I do for you?"

"Actually, we may have something of interest to you. One of our officers on routine patrol yesterday spotted a suspicious motor coach parked in a secluded area about a mile from the Creve Coeur County Park boundaries. The officer stopped by twice during the day without finding anyone present, although there were signs of another vehicle. We were going to send another car out last night, but we got busy with a multi-car accident on the interstate. Our captain contacted Dandridge, who thinks this might be a break in your case and asked us to invite you to join us this morning when we go back to investigate."

Lynch chuckled. "Did he really use the word 'invite'?"

The other officer laughed. "Not really."

"Didn't think so. Guess that means I'm supposed to accept your invitation, huh?" There was no direct response from the other end of the line. "So, what time does this party start?"

"As soon as you can join us."

"At the Maryland Heights station?"

"Roger that."

"Be there in 30 minutes, 40 max."

Lynch hung up and rushed into the bathroom for a quick electric shave and shower. Fifteen minutes later, he squealed out of his driveway, lights flashing, and headed toward the Maryland Heights Police Department. Early morning work traffic was heavier than he expected, but he pulled into the police parking lot half an hour later and linked up with Wilson.

"Sergeant Cully, these are Officers Meise, Hernandez, and Hoffman."

Lynch shook the officers' hands as he was introduced.

"Hoffman found the rig yesterday."

"Mike Hoffman. Nice to meet you." He pulled a map from a clipboard and held it out toward Lynch, while pointing to a place in the center. "Here's where I saw the motor coach. Basically farm land with some wooded areas. We have two access roads to the location, so we're doubling up and putting a car on each route. You can join one of us or follow us in your own car."

Lynch felt that high, which comes with hopeful expectation. Again. He knew he shouldn't expect the best. He'd been disappointed too many times on this case already. However, he now had new reason to want to be finished with this case.

"Let me follow you."

The others nodded, and after conferring further, they all climbed into their cars and started out. Ten minutes later, they were all in position, and in a coordinated effort, they converged simultaneously on the location, only to find it empty.

Lynch slapped his steering wheel in frustration as he came to a stop and parked next to Officer Hoffman's patrol car. He knew he should have kept his expectations in reign. As he emerged from his car, he heard the officers discussing their next move. Wilson and Meise would return to the station while Hernandez and Hoffman inspected the area. Lynch joined the latter two by their car.

"So, this was the place?" he asked.

"Yep. Parked right over there under the trees," Hoffman answered while Hernandez began scanning the area.

The officer pointed to the dirt and gravel roadway and started to walk over to the exact spot where the motor coach had been parked. Lynch noted the tire marks of a large vehicle, fresh marks it had left behind when it vacated the site.

He muttered something under his breath. "Mike!" he called as he moved to catch up with Hoffman.

The other man stopped and turned back toward Lynch.

"Can you give me a detailed description of the coach?"

"Sure." The man pulled a small notebook from his back pocket. "Forty foot Fleetwood. Black. Had a broad metallic silver accent startin' just behind the front wheel well and gradually curving up to hit the roofline just above the rear wheel well. Aft of the curve was kind of a sunrise pattern with the paint getting' lighter up to the line of the windows, then like a spider web pattern behind and above the windows and across the back. Pretty slick actually."

Lynch nodded. "License plate?"

"New York plates. Got the number right here."

"Run 'em?"

"No. We were told to look for that Barklage guy, not a vehicle, so I saw no need yesterday. Remembered the earlier alert about motor homes after I got home and started thinking, puttin' two and two together. That's when I suggested the sergeant call you guys this morning. I can do it now—"

"Won't help," Hernandez interrupted.

"What?" Lynch was baffled. Running the plates was essential at this point.

The other officer pointed to the edge of the grass about fifteen feet away. Lynch grunted. A set of New York motor home plates lay on the gravel.

"Whoever it was wouldn't have left 'em behind if they were legit. We'll probably find they're stolen or expired, or both."

Lynch had to agree, but knew they'd need to check the plates one way or the other. If the inquiry came back as lost or stolen, they'd be no better off than before. But, if not? Could the registered owner be their guy? Again, that seemed an unreasonable prospect. Still, Lynch wanted to hope for a favorable turn in this case.

He scanned the area to the left of the plates and noted more debris. He walked toward it, inspecting the ground as he moved. Two crumpled piles of metal and plastic appeared in the tire tracks as if the objects had been placed under the wheels as the coach backed out. He cursed as he recognized the solid-state electronics he saw under the crumpled casings and instantly knew who once owned them. There in the dirt and gravel were the smashed remains of a cell phone in one track, and the flattened fragments of a PDA in the other. He had no doubts that the serial numbers would lead them back to Elsa Dunleavy.

Ninety minutes later, Lynch arrived at the county impound lot after bagging, tagging, and delivering the crushed remains of the two electronic devices to the county police labs. He had little hope of discovering even a partial fingerprint, but protocol was protocol. As he had collected and bagged the pieces, the Maryland Heights police officer ran the discarded tags through a computer link to the New York DMV and confirmed that they had been reported stolen a little over three years earlier. They, too, had been dropped off at the labs for examination. And although he had few expectations of finding anything on the plates, their theft gave him a reference point in time.

Their quarry was in upstate New York 40 months earlier. With the local assaults having started eighteen months ago, he hoped he might develop a timetable that could reliably predict when their assailant moved to the area. He also planned to send queries to the Albany and Syracuse Police about any strings of attacks in their areas in the interval between the time of the theft and the date of the first local attack.

The adrenaline rush of the morning had worn off and the lack of sleep begged for resolution. He was early.

Maybe a short power nap in the car.

Yet, he realized the fatigue wasn't solely the result of one night's insomnia. This whole case. The prolonged loan to the squad. And . . . the decision he had to make. He yawned. If he could be honest with himself, he was tired to the bone. Maybe his parents had known something he had refused to acknowledge. Police work, by its very nature, focused on the dregs, the worst of humanity. And like any other profession or job, its nature could carry over to every other aspect of one's life.

Did he want his work to carry over into his marriage and family life? Amy had once talked about God's priorities in our lives. Lynch now questioned how his life fit that.

More importantly though, did he want to put Amy or their future children in potential danger from some crazed psychopath he had once put behind bars? Suddenly, the idea of teaching became even more attractive. He *had* been right to start putting out feelers in that direction. Yet, he reminded himself, again, that his current work required his full attention and chastised himself, again, that he found it so hard to give it that focus. At this point, he made a resolution. He would concentrate on this new career path later, once they solved this case.

With a new spring in his step, he walked into the lot's office and approached the desk. He recognized the young woman behind the counter as the same person who had been there when he had come to inspect the car of Art Barklage after its impounding from the airport parking lot. Her hair was jet black and cropped short. She had multiple piercings of both ears, the left eyebrow, and lower lip, although the pin in the lip was lost against the fiery red color of her lipstick. On their first encounter, she had presented herself with an air of absolute boredom, and today was no different. She looked up at him and placed her *People* magazine face down with the pages open to mark her place.

"Hi, remember me?" Lynch asked. It had been less than two weeks since his last visit there.

"Should I?" She rolled her eyes and frowned like a teenager being admonished by her mother.

"I'm—"

"Just kidding. Yeah, I remember. Thought you was supposed to be here yesterday."

"Something came up."

"Don't it always. You're here to check out the Dunleavy car, right?"

Lynch nodded. She flipped through a car file and pulled out a stiff, white, six-by-nine inch card.

"Here. Sign in. And don't forget to sign out when you leave. All this chain of evidence stuff. And if you find something, we have another evidence form you got to fill out. Okay?"

Lynch knew the drill. He signed in and noted the time next to his signature. She tossed a set of keys onto the counter.

"Lot two, in back. Slot 125. You gonna be long?"

"As long as it takes."

"Yeah, right. I take my lunch break at eleven-thirty. If

274

I'm not here, hit the page button there on the wall, and someone will come out to help. Have fun."

With that, she sat back down at the small desk and resumed reading about this year's 50 "most beautiful people." Lynch chuckled at the vanity involved in making such a list. If they wanted the truly beautiful people of the country, they'd have to look a lot further than Hollywood and professional sports to find people who made significant, real life differences in other lives.

Although the Chief had made it clear he wanted Lynch to check the car personally, he wasn't sure why he needed to do so. The crime techs had been thorough. He couldn't think of any place in the car that he could inspect that they hadn't already checked. Lynch was prepared to check the next couple of hours off to being thorough and to following a command.

It took Lynch about ten minutes to find the car, and it was squeezed into the slot so tightly he would have trouble getting into it, much less do a thorough inspection. Another fifteen minutes was required to get someone to move it into a work bay where he had the lighting and equipment to do a complete once over. Why they hadn't already moved it to a bay, when the clerk knew he was coming to inspect it, was a mystery to Lynch. But then, he realized this was his third call for the car and the previous two times he'd been a "no-show." This was his own fault.

He started at the trunk, pulling the lining to check the hollow spaces behind the wheel wells and then looked under and around the spare tire. He pulled the hubcaps thinking she could have taped the camera's memory card inside one of them. Although he doubted she would risk damaging her camera by hiding it anywhere in the engine compartment, he still looked.

Forty-five minutes later, he moved to the passenger compartment. He pulled the back seats, checked for any loose molding that might suggest a hiding place within a door or the car's frame. Naturally, the usual places like the glove compartment and various storage sites within the console were empty. He saw no evidence of the roof header being pulled loose at any point, so he proceeded to do that. Again, nothing.

He looked under the dash and at first glance saw nothing. He was about to pull the cover off the ventilation intake and in-cabin air filter when he saw the very end of a small loop of nylon cord. Reaching up into the recesses of the dash, he found a hollow space for mounting the pre-amp of a high-end stereo system. Filling the space was her digital camera. As he eased the camera free, something else dropped to the car floor, a small digital voice recorder.

He smiled and pumped his fist in the air once. This guy's arrest was as good as his.

With both items in plastic bags, Lynch felt ebullient. He was a major step forward to solving this case, taking down the "LA Rapist," and exploring a new life that included Amy. He left the impound lot after completing several forms in triplicate and drove toward the county computer forensics lab. Mike Jurgesmeyer was waiting to help him retrieve and analyze the images and recording. He resisted the urge to view the images on the camera's view screen and to listen to whatever digital notes the recorder held. He could not risk losing any data. A short while later, the two men sat in a small exam room where the two items sat on the bench in front of them.

Lynch lifted a small case onto a cleared spot on the counter and produced fingerprint dust and tape. "I need to dust each of these before we get started. I suspect we'll only find one set of prints, but you never know."

He felt assured that Elsa Dunleavy had placed the camera in that safe spot. Had it been taken by their unsub, the camera would have met the same fate as her cell phone and PDA, minus its memory card, which would have ended up who-knows-where. Fingerprinting the camera was mostly a formality. He suspected they would find but one set of prints.

He dusted and examined each item and lifted several prints that appeared closely identical on first look. He then removed the memory card from the camera and dusted it. One more usable print was found and retrieved.

"Okay, that's done."

Jurgesmeyer picked up the memory card and tried to insert it into a card reader on an adjacent computer.

"Shoot, be right back. I need to get a six-in-one reader that fits this card."

Lynch sat silently for Jurgesmeyer to return. He suspected, hoped, and prayed the camera would confirm that the motor coach discovered by the patrolman, the coach they'd missed detaining by just hours, was the same vehicle where Elsa Dunleavy met their infamous assailant. He could hope for little more than that, although the grand prize he really wanted would be a photo of the man himself. The voice recorder was another story. It was an unanticipated find, and his curiosity about what it held for them was boundless.

Lynch mulled over the fact that the two devices had been hidden within the car. Surely, that signified that Elsa Dunleavy had been suspicious about the meeting. Why else hide the camera and recorder? If she were afraid of theft, she could have secured them more easily in the trunk or glove compartment. And if she had been suspicious, how had she fallen prey to the man? If the medical examiner was correct, and the asphyxia was the result of a total nitrogen environment, how had he delivered it? And, as the examiner had questioned, how would you get an uncooperative victim to breathe pure nitrogen for the several minutes needed to starve the brain? Without drugs? Lynch was no closer in answering those questions now than he was when the M.E. posed them.

His cell phone interrupted his ruminations. A quick glance at the Caller ID revealed Janick as the caller.

"Hi, Bob. What's up?"

"Cully, you anywhere close enough to the office to come in to talk? I got some new information on the Payne case I need you to think about."

Lynch was a little surprised that Janick was actually

asking him to think over some information for him. There had to be something more.

"It'll take probably two hours before I could get there, but—"

"You or that girlfriend of yours know this Doctor David Koettering guy?"

I knew there was more to this, thought Lynch. "Can't speak for Amy, but all I know about the guy is that he's the neurosurgeon who leads the team caring for the victims of this serial attacker."

"Well, I learned some things. Payne's staff finally pulled together a list of past cases from county court records. Seems our Doctor Koettering arrived in town about two years ago, then joined the medical center staff about six months ago. Shortly after he arrived here, he was involved in a malpractice case brought on by none other than Edward Payne. Payne won the case about a month before his death."

Lynch wondered where this was leading.

"Okay, but neurosurgery's a high-risk specialty. Those guys get sued right and left."

"Yeah, yeah. I know. But I thought it too much a coincidence that this guy arrives right before this 'LA Rapist' character starts his gig and then ends up being the guy studying and caring for these women. You know I never believe in coincidence."

Every once in a while Lynch would agree with Janick, and this was one of those unusual occasions.

"Did some digging on this guy. Born some place called Falmouth on Cape Cod to a pretty well-to-do

Boston family. Upper echelons, if you catch my drift. Trained at all the best schools. Couple of siblings, but of interest is a twin brother, Matthew, who apparently died in a boating accident off Martha's Vineyard at age 22. Body never recovered. Both boys smart as whips and known for some minor delinquencies growing up. Parents got 'em off all charges. Hell raisers in college, but David seemed to settle down in medical school after his brother's death. Actually became somewhat withdrawn and moody at that point. Social life took a nosedive. That's what I want you, the wonder boy, to ponder. Does this fit your profile?"

Lynch ignored the slur. Janick had called him worse over their years of working together.

"Okay. I'll pass it on to 'wonder boy' to ponder. Anything else?"

"As a matter of fact, yeah. We've learned that one of Koettering's co-workers, their psycho something or other, Daniel Diehl, a PhD type, also has an interesting tie to these cases. Seems he was dating Patricia Shriver 'til he learned she liked it both ways. They had a major blow-up a week or two before her death, in front of several witnesses."

Thirty-one

❦✦✦❧

David sat behind the desk in his office at the medical center, his elbows on the desk as he leaned forward and rubbed his temples with his fingertips. The headaches were becoming more frequent and less responsive to non-steroidal anti-inflammatory medications. Yet, he couldn't risk anything stronger. He'd known too many surgeons, good physicians, who had destroyed their careers with the misuse of narcotic painkillers. It was just stress. He was convinced of that, and Dan had seemed to agree. Yet, the headaches over the past few days seemed to trigger the smell of blood when there was no blood around him. The coppery odor permeated his clothes, his car, and his home whenever his headache persisted longer than an hour or two. It was a haunting, sickening stench unlike what he was accustomed to in surgery.

Something else had happened that concerned him. He'd had another apparent time lapse. During college, he started suffering from fugue states, but they had eased during medical school. Hours would disappear that he could not remember. It had happened again last night. As best he could recall, it had been almost a decade since his last episode. But last night something had happened, and he had lost at least five hours, awakening at home unexpectedly, in bed, still clothed.

As he reached into his top drawer for another eight hundred milligrams of ibuprofen, there was a knock on his door. He laid the medication bottle back into the drawer and slowly closed it.

"Come on in!"

Dan opened the door and walked over to the chair nearest David's desk. Dan craned his neck a bit, moving his head back and forth, looking him over closely.

"Another headache?"

David nodded.

"When are you going to see someone about them?"

David shrugged. "Don't know. So, what's up?"

"Umm. Heard about your meetings with Royce and Cassidy. I thought Cassidy was on the Human Use Committee that reviewed our protocols. If they approved the protocol, what gives now?"

David gave his neuropsychologist a detailed rundown on his meeting with the head of the hyperbaric facility and their reasons for refusing a patient on high dose barbiturates.

"That doesn't make sense. I know of places that will do it. They may not like the extra precautions they have to take, but they're willing to do it."

David wasn't about to get into it with his own team member.

"Unfortunately, we're not at those places. I d/c'd her pentobarb and reordered the HBO."

"I know. I saw that." Dan shuffled in his seat and looked out the window briefly before returning his gaze to David. "Actually, I'm not here to talk about Esther Jacobs. I, uh . . . I've gotten an offer for a position closer to home, where I can be a little more available to help my sister care for my parents. It's not quite what I have here, but that's only one factor in my decision. I'll be leaving as soon as I finish the current phase of my project and . . ."

David held up his hand to stop Dan.

"Dan, you don't need to explain. I hate to see you go, but I fully understand and have been expecting it. Any idea how long?"

"Only a week, maybe two."

David nodded. "So, you're heading where? Somewhere around Rochester, right?"

"That's right. My folks live just outside of the city."

Upon returning home from the grocery, Amy placed the wine, cheese, and other perishables in the refrigerator and went to the storage room off the garage to find her picnic basket. She and Lynch would fly to the Bircher's farm on Stockton Lake and enjoy a romantic picnic. She retrieved a small cooler, returned to the kitchen before going to the hall linen closet for something to cover the picnic table.

While there, she made a brief detour into her bedroom to check her answering machine. The digital counter blinked six. She sat down on the edge of the bed and pushed "play." The first two were hang-ups. The third was an automated telemarketer that droned on and on until her time limit disconnected the line. There were two more hang-ups and finally a real person, Macy.

"Girl, did you turn off your cell? I've been trying to get hold of you all afternoon. When'd you get so popular? All kinds of folks are nosin' around here asking about the nurse from the helicopter. Thought I better warn you about them. We've gotten busy, but I get off at seven, and I'm heading straight home, so give me a call after seven-thirty. Bye."

Amy glanced at her watch. It was nearing five-thirty. She would have time to pack the picnic basket, fix a meal, and watch the six o'clock news.

After setting the basket, blanket, and non-perishable items onto the kitchen table, she turned her attention to dinner. She squatted before the open refrigerator and browsed through the various plastic containers of culinary odds and ends on each shelf. She removed a few containers that now held science projects and continued to rummage through the food until she found the leftover Greek food. *Just what I had in mind*, she thought.

With a plate of nuked leftovers and a glass of iced tea, she retreated to the couch in front of the television in time to see the start of the evening news. As she blessed her food, the station's female news anchor was beginning the lead story.

"We have previously reported that unconfirmed sources have linked the recent deaths of two prominent lawyers, Edward Payne and Patricia Shriver, to the long string of assaults by the "LA Rapist." In another twist in this bizarre and deadly saga, those same sources now link the recent death of a local air conditioning contractor, Art Barklage, to ..."

Amy closed her eyes and shook her head. *Lynch must be having fits*, she thought. It was the news anchor's next comment that redirected her attention to the TV.

"We have also learned that Barklage may have briefly awakened in his flight to the medical center. For that, we go to our field reporter, Dennis Kinney, in front of the Major Case Squad's operations center. What have you learned, Dennis?"

The scene switched to the reporter standing in front of a nondescript blond brick building on which the only thing you could read was "Police." The reporter simply repeated what the news anchor had stated, but added that the authorities were not commenting on the accuracy of the rumors, much less what might have been said.

"Our attempts to locate and talk to the medical crew on the MedAir helicopter have been unsuccessful so far, but we will continue to track down this story."

A burst of heartburn stopped Amy mid-bite.

Lady Law watched the evening news with renewed interest. He had long been scanning all four major local news stations for any and all information they had on his activities. Tonight he hoped they would become unwitting allies in helping him close this chapter of his life. Obviously, the word he had received earlier about Barklage surviving long enough to regain consciousness and say something to the flight crew had substance. Otherwise, it would not have endured the initial scrutiny of the news media. But then, only one station reported the story. Why only one? Were the others sitting on it awaiting verification of the facts?

He had moved into an adjacent county to a remote spot along the Big River. The landowner, a local farmer, was more than willing to accept his money in return for permission to park on his land for a week, maybe two if the "fishing" was good. In negotiating with the man, Lady Law had noted the home to be a simple one still heated by wood and with electrical requirements straight out of the nineteen-sixties. More importantly, there was no TV antennae, satellite dish, or cable access visible. It was highly likely the man had never even heard of the "LA Rapist."

Yes, this was going to be a good place to base his activities, despite its one drawback. It was far enough from the city and from even the most basic conveniences for that matter, that he required a car for every errand. Yet, he realized that, too, was to his advantage. The less he moved his motor coach right now, the less his chance of being noticed. He was concerned the patrolman who had stopped for two visits recalled enough of a description of his coach that it would stand out for even the dumbest of cops. A worse possibility occurred to him, that the officer had had the presence of mind to do more than write down a description of his wheeled home. He switched from the newscast to his recording of the officer's visits. Fifteen minutes later, he was satisfied from his surveillance footage that the officer had taken no photos and that the patrol car was not equipped with a video camcorder.

There remained one more job for the evening. Gathering a collection of electronic devices—small

river's edge. But he found he had no interest in exploring right then. The sudden location change somehow disturbed him, and he wasn't sure why. He found a large boulder a short leap away from the shore and jumped on top, sitting down Indian-style with his legs crossed. His mind wondered whether an Indian in the past had sat upon that very rock just to stare at the water and to think under the light of a full moon, as he was doing. The light breeze stirred the water and kept the insects from biting, but the swooping flight of a bat startled Markie and interrupted his thoughts.

He missed his sister and wondered why they never went to visit her anymore. Maybe it was because she did nothing but lay there, in that place called a nursing home, but that Matthew called a disgraceful vegetable garden. Markie continued to have nightmares of their father becoming a deadly beast and beating his sister. And beating and beating her. And then their mother making her the way she was now. He would awaken from those dreams, and most of the time Matthew was there to take control, to fight the demon in the dream. And then there was David, who had sworn to help people like his sister.

Thirty-two

❦❧

Thirty-six hours later, Macy's parting words echoed through Amy's mind. Lynch was late again, but he hadn't bothered to call until he was fifteen minutes past due in picking her up. The thought of one, maybe two, barrel rolls to teach him a lesson in timeliness crossed her mind. But, she had promised, and retribution was not the best way to win his commitment. To save time, she had agreed to drive to the airport and meet him there. She would have been surprised to see him there ahead of her, but that didn't happen. She had already stashed the picnic basket, some extra sodas, and the cooler and was completing her pre-flight checklist when he pulled into the airfield's parking lot, honked, and waved at her. He may have been late, but at least she had been busy and not kept waiting.

As he neared the plane, she walked around to the right side to meet him. He put his arms around her and gave her a lingering kiss that surprised her initially, but she gave in to her own desire quickly enough and didn't pull back.

"Ummm, now *that* makes me fly," he said as he eased back.

She smiled and returned the kiss with a quick peck on his lips. She broke free of his grip and put her arm through his to walk back to the plane.

"Pre-flight's done. We're ready for take-off. Are you up for this?"

"No acrobatics, right?"

After a brief but obvious hesitation, she nodded.

"Then up, up, and away we go. I do have a minor request, though."

She furrowed her eyebrows and questioned him with a look.

"I know you hate mixing business with pleasure . . ." He watched her closely for any sign of dissatisfaction. ". . . but while we're flying, can we keep a lookout for this?"

He handed her a full-color printout of a classy, dark metallic purple motor coach with abstract graphics along the back third of its body.

"We're pretty sure it belongs to our serial killer. We missed him by a few hours two days ago, but we came up with some photos."

"If you missed him, how—"

He smiled. "Courtesy of Elsa Dunleavy."

He was right; she didn't like mixing business with pleasure, but the fact that the woman the killer used to mock Lady Justice had somehow provided them with photos got her curious. The look on her face must have given her away.

"Yeah, Elsa Dunleavy. First major stroke of good luck we've had in this case. We found her digital camera and a voice recorder hidden up behind the dash of her car."

He proceeded to tell her how the digital voice recorder had a message on it outlining Patricia Shriver's suspicions that Lady Law on the legal forum was not who she alleged to be and that she believed Shriver's murder was somehow related to her bisexual, but mainly lesbian,

293

lifestyle.

"Unfortunately, neither one of them ever suspected Lady Law as being the 'LA Rapist' and killer. She had enough suspicions about Lady Law to snap a few digital photos of the motor home, leave a message, and hide both devices, but not enough to avoid the meeting altogether. Too bad."

"How did you miss him?"

Lynch told her the story of the police officer's discovery and how he'd found the camera later.

"But now we have a photo, and we've distributed it to all of the police agencies within a four county area. We're thinking about running it in the newspaper as well."

"Speaking of the news . . ." Amy responded. "I understand the news media is looking for me to make a statement about Art Barklage. Lynch, I-I don't think I want a bunch of reporters camped on my front lawn. Are you sure it's best to still keep this secret?"

Lynch grabbed her hand to reassure her.

"Sweetheart, I saw that news report, too. And I've talked with Chief Dandridge. We're going to announce what you told us. We think this photo is going to help us finally snare this guy, and Barklage's confession won't make much difference now. In fact, I think the Chief's going to hold a press conference late this afternoon, in time for the evening news."

Amy felt a weight fall from her shoulders and turned to hug Lynch.

"Hey, do you think I'd make a good teacher?"

His question hit Amy out of the blue. She gave him a quizzical look.

"Um, just thinking. Maybe teaching and consulting could give me a more manageable lifestyle."

Her eyes widened. Had he made THE decision?

"It's something I'm going to look into after this case is over. What do you think?"

"I . . . I . . ." She smiled and held on tighter. Her lips moved toward his, but she stopped short of kissing him. *Control yourself. He hasn't committed to anything.*

"Umm, we don't have to go flying if you want to do something else." He grinned.

She knew what he was implying and for a moment, wondered if she should forget the ultimatum she had given him just a few nights earlier. Yet, she strengthened her resolve to make good that challenge. She did not want lust and its casual intimacy to cloud his judgment and sway his decision, as hard as it would be to eliminate that factor from the process.

"Nope. Let's fly. We have a big ol' bus to find and a case to solve."

She grabbed his hand and pulled him to the right side door. Before opening it, she said, "My dad knew we were going up together today, so he prepared a present for you." She flung open the door. There, over the rip in the seat's upholstery, was a secure handhold fashioned to match the interior of the plane. "Your own personal sissy bar." She poked him in the ribs. "See, I told you he liked you."

Thirty-three

❧ ✦ ✦ ☙

Lady Law watched three different news programs that evening, and each delivered more bad news. The late afternoon police press conference had been the top story for the late night news.

". . . Yes, in answer to your question, Mr. Barklage was resuscitated successfully, but briefly, in the helicopter, and he did implicate himself in the death of Edward Payne. In our interviews with his family, we learned that they were aware of an unusual cash payment he had received, but they believed the payment was a bonus for completing the law firm's air conditioning work three weeks ahead of schedule. They also thought the payment had come from a member of the law firm and were shocked to learn of their loved one's possible complicity in the lawyer's violent death."

The news reporter came on. "That was Chief Dandridge of the Major Case Squad answering questions at his earlier press conference. We have also learned from another, more distant, member of the family that Barklage had been drinking heavily after Payne's death and had traveled to Las Vegas because he feared for his life."

There was something about this reporter that upset Lady Law. Not so much by what he said, but by what he implied, an implication that he himself strongly agreed with—if Barklage had confessed his role in the murder, what else had he said? What were the police not saying?

296

Lady Law sat there mentally recreating his meetings with Barklage. He had taken care to present himself as a representative of the law firm. The extra gas tanks, labeled "helium," were for children's balloons at an upcoming company picnic. He had indeed offered the money as a "bonus" for completing certain work ahead of schedule, for hauling the tanks from the warehouse where they had been stored, for installing a small box of electronics on the heating and air conditioning unit and for a few other minor installations. The man had been a moron, blinded by the money. Lady Law could not recall one point when he had identified himself to the man by any name, but that was not an ironclad guarantee that the man hadn't learned something. He might have contacted the law firm and asked some questions. He might have learned Lady Law's identity from some other, unexpected source. He had indeed fled to Las Vegas in fear, a move Lady Law had not anticipated. Had he underestimated the man?

Now, however, it did not matter. He was dead, but he had talked.

"She did what?" Lynch squawked into his cell phone. "I'll be right there."

Lynch stomped the accelerator and hurried to Richmond Heights and the Major Case Squad's operations center. Flannigan's comments from a few days earlier had just proven prophetic, and Lynch could see the Chief in livid living color. The Reilly woman's protection was paramount, and his bosses would hang Lynch out to dry if anything happened to her on his watch. In the last two weeks, he had learned some things about her brother and now found it difficult to believe he was cooperating. But he was.

If only he and Amy had spotted that motor coach the day before, they would have this guy in custody and no one else's life would be in jeopardy. The flight had been great, and the color of the changing trees throughout the foothills and around Stockton Lake was spectacular from the air. Her surprise picnic was the playful highlight of the day, and when she succeeded in pushing him into the lake, he resisted the urge to retaliate in kind, and Amy had rewarded him many times over for not dunking her. He had remembered just in time how much she hated cold water. He would have gladly remained wet all day to have their relationship back to where it had been when he so stupidly chickened out. And by the end of the day, he came to realize that he could, and would, put her first. As soon as this life-consuming case was over, there would be some changes in his life, and, hopefully, hers.

But the case wasn't over, and now the Reilly siblings were about to jeopardize their lives.

Lynch ran into the Ops Center and found Flannigan waiting for him by the Chief's office. Flannigan nodded his head toward the office doorway.

"He wants an update, so I thought I could fill you both in and save some time."

Lynch took a deep breath, nodded, and led the way to their waiting boss. He started to knock on the door, but the Chief's secretary waved them to go on in. They were expected. Still, he knocked twice to alert the Chief of their presence and opened the door. The Chief was in his shirtsleeves, rolled to the elbow, no tie, and watching absentmindedly out the window. Lynch could not recall ever seeing the man in anything but full uniform at work. Dandridge turned slowly to greet the two detectives and waved them into nearby chairs. His face seemed to sag from fatigue.

"Chief?" Lynch asked. He wanted to ask if the man was okay, but hesitated.

"Flannigan, give us an update. What's happened to the Reilly woman?"

Flannigan shifted in his seat and began to remove his ever-present notebook from a back pants pocket, but stopped and sat upright. Lynch recognized Flannigan's reliance on his notebook as a habit, but the man rarely needed it for recalling recent details.

"Uh, sir, nothing's happened to her yet. We still have her under surveillance, and we have someone monitoring her computer now. What's happened is that our contact on that Internet legal forum, the one used by Lady Law, called to inform us that Ms. Reilly used the forum to contact Lady Law last night and that she got a reply. They couldn't provide us with any text, so I tried to contact Ms. Reilly. I got her brother, and he informed us that they didn't want to wait around anymore for us to find this guy. They had devised their own plan and put it into action last night. In a nutshell, she told Lady Law that she now knew who he was, without revealing what she knows, which is nothing."

Lynch sighed. That act was paramount to casting a nose-hooked minnow right in front of a hungry fish. "Did he say what they planned next? After this guy takes the bait. Do they really know who or what they're up against?"

Flannigan shrugged, as Lynch realized none of them really knew who or what they were up against. Their prey seemed always a step ahead and able to become the hunter at will. More importantly, though, was that this guy would see right through her. If she knew who he was, why hadn't the police already picked him up?

"He's not going to take that bait. Did she tell him she was going to the police? He'll know that she hasn't already done so." Lynch paused for a moment. "Was she stupid enough to try to blackmail him? That would really be the dumbest of all dumb moves. Only in the movies does that ruse work."

The Chief said nothing at first and then asked, "So, how do we protect them?"

Flannigan looked at Lynch for the answer.

"We keep her under surveillance as we planned. But we also have to face the fact that they've taken a step of their own choosing, and if they decide to duck out from under our protection, we might not be able to save them. They'd be on their own."

The Chief nodded. "Lynch, go talk with them. Let them know what they might be facing and that we can't look after them if they stray from our safety net. Make it clear they'd be on their own and we can't, and won't, be

responsible for their well-being. Not after what she did."
He pointed to the door with his head. "Flannigan, stay
here. I have other things to talk with you about."

"Yes, sir." Flannigan looked at Lynch with eyebrows
raised and rolled his eyes.

Lynch left the office and flipped open his cell phone
on the way to his car. He keyed in Meghan Reilly's new
office phone number.

"Strasser and Beam," the receptionist answered.

"Meghan Reilly, please."

"I'm sorry, sir, she left the office early today and isn't
expected back until next Monday. Would you like her
voice mail?"

Lady Law smiled as he sat in his car a short distance
from the Richmond Heights Police Station. He recognized
Lynch Cully from the newspaper photos he had found
online. Now, he just had to be careful to remain
inconspicuous. One false step could be disastrous. He
watched as the detective left the building and walked to
his car.

So predictable, he thought. *And this guy's supposed to
be their wonder boy?*

When Lynch opened his cell phone, Lady Law picked
up a small electronic device and pushed a button on the
front face of the box. Static and a collection of voices
faded in and out until the scanner found the clear signal
he sought. The man was dialing the number at Meghan
Reilly's new job. He listened to the brief conversation

between the detective and a receptionist, made a mental note of the numbers on the digital readout, and placed the scanner back on the passenger's seat. The detective had just saved him an afternoon's work by using his cell phone so readily. Now he had the unique frequency of Lynch Cully's phone and could monitor his conversations at will, or even make calls on that frequency.

David felt better than he had in days, and there was a noticeable swagger in his step as he walked toward the Emergency Department. Outside the Radiology Department, he ran into Dan Diehl.

"Hey, you're looking remarkably chipper. Finally take my advice?" Dan asked.

"I did. Saw the head of Neurology about the recurring headaches and was gently reminded of the differences between the medical and surgical causes of headaches."

David realized that pride had kept him from seeing another physician. After all, he was a neurosurgeon; he should know all about headaches, he told himself.

"I was a little embarrassed to discover how much the medical side has changed since my training. All kinds of progress over the last five years. Do you know what it appears to have been?"

Dan shrugged his shoulders.

"A simple series of questions about diet opened the door to relief. It seems my diet soda habit and aspartame by the liter was my main tormentor. I eliminated the artificial sweeteners, and my headaches have gradually gone away."

Dan gave him a thumb up. "Anything new on the floor?"

"Haven't made rounds yet, so I don't know. I'm going by the E.D. first and then upstairs."

"Okay. See you there."

David's trip to the E.D. was not official but social. He found himself enamored with Amy Gibbs from the day he first saw her, the day she had delivered the Whiteside girl to his care. He thought her the most beautiful woman he'd ever seen, with eyes a man could fall into. And her personality, from what little exposure he'd had to her, seemed to complement his more taciturn disposition. His inquiry into her likes, dislikes, and availability had not provided him the answer he hoped for, but he had never been one to be cowed by a little bad news. Rejection, while unpleasant, was not a reason to admit defeat, but an obstacle to overcome. So, if she rejected his first invitation, well, in time there would be another one to follow. As a realist, he also knew when to stop. But to stop, he first had to start. He had enlisted the aid of a "spy" in the E.D. to alert him to her arrival there, and she had called only moments earlier with just such news.

As he walked into the E.D., he saw his accomplice sitting at the Nurses Station. When she spotted him, she looked about the department and then pointed toward the paramedic's workroom where David had first "met" Amy. He picked up a chart from a nearby desk and pretended to review it. Then he took it with him to the room where Amy was completing her paperwork. She was sitting, facing away from the door, and writing on the transfer form. He knocked on the doorframe.

"Hi, been flying lately?"

She turned and looked up. He was disappointed to note a slight annoyance at the interruption on her face.

"Oh, Doctor Koettering. Hi. As a matter of fact, yes. Flew over to Stockton Lake yesterday."

"Bet that was beautiful. That's one of the advantages of a smaller plane like your Skyhawk. You can fly low enough to enjoy the scenery."

She smiled. She had said she loved flying, and he knew he had picked the right topic to break the ice.

"True, but there's also something to soaring above the clouds."

"Maybe. But that's more like comparing a full-sized van to a sports car. Flying above the clouds is great for getting from one place to another. Flying above the treetops is like taking the curves of a country road in the fall, with the top down."

She edged forward on her chair, and her whole face brightened at his comment. She looked radiant.

"Yeah, I guess so. I like that analogy, and I have to admit I've always wanted to try flying something larger than my Cessna."

It was his turn to smile. He couldn't have asked for a better segue.

"Well, what about tomorrow afternoon? I have the afternoon off. I could get my family's King Air or even the Lear down here by noon. We could fly to Chicago, have dinner at this great Greek place I know in Arlington Heights, and be back before midnight. I know the pilot would be more than willing to let you sit second seat."

At first, her eyes widened, but when her shoulders sagged and she sank back into her seat, he knew what was coming.

"Um, look Doctor—"

"It's David, remember? The Labor Day picnic?"

"Sure, but we're in the hospital, Doctor. I really appreciate the offer and I'd love to take the controls on either of those two planes, but I'm committed for tomorrow."

"I see. Well, maybe someday next week?"

"I think you should know I'm seeing someone pretty seriously and . . ."

He nodded, trying to be as agreeable as possible and not wanting to burn any bridges before he crossed them. And there *would* be new bridges to cross. He was confident of that.

"I get it. Sounds too much like a date."

She nodded. He laughed.

"Rats! I didn't know I was that transparent. I have to work on some better pick-up lines. I'll make a mental note of that one—'come fly with me' didn't work." He mimed writing the words in a small notebook. "Tell you what. I'd still like to let you try your hand at one or both of those aircraft. You just decide what would satisfy you as *not* qualifying as a date, and I'll see if it can be arranged. Okay?"

She tilted her head and gazed at him quizzically for a

moment before nodding.

"Okay. Um, I need to finish my report and get moving. I'm sure my crew's waiting on me by now."

"Sure. Keep me posted."

David ducked out of the room and walked toward a nurse who was rummaging through the papers on the desk where he'd pulled out the chart.

"Here, looking for this?"

He handed her the chart. She looked at it quickly, frowned, and nodded. He chuckled, knowing she was most likely wondering what a neurosurgeon was doing with the chart of a woman with crampy, vaginal bleeding, but who cared?

Amy watched David Koettering, the neurosurgeon on a fast track to being department chair, as he left the E.D. What a difference between him and Lynch! He was so much more poised and conversant. He didn't bat an eye when she turned him down flat, but turned it right around into a second invitation, on her terms. Lynch had gotten sullen when she turned down his first invitation to dinner. And Lynch's come on was really lame, reflective of his street-wise attitude. Of course, whom did she know who could come anywhere close to a pick-up line like, "Hey, want to fly my Lear jet?" *Dear God, what a temptation,* she thought and instantly recalled that somewhere in the Bible it said God was not a tempter of man, but always provided a way out of any temptation.

Was Lynch her way out? It seemed so. They'd had a wonderful time at the lake, and he talked enthusiastically about teaching criminology and starting a consulting group. Would he actually carry through with the ideas he talked about? The hope he dangled in front of her almost swept her away, but she had learned one thing by his leaving. There were other fish in the pond. *She* wasn't going to be the party responsible for jeopardizing their renewed relationship, but if Lynch blew his last chance, at the least she might get to fly a Lear.

Thirty-four

Amy had spent the better part of her shift in the air. She now recognized the toll this serial assault case was taking on Lynch, and knew that the sooner the case closed, the sooner she'd have her "new" Lynch. At her suggestion, Lynch had circulated the photo of the motor coach to all the regional helicopter and paramedic crews in the hope that one of the teams might discover it.

Her thoughts were on Lynch when she first pulled up to the only four-way stop on her way home. She crossed that intersection coming and going to work each day and could count on one hand the number of times she had encountered another car there. She began moving through the crossroads when an inner sense told her to stop. She gazed to the right and saw a metallic silver sports car bearing down on the intersection at high speed, with no appearance of slowing down.

Her heart began to race and her breathing competed to match the pace. She quickly placed her car in reverse and scooted back, out of the path of the oncoming car. Only then did she take a deep breath and force a sense of calm on her tachycardic pulse.

She couldn't believe it when the car actually came to a full stop at the sign, flipped on its signal to turn right, and then waited to let her continue. She couldn't see the driver, as tinted windows and the angle of light aided his or her invisibility. She marveled at the customized Porsche as she passed by. It was unique and unlike any

911 she'd previously seen. The car pulled in behind her and followed her for the next five or six miles, riding closely on Amy's tail. She sped up, and it sped up. She slowed, and it slowed. Following the next stoplight, the pace continued for roughly a mile, until suddenly the Porsche pulled out and passed her as if she were still at the red light. As it passed, she noticed the unusual paint job along the back fenders and trunk area, and her mouth went dry. The car had a spider web pattern similar to that of the hidden motor coach.

Amy reached for her bag and fumbled to get her cell phone. By the time she got hold of it, the car was long gone, and she realized she had neglected to check the license. She wouldn't be able to tell him the state or the number of the tag. She couldn't see it on the road ahead, and as she passed each business and side road, she glanced from side to side to try to discover where it had headed, but could not find it. She closed her phone, but laid it on her lap for ready retrieval. As her nerves calmed, she told herself she was overreacting. The car's paint job couldn't be the only one of its kind. She was simply too preoccupied with the wanted motor coach. They couldn't possibly be related.

She stopped at her local Shop'n Save to fill her weekly list of groceries and household items and continued home. After pulling into the drive, she first unloaded her flight gear and bag, followed by her groceries. But as she came out of the house for her last trip, she stopped abruptly. Directly across the street was the Porsche 911, and as her heart rose to her throat, it peeled out and disappeared down the street.

"Whoa, slow down, Amy. Take it bit by bit and tell me again what happened," Lynch requested as he attempted to get her to calm down over the phone. In her current state of anxiety, she was less likely to remember details. Yet, time would also erode those details, so he needed her to cool off and let the facts come to her mind, without trying to force the memories.

The secretary at the Major Case Squad had forwarded Amy's call to Lynch, who sat at his regular desk in the Ladue detectives' bureau shuffling through and trying to reduce the mountain of paperwork accumulating there. He also awaited Janick, who had new information on the Payne case. All Lynch knew was that they had not been able to tie Barklage in any way to Ahmed bin Abdul Aziz bin Saleh al-Harasis, and with Barklage's admitted involvement, the case against al-Harasis had taken on water and floundered. Crime lab results were due soon, and Lynch suspected Janick wanted to pass on some of that data.

"Amy, look, you're jumping all over the place. We need to try to take it in order. Where are you?"

"At home. L-like I said, I was coming home from work."

This time, however, those results would take a back seat to Amy. She was upset, and it appeared she had a right to be. Lynch could also hear a mix of eagerness and anxiety in her voice, as if the final clue to a hidden treasure was within her grasp, but she was unsure of her ability to make the trek to find it.

From what she had told him, even in its erratic narrative, he became concerned. A sports car with the same custom paint job as the motor home could be a coincidence, for someone who believed in coincidences. Lynch wasn't one of those people. Neither was Amy. If the killer had learned that she was the flight nurse attending Barklage when he confessed, he might now know where she lived. Lynch didn't want to extrapolate that thought. He listened to her, taking notes intermittently.

He appreciated her help, but he most assuredly did not want her in harm's way. Especially not now. He would need to add protective custody teams to watch over her and her paramedic. He believed he could convince the Chief of that need, and the Chief, in turn, would convince the respective local police departments to do so. The hard part would be convincing Amy.

Amy hung up the phone. "Relax," she muttered. She sat in her recliner, legs folded beneath her, as she looked at the dead phone in her hand. *How does he expect me to relax?* She took a deep breath. Then another. How could she relax when they had another piece to the puzzle, another vehicle that might lead them to the killer? And that was what she chose to focus upon—that she had a new lead for Lynch and the Major Case Squad. Because she refused to acknowledge the thoughts she had struggled with when she first called Lynch—the killer now knew where she lived.

Amy stood up and walked to her computer desk, where she turned on her system. Her DSL line instantly linked her to the Internet, and she navigated to the page she used for flight weather information. It promised to be a gorgeous day for flying, and that's just what she was going to do. As soon as Lynch left, she would head to the plane and start flying a grid pattern, looking for that accursed motor home where she and Lynch left off. *Find that Fleetwood. That's the key to your safety*, her mind kept telling her.

That settled, she turned off the computer and walked to the front room. She hesitated to look out the front window, keeping the curtains drawn. Yet, holding her breathing, she peeked through a small opening between the two curtains. She released a lungful of air when she saw that no one was there. She turned back into the room and paced. *C'mon Lynch, get your butt over here.*

Lynch hustled to leave the office. He threw one pile of papers in the trash and handed another to the secretary. He had succeeded in cutting his 'In' pile in half. He grabbed his cell phone and unplugged the charging cord, but it refused to turn on. *Not now*, he thought. *Battery's shot.* Now was not the time to be caught without cell phone backup.

He disconnected the battery pack from the body of

the phone and walked into the secretary's area.

"Hey, Sue! Do we have a replacement battery for this Motorola phone?"

She took the old battery from him and jotted the number down. "Back in a minute." She left to search through their secure supply cabinet, and Lynch returned to his desk to finish gathering up his things. She found him there.

"Sorry. No spares. I'll order you a new one today. In the meantime, here's a different phone you can use. I'll let the Case Squad and dispatch folks know your temporary number."

"Thanks." He looked over the new phone. "Um, what *is* the number? So I can tell Janick or anyone else who needs it." The main "anyone else" being Amy. He did not want to lose his means of communication with her. Not under the circumstances.

Sue handed him a notepad sheet with the number already printed on it. Lynch nodded and tucked it into the inside pocket of his jacket.

One minute later, he sat cocooned inside his car and headed for Amy's house. His first course of action—call Amy.

"Hey, I'm on my way. My cell died, so here's my new temporary number." He recited it and confirmed she had it by having her repeat it back to him. "Be there in fifteen or so."

"I'm here. Nothing suspicious going on, but please hurry."

He could still sense anxiety in her voice and applied

a bit more lead to his accelerator. As he drove, he debated his various courses of action. He couldn't put out a 'BOLO' on the car based solely on her description. No actual crime had occurred, so he was limited. He held no doubt that the car had intentionally followed her home, but was it the killer? Was it even related to the case? And how common was such a paint job? At least that was a question he could get a rough "guesstimate" on.

As he neared her subdivision, he scanned adjacent streets and driveways as he passed. It was not a neighborhood accustomed to high-end sports cars, so any Porsche would likely stand out. Pick-up trucks and company vans dominated the visible collection of odd vehicles he passed as he drove.

He pulled to the curb in front of her home and hopped out of his car. By the time he stepped onto the walkway where it met the drive, the front door opened, and she stood on the stoop waiting. He scanned her from head to toe. She appeared calm. At least she didn't have her arms crossed, wasn't tapping her toes on the concrete, and wasn't crying. As he neared, she reached out for his hand, which he readily extended to her.

"Okay. I'm calm. What now?"

"What? Not even a hello, thanks for coming?" He smiled. She didn't. "All right. I have an idea. Get your car keys."

"Huh?"

"Yeah, get your keys. We're going for a drive. How far away is the intersection where you first saw the car?"

Now she crossed her arms and cocked her head to

one side, with her eyebrows slightly knitted.

"I don't have time to drive all the way out there and back. It's a good 20 minutes away."

Lynch knew better than to insist.

"Okay. Okay. Then we'll try the next best thing. It often helps to re-enact what happened. That's why I wanted to go back to the intersection where it started. But if that's out of the question, let's try it just driving through the neighborhood."

"I guess. I'll get my keys."

Amy was back with her purse and car keys in seconds. Lynch pulled the front door tight, and together they walked to her car. He got into the passenger's seat while Amy moved to the driver's side. A moment later they pulled onto the street and, at Lynch's suggestion, she slowly drove toward the nearest four-way stop.

"Now, as you come to the stop, provided there's no traffic, repeat what you did at the intersection and tell me what you did and saw."

From that point, she imitated what happened and narrated as she drove. Fortunately, there was little moving traffic to impede their progress or interrupt her story. By the time they returned to her home ten minutes later, Lynch was satisfied she had relayed as much detail as she could remember. She could always contact him with anything else she might later recall.

Sitting in her living room, Lynch broached the subject of her protection, trying not to show his worry.

"Amy, my real concern is your safety. We don't *think* this guy knows who staffed the flight when Barklage died. And we hope that the Chief's announcement about Barklage's confession has taken the focus away from you guys. And, we don't know that this car thing is even related. Could have been some guy just following a beautiful girl."

He smiled and took her hand. She smiled weakly in return.

"But?" she added. "There's always a but."

"Yeah. But we just don't know what this guy knows, or what he might do. And, worst case scenario, maybe that *was* him in the car."

He sensed a slight shiver in Amy and an increase in his own heart rate as he said it. It was the scenario he didn't want to think about, but knew he, they, had to face.

"I want to put you under our protection. I'm sure Chief Dandridge would authorize it under the circumstances, and—"

"No. No protection. I don't want a couple of policemen looming outside my house and following me all over."

It was the answer he expected.

"It doesn't have to be like that. I can have a female officer stay with you. You could tell people she's your cousin, or a friend from college."

Amy didn't reply right away. Lynch knew this was his best shot at getting her to accept his offer of protection.

"Lynch . . ." she started to say something and then stopped. Her shoulders became more rigid, and she held her head a bit higher. ". . . thanks, but nope. I don't need a babysitter."

He started to protest, but she put her fingers to his lips.

"Look, we may not know what this guy might do next, but we do know that if he's set on hurting someone, he probably won't hesitate to remove any and all obstacles. I don't want someone getting hurt on my account."

Lynch shook his head. "It wouldn't be 'on your account,' as you put it. It's part of their job."

"No. I think I understand this person well enough that being forewarned is being forearmed. I—"

"Do it for me," Lynch interrupted. "Give me the peace of mind in knowing you're—"

"It's not necessary!" she insisted. "I'll be fine. I'll have my pepper spray with me at all times and my cell phone."

Lynch knew she could outdistance him and most of his police buddies when it came to running. And she wasn't about to fall unsuspecting into any traps. Plus, she could hit anyone with pepper spray from ten feet. But, for him, that would not suffice.

Lynch stood up and began to pace in front of her.

"A cell phone won't do you any good if he already has you. Think about it, Amy, the cavalry would be 30 minutes too late, even if you managed a call."

She furrowed her eyebrows and frowned at him, shaking her head. Lynch stopped pacing and stood directly in front of her, hands on his hips.

"Why must you be so bullheaded about this? I'm just—"

317

She burst up from the couch, her face livid as she faced him down. "Bullheaded? Me? Look who's talking, Sergeant Cully. What part of 'no' don't you understand?"

He fought to control his own anger, but lost.

"Yes, bullheaded. Defined as stubborn and uncooperative. Amy, you need protection. Don't think you're better than this guy. Elsa Dunleavy felt she was prepared, even had her camera with her, and look what hap—"

"Get out!" She pointed to the door. "Now!"

Amy fumed as she watched Lynch drive away. She didn't know whether to throw things, hit the wall, or cry. She was right. She *was* emotionally and physically prepared. She didn't need his offer of a babysitter. And now, she questioned why in the world she had ever given him a second chance. But then she wondered why she had let her emotions get the better of her. She didn't want to be the one to spoil the rebirth of their relationship, and yet it had just happened. As she cooled off, she realized the depth of his concern. And that he was correct about the cell phone. It could very well be too little too late if something happened. Her mind was in a maelstrom of conflicting emotion, and pacing the living room did nothing to alleviate her mood.

She walked to her small home office and dialed her father. There was no answer, but she left a message asking him to call her ASAP. She needed his counsel.

As she hung up the phone, she noticed her hands

presented an interesting test. Did she initiate this move, or did the police? Each possibility posed its own set of rules and dangers, and his challenge was to find a countermove that accounted for both.

His chess opponent made his first foolish move, and he took the young man's bishop. If the return move came as expected, the game would be his in four moves.

Not so with the police, or Meghan Reilly. His motivation now was two-fold. She had been on his list of initiates for several weeks, but he had avoided her because of her ties to Edward Payne. Unlike Elsa Dunleavy who had indicated early on that she knew more than he was willing to risk her telling to authorities, Meghan Reilly had posed no such threat. Until now. Perhaps she had discovered something in whatever files she had at home. Or perhaps she had already talked with the detectives, with Lynch Cully. Maybe they approached her. He had half anticipated that move, reasoning that since he had claimed Elsa after Patricia's death, he might be tempted to do the same with Meghan after Payne's death. He had been tempted, but for reasons other than her relationship to the deceased ambulance chaser.

The other unexpected development was Detective Cully's sudden aversion to his cell phone. After going to the trouble of scanning him and finding his phone's unique signature, the man had ceased using his phone only a day later. It would be impossible to detect his phone being monitored, so why had he stopped? Had he finally become suspicious? If so, that redefined the rules of the game set by Lady Law, and those rules would require some new tweaking.

A beep from Lady Law's computer drew his attention back to the game. It was his turn, and his opponent had made the expected move. Checkmate would be his in four plays. With the game all but over, he focused again on Meghan Reilly. If she had become a pawn of the Major Case Squad, the scenario that held the greatest danger to Lady Law, using her to bait him was a move that bordered on mediocre. Check. They hadn't considered her new position, one that took her to one location almost daily where she could be removed from public view with some easy role-playing and a little luck. He smiled as he played the checkmate move.

It was fully dark now, and Amy huddled against the wall of her front room, sitting on the floor, her knees to her chest and her arms wrapped around her legs. Her home no longer seemed as much a castle as a prison with an unknown gatekeeper trapping her inside. What had she become? She'd always felt confident in her abilities. She had shown Lynch that strength just a day and a half earlier. Now she quivered in fear, huddled in a corner of a room, feeling as if she no longer knew who she was.

She looked at her watch for what seemed like the umpteenth time since calling her father. What was taking him so long? She stood and eased forward to the window where she sat on the edge of a small chest and peeked around the blinds and through the glass. She could barely see the SUV in the dim light of a distant streetlamp. It hadn't moved, and its interior light remained dark. There was enough of a shadow surrounding the vehicle that she doubted she'd be able to see anyone leave it unless the interior light announced such a departure. Yet, it required only a turn of a switch to deactivate that light when the door opened. She strained to watch the vehicle and the space between it and her home.

She blinked suddenly as the glare of headlights coming around the corner disrupted her night vision. She backed away so the lights wouldn't reveal her in the window. The lights moved slowly toward her house. *I hope it's you, Dad,* she thought, but it crawled past her driveway, and her front porch light exposed it as a local police cruiser. She wanted to run out of the house, flag it down, and ask them to check out the suspicious SUV, but she realized she was too late for that. She watched and prayed they would see the vehicle and check it out on their own, but the patrol car drove right past it as if it were invisible. She debated calling the police to report the suspicious car, but that's when another thought struck her. They drove by as if they expected it to be there. Lynch had set up a protective watch despite her protests.

A moment later, another car rounded the corner, ignored the stop sign, and rolled directly to and into her driveway. Her father had arrived.

Amy jumped up from her perch in the spare bedroom and ran to the front door. She opened it to find her dad standing there, preparing to ring the bell.

"Dad, quick. See that SUV over there?" She pointed to

the vehicle less than a block away. "I think—"

As her father turned to follow her point, the car's lights flashed on, and it eased away from the curb, turning down Amy's street in the direction away from her home.

"Shoot" she muttered. "I wanted you to go with me to see who was in that car. I—"

"Hold on. Just what is going on here?"

She grabbed his elbow, ushered him into the front room and closed the door. He walked directly to the couch, plopped down, and patted the spot next to him.

"Have a seat and start at the beginning," he said. The look on his face was one of concerned confusion.

Amy raised her hands to her face and rubbed her forehead with her fingers, taking a deep breath and releasing it as she lowered her hands. She took a second deep breath and then complied with her father's request and sat down next to him. She felt no urge to cry. In fact, she was so upset at the thought that Lynch had put her under protective watch against her wishes that she felt a slight heat rise to her head. She took a couple additional slow, deep breaths as she restrained her emotions and prepared to tell her story. Then, as asked, she started at the beginning describing the incident with the Porsche following her home, her fight with Lynch, the anonymous email, and ending with that night's suspicious SUV.

A brief period of silence followed her recitation.

"Why didn't you call me earlier?" he asked.

She looked at him, perplexed. "Dad, I *did* call you earlier. It took you a day and a half to return my call.

Remember?"

He looked down at the floor for a second. "Oh. I never have set the clock on that new digital recorder, so I didn't really know when you called. Sorry." He gave her a sheepish grin. "Flew to Omaha yesterday to pick up a quarter round of beef, and weather grounded us there overnight. I didn't get home 'til late this afternoon."

"What do you need a quarter of a cow for? With your cholesterol, you don't even—"

He held up his hand to stop her. "My cholesterol is back to normal, thank you. But we're getting off track. Look, if I were Lynch I'd probably do the same thing. He's got a vested interested in your safety, right?" She agreed with a lazy nod. "And it looks to me like he knows you pretty well. Might not be nice to hear it, but bullheaded is pretty much on target." She started to protest, but he continued. "Hey, I can say it. You inherited it from me, and I sure didn't discourage it when you were growing up."

She sat back in the couch, grudgingly acknowledging that he was probably right. It had required a soaring degree of stubbornness to survive her teenage years with her brothers. That tenacity also had enabled her to succeed on the basketball courts of high school and college. And basketball had paid for her nursing education in college. So, maybe being bullheaded wasn't so bad after all, as long as she didn't have to admit it to Lynch.

Her dad slapped her knee gently. "I have an alternative suggestion, if you're agreeable with it."

"What's that?"

"I can stay here with you for a few days."

She started once again to protest, but hesitated.

"Just a couple of days. I have no desire to move in permanently. You're a good cook, but lousy housekeeper." He smiled. "And I'm not about to intrude on your social life. I can fix a few things while you're gone, but more importantly, I'll be here when you are. You know, you've got two other people with you when you're at work."

Amy sat there contemplating his offer. There were some things needing repair. She hadn't mentioned them because she didn't want to intrude on his life.

"Hey, it's me or a bunch of strangers with badges."

That swayed her decision. "Okay."

"Good. Go call Lynch and tell him what we're planning."

Amy walked to the kitchen and picked up the phone. She dialed his new cell phone number and got him on the third ring.

"Hi, it's me. Um, look. My dad's here, and he's offered to stay with me for a few days. So you can call off whoever was watching my house earlier tonight."

"What?"

"Whoever was in the SUV watching my house. I don't need your protective watchdogs with my dad here."

"Amy, we didn't assign anyone to watch your house."

Eric Royce. And now that he assumed David Koettering to be competition, too, well, she didn't think he would stoop so low as to disparage David, or Lynch, in hopes of bettering his standing.

As she checked out, she saw him from the corner of her eye. He walked right past the express lane, empty handed, and left the store. As she thought about their conversation, she also realized the Marriott was at least two miles away, with one, maybe two, grocery chain stores located closer than the one she was standing in. It was difficult enough to try to follow him visually through the dark parking lot, but then the clerk pulled her attention back to the checkout lane, giving her the total of the bill. She pulled out her credit card and quickly glanced up as a dark red, or maybe maroon, SUV passed by the windows.

Thirty-seven

Lynch thanked the sales manager at Plaza Motors, the city's leading dealer of the BMW, Infiniti, Mercedes, Porsche, and other luxury auto lines, with a handshake and an acknowledgement that he would indeed consider their dealership when he bought his next car. *As if I could afford it*, he thought. Earlier that day he had visited a body shop where he had a contact, and between that man and the folks at the dealership he had concluded that finding the mysterious Porsche that had followed Amy home was a task bloated with job security. The "unusual" spider web custom paint job was unique, but not *that* uncommon. By the time he canvassed the other Porsche dealer and the hundred-plus metro area body shops, he could end up with a list of a couple of dozen, or more. Hopefully, the combination of colors Amy noted would help narrow down the list. That would still miss cars sold by independent brokers, at auction, or by used car lots. And it wouldn't even touch cars with out-of-state licenses, which Lynch believed was the most likely prospect if the killer owned the car.

He checked his car's clock. He still had time to grab an early lunch and make it to the MCS Ops Center before the early afternoon press conference. As he pulled into the lot of a local sub shop, his phone rang. The number was not one he recognized and only a select few had his temporary number.

"Lynch Cully."

"Lynch, good morning. Your department secretary gave me this number. It's Grant Waring, at UMSL."

Lynch felt a brief flash of surprise. Dr. Waring was the head of the Criminology Department at the university. He hadn't expected a call, having only put out his subtle inquiry a few days earlier. He hoped he hadn't mentioned the reason for his call to Sue, the bureau's secretary.

"Dr. Waring, thanks for calling."

"I understand you're interested in joining the faculty, and I'm calling because it happens we have two positions opening up fairly soon. I wanted to give you a direct call, because if you're serious, I'd like to talk with you about this."

The two men had met on three previous occasions, and the professor had called Lynch once to compliment him on an article Lynch had written about new trends in computer crime for the peer-reviewed journal, *Criminology*. After a brief discussion, Lynch reassured Dr. Waring that he would be in touch with him shortly.

Back at the Ops Center, he checked in and headed straight for the Chief's office to find the door closed. He knocked. No answer. As he silently opened the door to make sure no one was there, Chief Dandridge's secretary arrived.

"He's not here, Sergeant. Called in and said he's not feeling well."

"What about the news conference?" Lynch wanted no part of the limelight and was happy to stand *behind* the Chief, as a show of support, at these conferences.

"It's all yours, big boy. He said you two had covered everything, and he has the highest confidence in you to do a good job."

Lynch thought her grin a bit too sardonic.

"Great. Just great. Did he add anything else?"

She simply shook her head and handed him a prepared statement compiled from the Chief's own notes.

"Lights, camera, action. You have fifteen minutes to get ready. Want me to do your makeup?" She laughed and turned to her desk, picked up a compact of powder, and held it up toward him. "Hmmm, probably not your best shade."

"Ha, ha. Skip the comedy clubs and keep your day job."

He walked to the office he shared with three other detectives and found Flannigan on the phone. Stepping into the man's line of sight, Lynch waved to catch his attention. Then he moved both hands up and down in front of him, with eyebrows raised, and mimed two thumbs up, followed by two thumbs down. Flannigan smiled and held his free hand out parallel to the floor, palm down, and wobbled it up and down.

Lynch rolled his eyes. "Thanks. You're a big help."

He walked to the men's room and inspected his appearance in the large wall mirror. He straightened his tie, tousled his hair a bit, and fixed the collar on his jacket. It would have to do. He'd had no advance notice. At least he had shaved recently.

Lynch sauntered to the City Council Chamber, the only room in the building big enough to host such an

holding two open bottles of beer. Lester held a .357 magnum trained on the door. Lady Law stopped at the bottom of the steps and, for added reassurance, did a slow turn to make sure Lester saw that he hid nothing behind his back. He tossed the wallet to the farmer, who picked it up with one hand and flipped it open. He glanced quickly back and forth between the wallet and Lady Law, as he scanned the driver's license in a clear plastic pocket inside. He lowered the gun and slid it behind his back.

"Okay. I'm satisfied."

"Good. Hey, no hard feelings. How about a beer?"

Lester still appeared hesitant, but finally nodded and accepted a bottle. He took a small sip, seemed satisfied that it tasted like beer should, and took a couple of gulps.

"Hmm, that's pretty good beer. Never could afford this high-brow import stuff, but I might jes have to splurge every once in a while."

"There's more where that came from, my friend. Now, about these fish . . ."

Lady Law kept up the friendly banter as he cleaned the fish and kept up the supply of beer as well. He waited until Lester's third bottle to add the diuretic. Lester was half way into the fourth bottle when Lady Law saw that familiar look on the man's face.

"Guess this expensive stuff goes through you faster, too. Man, I gotta pee."

"Bathroom's inside on the right as you head to the back."

Lester gave him a funny look.

347

"You kiddin'? Who needs a bathroom in the middle of the woods? Be right back."

Lady Law hadn't anticipated this response as Lester disappeared behind a tree to relieve himself. He quickly came up with another ploy.

"Up for some pan-fried bass? I'm ready to cook."

"Hey, that sounds great. Thanks." Lester scratched his head and smiled. "Shoot. You're an all right kinda guy. I feel a little embarrassed. I come down here thinking you're some major criminal on the lam and end up drinkin' your beer and eatin' your food. I guess I should apologize or somethin'."

"No sweat." Lady Law handed him his fifth beer. "So, you ever been in a motor home like this one?" Lady Law began to detail its features as he led the man into the vehicle. "Take a look around. All the comforts of home. Bath even has a shower in it, but I'm not hooked up to a water supply so can't use it right now."

He watched the farmer nose around a little and retrieved his remote control box when the man's back was turned to him. As the man stepped in to inspect the small bath, he pressed a button on the console and smiled.

Lady Law recognized a potential risk in killing Lester. He knew nothing of the man's habits, his friends, whether or not he had a job somewhere in addition to his farming. Someone might notice the man's absence and, that could lead to an investigation with police combing his property. And if he showed up anoxic like the others, his death could lead to a more extensive search of the area. Neither option was welcome. And with the newspaper account depicting his motor home, he couldn't risk leaving the area right away. In a few days, most people would forget what they had seen in the paper, and he'd have a better chance of escaping, if needed.

So, after three minutes, Lady Law expunged the nitrogen and left Lester in a comatose state, still breathing. Gloved and hooded to reduce the risk of leaving trace evidence on the body, Lady Law used all of his strength to pull the man from his coach. Lester, although no more than five-nine in height, was a hefty farm boy who'd softened, sagged, and stuffed his medium frame to plump ripeness with age. Lady Law left the man outside the home and trotted to the abandoned tractor, which he then drove back to his campsite. He dragged the limp body up and across the front of the tractor and then carefully collected the empty beer bottles. Those he had consumed he wiped clean, and replaced with Lester's prints. Lester's empty bottles joined the others undisturbed.

He drove his collection back down the road, carefully crossed the main road, and continued down a similar lane that followed the river for about a hundred yards. There he approached a small stone-ringed fire pit near the river's edge. He scattered the bottles in a small cluster, as if they'd been discarded once emptied. He removed the man's shoes and left them near the fire pit and bottles. The body he then pulled across his shoulders in a fireman's carry, lugged it to the water's edge, and dumped the man into the river. Unconscious, the man would soon fill his lungs with water. He might be found the next day or next week. If found quickly, the inevitable autopsy would discover water in the lungs and alcohol in the blood, and Lady Law anticipated a ruling of an alcohol-related accidental drowning. And if found later, the abandoned tractor and empty bottles would lead to the same conclusion. He would not be implicated.

After building a moderate-sized fire in the fire ring, he left it to burn out and become one more piece of forensic evidence that Lester had enjoyed a private party at the river and had suffered for the lack of a companion to save him from his stumble into the water. He jogged back to his motor home three quarters of a mile upstream. He had work to do, to accelerate his timetable. The authorities were closing in, and he felt uncomfortable with them breathing down his neck. But he again smiled as he scanned the cell phone communications between Meghan Reilly and her brother, and plotted.

David sat at his desk at the hospital—angry, frustrated, and perplexed. The morning's call from his department chairman had not been pleasant, and it was obvious that the man had been talking with Royce. How a senior fellow, just two years out of his residency training, could stir up so much trouble for him was unfathomable. True, he had been at the medical center as a resident and had been handpicked for his fellowship, and that longevity had given him access to and credibility with many of the medical staff's upper echelon. But David knew that he, too, had been specially selected and was on the fast track toward a department chair. To have his credentials suddenly questioned and his research maligned was mind boggling, and yet he now found himself in the position of defending his work.

He had cancelled surgery and called in Sue, his nurse practitioner.

"What've you got?" he asked.

"Doctor, I've spent the better part of the last two hours reviewing the patients from the preceding year of our study. I've looked at their mechanisms of injury, pre-hospital down times and EMS care, E.D. interventions, and in-hospital care. Nothing different is jumping out at me. Here's my summary."

She handed him a sheaf of paper. He thumbed through the data, reviewing lab findings, MRI and SPECT scan reports, neuropsych evaluations, consultants' reports, and the discharge summaries of those who had left the acute care setting.

"What about Ester Jacobs?"

Despite her brief window of apparent lucidity, her fate had jumped into the same sinkhole of deterioration as the others. Nothing they had done subsequent to withdrawing the barbiturate had improved her condition. Yet, his use of the barbiturate now brought his research under intense scrutiny.

"Nothing new to report on Ester. Sorry."

"Man, I wish Dan was still here. Thanks, Sue."

As she left the office, David reached out and picked up the phone, hitting redial for the fourth time that morning. Dan had said Rochester, but he'd located no neuropsych programs there and moved his focus to SUNY, the State University of New York in Syracuse, just 90 minutes east. He had called the Upstate Medical University in Syracuse repeatedly that morning in an attempt to track down Dan Diehl. Dan was to have reported to his new job the previous Monday, yet no one seemed to know him.

"Neurosurgery. Anna speaking."

"Hi, Anna. This is Doctor Koettering again. You asked me to give you half an hour to try to find Dr. Diehl. Any luck?"

"I'm sorry, but no one in this department seems to know Dr. Diehl. Do you want me to transfer you to the Neurology Department, or maybe Psychology?"

Lynch sat in the Ops Center with Flannigan and Lorna Gregory, a female detective called in for special assignment to the MCS as a guard for Meghan Reilly. Lynch had complete trust in Detective Gregory, but he feared they might underestimate their foe yet again. The man's ability to stay one step ahead of them had been uncanny. He didn't want that to happen again.

"Okay, let's go through this one more time," Lynch said.

"Man, we've been over this like a hundred times. We checked, double-checked, and triple-checked the arrangements for her surveillance," Flannigan retorted.

Lynch glanced at Lorna.

"Hey, I've got my role down. I'll be a legal assistant working with her and I'll be at her side at all times during the day. I've got the part down pat. Shouldn't be hard being an obnoxious lawyer."

"Not too obnoxious. You're just a legal assistant. And outside of work?" Lynch asked.

"We've got over a dozen teams that will be switching intermittently so they aren't detected. We've tapped undercover detectives from all over the metropolitan area to work those shifts and act in different roles to blend into the daily life of a paralegal. They've all committed to it, and the schedule has been sent to everyone concerned."

Lynch nodded. "Good. I know I'm getting anal about this, but this lady's life is in our hands."

Lynch despaired at not being part of the surveillance. It was a dissatisfaction that weighed even heavier on him since he had devised the plan and felt personally responsible for her safety. Her brother, although anxious to help and concerned for her safety, also was to remove himself from the scene. It was likely the killer already knew who they were, and their presence around Meghan might deter the assailant from acting. Lynch also sensed an atypical degree of uncertainty in his own actions. His confidence had always been in his skill at being part of the action, not a behind-the-scenes coordinator. Now he could only observe from a distance. Meghan had set the snare with herself as bait, but it was up to Lynch to see she didn't find herself in a leg-hold trap chewing off a limb to get free.

Lynch stood and paced in the tight quarters between desks.

"I can feel it in my gut. We're tightening the noose around this guy's neck, and I sure don't want him winning any more battles before we win the war."

The media attention had produced dozens of leads, most of them days, weeks, and even months old, but several of them were consistent with the known attacks. These reports worked in concert with the known facts to confirm they had the right vehicle. Yes, the noose had tightened, but was time on their side?

The next morning, as Meghan left home for work, the ballet began. An electric company truck followed her halfway to work, while a battered pickup bearing the load of a painting contractor tailed her the remaining distance. The next morning it might be a satellite dish installer's truck and SUV bearing a realtor's magnetic door sign. When Meghan pulled into the law firm's parking lot, Lorna emerged from her car and waved as if to an old friend. She joined Meghan for the short walk to the building, the ride to the fifth floor in the elevator, and accompanied her into her inner hallway office.

"So far so good," Lorna stated. "Any problems or concerns on your end?"

Meghan shook her head.

"Good, let's go over rules of the road again."

"Hey, I'm good. I know what to do. I don't use my cell phone for anything other than calls I would usually have in a day and my computer may be monitored, so I use it only for business and real, low key personal tasks. Nothing about my surveillance is to be transmitted electronically or spoken of within any room with outside windows. During the day, you are my only means of communicating with the police, and at night I only call for an emergency. See? I've got it down."

Lynch left the office and collected a new undercover vehicle from a discreet county parking lot. From outward appearance, he looked to be a local cable company installer. Although he couldn't risk being seen interfacing directly with the surveillance crews, he could limit the distance he had to maintain from them. His plan for the day was to work a secondary perimeter several blocks out from wherever Meghan was at the time.

Lynch cruised the surrounding streets. At various points, he got out and walked behind a building or down an alley. He saw no places where a motor home could park, and while he spotted a dozen Porsche 911s, none had the custom paint job. He also saw half a dozen dark maroon, purple, and red SUVs of various makes, but he had less to go on about that vehicle than the Porsche. He jotted down the location of every one of these cars, so that whenever and wherever they triggered the trap, he could be close at hand for the catch.

An hour of cruising the streets around the law firm

revealed nothing truly suspicious. At mid-morning, his cell phone rang.

"Heading to the county courts." The voice gave no greeting or farewell and said nothing more. Nothing indicated who was calling or being called, in case the perp could monitor calls in the area.

Lynched sighed with relief at the news because security at the county courts added another layer of protection for the woman. He drove to the court complex and circled it once before moving further out along the side streets. Half an hour later, he parked and, clipboard in hand, he started walking, occasionally stopping to inspect cable company property and lines. He would make a quick note on the clipboard detailing time and nearby cars. He would use this list later in the day as he drove past the same spot, and by comparing, he could begin to develop a sense of which cars belonged in the area and which were transient. By lunchtime, he had canvassed an area roughly a half-mile in diameter surrounding the courthouse.

As lunchtime approached, he decided to grab a bite to eat at a small sandwich shop he had passed earlier and then switch vehicles to assume a new "identity" for his afternoon sweep. So far, everything sailed along as planned. As he entered the eatery, his cell phone rang again. He listened for a moment before saying anything, but the anger rose inside.

"You what? Hold tight! I'm two minutes away." He broke into a run back to the truck.

Thirty-nine

Her shift over, Amy should have left base two hours earlier, but with the troubling email and what it implied, that the killer knew *where* they worked and maybe *when* they worked, she was afraid to leave and took refuge in their temporary quarters. Commuting made her vulnerable, as she discovered when the Porsche followed her home. But at the base, she had constant companionship, and together they had instant emergency contact with local, county, and regional police, not to mention a quick airborne escape route if needed.

Amy picked up the phone and dialed her father.

"Hello, Gibbs residence." There was that female voice again.

"Umm, who's this?"

"This is Arianna Kendrick. Who's this?"

"This is Amy. Is my father there?"

Arianna's voice softened and became friendlier after Amy identified herself.

"Oh, hi, Amy. I thought it was you. Your dad's running some errands, getting parts for the car and something or other from the hardware store. I'm not sure how long he'll be gone, and he left his cell phone here. Again."

She had submerged her questions regarding this woman while treading the choppy waters of her current situation. Now they bubbled to the surface once again. Her use of the word "again" made it clear that she'd been at her father's house often enough to recognize he frequently left his cell phone at home.

"Is there something specific I can pass on to him? I'd be more than happy to try to track him down for you if it's urgent."

Amy wasn't comfortable leaving the message with a stranger so her message was only to request he call her at work or on her cell at his earliest opportunity.

At Reid's insistence, she had called Lynch earlier that morning and informed him of the problematic email. Lynch, in turn, contacted Mike Jurgesmeyer who was due to arrive at the base at any moment because Lynch was unable to assist personally. He hadn't given her any additional information, but she read between the lines. Something was happening in the case, and Lynch wanted in on the kill.

Reid, too, had stayed behind, insisting he wanted to see how the computer tech traced the email and where the trace might lead. But Amy could see it in his eyes and sense it in his voice. Like her, he lived by himself and had no desire to go home, to place himself at risk with no one around. The fear was real, and it was more obvious than Reid's machismo would like to accept. Despite his bravado at times, Amy could see the negative effects this case took on the paramedic. As he paced in the small central living area of the doublewide, pre-fab home, she reread the same page in her novel for the fifth time.

At the knock on the front door, Reid was on it in a split-second.

Amy had never met Mike Jurgesmeyer, but Lynch

had described him well enough that she had no doubts as to his identity when he entered the room. On formality, he showed his credentials.

"Hi, I'm Amy." She extended her hand.

Mike smiled. "Truly a pleasure on my part," he replied as he shook her hand. "Lynch has told me a lot about you. Sorry to see you going through all this."

She grimaced and nodded. "This is Reid McCormick. He's the paramedic who was with me when Art Barklage died. We, uh, got this gross email yesterday, and, well, I guess Lynch probably filled you in, huh?"

Mike nodded. "Not a pretty scene I understand, and I'm sure this digital instant replay isn't much better. Well, let's see what we can find out."

Reid led the way to their main workroom where the desktop computer and its purulent digital image resided. He pulled out the chair and stood aside as the computer-forensics lab supervisor sat down. Mike pulled a collection of compact disks from his disk carrier and inserted one into the drive.

"I've seen this guy's programming skills before, so I have serious doubts we'll be able to trace it. And if I run into any obstinate service providers, I might have to get a court order to get their help, which will take some time. Since 9/11, however, these folks have been a lot more compliant. They don't want to be tagged as helping terrorists, or murderers, whether knowingly or not." He launched a program from one of the disks and started to type. "All ready. Let's see what we can do. First, I want to make sure he hasn't put any of his spyware on this system."

A few minutes later, he started tracing the email. Starting with the header information on the email itself, he moved back into the company's mail server. There, he scanned the server's mail logs and found the next link in the chain. Methodically, he moved from one server to another, using each one's logs to find the next link. Forty-five minutes later, he hit his first snag.

"Rats. This one went through one of the digital satellite providers. Looks like the Dish One system. That means two things. I'll need to get the account information on whoever's account was used to upload the mail. I think I can swing that with a phone call. The bad news, however, is that the satellite dish could be anywhere on the ground and doesn't have to be stationary. It can be mounted to this motor home we're looking for, and that brings us back to square one—finding that bus. Give me a minute."

He pulled his cell phone from its belt clip and walked outside as he dialed. Amy and Reid sat silently in the Ops Center, waiting for his return. Five minutes later, he reentered the room, shaking his head.

"Another dead end. The mail originated with the account owner. Problem is, the account owner is our very own county court system. It was sent from inside the court building. The guy had to have walked right through at least two security checkpoints and tapped into the satellite system, right under our noses. Sonofa..."

"Mike, thanks for coming all the way out here to do this." Amy stood at the front door with the computer forensics technician as he prepared to leave.

"Hey, it's my job. Glad to help, but sorry we didn't get anywhere."

Amy simply nodded.

"I'll give a full report to Lynch as I drive back to the city. It was a pleasure to finally meet you." He shook Amy's hand and left.

She stood there, watching him leave and debating her reluctance in departing. She didn't work again for two days, and she couldn't very well move into their Ops Center until the police captured this guy. Yet, her feet seemed super-glued to the floor when it came to picking up her things and heading for the car. At Lyle's thoughtful insistence she stayed for lunch, but knew she had to take her leave soon after. She was tucking into her third piece of pizza when another knock on the door disrupted the meal.

Lyle rose to answer the door and returned a few seconds later, smiling.

"Looks like the Gibbs Escort Service has arrived," he announced.

Amy's dad appeared behind him. She felt a rush of relief and jumped up to greet him.

"More like the cavalry," she replied.

Lyle held up the pizza box. "Care for some lunch, Colonel?"

He hesitated and then took a single piece. "Maybe one for the road. Thanks." He took a bite, and after swallowing, continued. "Amy, I've got to get back. So, let's get a move on."

She looked at him askance. "My car's okay. I just . . . well . . . I . . . Do you think you could just follow me home?"

"Don't think so. I'll have to give you a ride."

"Huh?"

"Sweetheart, I just came in from the parking lot. Your car has four flat tires."

Lynch's anger had calmed a bit by the time he met Flannigan outside the main entrance to the courts building. Together, security ushered them directly through the entrance checkpoints and up to the third floor where district courtrooms nine through sixteen were in session. A crowd milled about the doors to number ten, and Lynch noted that many of the people congregated there were not happy at the delay. Their emotions couldn't begin to match his.

Lorna Gregory stood next to a balding, middle-aged man who, despite a convincing imitation of the Michelin man, was attired in an expensive and finely tailored, gray pinstriped suit. The two detectives walked up to them and introduced themselves to the man, Meghan Reilly's new employer, Walter Geiss.

"So, what happened?"

"We were on a brief recess while the judge reviewed a minor technical issue. Meghan needed to use the restroom and excused herself. Lorna will have to fill you in from there. Next thing I know, she's running back into the courtroom saying Meghan's disappeared and asking the bailiff to notify security to clamp down the building and secure all exits."

Lynch put his palms to his temples and squeezed. He couldn't believe what he was hearing. It was only day one of their plan. They were inside one of the most secure and heavily policed buildings in the county. There were hundreds of people both inside and outside of the building. And their "bait" had just been taken like a bluegill stealing a worm right from the hook?

"Lorna, you were supposed to stay with her." His frustration was strident in his voice, as was his implied condemnation of the female detective.

"I was. I went with her to the ladies' room. I even sat in the stall next to her, but I was done first and decided to wait for her just outside the door because the place was so crowded." She paused.

Lynch fought to hold his anger at bay and sensed that she, too, was trying to cap her emotions. He realized he needed to ease off, that laying into her too hard would be counterproductive. It had to be a team effort, and she was part of the lineup.

"So, what happened next?"

"When she didn't come out five minutes later, I went back in. She wasn't there. I found this on the floor of the stall. . ." She handed Lynch an iPhone. ". . . and I discovered an unlocked back maintenance door. It leads to a service hallway. I didn't take time to investigate, but ran back to the courtroom and put out the alert."

"Was it precisely five minutes, or is that a guess?" he asked.

"No guess. I monitored the time on my watch."

Lynch did the math. Five minutes. They were only on the third floor. The underground garage complex was but two stories lower. And it would take an additional one to two minutes to lock down the facility. Would that include the exits from the garage, or would they take longer to secure?

"Okay. That would give her, them, time to get out of the building, but maybe not the parking garage."

"You'd better check the phone," Lorna said gravely

At that moment, Lynch's phone rang again. He wanted to ignore it, but he also expected a call from Mike Jurgesmeyer. A quick glance at the screen confirmed that's who was calling. He held up a finger to his team. "One sec." He listened as Mike gave him a report on what he'd found at the MedAir base. What he heard, in light of the current situation, added to his frustration.

"Looks like our guy, or someone, has been here waiting since this morning. An intimidating photo of the Barklage crime scene at Creve Coeur Park was emailed to the flight crew this morning. The email came from this very building." He paused. "We need someone to start scanning surveillance video from today."

"You might want to check this phone," Lorna repeated. She looked a bit put out.

Flannigan spoke up. "We can start reviewing video, but who are we looking for? There'll be hundreds of people on these recordings."

Paul was correct. Who were they looking for? Lynch realized that whole exercise would be a snipe hunt.

This time, Lorna thrust Meghan Reilly's phone into Lynch's hand. "You *need* to see this. The last message. She didn't take time to erase it."

Lynch used the phone's menu to retrieve the last message. It chilled his heart. The text message read, "You know the drill. No police. Come to the corner of Central and Bonhomme NOW." That was on the opposite side of the building and one block south from its main entrance. Easily within reach in five minutes. It continued, "Your brother is now my guest." A digital image of an unconscious Sean Reilly followed the text.

Forty

Amy was surprised to see her father's "new" MG-B in the parking lot next to her car. As far as she knew, it hadn't left the garage at his home since he first drove it there. She gently tossed her gear into the space behind the front passenger's seat and then turned her attention to her own car. Her father's assessment was a little bit off. Only one tire was resting on its rim. The others were depleted of enough air to make it impossible to drive safely, but seemed able to take a new charge of air and regain shape. Amy felt just the opposite, overly pressured and ready to burst.

"Hey, I don't have time to work on it now, but maybe tomorrow morning we can come back and get it all fixed up. Okay?" Her father laid a gentle hand on her shoulder. "It's probably just a nail. With all the new construction between here and your house, some could have fallen into the road from any number of trucks."

Amy appreciated her father's attempt to lighten her concern, but his assumption didn't negate the very real possibility that this was another message, another warning from the killer. Just what *didn't* he know about her? He knew where she lived and worked and how to access the computers and most likely the phones and any other electronics, at both places. He obviously knew which car was hers. She shivered at the realization of just how vulnerable she was. She had told Lynch that being forewarned was as good as being forearmed. Now she questioned that judgment. She didn't feel safe anywhere except in the air. Who was it who said just because you're paranoid doesn't mean they aren't after you?

Her father lowered the top of the roadster and secured the black leather bonnet that covered the ragtop. He then hopped into the driver's seat and waited for Amy to join him. His presence eased her fear, but as she climbed into the vintage car, a new fear bolstered her paranoia. The car was of a vintage that neglected roll bars and even seatbelts. If the killer struck, could they survive an "accidental" rollover?

Almost by reflex, she reached down beside her seat for the two ends of a safety belt she knew would not be there. Yet, she found the mated ends of a lap belt just where they should be. Her surprise, or was it her relief, must have been obvious.

"Yep, buckle up. Had to add those to get it licensed. Well, I would have anyway, but they forced me to do it sooner rather than later. Ready?"

Amy snapped her belt together, tightened the excess, and nodded. "Let's go."

As they hit the open road, she released a smidgen of her fear and tried to enjoy the air blowing her hair and the warmth of the autumn sun on her face. Under other circumstances, it would have been a glorious drive.

"So, what do you think?"

His question caught her off-guard. "What?"

"How do you like the car?"

"It's great. Perfect for a day like this."

He nodded. "Yep. Dredge up any memories?"

She looked at him quizzically. "What, the car, or the day?"

"Either. Both. You wanted to know about Arianna, so I wondered if this car brought back any memories."

Amy recalled her father telling her that he had purchased the car from Arianna to help her out financially. But other than seeing it that one day in her dad's garage, she had no memories of a red convertible sports car. But she recalled a green one she loved to ride in as a kid. How old had she been? Maybe ten, twelve? It was before her mother's diagnosis of cancer.

"Um, I remember a green sports car when I was a kid. That's when we lived in Tacoma."

"That's right. I was stationed at Fort Lewis."

"Do you remember who owned that green car?"

"Sure. Major Ken. I loved it when he came to the house and gave all of us kids rides with the top down so it seemed like we were going a lot faster than we probably were. And I remember a picnic at Mount Rainier where we got to ride with him into the mountains, but we had to stop several times on the way there and back so each of us had a fair turn."

He chuckled. "I'd forgotten about that day, but you're right." Then his face turned serious and patted the steering wheel. "Same car."

He paused, and it took almost a minute for it to sink into Amy's mind.

"But I thought Major Ken died in Beirut."

* * *

"You sure you don't want me to stay the night again? We can get an earlier start to go get your car if I do."

Amy was lost in thought as her father drove her home. Amy recognized her father's concern, but she was exhausted, physically and emotionally. And she had no doubt he would want to pump her with questions.

"Thanks, Dad, but you don't need to tonight. I need some time alone to absorb this evening."

Amy also had no doubts that she wouldn't have answers to her father's questions. After all, dinner and an evening with Arianna just hours after learning she was Major Ken's sister, and that her father had "an interest" in her, was a bit too fast for Amy. Despite Arianna's warm reception of Amy, Amy felt odd trying to return the gesture. She wasn't her mother. In her mind, she'd always thought her dad needed and deserved another woman in his life. He needed a mate, not a doting daughter. Now that it was happening, she felt slammed by the strange, conflicting emotions inside. On one hand, she was happy for him. On the other, she felt as if this woman was trying to displace her in her father's life. Amy had not been cold or unfriendly, but "aloof" appropriately described her response. Still, she hoped she was not hurtful. Maybe if she'd had more time to absorb the news before actually meeting Arianna at the impromptu dinner set up by her father, her response might have been more tender.

Amy emerged from the car and headed for her door, but her father beat her to it.

"Dad, you don't have to stay. Really."

"Not a problem. But I *am* going to check the house

369

before I leave, for my own peace of mind."

A few minutes later, satisfied the house was empty and secure, he kissed his daughter goodnight and walked to his car.

"I'll be here at eight, and we'll go fix your car."

"Thanks, Dad."

Amy waved as he backed out of the drive, then double-locked the door, and went to her bedroom to change clothes. She thought no further of his offer to stay. She felt too worn out to feel any fear. And her father was, well, her father. She wanted Lynch there with her. She wanted to be held, to feel his strength, to be bolstered by his confidence and buoyed by his love.

Having fallen asleep in her favorite chair, she was startled awake by the phone ringing beside her. A quick glance at the clock told her it was almost eleven-thirty. *Lynch?* she hoped, but then she became scared that it wasn't him, that it would be an empty line, a reminder that the killer knew she was home—and alone. Or maybe it wouldn't be an empty line, but the killer taunting her, provoking her. She quickly turned off the answering machine. If it wasn't Lynch, she didn't want to preview the call, to have a digital reminder of her fear. Yet, maybe it *was* Lynch returning her call. She quilted together every scrap of courage she had into the fortitude necessary to pick up the phone.

"Girlfriend, where you been all night? You told me to call you, and I tried four times, getting that honky-tonk recording you call a message. 'Bout time you got home."

Amy felt a three-ton release from her chest in

hearing her friend's voice.

"Oh, Macy, am I glad it's you."

"Of course it's me. Who else would have the nads to call you this time of night?" There was a brief pause. "Never mind, don't answer that. So where've you been? And I want a straight answer."

Amy started with the email episode at work and worked her way through the morning's exercise in mail tracing, her flat tires, and finally her father's revelation and the unexpected dinner arrangements.

"Girl, guess I'm almost as relieved as you are about your dad. Thought I was going to have to start buying him perfume for Christmas, like my Aunt Diamond. Now I can just keep up his subscription to Popular Mechanics."

Amy laughed. She loved her friend's ability to lighten the tension.

"Yeah, he likes you, too, Macy. So, what's new from the war front?"

"War front. That's an interesting way to put it, 'cause I think that makes you the equal of Helen of Troy." There was another pause.

"Huh?"

"Get it? Troy? The town where you're based—forget it. Look, are you kidding? You haven't heard anything about it? A major battle of egos has erupted at the hospital, and the rumor machine is giving odds that it's all because of you, my dear friend."

"You are kidding me, right?"

"Not at all. Koettering and Royce are having the feud of the century, and your name keeps getting mentioned."

"Why? I haven't dated either one of them. I'm still seeing Lynch."

"I can't answer that one. All I know is that Royce has accused Koettering of academic fraud and endangering his patients, and his whole research protocol is now undergoing review. And Koettering is fighting back with his own charges against Royce about improper sexual advances on staff members and patients."

"He should have lots of staff support on that one. Royce is finally getting what he deserves."

"Maybe, but we all know he was mostly harmless hot air. Plus, he's really mellowed recently. Weird thing about it, though, is that he's left town. Word's out that he arranged some emergency vacation time and left for Boston."

Lynch looked at his reflection in the lavatory mirror and frowned. Leaning over the sink, he splashed cold water onto his face and rubbed down his cheeks. Lynch called the emergency squad meeting after consulting the Chief, who tasked him with leading the discussion because he remained ill and unavailable. He glanced at his watch. It was after midnight, and they were just about to start the meeting.

He walked into a conference room full of somber men and women, dedicated police officers who all felt the same dismay and guilt at "losing" Meghan Reilly despite their surveillance. No one felt that loss more acutely than Lynch, except maybe Lorna Gregory. She had not left his side, doing whatever task he asked of her short of going home to rest. He appreciated her dedication and had found her help invaluable that evening. Indeed, all of the officers there had spent hours in a fruitless search of the county court building and its adjacent neighborhoods. Not one grumbled at the late hour.

"Okay, let's get started. Lieutenant Harrelson, you took lead over the court building search. Anything?" Lynch asked.

The county sheriff's representative shook his head. "Other than the cell phone with her brother's photo, nothing. Her car was still in the lot and untouched. No prints other than hers, Gregory's and her brother's. Security camera footage showed a young woman of her description leaving the building on her own. Her face was not visible so we can't confirm that it was her."

They had reviewed step-by-step the events of earlier that afternoon and the subsequent, fruitless search of the county court building.

Lynch pointed to Jim Boyerton next.

"Jim, you took charge of canvassing the immediate area. What do you have?"

"We found Meghan's purse in a trash can at the designated street corner. Cash gone, but it still had the digital tracking beacon you guys had secretly slipped into her day planner. We showed her photo to everyone we could locate who worked in a two block radius of that corner, but no one remembers seeing her, much less if she got into a car with anybody."

"What about her brother?"

373

Another detective answered. "We found him safe and napping at the ambulance base where he was pulling a 24- hour shift."

Sean Reilly had arrived earlier that evening, insisting upon a full accounting. He was irate at first, blaming the police for screwing up and endangering his sister, and threatening to go public with the story. He mentioned lawsuits several times, until they reminded him that it was he and his sister who had initiated contact with and taunted the killer on their own volition. He was also informed that Meghan appeared to have had ducked out of the building on her own and had not been forcibly removed. The fact was that *she* had left her protection behind, not that her escort failed. He quickly quieted and asked only to be used somehow in saving his sister. If and how he might be used was yet to be determined.

Mike Jurgesmeyer pitched in.

"We analyzed the digital photo from the camera phone. It was manipulated and faked."

"Yeah, well, it was good enough to fool her."

Jurgesmeyer continued. "Phone company records show the transmitting cell phone as her brother's. Faked photo or not, you add the fact that she saw the caller's number as her brother's, and what else could she conclude? This monster has her brother. But the real take home message for us tonight is this guy has the technology to scan and duplicate cell phone transmissions, so we really need to be careful with our phone communications."

"Spyware. Internet hacking. Email intercepts. Cell

phone hijacking. You know, if it's electronic this guy seems to be a master of it. Anyone for carrier pigeons?"

No one laughed at the detective's attempt to lighten the mood.

The man had snatched Meghan Reilly from them through a clever ruse. However, catching the killer, although critical, was not paramount in Lynch's mind now. He had devised the initial plan to use Meghan as bait, despite the Chief's hesitation, and her safe recovery was squarely on his shoulders. True, "officially" he had been absolved of that responsibility when the two siblings took the initiative to step out of the box on their own and when Meghan left behind her protection, but in his mind, he was still culpable. For the first time in his career, he felt utterly powerless. His ace, the tracking device, had been played and gone bust. How could they find this woman in time to save her?

Lynch stared at the window and saw his faint reflection in the darkened glass. At the moment, he didn't like the man staring back at him.

Lady Law sat in a chair in the corner of the room, watching the young woman sleeping and bound to his bed. The sedation would last several more hours, hours he would use to set his own trap. He had seen through the smokescreen early on. She was no more than bait, and he was the quarry. But now, while she remained the bait, the hunter would become the hunted.

But a question lingered. Should she also become a

member of the privileged initiates? She had despoiled herself by volunteering to assist the police. That was a badge of dishonor that could tarnish the pristine legacy of those who had been sacrificed before her. There was also the uncertainty of David's research and the attacks on it that required consideration. If she could not contribute to the cause, what then would be her purpose? Still, he could not let her go unpunished. Or could he?

He thought himself one move from checkmate. He had played his queen through the squares of the county court building. He now had to confront the king. He mulled over possible moves and saw none on their part that might interfere, none that could turn the game against him.

He arose and walked to the front of the motor home where he pulled out every electronic and mechanical device he owned and arranged them like trophies around his state-of-the-art "command center." His goal was to make as impressive a display as possible for anyone walking into his home. Then he took his toolset and finished some changes he had started making to the bathroom door. The newly installed pneumatic device could automatically close the door behind anyone entering the space. With his remote control in hand, and the gas release mechanism disabled, he entered the bathroom and watched the door swing closed. He tested it three more times, increasing the speed of closure, until he was satisfied no one could react quickly enough to stop it.

He then walked to his computer console and sat

down. He activated the face recognition software he had recently acquired and tweaked and made sure the small video camera across from the main door was aimed at the entrance. He selected his own face as a target and left the motor home. Upon reentering, he sensed nothing unusual and pretended to look around. Upon entering the bathroom, the door quickly closed. He reopened it with his remote and set about a second test. He selected a new facial target for software identification and repeated the test. The bathroom door remained in manual mode. He reset the entire system and smiled in knowing the process was now fully automatic and fully armed.

He returned to the chair in his bedroom and turned his attention to the woman there. He had decided. He gathered a syringe and measured up a dose of medication, enough to keep her sleeping until his return. She was not a candidate for his club, and she would no longer be the bait. Instead, she would become a trade. Now he had only to decide the timing of the trade.

Forty-One

Amy's phone awoke her at seven.

"Hi, it's me," Lynch said. "Sorry to call so early, but I didn't know if you worked today or not and wanted to catch you before you left."

"That's okay. I need to get up anyway. Dad's coming to help me repair my car."

She enjoyed hearing his voice, but wished it were coming from inside her home, not from some unknown, distant site.

"What's wrong with your car?" There was concern in his voice.

She explained the situation with the tires, and her father's supposition that it was the result of picking up some nails on the way to work the other day. He didn't say anything to support or oppose her father's opinion.

"Is he going to be with you today, all day?"

"Well, at least until we fix my tires. Then I'm taking the Cessna up. I don't know if he wants to fly with me or not. Why?"

"Just want to make sure you're protected. The stuff's hitting the fan."

He explained the circumstances of the latest abduction and his fears for the young woman's safety.

"So, where're you flying to?"

"Nowhere, just flying. I figured I could help out and was thinking of doing a grid pattern south and east of the one you and I did together."

There was a pause at the other end of the line. Amy wondered what he was doing and thinking. She half anticipated an angry response, that he wouldn't want her taking any chances.

"Okay, I can swing that," Lynch finally replied.

"What do you mean you can swing that?"

"We've launched a massive search. Every department in three counties is calling in extra people and starting an intensive search for this motor home. It's still the only solid lead we have and it has to be around here somewhere. I was going to be working around Creve Coeur again, but I can move out so I'm reasonably close to where you'll be looking. If you see anything, call me on my new cell phone."

"You're not mad that I'm doing this, getting involved?"

"You're already involved." He sighed. "Plus, I need all the help I can muster. We don't have much in the way of air resources, so you can really help that way."

"Want me to get the medevac teams in the air? I think they'd be willing."

"Amy, I can't spring for any expenses, but if the company's willing to volunteer some resources, sure. I want to find this woman and nail this guy. Today, not tomorrow."

Amy's father needed no convincing to fly with her, and she felt relief that he was joining her, for several reasons. For one, she simply felt safer with him there.

And, with one person flying and another acting as a spotter, they could cover more territory more efficiently. Eager to get into the air, together they worked down their pre-flight checklist.

"Dad, I want to apologize for last night. I wasn't the best company."

He sidled up next to her and put his hand on her shoulder.

"Nonsense. You were fine under the circumstances. Don't you think Arianna knew what to expect? She didn't expect you to greet her like your mom, or even some long-lost sister." He moved to the front of the plane. "Prop's tight."

Amy nodded. "I remember your saying it was difficult to see Arianna as anyone but a friend at first. Well, I've decided to follow your lead. Friends. How about both of you coming to my place for dinner Friday night?"

He stopped his inspection and looked at her, one eyebrow raised. "Are you actually going to cook or are we ordering out again?"

"Thank you very much, but I plan on slaving all afternoon in the kitchen."

"In that case, I'll be there, but I can't speak for her. I'll have to ask."

"Hey, it's both of you or we order out. I'm not doing the gourmet thing just for—" His look stopped her mid-sentence. She rethought what she was about to say. "Okay. I guess I do owe you. It'll be epicurean delights for Friday night, but I'm going to invite Lynch and maybe Macy, too."

He glanced at his checklist and smiled. "Ready to fly?"

"Actually, why don't you fly while I spot?"

Her dad nodded and walked around to the left side of the Cessna. Amy climbed into the right seat and retrieved her cell phone from her purse, which she stowed behind her. Fifteen minutes later, they were airborne, and she called Lynch to inform him of their location and heading.

The afternoon dragged on as Amy saw nothing that could remotely qualify as the motor coach she was hunting. They spotted a number of campers and numerous barns that could house a 40-foot bus, but those ground objects would have to come under the scrutiny of local and county law enforcement agencies. The magnificent autumn color of a week earlier had faded with the passing days and was past its peak. Colder nights and shorter days had triggered the release of summer's foliage. To Amy's advantage, areas that had been hidden by a leafy canopy when she and Lynch had flown together were now more visible.

Her dad tapped her on the thigh to get her attention. "Wind's picking up. I think we're starting to see that promised cold front moving in."

She watched him dial in the frequency for a radio weather update and listened with him to the information on current conditions.

"This wind is going to make it harder to fly our grid.

Maybe we should head back," Amy said after hearing the weather report.

"Not at all," her father answered. "We just have to use it to our advantage. Let's head south, along the Big River and resume west from there. The winds will bring us back this way."

"But Lynch and I covered some of that area days ago." Amy saw the proposed move as a duplication of efforts.

"Maybe so, but it never hurts to look again. Plus, the wind will be on our side, as I said."

She couldn't argue against that comment. "Okay."

Her father set course and flew south. He calculated a new grid pattern and resumed flying a roughly east-west route and back again. As he predicted, the northwesterly winds moved them in a southeasterly direction with each sweep. Twice he had to correct his heading to avoid missing large tracts of territory.

"Winds are getting a bit dicey. We can get one or two—"

"Dad, turn back over that farm we just passed, along the river. And maybe drop to three, four hundred feet."

Her father made a sharp bank north toward the river and took the plane down as low as he dared within the river valley, as the ground winds buffeted the plane. A moment later, she pointed ahead.

"There, at one o'clock, just south of the river."

He adjusted his path and flew right over the dark object she had seen. Amy fumbled for her purse and plucked the color photo of the suspect motor home from it.

"I think that's it. Where are we? What road is that? Did you see any cars with it? Let's make another pass." Excited, Amy flipped open her cell phone and hit redial to get Lynch.

"Slow down. Let me see the photo again," her father requested. He glanced at the image she held up. "Sure looks like it. Get the road map. Let's try to figure just where we are."

"Go back. Make another pass."

"Nope. Might alert someone inside. I'll take us up to where we can get the panoramic perspective." He smiled as he put the plane into a climb, leveling off at seven hundred feet. "There." He pointed to the river on their port side. "There's a big school complex a few miles east of the bridge. I'll circle a couple of times until we can get the lay of the land." After a moment, he added, "Hey, that's Browns Ford Road. That's the public river access for fishing the river."

"Lynch." Amy clutched her phone to her ear. "I think we found it."

"What? Where?"

The excitement in his voice seemed double that which she felt. She felt an overwhelming sense of relief that the ordeal was about to come to an end.

"We're working on that. We're over Jefferson County and it's along the Big River, off Browns Ford Road. It's still partially hidden under the trees."

"Wait a minute," Lynch said. "You're farther north than you said you were going to be."

Amy explained the change in plans as she scanned the earth's surface and matched it up to the map in her lap. She waved at her dad to take it down for a closer look.

"Look, it's east of the Browns Ford bridge, off Engleford Road. Looks like you take a farm road to get there. Um, looks like second, maybe third, farm on the left after you turn onto the road. There's an old, abandoned house with a new doublewide next to it. Big hay barn behind them. They should all be visible from the road. Go past the barn to the river. I can't gauge the distance up here, but the road forks and you go left."

The Grandview R-II School complex stood at the crossroads of State Highways Y and C, about seven miles northwest of DeSoto, Missouri, and three miles east of the Browns Ford Bridge. The school district covered 73 square miles of southwestern Jefferson County and its 40-acre campus included the elementary, middle, and high schools, as well as support services, and handled roughly 800 students.

It was a typical, small rural school. Eighty percent of the high school graduates went on to college, and most of the teens and twenty-somethings thought of it only as a place to be from. Nothing exciting happened there. Yet, the school would play an important role for Lady Law. He would need a diversion when it came time to drive away, and to that purpose, the community would see more excitement than the University of Missou'rah' at homecoming with a surprise visit from alumnus Brad Pitt.

The surrounding area was a stereotypical farm community where everyone knew everyone else's comings and goings. So it was with some concern as he stood at the pumps at the Raintree Market & Grill, filling his car with the premium grade it demanded, that a middle-aged man from the store approached him.

"Hey there. Pretty fancy car. Sure don't see many of those in these parts."

"Thanks. I imagine they wouldn't handle the gravel roads around too well," Lady Law said with a grin.

"Nope. Tear the bottom up. Anyways, ain't you the fella what's been down on Lester Hargrave's place fishin'?"

The question jolted Lady Law. He had assumed a high level of anonymity from the locals. To learn otherwise potentially jeopardized his plans and definitely affected his timetable. He would have to take time to plot a new scenario, to map out potential moves with new pieces being played. But this wasn't like chess. The rules had changed and a new piece had suddenly appeared on the board. Would other fresh players arrive soon as well?

"Yeah, but I'll probably be pulling up this weekend, with the weather changing and all."

The man nodded in understanding.

"You seen Lester recently?"

Lady Law quickly calculated the best way to play this question.

"Couple of nights ago. Wanted someone to drink

385

beer with, but I couldn't join him."

The man chuckled. "Yeah, the man sure can hold his Bud Light. Well, if you see him, tell him his order is in. He'll know what it is. He can pick it up anytime."

"Sure. I'll check at the house on my way in."

The man touched the brim of his ball cap and ambled back toward the store, glancing back over his shoulder only once. Lady Law quickly completed his fill-up, paying at the pump with a stolen credit card, and headed toward the motor home. About halfway there, at the top of a hill right before the Engleford Road turnoff, he sensed an urgency to stop and pulled to the side of the road. From his vantage point, he saw a small, single-engine plane circling at a relatively low altitude and then dip down toward the farm. Alarms disturbed his thoughts. *Someone's seen the motor home and knows the police are looking for it,* he thought.

He no longer had the luxury of controlling the timetable, of calling the shots. He had to get to the Fleetwood. The coach itself was expendable, but there were papers, a computer, and other toys he needed to remove. Yet, he couldn't move. To drive into that farm with the plane circling overhead was tantamount to turning himself in. The car would be easily identifiable and explicitly linked to the motor home if they saw him there. How long did he have? A sense of panic arose within that he'd not felt in years. It was the same panic he'd had as a child in knowing his father would be home any minute and that the beatings might start without provocation.

He battled to control the terror, and upon realizing that his short conversation at the gas pump had delayed him long enough to prevent him from being on the farm and detected by the plane's occupants, an aura of calm settled on him. He glanced up and saw the plane change course to a southeasterly path, and he regained his confidence as he watched it leave the area. Maybe they hadn't spotted the motor home. Maybe they had circled the area for some totally unconnected reason. Maybe his timetable wasn't in trouble after all, but he could not take that chance. He reached behind the passenger's seat and pulled a small, rip-stop nylon bag up into his lap. Within it, he had a portable police scanner, which he now removed from the bag and plugged into the cigarette lighter. The receiver was already tuned to the Jefferson County police frequency, and with the press of a button, like on his car radio, he could switch to the other frequencies used by any of the several authorities who might be looking for him. With this, he hoped to learn how much time he had to escape.

As soon as Amy had mentioned that they were over the river in an area where they had flown together earlier, Lynch changed directions and headed for Highway 21, emergency lights flashing. He knew that would take him into Hillsboro and then DeSoto, southeast of the bridge. Perhaps he could find a shorter route. He accessed the map software on the car's police computer and tried to calculate how long it would take to reach the school, and from there, the Engleford turn-off. Traveling as fast as he dared on the twisting country roads, he was, at best, 30 minutes away. He needed a shortcut and he kept glancing at the computer trying to find one. Flannigan and others working on the squad were a minimum of an hour away, but Lynch dialed his friend's cell phone and alerted him to the new development.

"Paul, avoid the police frequencies. I'm sure this guy is scanning them. Let's coordinate by cell."

"Okay. I'll contact Jefferson County dispatch and start things in motion. The sheriff should be able to get some assistance from Hillsboro and DeSoto police. Where should we meet?"

"Grandview Schools. I'll be there in less than half an hour."

"Too soon. I doubt I can get this put together that fast. An hour. We need a plan, and we need to go in force, Lynch."

Lynch heard his partner and couldn't disagree, but if the Reilly woman was there, did she have an hour? She was not going to die on his watch. He played a quick game of "what if" and decided on his game plan.

"Okay, an hour. I'll be there," he said. *After I pay a visit to the farm.*

Forty-two
❧◆◆❧

Amy and her father hadn't touched down a moment too soon. The fast moving front now had winds at a steady 25 knots with gusts up to 40, not the kind of "breeze" best suited for light aircraft. In addition, a storm cell had developed, threatening rain and the potential for lightning and hail. The Skyhawk shuddered in the wind as her father taxied to their tie-downs. He pulled up to their parking space and parked it nose into the wind.

"C'mon, we need to secure her quickly," her father yelled as the wind blasted through his now open door.

Amy jumped to the tarmac and grabbed the wing strut on her side. Together they pushed the Cessna into a spot where they could attach the tie-down cables to the wings. She could feel the wind trying to pick up the plane as they moved. With the wings tied down, they placed chocks around all three wheels and stretched the nylon cover across the windshield and windows with rubber cords to hold it in position.

"All done!" she yelled into the wind. Her dad answered with a thumb up. She picked up her gear from the pavement and ran to her car. Her father joined her there.

"If we hurry, we can drive back there in about an hour," Amy said.

Her father shook his head. "Nope, I'll follow you to your house, or you can come to mine."

"But, Dad, we can—"

"No! As your duly unelected bodyguard, we'll do no such thing."

"But, I want—"

"Amy, I'll sit on you or tie you up if I have to. We're staying out of the way. Lynch can call you when it's over."

Amy saw no way past her father and grudgingly knew he was right. Disappointment filled her. The stress of the previous weeks had mounted to a level she refused to accept, and with the serendipitous discovery of the suspect motor coach, the floodgate holding back the waters of deliverance from that anxiety had begun to crack open, only to now seize up with the flow at a trickle. She wanted to be there, to celebrate the victory with Lynch, to see firsthand the monster behind the months of terror and torture.

"My house. He'll call there first, before he tries my cell," she replied, and she wouldn't be far from the phone, waiting in anticipation.

Lady Law eased his way down the gravel farm road. The guy from the store was right. These roads could tear the bottom out of his car, and he didn't have time to take it so slowly. As he got to the fork in the road, he had an idea, but the weather had worsened, and he didn't have much time. He turned to the right and pulled into the clearing where Lester had held his final party. The beer bottles remained undisturbed and the tractor was right where he'd left it. He gloved up and mounted the tractor. With a couple of turns of the engine, it sputtered to life, and he put it in gear and headed toward the motor coach. There had been no traffic on the police scanner, but that didn't mean no traffic coming in his direction.

At the motor home, he first checked on his guest. She was semi-conscious and a look of fear captured her face as she opened her eyes and saw him. Her terror was brief, however, as he administered another dose of sedative. He pulled a duffel from under the bed and emptied the winter clothing it contained into a drawer in the built-in dresser. He stuffed the clothing tightly into the limited space and jammed the drawer closed.

Then he took the duffel and moved to the bathroom. He quickly collected anything and everything that might hold his DNA traces and dumped them into the bottom of the bag. He took a washrag, soaked it in the available bottled water, and washed down the sink. He would have preferred bleach. He'd have no time to attend to the shower, but he'd cleansed and disinfected it since last showering, and it would have to be clean enough.

He moved to the front room, powered down his main computer, and unplugged it. He unlatched the side of the box and deftly removed one of the two hard drives. The remaining drive could control his command center, but contained nothing of his financial or personal data, or valuable software that he could not easily replace. He wrapped the drive in bubble wrap and eased it into the duffel. He turned the system back on, and once rebooted, the software took control. His home was once again armed and ready for intruders.

He looked at his watch. Twenty minutes had passed.

He glanced around the room, selected a dozen other custom-crafted devices, and placed them into the bag. The other items he could replace easily. Lastly, he retrieved a small, flip cell phone from a drawer in his desk. Today's generation would call the Razr an antique, but he had no need for a smartphone for this task. He opened it and pressed a button sequence that connected it to a small transmitter on the top of his home. It was more like a wireless intercom that linked directly to his command center computer. This he placed inside the shower, on the floor.

He took one final look into the bedroom.

"You disappointed me, Meghan, but at least you'll get to live with that. Sweet dreams." He turned and gently closed the door behind him.

As he left the home, he felt a sense of melancholy. It was hard to say good-bye to the place. But not impossible.

He heard a noise from the direction of the farmhouse, the sound of tires on gravel. He had no time to waste. He mounted the tractor and headed into the adjacent field, away from his car. If things worked out, he could come back for it later. If not, he had spied Lester's two-year-old F-150 parked inside the barn, with its keys in the ignition. As he worked his way through the field of drying corn stalks waiting to be cut and shredded, he noticed a cloud of dust moving slowly toward the river. The clouds in the sky darkened and rain seemed imminent, but no precipitation had fallen for days, and the dry conditions remained his ally. When the dust cloud stopped near what he estimated to be the fork in the road, he stopped the engine, climbed down from the tractor and retrieved his remote control from the duffel bag. Although his system was now on automatic, his curiosity won out over the urge to flee. He turned on the three-inch monitor and waited.

Lynch's heart raced. He was so close to ending this, he was already thinking ahead to classes he could teach and research he could do. Of course, he'd need to complete his Ph.D., and that would take two years. As soon as he had a position confirmed, he would resign from the department, take Amy out for an elegant evening and propose.

He missed Engleford Road the first time and had to swing around in a three-point turn to go back. Amy's description of the farm was clear and on target. It was the second farm, and the old farmhouse appeared to be the original homestead. No doubt it had deteriorated to the point where it was cheaper to buy a doublewide, pre-fabricated home than to repair the first.

He pulled up to the house at first, but it appeared empty. He drew his gun and slowly worked his way around the house. In the late afternoon light, there were no lights evident inside and, curiously, there seemed to be a couple of days worth of mail and newspapers stuffed into the rusty metal mailbox. Lynch doubted the family who lived there received that much mail in one day. He also noted only a single phone line accompanying the power lines to the house. No satellite dish or cable TV, and certainly no DSL that far out. A family who lived so simply might possibly have no knowledge of the "LA Rapist," making this farm a perfect hideaway.

Lynch worked his way around the outbuildings and cleared the smaller ones first. Nothing out of the ordinary there. He took extra precaution as he approached the main barn. There were no recent tire tracks in the dust by the large door nearest the house, but the place was typical in that you could open front and back main doors and pull your equipment through. He saw that the hasp for a padlock had been pried away from the wood of the door, the padlock still connecting the two pieces. That did not bode well for the owners. They most surely had a key and no need to force their way into the building.

As quietly and quickly as he could, he entered the barn and discovered an old pickup, its engine cold and keys in the ignition. There was evidence of a tractor having been parked inside, but it was missing. A quick look out the back door revealed relatively recent tracks heading for the nearby lane, which was currently blocked by a metal gate. A fast search of the building exposed no new discoveries.

Lynch ran back to his car, pulled up past the barn, got out of the car and opened the metal gate to the lane, dragging it along the ground for the last couple of feet in order to gain enough clearance for his vehicle to pass through. He slowly worked his way down the rough, pitted road and soon found the dust so unbearable he had to close his window. The gusting wind added to the dust storm around him instead of clearing it away. He strained to listen to what sounded like a tractor in the fields, but the crunching of his tires on gravel made it difficult to confirm. Maybe the farmer was alive and working his fields after all. It seemed likely he'd be working his fields, preparing for winter.

About a mile down the lane, Lynch finally saw the river and what seemed to be the fork in the road that Amy had mentioned. She had said to go left, but as he got to the fork and peered right, he saw it. Approximately 100 yards away, in a clearing and partially hidden by brush, was a silver sports car, a Porsche 911 Carrera 4. He couldn't see the back end, but common sense told him that was unnecessary. The mysterious car that had tailed Amy home, combined with the presence of the suspect motor home could only add up to one thing. He had the right spot, and someone was home.

He turned off his engine, eased out of the car, pulled his service nine-millimeter again, and cautiously headed down the left fork in the road. Only yards into his trek, he spied something metallic to his left. He quickly rolled to his right and came up with his gun pointing toward the spot. He craned his neck for a better view. There was no movement except that induced by the wind. He slowly rose to a crouch, still intent on his quarry being in the bushes. He inched forward until the cause of his alarm became clear.

"What an amateur," he muttered. *I might as well walk in with an engraved invitation.*

Attached to a tree was an infrared device, pointing

toward a reflector across the road. Lynch had walked right through the simplest of early warning devices, one sold in many hardware stores to alert homeowners to someone entering their driveway.

He had left his caution to the rising wind. So intent was he on getting to Meghan that he'd forgotten the most basic approach tactics and that this killer was an electronics gadget freak. He retrained his focus on the task ahead, and allowed his training and experience to reassert itself. He moved stealthily to his left, into the adjacent cornfield, and stalked his way parallel to the road toward his target. Ten minutes later, he saw the motor home for the first time. It was both impressive and hideous at the same time.

He checked his watch. The cavalry would be mounting up at Grandview School soon. He spent five minutes watching the coach. There was no sign of activity. He moved a little bit past the bus and still saw no sign of life. Yet, the Porsche sat parked not far away. Where was he? He then realized there were no sounds of a generator and no obvious external source of electricity. He saw no portable gasoline cans for replenishing a generator and knew the man couldn't risk taking the coach itself out for refueling. Did the man have a battery array somewhere, or was he unsuspecting and operating in the blind at the moment? Lynch moved into the woods behind the home. He detected no monitoring devices as he scanned the area and moved more freely toward the front of the bus, facing the river. Again, he waited. He could see a glimmer of light inside, but that was to his advantage. It allowed him to see in through the broad front windshield. He could see past the front living area and into the kitchen. There was no one there. He decided to take a chance and enter the coach.

Swiftly he moved to the main door and finding it unlocked, opened it quietly but quickly. Gun raised, he mounted the first step and glanced back and forth. Nothing. He took the second step and swept his gun back and forth, parallel with his line of sight. He stepped fully into the front end of the motor home and put his back to the nearest wall. The kitchenette and main living area were empty, and there seemed to be no response from the back. The living area was crowded with state-of-the-art electronics. The man not only knew his stuff, he spared no expense for the best equipment.

Lynch had no time to inspect the layout further. The door to the bedroom was closed, holding a possible trap. He inched his way past the galley. There were several small doors leading into storage closets and a pantry. None could hold a man. The bathroom door was partially open. He nudged it open all the way and found it empty. One last stop.

He kicked in the doorway to the bedroom. He stood there for a fraction of a second, long enough for his mind to register someone on the bed, before he ducked out of the line of potential return gunfire and into the bathroom. As he realized the body on the bed was that of Meghan Reilly and that no response was coming, the door whirred shut on its own accord and he heard the click of a locking mechanism. He tried the door, but it remained frozen in place. He looked around frantically. Was the door reinforced? Could he risk a gunshot? The ricochet could kill him.

He noticed a small cell phone on the floor of the shower and picked it up. Holding it to his ear, he listened to a computer-generated voice. He started feeling lightheaded. Did it address him by name, or was he imagining that? His breathing became more rapid as he struggled to get more air. The voice thanked him for giving up his life for that of Meghan Reilly. She had been a disappointment. *A disappointment in what?* he thought as he sank to the floor. Then the voice told him something he didn't want to hear. Amy! He tried to scream, but there was no air to produce sound. Amy! Amy! No! He tried to hold onto her image, her scent, her touch. In a final desperate move, he lifted his gun and fired at the window—and then at the lock in the door.

Lady Law heard the gunshots and broke into a run toward the motor home. He could not let that detective beat him. Not now. He was so close to finishing his "work" here. He eased up to the door of the coach and peered around the edge into the main living area. No one there. He glanced again at the three-inch monitor on his controller, and saw no one inside the bathroom.

Where was he? The gun might have foiled his locking mechanism with just the right hit. He had never designed it to be bulletproof.

He worked to calm his heart. He needed to regain

control over his fear. He needed to think through what had happened. Cully had been inside at least three minutes. No four. He heard the first gunshot after the four-minute mark. But how long after?

Confident that the policeman would not be able to put up much of a fight, he slowly entered the coach and checked the hallway. The bathroom door remained closed. He pressed the lock release and waited, ready to jump out the door and run if the man emerged with his gun at ready.

He heard the lock release. Nothing happened. Still cautious, he moved to the door and found he had to force it open. The man lay in the corner below his camera. The gun had fallen from his hand. A quick check revealed he was still breathing, although the breaths were shallow.

Lady Law grabbed Cully's wrists and pulled him to a different position that allowed him to open the door fully. Then he dragged the detective by his arms to the main door and pushed him out onto the ground. From there, the river's edge sat only 30 feet away.

Thankful that the man weighed less than the old farmer, Lady Law pulled him to the shoreline and rolled him into the river. He used an old, weathered plank to push Cully's body farther out, but still the current didn't take him. He had no choice but to get wet.

The water was freezing cold, but Lady Law had no choice. He pushed the body farther away from the shore, waded after it, and pushed it farther still, until the current finally caught the body and took it downstream. He clambered to the shore and followed the body. Soon, it hit the main channel and quickly floated away.

Lady Law rushed back to the motor home and erased all evidence of dragging the body away. Those coming now would find the girl, but nothing more.

Forty-three

༄· ♦ ♦ ·༅

Amy startled awake, arose from her chair, and moseyed to the living room as she twisted and rotated her shoulders and stretched the kinks out of her back. Her father was dozing on the couch, yet he opened one eye as she neared.

"Hi. You okay?" he asked.

She nodded. "Any word at all from Lynch?"

Her father shook his head. "No calls at all. Try his cell phone again."

As she dialed, she used the remote control to turn on the television. She had missed the first few seconds of the lead-in, but it was something about late-breaking news from the Major Case Squad. The show's beginning credits and logo began to their familiar theme music.

"Good evening. As we stated, there's late breaking news from the Major Case Squad tonight. Based on a solid lead late this afternoon, authorities closed in on the motor home linked to the "LA Rapist." It was spotted on a farm in Jefferson County near the Big River. Then, as police joined up at Grandview R-II Schools to prepare for the raid, a huge explosion ripped through the middle school there. Fortunately, the students had been sent home early. However, two county sheriff patrol cars were destroyed and the deputies seriously injured. They were evacuated by air to Barnes Hospital, where a spokesman tells us they are in serious but stable condition and expected to make full recoveries. For more, we go live to

Erin Broder at the Grandview R-II High School.

The scene switched to an ill-defined location where the reporter was illuminated by artificial lighting, and the background was one of smoke, flashing lights, and emergency vehicles.

"Thank you, Marshall. We're here at the Grandview School campus in rural southwest Jefferson County where an explosion appears to have leveled a portion of the middle school and injured two sheriff's deputies."

The broadcast changed again to video taken earlier showing fire crews battling the blaze that consumed a portion of the school building. The reporter's commentary focused on the immediate events, and Amy's frustration level rose as they said nothing about the motor home or the search for the killer. The reporter quelled her anxiety moments later.

The reporter continued, and the scene became one from a news helicopter over the farm. "The story, however, began hours earlier. Based on a tip from a recreational pilot . . ." Amy and her dad smiled and gave each other a high-five. ". . . the suspect motor home we reported on several days ago was located on a farm three miles from here. Members of the Major Case Squad were coordinating a raid on the site when the explosion occurred. Authorities believe the two events are linked."

Amy edged forward in her seat and pointed to the screen where the view clearly showed a car parked at the fork in the farm lane and the motor home to the left of the screen.

"Dad, there, there's Lynch's car. Way to go. Did you

get the guy?" She was talking to the TV as if Lynch could hear her through it.

The reporter continued. "We have with us Sergeant Paul Flannigan of the Major Case Squad. Sergeant, what can you tell us?"

Flannigan looked somber and fatigued. Amy wondered why he, and not Lynch, was the evening's spokesman.

"Our raid, although delayed by events here, was a partial success. We can confirm that the motor home is the one used by the 'LA Rapist' and we found his latest victim there, sedated, but alive and unharmed. Unfortunately, we did not capture the killer."

"Can you tell us who he is?"

"We hope the motor home will provide us the information we need to learn his identity. I have no further comment tonight. Thank you." Flannigan turned and walked away from the camera, which guided its focus back to the reporter.

"Yes, the good news is that they saved a young woman from the wrath of this killer. Unfortunately, he remains on the loose. We have other bad news to report tonight. An unnamed member of the Major Case Squad is now missing. Officers found his car on the farm, but so far, he is unaccounted for. Back to you, Marshall."

Amy's heart stopped.

Matthew sat back in the recliner in the den of his brick-and-mortar home not far from the medical center.

403

He watched the evening news on four different stations, and all carried the story out of Jefferson County. His system at the house was not as state-of-the-art as that in his motor coach, but it would suffice until he had time to rebuild. His getaway had been uneventful and he had even slipped through in his Porsche. Driving east, he passed the school and noted the building police presence. A mile north on Highway C, he used his cell phone to dial another phone, one stashed just within an outside vent in the school's crawl space and accompanied by a moderate charge of explosive which the phone's ringer detonated. He had heard the explosion as he drove away scot-free.

During the Major Case Squad detective's interview, he smiled in complacent confidence. His motor home would yield no clues. Its registration was falsified, as were its tags. Everything about its ownership was fiction and added electronically to those databases that needed the data. As for physical evidence, well, he glanced at his watch and calculated that in one hour and 50 minutes, at the stroke of midnight, that too would disappear into an inferno of toxic gas. His last phosphine tank's timing mechanism was still sending him its signal. It remained online and on time.

With that blast, "Lady Law" would be no more. Matthew would assume a new online identity, and his two remaining loose ends would soon be resolved.

"The line's still busy," Amy stated after her fifteenth attempt over 30 minutes to call the Major Case Squad's emergency number.

"Why don't you try the Ladue police and see if they can track him down?" her father suggested.

Amy pulled out the phone book and looked up that number. After talking with a dispatcher, she remained frustrated.

"What'd they say?"

"All of Lynch's calls are being taken by someone else. They wouldn't tell me who, but promised someone would call me."

Amy resumed pacing the living room floor, phone in hand. Fifteen minutes later, it rang.

"Miss Gibbs, Amy, it's Bob Janick."

"Lieutenant Janick, thanks for calling. I saw the news tonight, and I'm trying to get hold of Lynch. Have you heard from him? Do you—"

"Amy, I only know what you know. Tell ya what, let me contact Paul Flannigan. He was working with Cully on the squad. He'll know more. I can't promise you he'll call right back, but I'll find him for you. Okay?"

"I-I . . . uh, okay. Thank you, Lieutenant."

Paul Flannigan was a name she'd heard two, maybe three times from Lynch, but a man she'd never met. His call came in just before midnight, leaving her in agony for nearly an hour.

"Ms. Gibbs, I'm sorry to have to tell you that we haven't the foggiest idea where Lynch is. From what we can tell, he went ahead to the farm without backup. Why? I can't say for sure, but I know he felt personally responsible for Meghan Reilly's safety. We found his car

405

by the river, about a quarter mile from the motor home, but we have nothing on him. We've got dogs coming to help, but that won't start until daylight."

Amy's brain turned off after hearing the words "haven't the foggiest idea where Lynch is." How could he just disappear?

"Ms. Gibbs, are you still there?"

Amy replied with a faint, "Yes."

"I hate to say this, but we have to be prepared for the worst. We found two bullet holes in the motor home's bathroom. We don't know if they're new or old, from Lynch's gun or some other gun. We haven't found the slugs yet, and the crime scene techs have called it a night. They'll be back in the morning with better equipment." Flannigan paused again. "Ms. Gibbs?"

Amy could not respond.

"I guess you're still there. Hey, I know you two were getting things back on track, and I know Lynch really cared about you. I promise to keep you posted. If you've got some paper, here's my cell phone number."

He started to rattle off his number, but Amy couldn't move, couldn't make her hand copy the numbers. His offer never really registered, but she reflexively said, "Thank you," and hung up.

Some of Flannigan's words—nothing on him, expect the worse, bullet holes—bounced through her head like those yelled into a well, echoing back and forth until they were absorbed and dulled by the water at the bottom. But this well's water would bring no relief to her thirst.

The thought of a well brought to mind the scripture

about Christ providing water that would quench all thirst. Yet, where was God in all of this? Had He allowed Lynch back into her life only to take him away again?

She stumbled into bed, leaving her father to fend for himself in the living room. She wanted to jump into the well with chains wrapped around her, never to surface. It was her fault. If Lynch was dead, she was to blame. The fingers of guilt would all point to her. She had discovered the motor home. She had called him directly with the information, an act that had given him the time to precede his team to the farm. If only they had retreated from the advancing weather earlier that afternoon. If only they hadn't gone flying at all. If only she hadn't been so insistent on helping in the search. If only, if only, if only . . . no more 'what if.'

Forty-four
❦✦✦❧

The young woman sat alone in the cabin, tears filling her eyes. Her benefactor had left her there three weeks earlier with plenty of food and a warm place to stay. Yet, he hadn't contacted her in over a week, and she feared for his safety. One didn't cross the man he had once worked for and expect to go unpunished.

She gazed out the picture windows and watched the river's water flow past. As the sun descended, long shadows began to ease across the river, and she had noted before how these sometimes played tricks on her eyes. Too often she saw things in those shadows that made her tremble in fear. She disliked being alone under these circumstances. Where was Ibrahaim?

Suddenly, a mass of something floated up to the bank nearby. Were the shadows deceiving her again?

She stood and moved closer to the window. No. There was definitely something floating there. She startled. Did it just move?

Curiosity got the better of her. She grabbed her coat and walked outside, taking the iron poker from the wood stove for protection. She eased up toward the water's edge and moved to catch a better view.

It was a man!

She dashed to the body and saw that he was face up and appeared to be alive. She ignored the temperature of the water and charged into the river. She grabbed his arms and tugged and tugged until she had him on dry ground. His lips looked blue, but he seemed to be breathing. She hesitated, but finally placed an ear to his chest. Yes, he was breathing. How was she going to get him inside? And then what was she going to do? Under her circumstances, she couldn't call the police.

The wood cart. Ibrahim had a small cart for hauling firewood. She ran to retrieve it, dumping the wood that occupied it at the moment. In less than five minutes, she had the man inside and next to a cot by the stove. Again, with some effort she managed alternately to pull and push him from the cart onto the cot.

She then rolled him back and forth to remove his wet clothes. She ran to Ibrahim's bedroom and gathered his blankets. She wrapped the man with the dry linens and began to drape his clothes over the wooden chairs that accompanied the dining table. They had been torn and battered by his time on the river. What had happened? How long had he been in the water?

As the man opened his eyes, the world around him spun, and nausea engulfed him. Instinctively he knew it would pass if he kept still. His chest burned with each breath. Why? The fire inside overwhelmed him as he tried to inhale deeply, so he continued to breathe at a level where he could manage the pain. As the whirling eased, he turned his head. The room was unfamiliar. He groaned as the vertigo returned. What had happened? Where was he?

He raised his hand and gazed at it. He knew he

should know the name of that body part. What was it? He wiggled his fingers. What were they called?

He could recall some things. He knew he was lying on a bed. Above him was a roof. No. A ceiling, then the roof. If he could sit up, maybe he could find a chair to sit in. Still, other names escaped him. Glass filled something that let light into the room. A raised, flat thing was used to eat on, using something to spear the food.

More importantly, who was he? He recalled nothing about himself. His age? Where he came from? Parents? The word came to mind, but what were parents? He struggled to recall "parents," as part of his mind told him that this was something everyone knew from their youngest days. Why couldn't he remember?

He sighed in frustration and regretted it as the burning hit. He moaned again.

"Awake?"

He didn't want to move his head, but found himself nodding. And spinning.

"Hurt. Yes?"

The woman's voice seemed to come from a distance, certainly not next to him.

"Yes." His reply emerged as a coarse whisper.

"You hurt me?"

The question puzzled him. He could barely move. What kind of threat could he be?

He shook his head and noticed the spinning had lessened. A moment later, a young woman with long, coal black hair came into view. She held something with water in it. *A glass.* He remembered the name.

"You sit up?"

"I don't think I can," he whispered.

"Here. Put in mouth. Then I help."

She handed him a small white thing, and he looked at her, questioning.

"Is medicine. Ibuprofen. For pain."

He placed it in his mouth. It tasted bitter. The woman placed one hand behind his back and helped him sit. He closed his eyes until the spinning stopped and reopened them. The woman handed him the water. He took it and washed down the pill. *Pill! Yes, that's what it's called*, he thought. Instinctively, he gulped down the rest of the water and handed the glass back to the woman.

"More, please?"

She nodded, stood, and walked across the room. To that place where she got the water. He struggled for the word. Greedily, he repeated the process until he'd downed five glasses of water. The spinning definitely seemed better.

"What is name?" she asked.

He shrugged.

She pointed to herself. "Danijela. Spelled . . ." She spelled it for him. "Is Bosnian."

He moved to put his feet over the side of the bed, and Danijela jumped back. She grabbed a sharp, metal thing from that flat-topped thing you ate on.

"I won't hurt you," he whispered. She remained alert. "Honest."

She seemed to relax, but did not give up the sharp thing.

411

"Thank you. For the water. For helping me. I-I don't remember."

She eyed him closely. "I fish you from river. Yesterday."

He didn't remember any of that. Why had he been in the river in the first place? And what river was it? Not that it mattered. Even with a name, he realized he wouldn't know where the river was or where he was.

"Where am I?"

"Here. This place," she answered.

"Where is this place?"

"Is here." She looked around the room and shrugged. "Ibrahim's home. He rescue me. Bring me here. Protect me. Good man."

"Where is Ibrahim? Can I talk to him?"

Tears welled up in her eyes as she shook her head. "I think dead now."

"I'm sorry." Somehow he sensed and understood the woman's fear. "I won't hurt you. Promise. Will you help me try to remember things? I need help. Can you help?"

Danijela shrugged again before nodding. "Maybe. My English not good."

He smiled. "Right now, it's better than mine. Like that, that thing. Next to you. I can't even remember what it's called."

She looked puzzled. "This?" She placed her hand on the table. He nodded. "Table."

Yes, table, he thought. He pointed to several other things in the room, and she named them for him. "See? You are helping already."

She smiled. "You need name, too. I call you Jusuf."

Jusuf somehow knew that wasn't his real name, but it would do. He decided he would stay with Danijela until . . . until when? He would know when he was ready to leave.

Forty-five
❦ ✦ ❧

Amy's alarm droned on for close to half an hour before her father gently woke her and asked if she wanted him to call in on her behalf. She shook her head.

"No. I, I need to get out of the house. I need to try to stay busy."

Her dad stepped away from the bed and eased toward the door. "If there's anything you want me to do, just say it."

Amy nodded. As her head cleared, the smell of brewing coffee registered, and she could hear the low murmur of voices from the morning's television news shows. She padded down the hall to the kitchen, poured a cup of coffee, and headed for the bathroom, resisting the temptation to plop down into the couch and watch the news. She splashed cold water on her face and worked on her hair. She had little interest in fine-tuning her appearance that morning, and her makeup went untouched. And if necessary, she could always shower at the base, although that always felt a bit awkward.

By the time she had dressed and accumulated her gear near the front door, her father appeared with a toasted bagel and cream cheese. He handed her a brown paper sack containing her favorite sandwich—Cajun-spiced turkey with lettuce, tomato, alfalfa sprouts, and bacon on toasted seven-grain bread smeared with mayonnaise—and an assortment of chips and fruit. That produced a faint smile. She felt like a schoolchild heading off to class again.

"Need me to follow you?" he asked.

She shook her head.

"Then, get going. I figure that detective will call here if anything comes up, and I'll call as soon as I hear something, or pass him on to your cell."

She walked up to him, placed her hand on his arm, and leaned forward to kiss him on the cheek. "Thanks, Dad. For everything." She held up the sack.

She gathered her gear, stepped through the door, and froze in place on the stoop. A maroon Jeep Grand Cherokee sat parked in the cul-de-sac. She turned to get her father, and as she did so, the vehicle pulled away and left. Her dad was already there, standing in the doorway.

"Yeah, I saw it. I'll get my keys and follow you to work." Amy started to protest, but he held up his hand. "I'm following you to work. No ifs, ands, or buts about it."

Unsurprisingly, the news about Lynch Cully's disappearance had preceded her to work, and her crew danced around the subject as if waltzing on fine porcelain teacups. Amy felt more miserable than she might have been at home. Reid and Lyle made small talk, but largely avoided her. As much as she liked both men, she found herself wishing she had a compassionate female ear to bend, someone who would understand. One other realization hit her that morning. This was the first time all three had been teamed up together since the flight with Art Barklage.

By noon, Amy had single-handedly restocked the helicopter, their medic bags, and the stock room, as well as scrubbed down the stretcher and patient bay inside the aircraft. She had cleaned the kitchen, her call room, the spare call room, one bathroom, and the living area. She had been a whirlwind of activity, but it hadn't dulled her worry. Shortly after lunch, she heard Reid calling.

"Amy, where are you? Let's go. We got a call."

She laid her paper sack on the kitchen table, rushed to her call room, and grabbed her gear. Both men were at the aircraft by then. She sprinted toward them.

"What's up?" she yelled.

Reid was already climbing into his seat, and Lyle was powering up the engine. Reid signaled for her to get in. She lifted herself into the aircraft. Once secured, she donned earphones and flipped on the intercom channel.

"It's a rollover out on Highway ZZ. Another pickup truck and the usual bad combination of high speed, curving road, and no seatbelt. Driver went out through the windshield. He's awake, complaining of left thigh pain and chest pain. Paramedic says the femur is obviously deformed, and there are bruises noted on the chest wall. Steering wheel was bent, so good chance of cardiac contusion."

Amy nodded, and her mind clicked into gear, thinking about the potential complications and what they might need to intervene should the patient crash in flight. She welcomed the business, and how it forced her mind to focus on someone other than Lynch, or herself.

* * *

416

The action at the accident scene went a long way in normalizing the teamwork of the flight crew. Reid's banter was back. Lyle's deadpan humor returned. The tension of the morning faded with their need to attend their patient. Amy radioed in and learned the E.D. had two full codes in progress and that security would meet them on the helipad with a stretcher and oxygen.

"Guess it's up to us. Lyle, we're going to need your help moving this guy into the E.D."

"No problemo, Amy. I'll just need to power everything down before leaving her."

Amy understood. Lyle was always reluctant to leave his aircraft, but never hesitated to help when needed. After a smooth landing, he turned all systems off and assisted his medics in off-loading the patient to the awaiting gurney. Together, all three rolled the man into the prepped trauma bay inside.

Brad, the paramedic, walked into the bay to assist. She hadn't seen him since the Labor Day picnic.

"Hey, Amy, Reid. Man, this place is a zoo today. We're getting slammed."

Lyle touched Amy on the shoulder. "I'm going to the cafeteria for something to drink. Want something?"

She turned her head toward him. "No, but thanks." She moved to the curtained entrance. "Brad, is Macy here today?"

"Not that I know of, but I heard they might be calling some people to come in and help. I've been in with Doctor Royce on a pediatric code. Five-year-old boy found in a motel pool. Doesn't look good. Police and family services folks are talking to mom in conference room A. So, what's new with you?"

She brushed off the question and moved into the main area of the nursing station. She was talking with another nurse when she saw Royce, looking frustrated and unhappy, walk out of another trauma bay and over to his work station. He collapsed into the chair.

The other nurse noticed Amy's attention to Royce.

"Came in late this morning. Said he was up most of the night helping a friend. This has not been a good day for coming to work like that." She inched a bit closer to Amy. "Hey, can I ask a personal question?" Amy looked at her quizzically. "Any truth to the rumor you've been going out with Doctor Koettering? He was down here earlier asking if you'd been in, and—"

Tears formed in her eyes as she shook her head and walked away. She used her sleeve to wipe her cheek. She fought to maintain her composure as she walked to the workroom to join Reid. As she passed the doctors' work desks, Royce jumped up, but instead of approaching her as she half expected, he marched out of the E.D. into the ambulance drive. He did not look pleased.

Amy and Reid, both eager to leave the madhouse behind, quickly worked through the report. Lyle appeared in the doorway and walked over to the desk to hand Reid a large cup.

"You guys almost done?"

"Five minutes, tops."

"Okay. I'll be outside. We'll take off as soon as you're ready."

Reid gave the pilot a quick thumbs-up as Amy continued to write. They finished their task with a minute to spare, and Reid picked up the report and volunteered to find the chart or the nurse, or both, so the report could be added to the record. As he walked off, Amy saw an older gentleman walk in through the ambulance entrance. She recalled meeting him in the E.D. once before, but it took a few seconds before his identity came to her. She ran to meet him.

"Chief Dandridge! I don't know if you remember—"

"Of course, Ms. Gibbs. I—"

"Have you found him? Is he okay?" The tears reclaimed their positions on her cheeks as she fought to control her emotions. She couldn't break down, especially not there, not in the E.D.

"Amy, I'm so sorry, but we still have no clue."

"What about the motor coach? Have they found anything? Flannigan said the crime investigators would be going over it this morning."

She noticed a distance in his eyes, eyes framed by a haggard face, gaunt from lack of sleep, illness, or maybe both. She remembered a comment by Lynch that the Chief had not been in the office recently.

"There is no motor coach anymore."

"What?"

"That's why I'm here. At midnight last night, the motor home exploded in a fireball. The force flipped the car my two men were in at the time and injured them. Whatever we might have learned that could lead us to Lynch went up with the flames."

419

Forty-six
❦◆◆❦

Amy sat in her seat, numb to the vibration of the helicopter, and stared out the window as they took off from the medical center. Her conversation with the Chief had been overheard, and before she could leave, she had received numerous comments, questions, and condolences, all of which added to her torment. She felt no longer capable of tracking time. Leaving the E.D., climbing aboard the chopper, and taking off were all a blur. At some point during the flight, Reid leaned over and tapped her on the shoulder. She flipped on her intercom.

"Sara's coming in to relieve you as soon as we get back. And I called your house to talk with your dad. He's coming to get you."

She nodded, dazed.

She returned her gaze to the landscape passing below. They had climbed in altitude. Amy watched as the trees and subdivisions below became smaller. She wondered why they were climbing and looked forward. Lyle was taking a more direct route back to base, one that took them over Creve Coeur County Park. Lambert International Airport's flight lanes typically prevented them from taking such a direct route. Amy watched as homes and businesses gave way to trees below. The remaining autumn beauty of the trees was not lost on Amy, but that appreciation was buried by her other memories of the park beneath—Elsa Dunleavy with her hand screwed to the car roof, and Art Barklage, mutilated, cut and left to bleed to death. A shudder passed through her. She doubted she could ever enjoy the beauty of that park again.

Then the shudder occurred again, and she realized it was a physical sensation, not an emotional one. The aircraft shook a third time. She looked at Lyle and saw him fighting the controls.

"What's that, Lyle?"

"Gimme a sec. I hope it's not what I think it is."

The vibration came again and lasted close to a full minute.

"Lyle?" Her worries, doubts, and self-pity flew from the cockpit.

"The compression's falling. Now the temperature gauge is fluctuating. If it—oh no, hold on folks, we have a flame out!"

Lyle methodically tried to restart the engine. Amy looked below. They had no obvious landing site beneath them.

"Lyle, where exactly are we?"

He didn't answer as he tried again to restart the engine. And again, he was unsuccessful.

Amy tried to think about the terrain they had passed. Had she seen a clearing along the way? Helicopters can't glide. They fall out of the sky like rocks, but unlike a rock, they had a little control. As long as they maintained a critical airspeed during the autorotation freefall, they could turn and possibly land with minimal damage. But not in trees. They tore everything apart and came up through the floor to tear you apart.

Lyle turned the aircraft in a wide arc back toward the county park. Of course! She intuitively knew where he was headed, back toward the lake where the parking lot for the picnic grounds offered their only apparent landing zone. And it was late afternoon, in late October; the parking lot was likely to be clear of traffic. She watched again as he attempted to restart the engine, unsuccessfully. The parking lot was their only chance. Death lay in the trees.

But then she realized that next to the trees, water was their second worst enemy. A helicopter was top heavy, and upon hitting the water, inertia drove the blades forward into the water, tearing them off. The engine on top would then flip the aircraft, which would sink upside down as fast as it fell out of the sky. Amy began praying for supernatural deliverance. *Lord, please help us to a safe landing.*

The earth approached them at a rate she had never experienced. They had seconds left.

"Open your doors and latch them," Lyle barked into the intercom. "Put one hand on the door frame, the other on your harness latch. If we hit the lake, we'll flip faster than you can imagine. Hold tight and pull yourself out as soon as it stops turning. You'll be upside down and disoriented. Remember that! You need to swim for the surface. Swim for the surface!" He paused. "Hold on. All we have left is water below us!"

The impact of hitting the water at 55 knots jammed Amy into her harness and drove the blades forward into the water. The sound was deafening as one by one the blades ripped from the main rotor shaft. But water quickly muffled the sound as they flipped and began to sink.

Amy took a rapid deep breath just as the water came over her head. With one hand she unlatched her harness, while holding onto the doorframe with the other to keep her bearings. They were sinking fast. She pushed her body out through the open doorway and for a moment could not tell up from down. Swimming in the wrong direction would mean drowning. She twisted around and soon recognized where the light was the brightest, her only indication of the surface. Her body craving oxygen, she struggled . . . toward . . . the light.

Forty-seven

❧ ✦ ✦ ☙

Amy awoke to the whomp-whomp-whomp and steady vibration of the helicopter. *Lyle got the engine started*, she thought. She tried to shake her head, but couldn't. Where was she? *He couldn't have gotten the engine restarted, we hit the water*, she remembered. Her chest ached, and breathing caused a pricking sensation in her lungs with each breath. As she became more lucid, she could feel the plastic mask covering her mouth and nose. She reached up to touch it, but something restrained her arms. Her vision began to clear, and she saw the inside of her helicopter, but she was lying on the floor looking up. No, she was in the patient stretcher. Was this her aircraft? There were subtle differences in the equipment layout. She felt a hand on her shoulder and looked up and aft. It was Nancy, another MedAir nurse. What was she doing in their helicopter? *Wait a minute, I'm in her helicopter,* she realized.

Amy tried to talk, but no sound emerged.

"Shhh."

Nancy was down by her ear, talking. *What is she saying?* Amy closed her eyes and focused on Nancy's words.

"You'll be okay. Reid fished you out of the water. He said you started swimming the wrong way, but he got to you. He says he got a bit of water out of you before you started breathing again. He's fine. Lyle has bilateral femur fractures, and they're flying him to Central

424

Regional. Can you understand what I'm saying?"

Amy nodded, although she now realized her neck was immobilized and she was strapped to a backboard.

"I think that was a nod," Nancy continued.

Amy nodded again, more forcefully against the no-neck brace.

"Good. Look, the police don't want anyone to know you guys survived. They've told the press the crew died in the crash. That's why Lyle's being flown out of town. Reid's going into protective custody. We're going to fly you to base one, and then move you to the medical center by ground ambulance. Central wouldn't take you because they don't have as good a facility for handling a near drowning. Doctor Cassidy has agreed to care for you personally, and the police have a roster of nurses who work with them in cases like this. You'll be in a private room, and no one will know you're there, except the nurses and two technicians in the hyperbaric facility."

Lady Law watched the evening news and was disappointed to see that a warehouse fire had beaten out the crash of a regional medical evacuation helicopter as the top news. But then, they had no footage of the actual crash, and the warehouse fire produced some impressive video with flames, smoke, and active firefighters battling the blaze. He envisioned the chopper's freefall from the sky. It was amazing what one single cup of water dumped into the fuel tank could do. The water eventually gets to the turbine and suddenly, no fire. Flame out. And if there's enough water clogging the line, well, there's no way that engine is going to restart in time. Pilots took special efforts to purge their tanks when they refueled, but few rechecked it in between those times.

He had hoped the crash would be something spectacular. A crash into the trees with its resultant fireball might have captured the top news position. Or, had some amateur caught the crash on a home camcorder, it might have made the top spot. But he realized their plunge into the lake was an unexpected bonus. Now, no one would ever be able to prove the helicopter came down because of his simple act of sabotage. How do you prove water in the fuel line caused the flame out after the wreckage is pulled from a lake? He smiled at that unforeseen stroke of luck. With three fatalities on board, he now had his loose ends soldered tight. Maybe it was time to change his online handle to Lady Luck. As the story ended, he lifted his glass of wine toward the TV and toasted his rebirth. Time to move on.

Forty-eight

৵✦✦৵

They admitted Amy to the hospital under the name Lucy Taylor. Her medical history went something along the line that she was a celebrity who'd nearly drowned in a hotel pool and was there in anonymity to get hyperbaric care. They even went to the lengths of hiding her face whenever she was in public view. Her first hyperbaric treatment, under the supervision of Doctor Cassidy late that evening, was uneventful. He had explained that the use of hyperbaric oxygen in near-drowning was still a research topic, but he saw no reason not to take full advantage of the facility. Amy had been scuba diving a couple of times, and the pressure of the chamber caused her no concern or ill effect, but the isolation and feeling of being trapped disturbed her. She still had her doubts that her presence in the hospital would remain secret. She knew too many people there. And the last place she wanted to be was "locked" in a tightly sealed metal box should the killer discover she was there.

Doctor Cassidy woke her the next morning by wiggling her toes through the thin hospital blanket. She rubbed her face with her fingers and glanced at the clock on the wall opposite her bed. It was only six-thirty. *Haven't these doctors figured out that patients get well faster with sleep?* she wondered.

"Good morning, Ms., um, Taylor. Sorry to wake you so early." He smiled. She could tell he didn't really mean it. "How do you feel today?"

"Might have been totally healed with another two hours sleep," she replied.

He came around to the side of her bed. "Let's take a listen." He placed the earpieces of his stethoscope into place and palmed the head of the device against her back. The cold metal against her warm skin jolted her. She wondered how many times she had surprised a patient with a cold stethoscope. She empathized with them now. After listening across all of her lung fields, he lowered the stethoscope.

"Still have some wheezing. As you probably know, the first 24 to 48 hours after a near drowning are the most dangerous, so today's kind of a critical day. We'll plan on two treatments, one this morning and then again later this afternoon or evening. If you're still doing this well or better tomorrow, I think I can safely let you go. Any questions?"

She shook her head. She had no doubts she'd be leaving tomorrow. He walked toward the door and turned back to her before leaving.

"You're first on the schedule this morning. One of the techs will be up to get you shortly."

Amy jumped out of bed and walked to the bathroom. First things first. No way would they lock her into that tank with a full bladder. It was too early for breakfast, and, fortunately, she wasn't at all hungry. She prepared her scarf, sunglasses, and surgical mask. It was the disguise *de jour* for traveling the halls. She then pulled on some scrubs. She wasn't about to leave her rear exposed to the breeze again by wearing a hospital gown to the chamber.

There was a knock on the door.

"Just a minute." She quickly donned the scarf, mask, and sunglasses. "Okay."

She was glad to have made the change. It wasn't one of the HBO Chamber techs, but an orderly she knew only too well. Had he seen her unmasked, the word would have been out within minutes after he left her.

"Ms. Taylor?"

She nodded. He reached for her wrist and compared the name and number on her ID band with that on his transport slip.

"All right. Let me get the wheelchair. It's just outside."

He wheeled the hospital chariot into the room and assisted her into it. He then covered her legs and lap with a blanket fresh from the blanket warmer.

"Kinda cold in the lower hallways. Thought you might appreciate that."

What game was this guy playing? He was never known for caring about his job, or his patients. He was the wheeler-dealer type. *Ahh*, Amy understood now. She was a celebrity, and he wanted to make sure she thought the best of him. The way he pushed her through the halls confirmed her suspicion, careful at each intersection to avoid any collisions, giving her a running commentary and tour of the hospital as they passed different departments. She laughed inside. If only he knew the real identity of the person he was pushing through the corridors. Her father had often commented on identity and deceiving looks. Only now, she was the one in disguise, and she felt something of the power it held, even though it was simply an illusion.

At the hyperbaric lab, the orderly went out of his way to make her comfortable before he left.

"One of the techs will be with you in a minute," he said before exiting.

Amy sat there, alone, for five minutes before she heard a door open from within the lab. Footsteps approached her from behind, from the short wing of offices and workrooms that supported the chamber. Seconds later, someone grabbed the handles of the wheelchair and started to push her to the door leading to the main lab. She tried to turn to see who it was, but the scarf covering her hair got in the way.

"Ms. Taylor, I presume."

The voice was oddly familiar, yet distinctly strange at the same time. The automatic doors to the main chamber opened, and Amy felt fear engulf her. It grabbed her by the throat as if an assailant had gripped her windpipe in a strangling clench. She jumped up from the wheelchair, only to fall to the floor, tripped by the footrests. She struggled to crawl away, but two powerful hands pulled her up by the waist. The man dragged her to a nearby chair and dropped her next to it.

"Sit, and look straight ahead." He remained behind her, out of view.

She felt the icy surface of a metal tube against the back of her neck, but this was no stethoscope. She would have welcomed the cold diaphragm of a stethoscope at that moment. She rose slowly and sat down as instructed. An instant later, a band of hospital sheet dropped across her waist, tightening into a broad restraint that held her tight to the chair. The end of the gun nuzzled her neck again.

"Hands behind your back!"

She refused and in defiance, folded them across her chest. In response, she felt the sudden pain of the gun slamming against the side of her head. Her head felt woozy, and her vision blurred. The man yanked her hands behind her back, but she was unable to resist.

As her mental faculties cleared, she realized she was not seriously harmed and had been moved. She found herself bound to a chair inside the center's large hyperbaric oxygen chamber. Unlike the modern, Plexiglas, single-patient cylinders for wound care, this large cylindrical chamber was similar to those used by the Navy and deep-sea contractors and could manage up to six patients. The floor was non-skid and designed to prevent any static electric discharges. Portholes, like those on a ship, studded the wall to allow easy visibility both ways.

Her captor still had not revealed himself, and she struggled to identify the voice. She looked about and noted a clock just outside one window of the chamber. She had been "out" for no more than a few minutes. Her session was scheduled for 90 minutes. She would not be missed for over an hour. She prayed someone would come calling—a sales rep, maintenance worker, anyone

431

who might run for help, but the lab was in a remote section of the lower levels of the hospital, and she knew her chances of being randomly discovered were slim.

She tested her bonds and noted they were a little loose. She could see that her ankles were duct-taped together and assumed her wrists were as well. The chair was all aluminum so that it could produce no sparks within the high oxygen environment of the functioning chamber. That kept it light, but made it no weaker. As she wiggled about, the right side of her scrub top snagged on something in or on the chair. It wasn't much, but it indicated enough roughness that maybe she could begin a tear in the tape that secured her wrists. She twisted about and began to rub the binding across the area where she guessed the coarse edge to be. From the border of her peripheral vision, she perceived a change in the light outside the tank. Someone had just entered the lab through the main door. She quickly settled back into her seat and feigned a sedated sleep.

The squeal of the hinges on the heavy steel door to the chamber grated on her like fingernails on a blackboard. And it must have been obvious to her captor.

"Nice try, but you aren't any good at faking sleep."

She still couldn't identify the voice, yet there was a subtle familiarity to it. She didn't have to struggle long. The man walked around her and took a seat in front of her. She was stunned. Her breath evaporated. Her mind reeled in learning the identity of the killer.

"What? Speechless?" He laughed. "They always are." Then his demeanor changed, and an evil aura enveloped his face. "So, the question remains, what do I do with you?" He watched her closely for her response. "I still don't know what David saw in you, but he really likes you, you know. That's the only reason you've lived this long."

Amy was confused. *David?* Were her eyes playing tricks on her? How could someone's looks be this deceiving?

"He's such a weakling. I keep him around for the legitimacy he provides me. But *I* call the shots."

"David?"

He laughed again. "I'm Matthew. Did he ever tell you about me? Of course not, he doesn't even know I exist. But then, he doesn't know about the other one either."

The other one? Amy felt a new level of terror invade her mind. She sensed the instability of the person across from her, whoever he really was.

"Really, Amy, did you think I could just let you slide by?"

Amy struggled with her bonds, the duct tape around her wrists and ankles unyielding. She was tempted to spit in her captor's face, but knew it might antagonize him into just the type of violent reaction she hoped to prevent.

"Wh-what are you going to do with me?" She castigated herself for the unexpected waver in her voice, a sign of weakness. Yet, her fear was real and mounting with each minute. She had seen the despicable actions this man was capable of. "I—"

"You'll what?" Promise not to tell? Do I look stupid?"

A sardonic smile flashed across his face. "I've been watching you, Amy, ever since Barklage died on your medevac flight. I wondered what he might have told you before he died, so I've been watching. Closely. Looking for any sign that you knew something he was supposed to take to the grave with him."

Amy looked into his face and saw something different in his grin. His watching had been a source of pleasure. She felt revulsion at the thought of the voyeuristic gratification he must have enjoyed at her expense. Her fear jumped to a new plane and her gaze lowered to the floor. She had to figure out a way of escape.

He seized her chin and raised her face to meet his.

"Yes, it was quite a pleasure watching you. Maybe that's what David liked as well."

His index finger slowly eased down her neck, pushing the bottom of the V-shaped collar of her scrub top into the crevice of her breasts. She felt a wave of nausea and tried to jerk her body away, chair and all, but it only served to rip open her thin cotton top, leaving her exposed to his leer, and lying on the floor.

There was a sudden, loud noise at the main door to the lab, and the man jumped to his feet. He bent over to look out the nearest porthole and then rushed out through the entrance to the chamber.

Amy lay on the floor, unable to right herself. Her hands felt the floor. It was the rough, no-skid type of flooring she had seen on some military choppers and ships. She concluded that this was an adhesive mat, because she found one edge of it curled up. She quickly scooted around and frantically began rubbing her wrist restraint against the edge. She felt the tape give just a fraction. She had started the tear. Could she now pull the tape apart?

She heard the noise of something battering against the main doors. He must have locked or barricaded them somehow. She glanced out the chamber door and saw the man huddled behind an overturned table. He had the gun drawn and aimed at the door. Amy took one look at the weapon and rage replaced the fear. She knew that gun. It was Lynch's nine-millimeter service gun and he would never have given it up freely. In that instant, she knew Lynch was dead, and there was no way that monster in the room outside the chamber was going to take her as well.

With every ounce of strength she had, she began to work the small tear in the tape holding her wrists. Slowly it gave way. Her wrists were bleeding from the effort, but she was free. She quickly removed the tape from her ankles and stood. She reached down and picked up the aluminum chair. With it in both hands, she crept out of the chamber while her captor's attention focused on the door. She moved up behind him and swung the chair down hard.

At the last moment, he dodged the strike, but she had succeeded in knocking the gun from his hand. She recovered quickly and struck again, gaining a glancing blow across his right shoulder. He was on his feet now, and she expected him to fight back. She backed away to prevent his grabbing her only weapon and her only defense, the chair. But instead of anger, a look of absolute terror crossed his face and he cowered in front of her.

"Lady, pl-please don't hit us. I'm Markie. I'm only nine. Why are you mad at me? Is it something Matthew done? I don't like what he does."

Amy stood there puzzled and confused. *Markie? Us?* She let her guard down for a second, but that's all it took for the man's face to change again. He lunged toward her. She lifted the chair and evaded him at the same time. She brought the chair down across his back, and backed away again.

A new countenance surfaced as the man staggered to a crouch. "Amy, where are we?" He held his hands to his temples. He looked around, dazed. "Amy? It's me, David, what—"

Anger took control and contorted his face again. She had no trouble recognizing Matthew this time, and swung the chair violently at him. He backed off. She swung again. He tried to fend it off and she caught his right arm. He cried out in pain and backed away.

Step by step, she drove him toward the chamber. His arm hung useless by his side. She swung again and hit him across the left upper arm. He jumped back and moved to evade her by rushing into the chamber. It was his only avenue of escape; he was cornered and she would have no room to swing the chair in its cramped quarters. But she didn't need to. She saw her opportunity and rushed to the entrance. With rage fueled by vengeance, she forced the door closed and pulled down the locking lever to seal it.

Breathless and shaking, she felt a surge of relief flash through her body. She leaned back against the outer wall of the chamber, and her body sagged in fatigue against an instrument panel. The instant whirr of motors hummed inside the room, and the "Do Not Enter" light flashed on above the door to the chamber. Amy turned to the panel, but the lights and gauges were a mystery to her. She had no idea what she hit, how to turn it off, or what it would do.

There was a pounding at the door to the chamber, but she dared not open it. Within a minute, the pounding stopped, and she rushed to the tank's nearest viewing port. The killer had slumped to the floor. A look of fear and surprise filled his eyes as the vacuum enveloped him and wreaked its damage to his body. Amy turned away from the ghastly image.

New noises at the main door caught her attention. She ran to the doors and pounded back. "I'm okay! I'm okay!" she yelled. She looked around to see what the killer had used to lock the doors, but couldn't see how he had accomplished it.

"Stand back!" she heard from the other side. The subsequent pounding against the metal doors was deafening, but within minutes, they gave way to a police battering ram. Robert Janick was the first through the door, gun drawn. Amy sagged to the floor.

"All clear," Janick screamed, and a small flood of officers flowed into the room. Doctor Cassidy and a technician were the last in.

As Janick supported Amy, she pointed to the chamber. Doctor Cassidy and the others rushed to the tank and peered through the small observation windows. Amy watched as one by one they turned away, guns lowered, some pale, some struggling to contain their gag reflexes as their stomachs lurched up inside them. Doctor Cassidy operated the controls, and the hum of machinery filled the silence. A minute later, the technician opened the door, and the doctor entered the chamber, stayed briefly, and emerged.

The doctor, his face grim, strolled back to Amy and the detective. He had something in his hand. "He's most certainly dead. The vacuum line was activated, and, well, it's not a pretty sight." He handed Janick what appeared to Amy to be a playing card. "I found this laying next to him."

Amy leaned over to see what it was. Janick flipped the card to find an Ace of Spades, and scrawled unevenly in the white space was "Lynch Cully is . . ."

Forty-nine
❧✦✦☙

The attendance for Sergeant Lynch Cully's memorial service was the largest the state had witnessed in many years. While the body of Lester Hargrave had been discovered downstream in the Big River, snagged against a bridge pier, the detective's whereabouts remained unknown, that information taken to the grave by the killer. A desperate but thorough search of the farm and river, as well as David Koettering's residence in Ladue, failed to uncover his body, and a meticulous analysis of the motor home debris yielded no DNA evidence that Lynch had been hidden in the coach when it exploded. So, after six weeks, he was presumed dead with the expectation that the river would give up his remains when it was ready to. He was being given full police honors, and Amy rode with the Governor, Chief Dandridge, the mayor, and Lynch's parents at the head of the two-mile-long procession. Every police department in a three state region had sent representatives. The federal government—FBI, ATF, DEA and others—also came to pay tribute to a man with whom many of them had worked.

Outside the church where the memorial was to be held, Amy joined hands with his mother as they stoically consoled each other and preceded his father while walking toward the front doors. It was a beautiful day for flying, and Amy gazed upward knowing that his soul now soared above all of them. After a short service, they returned to the front plaza where Lynch was honored with a 21-gun salute, and his father, mother and Amy were each handed a large white helium-filled balloon. They tied a long-stemmed red rose to the ribbons trailing their balloons and, then, holding hands, they launched the balloons upward in unison.

"I got him, Lynch. Just for you," Amy said as she watched the balloon lift toward heaven.

Arm in arm, the women left the site and walked toward the lane where family members waited to take them home. Her father was there, talking with one of Lynch's uncles. The two women parted with a few words and a hug, and Amy walked toward her dad. But when she saw Robert Janick a short distance away, she redirected her steps toward him. She walked up to him and gave him a hug. As she backed away, he surprised her with a tear in his eye.

"Yeah, I'm gonna miss him, too, no matter all the grief he gave me," he said.

She nodded. "I never had a chance to thank you, for coming to my rescue."

He offered a subtle shake of his head in acknowledgment. "I'm not really the one you need to thank. Someone else was watching over you. He's the one who first tipped us off that Koettering might be the guy. He even did some of the footwork for us, to convince us, 'cause we weren't taking him seriously. Then, we finally located a co-worker, a Doctor Daniel Diehl, in Rochester, Minnesota. Said Koettering had frequent fugue states or something like that. He'd have headaches and lose whole hours of his life. But ends up 'David Koettering' was just another made-up identity. His real name was Mark Crawford. Your guardian angel found Crawford's father imprisoned for child molestation and abuse near Boston and learned the truth about Crawford's multiple personality disorder. Dissociative Identity Disorder they call it now."

The detective paused and looked about as if trying to find someone.

"Anyway, all the stuff in Koettering's file about his identity, his family, his twin dying in a boating accident, and so on, was manufactured and seeded into various electronic databases for us to find. Only two things were true. As his 'alter' named David, he really did go through medical school and neurosurgical training, while Matthew was an electronics mastermind who amassed an incredible fortune, all stolen. He was also the dominant personality. For someone so warped, he was an absolute genius."

Janick tipped his hat to leave. Amy placed her hand on his arm to stop him.

"Who was it? Who should I thank?"

Janick turned toward the phalanx of cars crowded along the road outside the church. He pointed to a man walking alone toward the vehicles.

"Thank you," Amy replied, and she rushed away to catch up with the man. His back was toward her, and she couldn't see his face. She caught up with him as he started to open the door of a maroon Grand Cherokee. "Excuse me! Wait! Please wait!"

The man stopped and turned toward Amy. It was Royce.

In a moment, Amy understood. The car outside her home. The sleepless nights helping a friend. His presence in the grocery store. Despite how she had treated him, he had watched over her, given up his valuable time to keep her safe. She was overwhelmed. She truly did not know this man. "Looks really can be deceiving," her father had said. "Only God knows our hearts and thoughts and motives, what's on the inside. The outside usually tells us little."

"Thank you," she said quietly, tears welling up in her eyes.

Sheepishly, he shrugged and smiled. "I guess I should say you're welcome." He shrugged again and turned to enter his car.

Amy put her hand on the top of the door before he could close it.

"Hey, Royce, sometime next week, how about dinner together?"

Epilogue
❧ ✦ ✦ ☙

Jusuf. In the past three months, he'd become known as Jusuf, but his real name eluded him. As had all events prior to three months earlier.

Yet, after weeks of frustration, he no longer felt disheartened. He'd made progress. Three months ago, he walked dragging his left leg. Now, his motor coordination had improved to the point he could jump rope, walk a wooden beam, and more importantly, chop the firewood they needed to warm the cabin. Two months ago, he still fumbled with dinnerware. Now, he could spin a fork in his fingers, not to mention that he actually knew the names of each utensil he used. Somewhere from the recess of his mind, he recalled how to set a table properly, a task he taught Danijela, while feeling surprised that she didn't already know how. He had even learned what parents were, although he couldn't remember much about his.

Danijela. He remembered his first night waking up in her cabin, with her holding a kitchen knife for protection. She had looked awful that day. 'Run hard and put away wet' was a phrase that came into his head, even though he didn't remember exactly what that meant. Still didn't. The meaning would come to him at some point. Of that he felt confident.

Those first few weeks had been difficult in many ways besides the frustration tied to his failed memory and physical disabilities. Danijela lived in a constant state of fear, of him and of monsters from her past. She didn't trust him, and in turn, he often wondered if he could trust her. Yet, just as he made progress, so had she. In time, he finally learned some of her story.

At the age of sixteen, Danijela had been promised a job as a nanny here in America. A place called Wildwood. Part of some bigger city called St. Louis. An American education was to be part of the package. Her best friend, Tatjana, had been offered the same opportunity. Together with a dozen other girls from surrounding villages near Tuzla, in Bosnia, they traveled to the port city of Dubrovnik, Croatia. She recalled the beautiful cruise ships at dock and imagined them taking her group to America. Instead, a battered launch with a smelly, leaking diesel engine took them to rusty cargo ship where they joined two dozen other girls in a stinky hold outfitted with crude bunks and smelling of vomit. After two seasick weeks of contributing to the detritus in that hold, they'd been herded up top and, in smaller groups, pushed onto four old, sport fishing boats in the middle of the night, and brought ashore somewhere near a city called Houston.

That was when the warning flags of concern began flapping in her head. She knew they were supposed to pass through Customs, to have work Visas and the papers needed to grant them entry into America. They had given her no such documents. Instead, they had confiscated their passports, and she, Tatjana, and four other girls were hustled to a windowless white van. No food. One bottle of water to share. One lone bathroom break, at something called a 'rest stop,' while it was still dark. They allowed them out of the van the next night, when each girl's prospective "employer" took control. She had been allowed to talk with Tatjana only once since, and that conversation had not gone well. Tatjana had been scared to talk, even in their native dialect, which Danijela did not believe either "employer" could understand.

Beyond that, Danijela refused to tell Jusuf anything more. Only that Ibrahim had rescued her from a life in hell, and that he'd gone to get Tatjana three weeks earlier. He had contacted her regularly until a week before she fished Jusuf from the river. Ibrahim never returned.

Today had been a good day, a remarkable day. Danijela had smiled at him for the very first time. Yet, Jusuf still had much to learn about Danijela, and everything to learn about the things in her past that she feared. He gathered these "things" were really men, although she never addressed them as such. Maybe it was easier for her to deal with her fear by turning them into inanimate objects. Intuitively, Jusuf knew that in time she would come to trust him. He would certainly never do anything on purpose to violate such trust. And he pledged to protect her. After all, he owed his life to her.

Sneak Preview:
RESCUED AND REMEMBERED

One

As the 206L-4 LongRanger IV helicopter circled the farm field a second time, the MedAir-12 crew knew they had a bad one waiting. In direct radio contact with the paramedic team on the ground, they surveyed the scene below and wished they were somewhere else. Amy Gibbs, the flight nurse, had had enough of the "bad ones." Her run-in with the "LA Rapist" three months earlier had shown her what she thought was the worst of what one person could do to another. She didn't want this case, any case, to prove that wrong.

"They're setting up the LZ now," said Sanders, their new pilot on loan from MedAir-24, into the com system. Lyle Henderson, the crew's regular pilot, remained benched from the bilateral femur fractures suffered during the helicopter crash they'd experienced during that earlier, traumatizing case.

Amy gazed at the fallow field below. The remnants of an earlier light snow framed the fencerows where the wind could blow it no farther, and that day's sun had not melted it. In the dimming light of dusk, she could see a wide figure eight etched into the dirt. At one end, the lights of the sheriff's cruisers and EMS vehicles lit up the field. Not far from them, she saw the first flare ignite. Within two minutes, all four flares illuminated the makeshift landing zone, and Sanders touched down with the typical finesse of a MedAir pilot.

Not. The jolt of landing almost knocked Amy from her seat.

"Sorry. The long shadows threw me off." Sanders powered down the bird as Amy and Reid McCormick, their paramedic, unbuckled and gathered their bags.

Upon entering the aurora of the headlights, Amy noticed that tire ruts had made the figure eight in the rich, partially thawed topsoil of the Cuivre River floodplain. She saw the county paramedics working over the victim and hesitated. She saw no person there, just a mangled version of one. Images from three months earlier flooded her mind. She needed to focus. The young woman needed her care, but nothing visually told Amy that this victim was female. She took a deep breath and fought the fear rising within. Her shrink had told her she was returning to work too soon after her ordeal. Until now, she'd thought Doctor Lange was the crazy one.

She had a job to do, and she rushed toward the scene.

"Hey, Amy. As we radioed, young female, age unknown. It appears she was bound and dragged behind a truck for who knows how many laps around this field. Farmer was moving some equipment and saw headlights. Thought it was joy riders. Found her when he came to investigate. Saw a dark pickup leaving."

"We got here within five minutes of the call. Blood pressure was 40 systolic. Pulse barely discernible. Shallow breathing. Found one cephalic for an 18-gauge. Had to do an IO on the opposite side's tibia. We've squeezed in two liters of saline so far. Third and fourth are running. Blood pressure, maybe 60 now. Difficult reading it. Intubation was a bitch. Blood filled her throat every time we managed to clear it. But, Jazz there managed to snake in a seven. She's circling the drain and needs to get out of here STAT if we have any chance of saving her."

"Thanks, Paulie. Injuries?"

"Haven't had time to really inventory them. I mean, just take a look. What *isn't* torn up?"

Amy saw the form of a young woman, but little else could identify the gender. Her hair had been shorn. Face, scalp, and exposed extremities appeared more like raw hamburger than human flesh. The generic jeans and t-shirt were as mangled as the flesh. Right femur appeared broken and angulated, as did the left upper arm. The wrists revealed wounds consistent with coarse bindings of some sort. Amy saw little oozing from the wounds, a good indication of the low blood pressure and the bad warning of a body shutting down. Amy held little hope that this girl would even survive to the trauma center.

"Quick, let's get these extremities splinted. Reid, get the . . ." She stopped when she saw that Sanders had brought their stretcher to them and was preparing it for their patient. "Get the ventilator and hook her up."

Amy took her penlight and lifted the girl's eyelids. She gasped. The globes were flaccid, the corneas gone. She returned her focus to starting her initial assessment while the others immobilized the girl. The airway was good, but the lungs sounded full of fluid. Heart sounds were muffled. Tamponade? Her condition made the usual clinical signs of cardiac tamponade unlikely. Amy had little choice but to put a needle into the pericardial sac and check. To miss a tamponade would guarantee the girl's death while relieving one could prove the turning point in her resuscitation.

She grabbed an 18-gauge needle and pulled open the tattered shirt. Again, she startled. A large incision in the right upper quadrant of her abdomen gaped open, its sutures torn amidst the battered flesh. What had this girl gone through?

Amy's pulse quickened, and her breathing seemed labored. Focusing on the patient became harder. Reid brought her back by swabbing the area just below the woman's breastbone with antiseptic. He'd read her mind. Amy unsheathed the needle and inserted it just below the xiphoid of the sternum, angling it at roughly 40 degrees toward the heart. She felt the needle puncture the pericardial sac and immediately saw a return of fluid. With a large syringe, she removed 50 milliliters of serous fluid.

"Pulse?"

Reid was already on it. "Seems stronger. Good call." He moved on to check the blood pressure. "Up to 80 systolic."

Amy felt mixed emotions. Were they going to save this girl to a life of disability? Blind and who knows what else. She slipped the plastic catheter off the needle and left it in the pericardial sac, burying the hub in a wad of sterile 4x4's that would absorb further drainage in route.

She grabbed the antiseptic, doused the abdominal wound, and placed a bulky dressing over it as well. Then a sickening thought hit her.

"Guys, did you inspect her back?"

Both paramedics shook their heads. "Didn't get to it yet," answered Paulie. "Higher priorities."

With the victim's extremities splinted and her neck immobilized, the team gently rolled the girl to her side. The ripped shirt fell away from her body except in the areas where it had been ground into her skin. Amy gagged at the site of two more gaping incisions, also torn apart by the trauma of being dragged behind the truck, the frayed ends of their sutures barely visible above the macerated skin.

Amy jumped up and ran, fighting the bile rising into her throat. Tears welled up and cascaded down her cheeks. As she neared the helicopter, she bent over and began to puke. She couldn't take it. She emptied her stomach, but the retching continued. Why? What had this poor girl done to deserve this? She kneeled, sobbing. What? The question would go unanswered.

"Amy!"

She turned to see Reid and the paramedics loading their patient onto the bird. Sanders had started the engine. She knew she had to join them, do her job, but she couldn't move. Reid finally came, pulled her up, and helped her into the bird. By habit, she strapped in and donned the headset, but the tears continued as Reid managed the patient.

"W-we're not going to save her, Reid. She's n-not going to survive the flight."

Reid looked at her, questioning.

"She's been har . . ." She choked back her tears and continued. ". . . harvested, Reid. Corneas, liver, kidneys.

Who knows what else! All taken." She bowed her head. They'd even taken her hair, a woman's crown of glory.

A quick note from Braxton . . .

I hope you enjoyed *Looks that Deceive* and thank you for purchasing it. Please consider writing a review at my website, Amazon, Barnes & Nobel, iTunes, Goodreads, or elsewhere. Reviews are crucial to Indie authors. It doesn't have to be lengthy. Just a couple of sentences will do.

Also, if you'd like to stay informed about my new books, book signings, and more, please sign up for my newsletter. You can do that at my website: **www.braxtondegarmo.com**. As my thank-you for signing up, you will get a free eBook, *And Then One Day*, a prequel to the series. Have you wondered how Lynch and Amy first met, and what led to their breakup? This is the book for you.

And did you know you can purchase signed copies of my paperbacks at my website? With shipping included in the price, ordering them directly from me is typically cheaper than ordering them online.

**Books by
Braxton DeGarmo:**

MedAir Series:

**Looks that Deceive - 1
Rescued and Remembered - 2
The Silenced Shooter – 3
Wrongfully Removed - 4
A Zealot's Destiny – 5
Kidnapped Nation - 6**

Others:

**Indebted
The Militant Genome**

ABOUT THE AUTHOR

 Braxton can't lay claim to wanting to be a writer all his life, although his mother and seventh grade English teacher were convinced he had what it would take. A bachelor's degree in Bio-Medical Engineering led to medical school and a residency in Emergency Medicine. He served for a decade in the U.S. Army Medical Corps with tours such as the Chief, Emergency Medical Services at Fort Campbell, KY, and as a research Flight Surgeon at Fort Rucker, AL. Who had time to write?

By the 1990s, as a civilian, his professional and family life had settled down, somewhat, and his mother once again took up her mantra, "Write a book. You're a good writer." In 1997, a Valentine's Day writing contest convinced him that maybe he could write fiction. He spent the next fifteen years learning the craft of writing.

Now, nineteen years after that first hesitant start, he has seven novels published and can't find enough time to write. As a Christian, he writes "true-life" Christian fiction (suspense and thrillers) that many call "cutting edge," as he's not afraid to take on such issues as human trafficking, racism, and more. His characters are real-life as well. As such, his books are never likely to gain acceptance by the Christian Bookseller Association. But then, he never intended to tell stories just to the choir.